D1736194

The Healers' Road

The Healers' Road

S.E. ROBERTSON

For Jay, who always believed.

Part One

Agna: Arrival

Agna stood outside a stranger's door. She had brought along her old friend Rone's most recent letter, slipped safely into an inside pocket. Now, as the lamps flared to life in the houses up and down the street, Agna decided that she had been childish to carry the letter along. She had come halfway around the world to serve her time as a charitable agent; she couldn't indulge in silly things like carrying a letter like a talisman.

She was having quite a bit of trouble knocking.

The windows of this house were half-lit, as if by a lamp or two deeper inside the rooms. Rone must have been reading a novel or some philosophical text after dinner. Agna wished she were back in her dormitory room, reading after dinner. Even a quiet night back at the hotel would be an improvement over lingering on the street. Agna's skin felt as though it had absorbed salt all through her weeks at sea, and she hadn't been able to scrub it out.

She tapped her knuckles against the wood, then, noticing a brass knocker, gave it a couple of firm knocks. She remembered how to breathe. Rone had said he'd missed her, in his letters; he'd be as happy to see her as she was to see him.

The stranger's door opened, and a stranger looked out. An adult – his chin was scruffed with the beginnings of a beard. The authority of the Academy shored up her nervousness. Standing up this straight, her head would have reached the stranger's chin. "I am Agna Despana, healer of the Church of the Divine Balance," she declared in carefully studied Kaveran. "Is this the residence of Rone Sidduji?"

The stranger's mouth quirked. "Yeah. He's working at the moment. You're one of his little sisters?"

Agna felt her ears pink at the term. "Not literally, no. At the Academy, he was my mentor."

"Right, that's the one. Come on in if you like. Tea?"

Agna hesitated. She had received letters from this country for four years, but it still seemed as though Rone should live in the upperclassmen's dormitory at the Academy, or in the Islander neighborhood with his parents. It seemed wrong that he lived in this bearded man's house, where one could just invite a visitor in and make tea.

She thanked the stranger and followed him inside.

In the vestibule, she remembered to take off her shoes. The stranger had gone on ahead. She padded after him, her silk-clad feet slipping on the polished floorboards. The fireplace was unlit, leaving the room in the chill that seemed to pass for early spring in this country. The stranger – Rone's friend, somehow – clanked around in an adjoining room, pumping water, lighting the stove. Agna clasped her hands behind her back, tried not to nod in exhaustion, and waited.

He'd said that Rone was working. So he'd taken the evening shift at a shrine. That was, as usual, selfless of him. She wondered whether she should drop by the shrine tonight, or come back here in the morning.

Agna cast a look around, gathering what she could about the state in which her friend lived. It was a humble city house, no more than three bedrooms. It had a modern kitchen with an indoor water pump, by the sound of the Kaveran's preparations. There were bookshelves along most of the walls, and the floors were clean and polished. It wasn't so different from Rone's parents' house in Murio: small and vicariously embarrassing, but safe.

Eventually, the bearded man came back with a pot of tea and two cups. "No doubt you've guessed already, but I'm Tenken Grim." He set the pot on the table on one side of the room and waved at the chairs.

Agna took the seat that Tenken Grim did not claim for himself. "Yes. Rone mentioned you. Pleasure to meet you." She thanked him for the tea and waited for it to steep. The scent of the leaves rolled up from the hot water – Kaveran tea, that dark, acrid stuff, not Nessinian herbal tea. They'd served it in the hotel, too.

"Do you take it with honey like he does?"

Agna's throat constricted, remembering Rone's over-honeyed cups of tea, crowding in with their textbooks and notes. Honeyed verbena tea for Rone, cold mint tea for Esirel, hot chamomile for Agna, at the last table along the right-hand wall in the Direzzo Café. Once a week for four years, the three of them had met to study, until Rone had graduated. And now Agna and Esirel were off in the world, too. It might be a long time until they all met again.

Agna found her voice and held it steady. "No, thank you."

"Hm." Tenken's solid brown hands cradled the teacup, soaking up its heat. "Always wondered whether that might be a Nessinian thing, or just him."

Agna's laugh hurt a little. "Just him."

Tenken seemed to lose himself in thought. Agna watched the drifting tea leaves. All she wanted was to ask about Rone, to make sure he was well, to grasp some sense of his life in this place. Yet asking might look desperate and immature. The thought of this stranger's disapproval – or, worse, amusement – made her jaw tighten. She shouldn't care. But she would rather ask her old friend personally. She knew she could trust him, and he was too noble to think ill of her.

She swallowed. "So... where is the shrine, if I might ask?"

"The shrine?" the Kaveran echoed. "Well, there's one up in Prisa. Three days' ride from here."

Agna squinted, parsing the answer. "Does he travel back and forth, then?"

"Rone? No – well, he went up once for a festival."

"I thought you said he was working."

"Yeah. He works a lot of places. Three jobs right now, I think."

"But..." She swallowed the rest of her protest. Rone was the greatest swordsman in his year, if not the greatest ever. He was dedicated to the service of his Church and its missions. That was why he'd come here originally, on his own assignment. Now that he was finished, why would he work all over the city, like a common ditch-digger? This foreigner didn't understand. But the point was that Rone wasn't here, and that she had come here for nothing. Here to this house, she reminded herself. Not here to this country. No need to jump to such conclusions yet.

She sipped her bitter tea. There was nothing she wanted from Tenken Grim but answers, and she hated her own sense of desperation. She was out on her own now; she was supposed to be an adult.

Agna turned her questions over and over in her mind until they seemed innocuous, smooth as river stones. "So... how long does Rone intend to stay here?"

Tenken shrugged. "Until he makes enough to move out on his own. Doesn't bother me. Nice to have some company."

Until he can move out on his own, Agna noted, not *until he can go back to Nessiny*. She intended to ask Rone about that in her next letter. Perhaps his new roommate was mistaken.

"You're the healer, then?"

She looked up and squared her shoulders. "Yes, healer second order of the Academy of the Divine Balance."

"And the other one was a swordmaster, like him."

Agna chose not to take offense at *the other one*, as though she and Esirel were somehow interchangeable. "Yes. Esirel Relaska was his other – little sister, as you put it. She's on assignment in Achusa." She took a deep breath and sipped more of her tea. Her assignment was almost manageable compared to Esirel's. Esirel was closer to home, true, but her term was four times as long. And Agna didn't have a sweetheart to leave behind, of course. As much as it grated on her soul to be overlooked her whole life, Agna could at least take solace in having missed the traditional graduation separation.

"Going to work in one of the hospitals here?" Tenken asked.

Agna turned her cup around on the saucer. "It depends on the Benevolent Union. I'll leave it up to them." *Like he did*, she finished silently.

"Ah."

3

Tenken was quiet as he drank. Agna struggled to the bottom of her teacup in silence.

At the end of it, there was nothing else to say. "Thank you for your hospitality," she said, scraping her chair back. "Please tell Rone that I will be in town for four more days. I'm staying at the Bluethorne Hotel."

"All right," Tenken allowed. He saw her to the door. "Good to meet you, then. Safe travels."

Agna fled into the strange city alone.

Keifon: Exile

Keifon watched the sky turn gray and pink and blue from the window of his room in the Benevolent Union base. After a week in Vertal, he had learned the layout of the neighborhood, and the positions of the restaurants and bars and theaters. He did not trust himself outside. It had not been this hard in a long time.

He read his Kaveran phrasebook again, dusting off the words that he had learned in another life. He read his other two books when he tired of that one. The sacred texts and the medical terms slid through his brain in the same way.

One day, after he had managed to get some sleep, he ventured out to buy cooking equipment. Buoyed by this small victory, he practiced the nanbur that had lain neglected on a side table in his room. His fingers flexed around the notes of the scales. The strings were still sound in this southern climate. The nanbur was undamaged by its time on the ship, crammed in next to him on a narrow bunk alongside sacks of wheat and bolts of silk. That was something. He should have left it with Nachi, so that she might grow up to learn how to play it and remember him by it, but he had lost his nerve.

He sat at the table later that evening to write a letter to Nachi – or to her mother, as Nachi was still learning to read. He had to believe that Eri would read it to her. She had agreed to let him visit on his way out of the country, though her eyes had betrayed her worry. He had not broken down in front of Nachi. He had put on a brave front for the last time he would ever see his little girl.

Remember me, he wanted to write. *I know you'll be nine by the time I get back, and you'll forget you ever had a father, and maybe that's for the best. Maybe you'll have a new father by then. But don't forget me.*

He didn't waste the ink. *Have fun in school,* he wrote. *Listen to your mother and your grandparents. I love you. Always.*

Keifon couldn't cry afterward. He could feel for Nachi; he could love her and miss her. The rest was blank.

He tried to pray instead. He remembered the right words and the proper placements of his hands. The prayers echoed through his head. The gods didn't hear him. They couldn't. If the gods loved him, he would not be here. Kazi would not have sent him away.

It doesn't mean I don't love you, he had said.

It's for our own good, both of us, he had said.

5

I know it's sooner than we expected, but this is a perfect opportunity for you, he had said.

Someday I'll make enemies, if I haven't already, he had said. *I want you out of harm's way.*

Keifon did not feel out of harm's way. He felt very much under harm's boot. He counted hours and waited. Four years. He couldn't see the end.

Agna: The Golden Caravan

The world headquarters of the Benevolent Union were unassuming from the outside. Agna had mistaken the building for an inn the first time she'd visited, following the address that she'd been given at the Academy. But she had noticed afterward that the Benevolent Union's sigil was carved into the sign over the door, and stitched into the jacket of the receptionist at the desk. She returned on the appointed day, feeling like an expert.

"Name and affiliation?"

"Agna Despana, healer second class, Church of the Divine Balance. I have an appointment," she added. "With Agent Harnal."

"Mmhm. Down this hall, third door on the right."

Agna inclined her head and hurried past him. She closed her hands in her skirt as if to lift it out of the way of her shoes, wicking the sweat from her palms.

The Benevolent Union was a well-established charitable organization. The Academy would not partner with it if it weren't competent. Its agents would find a fitting assignment for her abilities, something that would serve the people of Kavera and the missions of the Benevolent Union and the Church. She would join the long line of Academy graduates who had gone before her in serving, as Rone had.

Agna paused and steadied herself with a hand against a doorframe. She took some deep breaths and murmured a prayer, as Rone would have. "Let my hands and my mind serve the world's need." Agna had never been particularly observant, but it couldn't hurt.

The agent's office was a small room, and three walls were lined with bookshelves loaded with logbooks and bound papers. The only other furnishings were a massive wooden desk, with one chair behind it – where the intake agent studied some papers – and two chairs in front of it. Behind the desk loomed a noticeboard, as big as a banquet table, plastered with paper notes. As Agna peered at it, the chaos resolved into order: the notes were sectioned into columns, with subheadings under that. Over the largest divisions, she made out some names – Vertal, Prisa, Laketon, and Wildern, all Kaveran cities. Most likely, the notes represented the Benevolent Union's openings at each location. Agna stared at the board. There were hundreds of notes. All of this happened in a mostly modern country, in peacetime.

The agent, a middle-aged Kaveran man, looked up and motioned to the empty chairs. "Do have a seat." He spoke her native Nessinian quite clearly, despite his accent.

Agna sank into one of the chairs, as the grandiose introduction she'd planned – citing her honors, insisting upon the best of assignments, expressing her displeasure with being made to wait for days – withered in her mind. A familiar voice replaced it. *That's why the Academy exists. That's why they send us out.* Rone had been so proud to go overseas, to do his duty as a graduate. He probably hadn't thought about his own importance. He had probably looked at that board and said *Let me work wherever the need is greatest.* Agna felt selfish and small. For all her accomplishments, she was still inadequate.

The agent paged through the file on his desk for another minute as Agna regained her bearings.

"So, Healer. I've read the Academy's report on you. We're glad to have more of the Academy's graduates working with us. And healers are always appreciated." He consulted a nearby logbook and dipped a pen in his inkwell. "Now. Do you have any requests for your assignment?"

Agna swallowed. Part of her wanted to ask where Rone had been assigned. Part of her wanted to beg to go home. She revised her goals for the conversation: don't cry in front of the intake agent. And remember what Rone would do.

"Wherever I can be of use, sir."

The agent smiled. "Well then." He turned to untack a note from the board behind him. "We have a need for medical workers on one of our more challenging assignments. The Benevolent Union runs a mobile clinic that travels with a merchants' caravan." He found another sheet of paper among the stacks on his desk and handed it to her. Agna stared at it: a map of Kavera with a path traced over it, crisscrossing the network of canals that fanned through the country like the veins of a leaf.

The agent went on. "Some of the areas that it visits don't have resident doctors or healers of their own, so it's important to our mission to supply these places with medical care." He paused, and Agna nodded, looking up from the map. She was listening, whether or not she understood fully yet. "It's not more dangerous than any of our other details – though it is difficult. But it's needed, and greatly appreciated."

Agna found her voice. She sounded meek and distant to herself. "That doesn't sound so bad."

"Well. The caravan doesn't have top-notch accommodations. They have water and various other conveniences, and the trading company will supply guards and transportation. The Union supplies you with some camping equipment and the mobile clinic. When the caravan sets up shop, you and your partner will open the clinic and treat anyone who comes to it to the best of your ability. When the caravan comes back to Vertal, we will account for the fees you've collected, all applicable taxes, and the expenses that the Union owes to the trading company. You'll be paid out of the remainder."

Money was not interesting in the slightest. He was getting off track. Camping? The world-famous charitable organization resorted to *camping*? Agna throttled her initial reaction. "...I have some questions. Please."

"Go ahead."

"When the caravan comes back to Vertal, you said – how long is it on the road?"

"The circuit is a year long. If you want to be reassigned elsewhere for your – second year?"

"Yes."

"When the caravan comes back around this time next year, if you want to be reassigned, we can arrange for that."

"I see. And... my partner, you said? I don't have a partner. There were a couple of priests coming to the west from the Academy this year, but they're going on to Warma. And there were two other healers that were going to a new hospital in – Wildern, is it?"

"Yes, Wildern. But I'm afraid we have a greater need for healers on this assignment, if you're amenable."

Agna sighed. "Go on, then. Partners."

"Yes, well. The Benevolent Union's procedure is to work in pairs or teams. One doctor can't cover the whole caravan route alone. There are some areas where you'd have them queued out the door." He drew another logbook from the stack on his desk and opened it. "We've had an agent from the Yanweian National Army sign up already. You'll need to be ready to meet the caravan before they leave town. They arrived last night, so they should be moving on by this time next week."

"A Yanweian?" she blurted.

"Yes. The Yanweian National Army sends agents to work with the Benevolent Union, much as your Academy does. They've sent an agent who is fluent in Kaveran and has trained as a medic. "

"I see." Agna racked her brain for everything she knew about Yanweians. Yanweian artists had been in and out of fashion in some of the galleries in Murio; she could recognize their style of brushed ink on vellum and their idiosyncratic color combinations. She had read Yanweian poetry in some of her classes, and had once heard it read in their strange, lilting language. There were a few Yanweian students in the Academy, but no one that Agna knew closely. The Yanweian immigrants in Murio didn't mix with outsiders. Agna realized that she knew nothing else about them. They were... foreign.

"Do you have any problems with this arrangement, Healer? Do you accept?"

"I..." She tore her eyes from the map in her hands. She would have to spend a year riding around the country like an itinerant trader, on a horse? In a wagon? – and ply her healing in the Kaveran hinterland, accompanied by an incomprehensible stranger from a foreign military. This was not why she'd become a healer, to tread dirt in the back of beyond. And then the noticeboard caught her gaze again, and she remembered Rone's voice, just before he went away. He hadn't spoken a word of Kaveran. He had asked the Church and the Union to make the best use of his talents, to serve the greatest need. He had trusted his life to them.

And somewhere out there, he was still serving, humble and devout, lending his sword and his soul to the cause. Agna couldn't hope to reach his level. The thought made her mouth go dry. Rone would tell her to go, to give her abilities to the people who needed them, no matter how hard it would be for her. That was what the Church and the Academy meant to him: defending the weak and saving the lost. To Agna it had been a refuge where knowledge was paramount, where she could prove herself through hard work and intelligence. They'd had so many long discussions in the coffee shops in Murio about the nature of the greater good and the best uses of Church resources. Agna cherished those memories of her peer mentor; they meant infinitely more to her than his advice about finding her way around the Academy.

She had come across the ocean in his footsteps, trying to follow his example. And in this assignment, Agna might be able to pursue both knowledge and selflessness. She had trained as a healer since she was twelve, and now she had an opportunity to find people who truly needed her expertise. Agna hoped that she could set aside her pride. She hoped that she wasn't making a terrible mistake.

She took a deep breath. "I accept."

The agent nodded, smiling as he drew a form from a drawer in his desk. "For the Benevolent Union and for Kavera, thank you for your service, Agent Despana."

She bowed her head and hoped she wouldn't cry as he filled in some blanks on the form. This was a terrible mistake. "Thank you."

He waited as she read the contract, explaining the terms. She was to work for the Benevolent Union, by the good graces of the Church and Academy of the Divine Balance. Her pay would be minimal, her living conditions the best that could be managed under the circumstances – at least that was encouraging – and after this term and that condition were met, her contract would be fulfilled. Agna let the dry, formal words cool her mind back down. She signed and dated it and turned it over to the agent, who signed it again. And so it was done. She was an agent of the Benevolent Union for two whole years.

"Now. Get some rest, see the city if you like. Meet the other medic back here five days from now, at eight in the morning."

"Yes, sir." She sat dazed, then shook it off. The task lay before her. She would do whatever she could.

■ ■ ■

The morning of her departure, Agna woke up too early. She got dressed, descended to the lobby, and asked one more time whether any mail had arrived for her. One more time, the desk clerk said no. Sighing, Agna called for a carriage and her trunk, and settled her bill. The porters loaded her trunk onto the carriage, and Agna gave the driver the address of the Benevolent Union base for the third time.

She was alone in the small carriage they'd sent, and so Agna rested her head against the window frame. The doors and windows and signs and pedestrians flowed by outside. On the first day Agna had sent all of her clothes out to be laundered, which had been a great relief. She had stopped by a library to copy out a map of Kavera onto some of her drawing paper, and learn what she could about the trade routes. She had spent one full day in an art museum, wandering delightedly from one room to the next. On that day, she had managed not to worry about Rone until she checked for mail.

Rone had never come. Every day Agna set out to see the city and to try to prepare for her trip, and every day she resolutely set her feet away from the neighborhood where Tenken Grim lived. Rone must have his reasons. Was he disappointed that she'd come, that she'd followed him? She waited for his next letter like a child awaiting a festival.

At the Benevolent Union base, Agna had the footman carry her trunk into the lobby, and gave the receptionist a few coins to watch it until her meeting with the Yanweian agent. She would have to pull it along herself soon enough. She could move it, just barely, thanks to the wheels bolted to the bottom, but it was tiring and undignified work.

There was enough change in her purse to pay for breakfast, and there was plenty more where that came from, anyway. Agna shrugged to herself and headed across the street to a cafe. The morning was cool and clear, so she decided to claim one of the outdoor tables. Since they did not offer Furoni coffee on the menu like a proper cafe in Murio would, she ordered tea and toast and a newspaper. Were it not for the dark, bitter tea, the Kaveran chatter of the occasional passerby, the news about Vertal in the paper, and the block-long edifice of the Benevolent Union headquarters dominating the landscape, she might almost be home in Murio.

Agna had had so few opportunities to travel, being busy with her Academy training. That was the only thing she'd looked forward to, among all of the duties she'd have to undertake in her father's agency. Currying favor with patrons was dull, buying new art was intriguing, but her interest was truly captured by the thought of traveling to museums and galleries and studios to collect new acquisitions. Agna had read countless books about the sorts of places that she would be able to see in person once she was an art dealer.

She suspected that museums, galleries, and studios would be in short supply on this trip, once she left the capital. But travel was good for one's horizons. Even if the people she met in the countryside were not the best-educated or most refined people in the world, she could make do. There would always be something to learn.

Agna paid for breakfast, leaving a handful of coins on top of the discarded newspaper for their trouble. She had read in her cultural briefings that such things weren't customary here, but it felt wrong not to do it.

The clock in the lounge area of the headquarters read five minutes to eight. An agent appeared at the bottom of the stairs. Agna addressed him. "You. Will you help me with something? I'll pay you. I'm in a hurry."

The newcomer frowned vaguely and rubbed his temples with one hand. "I'm running late, too. I'm sorry." Between his soft voice and his lilting accent, the words were hard to make out.

"It won't take a minute. I just need to have my trunk loaded onto a carriage outside. I'll pull it out there," she offered.

The agent sighed. "All right." He shrugged the strap of a long, angular case higher on one shoulder. Agna grabbed the handle of her trunk and bore against it, leaning hard to get it rolling. The other agent darted around her to hold the door open, and Agna hauled the trunk through the door, feeling clumsy and ridiculous, trudging through the door bottom-first.

"Now. When the Yanweian agent gets here..." She looked at him again as he closed the door. Just a bit taller than herself. About her own age or a bit older, on the young side of adulthood. Clearly in a physical trade, though not as graceful as the Academy's swordmasters. He wore a light cloak of gray material with a sigil pin – a quartered shield – holding it together at the shoulder. On the opposite hip from his money bag, he wore a sheathed knife half as long as her arm. The valise in his hand was marked with the international symbol for medical aid. On his back, along with the long case, he carried a large hiking backpack. The stranger had dark hair cut short, and dark, guarded eyes. Dark eyes, amber skin, and... a Yanweian accent.

"...Oh."

"You're the Nessinian healer, aren't you."

"...Um."

"Do you know the way to the caravan?"

"Uh."

"Follow me, then." He turned and set off along the street.

Agna froze. *"Walking?"*

He turned. "It isn't far."

Agna scrambled to follow. It was a long walk to the caravan's campsite, beyond the open-air market and the warehouses behind it, and through a gate in the city wall. Agna gritted her teeth and hauled the trunk. The wheels made a terrible clatter on the cobblestones. At long last, the street emerged into a field full of wagons and tents, people and horses, flags and banners. She caught a glimpse of a herd of goats. People were dismantling tents, hitching horses to wagons, fitting them with saddles and bridles for riders. The Yanweian scanned the crowd and gave a small wave to a stranger at the edge of the field. The stranger jogged over to meet them. The Benevolent Union seal was embroidered on his jacket – another agent.

"Good, good." The agent opened a satchel slung over his shoulder and extracted two cardboard-bound books with the Benevolent Union seal embossed on their covers. He passed one to each of them. "These are for your records. You'll need to keep logs of your patients, their conditions, any treatments that you perform, and what you've charged for them. The Benevolent Union will need this information when you return." He reached into the satchel for another book, if it could be called that; it was not much more than a packet of bound paper. "This is a summary from the last team of spring healers." The Yanweian reached for it first, and slung his backpack to one side to slide it inside.

The agent turned toward the campground. "Follow me, please. I'll introduce you to the caravan master and the passenger wagon's driver." He led them to one of the larger wagons, a proper enclosed traveling coach with a rectangular sigil painted on the side in gold. A guard in a short brown cloak waited in the driver's seat, yawning; another loaded boxes into a storage compartment over the wagon's rear wheels. The agent waved to both and knocked on the wagon's door. "Agent Chesler, Captain. I have the new healers."

The door swung open, and the caravan master dismounted. Once on solid ground, she was barely taller than Agna, a fact which hardly dampened her commanding presence. The Benevolent Union agent bowed his head. The caravan master nodded her acknowledgement and scanned Agna and the Yanweian. Agna felt her nerve withering, as though she'd blundered into the wrong practice room and was about to be mocked in front of a class full of swordmasters. It might have been the caravan master's close-cropped silver hair, leather riding clothes and compact build that gave her that impression. More likely, it was the unspoken, yet non-negotiable, air that the caravan master was very much in control of the situation.

"Another Nessinian – another Balance healer, are you?"

"Yes, ma'am," Agna replied, faintly irritated by the shortcut through the Academy's name, but not at all inclined to raise her voice in protest.

"And a Yanweian?" the Captain went on.

"Yes, ma'am. Keifon the Medic, from the Yanweian National Army."

"Interesting. Talina Tego," she added. "I run the spring caravan. Welcome aboard."

Agna bowed in proper Kaveran fashion, and from the corner of her eye she saw the Yanweian make some kind of salute.

"Agna Despana, second-order healer, Academy of the Divine Balance," Agna added belatedly.

"Thank you, Captain," Agent Chesler concluded, and craned his neck to peer through the mob. The caravan master rounded the wagon to speak with one of her guards. Chesler pointed ahead, and their sad little Benevolent Union contingent soldiered on.

"Captain?" the Yanweian asked the agent, once they'd left the caravan master's wagon behind. "Is the caravan associated with the military?"

"It's an honorary title. A nickname, if you will. Because of the comparison to running a ship along the trade routes."

"I see."

"And here we are." Chesler turned to face them beside a long, open-sided wagon with a canvas roof. Some workers loaded rucksacks and trunks through the open gate in the back of the wagon. Agna aligned her trunk with the waiting luggage as Chesler hailed the driver.

"If you will, please." Chesler waved Agna and the Yanweian closer. The Yanweian stroked the nose of a nearby draft horse as the driver looked them over. "The Benevolent Union will pay for your passage. The rest of your equipment is already loaded. It's labeled with the Benevolent Union seal, so just look for that. There should be two tents as well as some tables and chairs for the clinic. Anything else you might need can be bought in the caravan. The mail riders stop by the caravan whenever their paths cross, so send word back to headquarters any time you like. Good luck. The Benevolent Union thanks you."

He shook hands with each of them, as Kaverans did, and left.

The Yanweian heaved his backpack into the wagon and jumped up with his valise and the case across his back. Agna turned. Her trunk sat behind the wagon, neglected. "What – you forgot mine. Excuse me?" A few faces turned inside the wagon and stared. The Yanweian turned to look back at her.

"Do you have some issue with carrying your luggage?" he asked, a cold tone underlying his polite words.

Agna crossed her arms. "The porters forgot mine. It's very unprofessional of them."

"*Porters?*" He folded his hands together, breathing deliberately. When he spoke again, he had reined in his voice to the point of monotone. "Agent. Everyone here is a passenger. There are no porters."

Hot tears spiked behind her eyes. How was she supposed to *do* this? Why had she agreed to any of this? Why did it have to be so scrabbling and awful? She set her jaw and, propping the trunk against her foot, tipped it on its end. Nothing inside was that fragile, she reminded herself. Things might get shuffled out of place, but that was worth proving to this arrogant stranger that she didn't need anyone's help.

The Yanweian bent over the edge of the wagon to grab the trunk's handle, and Agna bit back her impulse to snap at him. Her humiliation may as well reach its peak. Why hadn't any of the swordmasters been sent to Kavera this year? Curse everyone in this backward country.

The Yanweian pulled as Agna hauled upward with every muscle in her body. Her arms ached, but the trunk tipped up until the wheels made contact with the deck. The Yanweian stepped back along the narrow aisle between the benches.

"I'll get it from here." Her voice wavered, and Agna's cheeks burned. She wiped her eyes with her handkerchief and scrambled up the ladder on wobbly legs to the deck of the wagon. She felt the wagon shift under her weight, and felt thick and clumsy as well as weak and conspicuous. She pushed the trunk in front of her through the rows of benches.

"You're welcome," a soft, sarcastic voice said as she passed. Agna grabbed a few coins from the pouch on her belt – she didn't see what they were, and it didn't matter – and shoved them at him. She ignored the disgusted sound he made and straightened her posture.

The passengers of the wagon sat in the ranks of wooden benches with their luggage piled around them. The Yanweian settled into a seat in the back, propping his feet up on his backpack and cradling the angular case on the bench next to him. Agna pushed her trunk four rows past him and sat on the opposite side, where a pile of luggage branded with the Benevolent Union seal was stacked near an empty bench. She slapped her blank logbook on the bench and took her seat.

The activity in the campsite intensified. Good-natured shouting mixed with laughter, creaking leather, banging wood and a thousand other things that Agna was too drained to care about. She tried to reason through the situation. The Benevolent Union had supplied her with some equipment. She'd read adventure stories before. They could make anything out of sticks and cunning in that sort of story.

She had agreed to this, in the most foolish decision of her entire life, and now she had to rise above it. She had come here to this stupid country to do the right thing. And Rone's stupid friend must not have even told him that she'd visited. She would have to prove that she had made the right decision. She would have to prove that these backward, small-minded people could not best her. She was a graduate of the Academy. She was capable of more than they could ever imagine.

Keifon: Traveler

Keifon watched the last preparations through the open side of the wagon, between the supports that anchored the canvas roof. The tents were being packed up, the horses were being hitched to wagons, and men and women in matching reinforced leather and short brown cloaks roved through the grounds. Most of them were armed with short blades, though a few of the mounted guards carried muskets on their backs – modern, expensive pieces, the kind that the Yanweian National Army would only hand out to officers. Keifon wondered whether the caravan guard carried them mostly for show.

A bell rang somewhere in the middle of the camp, echoed by more bells around the edges. The passenger wagon driver barked a command at her horses, and the wagon lurched into motion. A cheer went up from the other passengers. Around them the other wagons began to roll as the mounted merchants and guards rode at an easy walk.

Keifon watched the receding city wall until a turn in the road put it squarely behind the wagon. Around him, the other passengers talked amongst themselves about their destinations and their homes – going back to the country from Vertal, or to the patrol garrison just up the road. A few were going as far as Laketon, which he remembered as a ranching hub in northern Kavera, just over the border from southern Yanwei.

His letter to Nachi would take several more days to reach her; he thought about the mail riders running north, cutting through the land he'd bypassed by sea, heading toward the home that wasn't home anymore. Ceien had never really been home, after all. It was Eri's family's home, and Nachi's now. The base had been home, and now he could not return for a long time.

Keifon had stopped listening to the other passengers. To distract himself, he turned his attention to the wagons and riders around them. He had visited the camp once with Chesler, briefly, introducing himself to the retiring Nessinian healers and helping them pack up their clinic tent. They had been gracious in showing him the quirks of the equipment that he had since inherited. They were middle-aged, looking forward to settling down – one in a private office in Vertal, the other in a hospital. Keifon had politely listened to their reminiscing and their good wishes. They had spoken to one another in half-sentences in their syncopated Nessinian accents, hardly needing to finish their thoughts before they were understood. They had clearly worked together for a very long time. At the time, Keifon had fought the rising dread that he would be forced to work with a partner. He wanted to work alone; he wanted to live alone. If he could not be with Kazi or with his daughter, he did not want anyone else near him.

He had his solitude for now, at least. The order of the procession slowly shifted as one wagon or rider passed another, moving as a loose body to the northwest. He spotted a textile merchant, a livestock driver with a herd of goats, the bookseller that Keifon had noticed on his first visit, and several merchants who dealt in whatever they could fit on their carts, tarpaulined over to keep the piles of scavenged odds and ends from spilling out.

In the early afternoon, a rider picked his way around the wagons, tailed by a young apprentice. The pair called out like street vendors. As they pulled alongside the passenger wagon, the apprentice handed up paper-wrapped packages and glass bottles. A wine vendor? Keifon's hand tightened on the bench back until he caught a rising savory smell from the rider's saddlebags. A food vendor, food and drink. Keifon caught his breath and considered what he could afford and what he could digest. He noticed a passenger two rows ahead buying bread and two hard-boiled eggs, so when the rider passed his way, he bought the same, with a flask of water. He downed half of the bottle of water first to muffle his stomach's complaints, then slowly finished the food. It settled his hunger without too much pain. He leaned against the roof support and watched the road as his body finished its ritual war with itself.

Along the road a series of inns, horse traders and general stores gradually thinned out. Keifon remembered the notes that the Benevolent Union had copied; the Nessinian healers had mentioned that they'd drawn maps. This ride would seem less interminable if he knew how long it would take.

He extracted the notes from his backpack and flipped through. They were written in Kaveran – translated, perhaps – and many of the treatments referred to Nessinian energy healing. A faint sick feeling swam through Keifon's gut. The Nessinians had seemed kind and even welcoming, but they were still unbelievers in the end. They called on Tufar's holy energy without proper training or attribution, an affront to the bronze god that could not be overlooked. Still, Keifon could learn something from their experience, however ill-gotten it might be.

The map folded out from the back of the logbook, with three dense pages of notes following it. The roughly rectangular trade route was heavily annotated, numbers and symbols peppering the countryside, each referring to the following text.

The caravan now pulled out of Vertal, the port in the south; Keifon located that. The route ran northwest to a city called Prisa, not far away, where the notes mentioned Benevolent Union clinics and a Church of the Divine Balance shrine – something the Nessinians would care about, but of no use to Keifon. From Prisa, the route turned east to the mountains, north to run near the border with Yanwei, then south again to return to Prisa and Vertal. Line after line, note after note, sprawled across the country. *Mining villages all over this area, will come to the Feast of Darano market. Ask for the doctor here, will appreciate help. Risk of bandits in this wood. Refused treatment at first, came to trust us. Caravan might look into rerouting here; hard going. New BU road? Recommend permanent doctor in this town, lots of business. Water sickness common here. Tried to educate.*

Ten years of experience had been distilled down to this. Keifon carefully closed the book. He couldn't imagine traveling with the young, pampered Nessinian girl for ten years. He couldn't imagine her sticking it out for ten years; she was throwing enough fits after one day. He fingered the outline of the coins in his belt pouch and wondered whether she realized how much she'd given him – enough to buy food for a week. His cheeks warmed with the memory. Had she meant to humiliate him? Or was she getting revenge for having been embarrassed? He had been harsh with her about calling the passengers porters. It seemed unbelievable that someone could be so thoughtless, and he was offended on the other passengers' behalf. It was all part of the gods' punishment, that he should be matched up with such a spoiled patrician.

The conversation on the wagon quieted as the afternoon wore on, a few murmurs blending with the wheels' rattle and the hoofbeats of the horses. The members of the caravan kept more or less the same pace with one another, and the mounted guards in their leathers and brown cloaks weaved back and forth between them. The passenger wagon now rolled alongside an open-topped wagon stacked with furniture, cooking implements, barrels, crates, small plaster statues of gods and demigods, farming implements, and canvas-wrapped packages of unclear purpose.

When the sun slanted in from the left front corner of the wagon, the food vendor came around again. The other passengers bought more food, and this time, Keifon noticed several bottles of wine being passed up as well. He could afford to splurge with what the Nessinian had given him, so he bought one of the vendor's Kaveran crepes – full of cheese and mushrooms and herbs – and more water. The passengers behind him uncorked a bottle and passed it back and forth, laughing as they opened their picnic baskets. Keifon could smell it from here, and his throat clenched. His feet were moving before he finished forming the thought.

Agna: Advice

As Agna started eating, she wondered whether the vendor would sell her any advice about cooking over a fire. Her family had always had modern enclosed stoves in their kitchen; Tane, the housekeeper, only cooked things like mulled cider over the fireplace, for the ambience. Agna had helped in the kitchen sometimes for the sake of learning about it, but she knew nothing about campfire cooking.

Footsteps creaked on the floorboards behind her. Agna turned; it was the Yanweian, grim-faced as ever, laden with his luggage.

"May I?"

"Oh. I suppose so." She shifted down the bench toward the wall, and shoved her luggage over to make room for his.

"Thank you." The Yanweian set down his backpack and valise on the floor and perched his case on the bench between Agna and himself. Agna realized that he had also bought dinner from the vendor, and he started to eat without another word.

Agna wondered whether his rudeness could be chalked up to a Yanweian cultural trait, or his personality. She wondered whether he were still angry at her. It wasn't her fault that she had mistaken the passengers for porters. They dressed like porters. She had, of course, noticed that she was the only well-dressed person on the wagon; everyone else wore plain clothes, mostly linen and wool and leather. They wore little jewelry, apart from some marriage torques, as people wore instead of rings in this part of the world. Even the Yanweian was simply dressed. She saw a glint of metal under his open collar and almost startled. He was married? With *that* rude attitude? Why was he traveling alone? Or maybe that accounted for the attitude –

"Is there a problem?"

Agna jumped and snapped her gaze back to her own hands. "N-no. Just – drifted out to sea."

"Hm."

The passengers behind them erupted into laughter, and she felt the Yanweian's posture tighten. She glanced around. None of the others were looking their way; they were engrossed in their own conversations, passing the vendor's wine around. Agna finished her meat pie and the half flask of water that she had saved from lunch. She sighed contentedly, crumpling up the paper wrapper. The Yanweian was halfway through the crepe he'd brought. It seemed rude to talk to someone who was still in the middle of eating, and besides, he probably didn't want to start a conversation. She had no idea why he'd come to sit by her, either.

Eventually he finished and drank a little water. He hadn't bought any of the wine, either. Maybe he had refined tastes, too; Agna certainly didn't intend to drink some homebrew from who-knew-where.

"So," she began, "do you know much about camping?"

He watched her before replying, his tone guarded. "I know some things."

"Oh, that's good. I've never had to camp before, you see. If you could help me learn how to put my tent together, I would be happy to pay you for the privilege."

"Hm. I suppose so." He was looking at the Benevolent Union tents at their feet, bound up in cords. "I helped the previous healers to take this one apart, a few days ago. It's a two-person job. I'll show you how it works."

"We'll help one another, then." She felt magnanimous and optimistic. Perhaps this wouldn't be so bad. "If you help me put up mine, I'll help you with yours."

"They aren't mine or yours. They're ours. One tent for the clinic, one for camping."

Agna couldn't help but stare. "What?"

The Yanweian lowered his water bottle slowly. "The Benevolent Union only pays for one place at the campsite for both of us. They didn't tell you that?"

"They just told me that they sent out teams," Agna said. "That there were too many patients for one person to handle."

The Yanweian's voice picked up an edge of disbelief. "Yes, and we're to camp together. The last pair, your Nessinians, bought a wagon – but they sold it off to another merchant before they retired. It wasn't Benevolent Union property. They didn't tell you that?"

Agna thought back to the briefing in the Benevolent Union headquarters. The intake agent had spoken perfect Nessinian; everything had been clear. She had scrambled behind the idea of the caravan itself, of not having a proper assignment with a clinic or a shrine, of traveling around the country and who knows even what else. They hadn't gotten down to details. "They did not tell me that."

The Yanweian sighed quietly. "That's not your fault, then."

Agna's mind scrambled the rest of the way. She would have to room with this sour stranger who seemed to regard everything she did with contempt. They most definitely had not briefed her about this. She would draft a strongly worded letter to headquarters. And that still left her with a whole year before she could be reassigned. She wondered how much another place on the caravan campsite would cost, along with another tent. She had brought enough money, and she could ask her parents for more. – But that wouldn't do. She could not complain to them, after they had barely put up with her decision to take an assignment overseas. It would be like admitting that they were right. All she had to do was to hold out until she found another arrangement, or thought of some way around this problem.

The Yanweian reluctantly continued. "They should have prepared you more than this."

Agna was almost grateful for that flicker of sympathy, but she considered the possibility that the Union had expected her to research camping on her own. She hadn't. She had gone sightseeing and moped around the hotel. She had looked up the history of the Golden Caravan and brushed up on her Kaveran history. There was so much more she could have done. "I... suppose they didn't."

"I'll help you get set up in camp," the Yanweian offered.

Agna waved a hand. "I'll be happy to pay you."

The Yanweian's shoulders tightened. "No need. The Benevolents assigned us both to this task. For the success of the assignment I'll do what I can."

How not selfless at all. "Fine." She paused, reluctant to ask him for help outright. "What do you think I'll need for camping?"

"What do you have?"

"Some clothes, a few books, personal items."

"No camping supplies?"

"I didn't know that I was camping when I came here," she retorted, the disbelief in his voice inflaming her temper. "And I don't know what to buy. Are you going to help or not?"

His jaw clenched. "Yes. Fine. ...I have most of what I'll need for cooking. I don't mind if you use it as long as you take care of it."

"I'll pay for half."

He waved it off. "Fine. You'll need something to sleep on." He hauled his backpack upright and patted a thick parcel lashed to the top. "And blankets. And we'll need something to keep food and water in. You can split that, if you want," he added, as if cutting off her question before she could ask it.

Agna took a deep breath. "I understand. I can do all of that."

The Yanweian didn't reply. He seemed to consider the conversation concluded. He didn't make a move toward returning to his previous seat, however. She saw him glance toward the case between them.

"What is that?"

"It's a *nanbur*," he said. She didn't understand the word, which tilted like the rest of the Yanweian language did, each syllable like a note in a song. He laid the case over his lap and unbuckled the latches holding it closed. The lid lifted away from an unadorned but beautifully made stringed instrument. She resisted the impulse to touch the glossy wood, but saw him stroke the strings at the neck.

"A lute?"

"It's similar to a lute, I suppose." He closed and secured the case again.

"It's pretty."

"Thank you," he said uncomfortably.

"Will you be playing for everyone when we make camp?"

"...I don't think so."

21

"Why did you bring it, then?"

His voice hardened again. "Because it's mine."

Agna blinked, caught off guard by the nonsensical yet vehement answer. Perhaps her question had been too prying, but it seemed to stand to reason. If he wasn't planning on playing it, he could leave it at home for safekeeping until he returned. She gathered her dignity and leveled her gaze past him, toward the front of the wagon. "Well. Suit yourself."

He didn't answer after that, and they rode until dark in silence. It was their last conversation for three days. Their interaction dwindled back to "excuse me" when they had to climb over one another during the brief stops. Agna knew that the state of things was for the better, even as his silent presence chafed her nerves. She seemed incapable of forming a sentence that did not offend him. He still seemed convinced that she was an idiot, which spurred vengeful fantasies of clubbing him in the back of the head with her nearly-memorized copy of *Blackhall's Human Anatomy and the Workings Thereof.*

There were no proper campsites – if such a phrase even made sense – for three days. The caravan simply pulled aside from the road so that the horses could be rested and watered and fed. When morning came they moved on. For three days the Yanweian did not move back to his original seat, and showed no intention of doing so. Agna refused to move herself, to spite him. She'd been here first, after all. They read, stared into the distance, ignored the other passengers, and ignored one another. Agna's back cramped into a creaking mess after one night of sleeping upright in her seat, and her limbs went numb if she didn't attempt to find new and undignified postures every few hours. It was the longest span of time in her life that she had been without a bath or a change of clothes – even the ship had allowed for sponge baths. Her head ached when the sun shone in her eyes.

The Yanweian's silence took on an increasingly impatient tone. He was tense in the morning, at the dinner hour, at night, and any time that Agna muttered or sighed about the deplorable conditions. After the second day on the road, he put away the medical reference book that he'd been reading – it was printed in that dense Yanweian writing, but Agna had glimpsed some anatomical illustrations. He then started in on some Church of the Four tome with closely spaced text and somber woodcuts of gods and heroes. Sometimes he would pray silently, his hands making the prayer signs of one god or another. Sometimes he would stare into nothing and toy with the links of the marriage torque at his throat, sliding them between his fingers. The tiny sound of the metal clicking against itself, barely audible over the rumble of the wheels, aggravated her.

On the third day, Agna glimpsed a high log wall in the distance, between the edges of the carts. A city, or at least a town. The caravan would finally stop. Hot baths, and proper sleep! And getting off this wagon was a reward in itself.

By noon they had drawn within sight of a wide, level field of bare ground, fenced off from the surrounding fields. A rumble of talk and cheering rose from the leading edge of the caravan, and bells rang from the carts, piercing Agna's foggy head.

"Fort Unity," the passenger wagon driver called over her shoulder. "Caravan camps here for one day, two nights. Next stop, Prisa."

Agna could have leaped up, or sat backwards on the bench like an excited child, or even talked to the Yanweian if she had to. She managed to wait, and made sure that the lid of her trunk was locked. The caravan flowed into the field like a breaking wave, each wagon and rider finding a predetermined place. Agna noticed that the field was already dotted with open-air fire pits, small stone rings with the remains of old ashes in the center of each. They made a grid across the campsite, with a large fire pit in the center. These, then, would be the assigned spaces rented out by the trade company.

The passenger wagon found its place and finally, blessedly, stopped. Some of the passengers bustled around, collecting their things; several of the younger passengers picked up identical rucksacks, slapping one another on the back. The remaining passengers eyed the vacated seats and sneaked around to claim better spots. Agna would leave them to it. She was free. Her back howled when she stood up, but no matter. Rest, and hot water, and freedom!

The Yanweian hefted one of the Benevolent Union's tents on the opposite shoulder from his lute. "I can come back for the other one," he said, the first words he'd spoken to her in a day and a half.

"Yes. Good. I can help once I get all of this unloaded, and buy what I need, and find out where I can have a bath–"

He was already turning away down the aisle. So rude. She reversed the boarding process to bring her trunk back to solid ground – lining it up at the edge, climbing down and breaking its crashing fall as best she could – and scurried after the Yanweian. She assumed that he knew where he was going, the way he'd known about camping and the caravan and every other twice-cursed thing they'd encountered thus far, but his path turned out to lead to the nearest guard. Agna groaned aloud and hung back while he conferred with the guard, then trudged along where the guard pointed.

"Do you know what you're doing?" she panted, as the Yanweian stopped beside a small enclosed cart painted with the trading company sigil.

"Yes," he snapped.

The owner of the cart emerged – a thin, distracted Kaveran man with glasses. The Yanweian was polite with him, she noticed darkly. After consulting some papers, the trading company representative waved at them to follow him, around the rows of wagons and fire pits.

The trio reached one of the unclaimed spots; the trade company representative nodded at them and headed off. Agna dropped the strap of her trunk. Her knees wobbled, and she struggled to stay upright.

The Yanweian sighed, unstrapping the tent from his shoulder. "Stay here, then. Take all the straps off of this, and get it unrolled. Can you do that?"

"Of course," she snapped.

"Good." He piled up his backpack and lute case, leaned the Benevolent Union's tent against them, then headed back the way he came.

Her fingers still obeyed her commands, more or less, so Agna unbuckled all of the fastenings lashed around the tent. The carrying strap came off with them, leaving a long, heavy roll of canvas wrapped around several wooden poles. She dragged it to an open patch in front of the fire pit and shoved it open, half a turn at a time. Once it was unrolled, the construction made a little more sense. It was a few paces to a side, a heavy canvas envelope with a sloped roof, propped up with poles at the corners. There were ropes and metal stakes connected to it at some points, as well. She had seen enough drawings in books to get the general concept. She located the door – such that it was – and dragged the tent around so that it faced the fire pit, like the other tents being built around them. She laid the poles out parallel, and uncoiled the ropes. And there her expertise ended. She couldn't leave the trunk unguarded, even locked. Agna sat on her heels by the deconstructed tent and waited. If the Yanweian said one sarcastic thing when he returned, she would kick him in the shins, or throw one of the stakes at him.

In a few minutes he returned with the other tent slung over his shoulder, lugging some folded wooden contraptions in his arms. Those made yet another pile. At close range, Agna identified a folding table or two and a couple of stools. Equipment for the clinic, as the agent had mentioned.

The Yanweian stretched his shoulders and swung his arms. "We don't have to set this up until tomorrow. Let's just get the camping one up."

"Fine," Agna replied.

With an almost admirable lack of bile, he directed her to hold here and pull there, and in this manner they assembled the tent. Agna followed him inside and sank to her knees again. It was half the size of one of the dormitory rooms. One door that tied shut with canvas straps, no windows, no interior walls. Just the door and a flap in the roof – the only source of air or light, apart from the door.

Agna crawled back outside to breathe. She could rent a carriage back to Vertal. She had plenty of money for that. She would even have enough after that to buy passage back to Nessiny.

Rone would be disappointed with her. Her parents would be proven right. It would be the same as giving up.

She breathed in the open air until the urge to cry subsided. Not now, not yet. She could rise above this. She had trained at the finest institute of higher learning in the entire world, and her mentor was the greatest swordsman in the modern age, and she would not disappoint him. She had learned everything there was to know about healing, and history and business management and Kaveran grammar besides. She could do this.

To calm herself, Agna made a mental list of the other things she had to do. She had to find somewhere to take a bath. She had to buy something to sleep on. She would need clean clothes for after the bath. She would need her mirror and soap and hairbrush. Her toiletry kit, apart from the mirror, was held together in a bag with a clasp. She unlocked the trunk, located her kit and her mirror, and untangled a fresh dress, underclothes, and her towel from the tumbled morass.

The Yanweian's voice was cautious as he picked through his backpack. "If you want the bathhouse, it's at the back of the campsite, on the opposite side. Closest to the hill that goes down to the stream. It's a big tent with a steam cloud design on it." His finger wiggled along a wavy line in the air.

Agna blinked. "Oh. ...Thank you." She gathered her armful of belongings and turned to go.

The Yanweian's voice stopped her again. "I asked where you could buy a bedroll, too. There's a clothes and linens seller who has them."

Agna turned. He wasn't looking at her. He had laid out a cooking pot – the inane thought ran through her head, *so that's how it works!* – and a teakettle. The ordinary, civilized objects were jarring on the bare ground, next to a circle of stones.

A hot bath and some sleep. And no more backbiting. That was all she could ask for. "Thank you," she said again. She didn't have the heart to add, *of course you'd know what to do, you apparently know everything,* or *did you think I couldn't figure all of that out on my own?*

Agna walked across the camp toward the baths. All of the water was still cold, the bathhouse owner explained; they hadn't stoked the stove yet to heat it. So the fee to rent a cubicle in the tent was halved. It didn't matter, Agna insisted. The bathing facilities were rudimentary, just small wooden tubs for soaking and stools and basins for washing, but at least they were private. In another half hour she was clean again, and redressed in fresh clothes. She was shivering, and her hair was damp against the back of her neck, but she didn't care about that.

She nearly skipped back to the campsite with her bundle of laundry. The Yanweian had built a fire in the pit and was heating water in the teakettle. She forgot to say something superior. "Where did you get the water?"

"From the stream. The food vendor seems to sell it when the caravan is moving, too. This water is good for now, though."

Three whole sentences. "I see." Agna pulled her trunk into the tent and parked it on one side. The Yanweian's luggage was already stacked on the other side. So they had claimed sides, like a dormitory. That, at least, made sense. She tossed her laundry in the corner, unlocked the trunk, and refilled her purse from the money box inside.

"You wanted a water barrel and something for food, right?" she asked breezily, emerging from the tent.

The Yanweian looked up. "Oh. Yes. Are you going now?"

"I don't see why not." She had revived; she had a plan; she could take anything.

"Mm. I don't know where the textile merchant is. Just that there is one."

"I'll find it," she shrugged. "Easy enough."

■ ■ ■

Agna carried an empty water barrel stacked on top of a latching chest full of dishes and utensils, with a tied-up bedroll slung over her shoulder and a blanket draped over her arm. It was awkward to slog all of it across the campsite, but the triumph of doing so without the Yanweian's help outweighed every bump and stumble. Agna plunked her armload down by the fireside.

"Ha."

The Yanweian drank the last of his tea and got up from the ground – the ground! "Oh... you didn't have to get such nice things."

Agna stretched her back. "Tch. They're not that nice. Besides, you have to have some self-respect."

The Yanweian weighed the barrel in his hands. "I'll... I can pay you back. Not right now. When we open the clinic, I'll start."

She would have been offended by his stinginess, had his demeanor not been so hesitant and subdued. Maybe he didn't have enough money, somehow. How embarrassing. Agna shrugged. "I don't mind if you owe me. I'm sure that it will all come out evenly in the end. I didn't add it up, anyway."

He didn't answer at first, looking at the things she'd bought, and irritation clouded her sense of accomplishment. She'd done it right. She'd taken care of things. He had no right to ruin that. Finally, the Yanweian set the barrel down just outside the tent door and poured the rest of the boiled water into it. "I'll go and get some more water."

Agna merely nodded, hiding her relief at not having to carry anything else. The Yanweian took the cooking pot and teakettle and headed off toward the stream.

One task down. She could buy some food next; she'd passed a few carts selling basic edible things – cheese and eggs and rustic bread. Enough to make a start.

First, though, setting up – furnishing her room, she thought, and snickered to herself. Her new bedroll was of higher quality than the Yanweian's, which appeared to be military issue, but it was still inadequate for any reasonable person. Agna unrolled it across the floor on the side of the tent that she had claimed as her own and stretched out to test it.

Agna startled awake when a beam of orange-gold light hit her in the face. "Ow!"

"Oh, I'm sorry. I didn't–"

"Ugh." She sat up. Her head seemed to be stuffed with salt and rocks. The Yanweian had opened the tent flap, and the light slanted in over his shoulder.

"Err... I, um. Got some food if you'd like to make yourself something to eat."

She stretched; her muscles were somehow less cramped, despite having slept on the ground. "I'll subtract that from your debt for the storage containers."

She'd meant it as a jab, but he smiled faintly. "Thanks."

Agna emerged into the early evening and sleepily rifled through the food he'd bought. There wasn't much, but then, they would be on the road before long. She managed to toast some bread over the fire and melt some cheese over it, and brew some tea in her new teacup. Even that was a small victory. The Yanweian, meanwhile, wandered off.

When her dinner was finished and all of the pots and plates had been washed, the daylight was still strong enough to read by. Agna dug through the ruins of her trunk to find the flat wooden box that held her writing paper and pens and ink, and settled by the fire – on the ground! – to write.

Dear Rone,

I hope you are well, so that at least one of us might be.

The Benevolent Union has placed me on an assignment that I can only describe as loathsome. I'm following the trade caravan as it makes its way around Kavera, to give healing aid to the people. It's boring and dirty and hard, there are no proper – anything, I am expected to sleep on the ground, and the fellow agent they've assigned to me is sullen and inclined to offense.

I miss you and Esirel, and my family, and the Academy, and Murio, and civilization.

I will be here for a year. I will finish my contract with the Benevolent Union at a proper assignment, and until then I shall make the best of what little I have. My thoughts are with you, also, because your work now must be more meaningful and dignified than this.

Yours, etc.,

Agna

She sealed the letter, addressed it to Rone in care of Tenken Grim – who now, at last, seemed like a real person – and pondered the idea of drafting a letter of complaint to the Benevolent Union headquarters. Perhaps later; she lacked the mental stamina to truly take them to task.

Agna fetched her shoes from the tent and set out to survey the camp and to determine which merchant could handle her mail. A few questions directed her to the master of records, who turned out to be the highly strung trade company employee who had shown them to their campsite. The mail runners, he informed her, would deliver mail to him. She could pick up any incoming letters at his wagon when they were camped.

She completed her slow circuit around the camp, wandering back and forth along the lines of tents. The rows closest to the road were incomplete, with a few tents and shuttered wagons bearing apologetic signs: *Closed, Open Dawn-Dusk, Please Come Back Later.* Beyond the first few lines, the camping tents began, mixed in with some smaller wagons and a few larger coaches. The Captain's wagon was parked near the middle of the camp, along with the passenger wagon and the master of records' wagon. In the center of the camp, some of the merchants were building a bonfire while others gathered around to talk. Agna kept moving.

Back at the Benevolent Union tent – Agna could not yet think of it as her tent – the Yanweian huddled sullenly next to the fire.

"The others are starting a bonfire," Agna offered archly. "You might find more agreeable company there."

His eyes narrowed a fraction, but his voice was polite. "No, thank you. I don't want company."

"At least we agree on something." She slapped open the tent flap and discovered, upon stepping into the tent, that it was nearly pitch dark inside. So much for reading, or repacking her trunk. She would have to either stay here in the dark – limiting her activities to sleeping or fuming – or venture back outside.

Fine. She rolled the trunk through the door and turned it to rest across the fire from the Yanweian, where its raised lid would block their view of one another. Perhaps it was childish. So be it.

She extracted the entangled articles of clothing, tumbled books and other articles and sorted them out into piles. She devised a new system that would, with some luck, survive the next leg of the journey. The bedroll had to be carried across her shoulder or under her arm – it wouldn't fit inside the trunk – but everything else fit, somehow.

Agna took a deep, satisfied breath, locked the trunk, and took a seat on its lid. The perch put her head a couple of feet over the Yanweian's, which helped her mood as well. She felt self-conscious slipping the key on its chain back into the bodice of her dress, but he wasn't looking.

"Might be a good time for a song," she offered.

"I practiced for a while when you were out posting your letter," he said, flexing his hands.

She looked at him again; he'd also changed clothes and shaved. At least he was as civilized as that. The silence rolled over her, and in the distance she heard chatter and singing. It was a world in which she had no interest, even though they were relaxed and entertained there. Agna got up and left.

Fifteen minutes later, she returned with a lantern and a bottle of oil. The Yanweian swallowed whatever complaint or demurral he'd been preparing, and she chose to grant forgiveness for it.

One small lamp lit the tent well enough to read. Agna settled in with her copy of *The Wanderer*, wrapped in self-satisfaction. The smell of damp smoke drifted in from the outside a minute before the Yanweian slunk in. Agna said nothing; it was triumphant enough to watch him curl up with one of his books and read by her light. She'd add that to his tab, too. Then again, what might irritate him more than that?

"I'll call it even for the lamp," she remarked. "Since you knew how to set up the tent."

"All right."

No good. He was barely listening. Agna gave up and turned her attention to her own book. It was still irksome that she'd only been able to bring a few books, and would have to cart around any more that she bought here. She might part with some of her own eventually – she could always buy another copy of most of them – but the dictionary and *Blackhall's Human Anatomy* would have to stay. She would keep her copy of *The Wanderer*, because it was her favorite. And she would keep the book that she'd bought on the waterfront back in Murio, the one at the bottom of her stack of books. She didn't want to admit that she had brought it in lieu of something more dignified. She wouldn't admit the fact that it was one of her favorites, too.

But until she ran out of space or became sick of them all, she could read the books she had brought a few more times. Besides, she supposed that it could be worse; the Yanweian only seemed to have two or three books on hand. He'd spent some time on the passenger wagon paging through his own reference books, and he joined her now, even though Agna took it as a tacit admission of defeat.

The Yanweian clearly enjoyed reading. He looked relaxed for once, sprawled out on his bedroll with his book open on the floor. The lamplight was kind to his face, as was the rare absence of suspicion and tension. Rude, incomprehensible, scornful, impatient and strange, yes, but not stupid, and, despite her early assumptions, not uncivilized. Agna realized that she was staring at him, and snapped back to her book as her face grew warm. She turned toward the wall, holding her book high enough to catch the light, until she was too sleepy to prop it up.

She yawned her way back up to find the Yanweian sitting by his bedroll, hands folded in one of the Church's prayer gestures – Agna remembered her Survey of Polytheism class, and the Church of the Four followers back home. That particular position was the prayer sign of Darano, the warrior god of order and power. The Yanweian's eyes were closed, and he did not react as she gathered her nightclothes and dressing gown and slipped out to the bathhouse to change.

When she returned, he still hadn't moved, except for his hands – Eytra's sign, now. He looked up and then closed his eyes again. Agna hurried to pack up her clothes.

The Yanweian regained his concentration, shifting to the prayer attitude of Tufar. There were only four gods, for goodness' sake; how long would this take? At the same time, some part of her found it reassuring. He wasn't making a show of it – he didn't seem to care whether she even noticed. He was serious about it, and he might even be the sort who prayed every day without fail, like Rone. She had seen the Yanweian praying during the ride, especially as night fell, when both of them were enveloped in their own thoughts. She had to respect his dedication. And the Church of the Four practiced sound ethics most of the time. If he was this serious about his faith and not observing it to keep up appearances, he was more or less trustworthy, or at least ethical.

Rude, incomprehensible, and so on – but ethical.

The Yanweian unfolded from the floor, took some clothes from his pack and stepped outside. Agna relaxed and, finally, shucked off her dressing gown in a pile next to the bedroll. She pulled her new blanket – thin, but of reasonable quality – up over her shoulders and huddled in. She should follow his lead and pray for a while. Following Rone's lead had been intermittently successful at the Academy. She wasn't sure she believed in the Divine Balance, but it was nice to try to meditate sometimes. Sometimes she could clear her mind, ponder the interconnected nature of creation, and call upon it for guidance and sustenance. Sometimes she got stuck in a loop of classes and dormitory insults and unwritten assignments. Her mind wouldn't cooperate now, at any rate. Maybe in the morning.

Keifon: Open for Business

When Keifon stumbled from the tent on their first day of business, the Nessinian was seated by the campfire, dressed in dark brown robes, reading a weighty book with a foreign title. She raised a cup of tea to her lips and continued reading. Keifon groped for the teakettle and poured himself some hot water, then looked for the tea leaves. His mind was muddled after his fragmented sleep, and he pawed through the larder chest randomly.

He couldn't handle breakfast, so he extracted the box of tea and left the food. Waiting for the tea to brew gave him a chance to finish yawning, and the hot liquid soothed his jumping stomach a little. It would have soothed his jangled nerves, as well, were it not for the disapproving presence of the Nessinian and her book. Keifon half-recognized the robes; they looked more or less like the heathen priests' robes. They were nearly the same color as her hair, and the monochromatic contrast against her pale skin underscored her grim expression.

Keifon finished his tea and headed off to shave and change, feeling more alert, if not any more settled. Back in the tent, he gathered the blank logbook from the Benevolent Union and slipped it into his valise, along with some pens and ink. He fastened the medic's pin just below his collar. The Nessinian met him outside the tent, her own logbook under her arm. For a moment they faced one another, unspeaking. Then he picked up the pile of folded equipment, sliding the valise handles over his wrist, and headed toward the road. When he glanced back at a crossing in the path, she had slung the Benevolent Union's clinic tent over her shoulder.

Their assigned spot in the camp layout was placed close to the main flow of traffic, perhaps to give any sick patients the shortest possible walking distance. On one side, a bookseller checked over his inventory. The booth on the other side was a simple table and chair under a canvas sun shade. Its proprietor glanced up from his unpacking to gesture a greeting in the Kaveran style. He was too pale to be Kaveran – Achusan or Nessinian, something eastern. He and the Nessinian would have to be chums, Keifon thought irritably. Weren't their countries more or less the same?

Keifon stacked the tables and stools on the ground, and they set about the construction of the tent. It was larger than the camping tent, emblazoned with the Benevolent Union's seal and the medical aid symbol on all four sides, and fitted with a curtain that slid over the door. He unfolded the tables, leaving the stools to the Nessinian; she could at least handle that much. Eventually they had produced an examination table, a small table for writing or holding supplies, and a set of four folding stools. They arranged a pair of stools on either side of the table, so that both could see patients at the same time.

"We should have water," Keifon mused aloud. "And more light. I'll go."

The merchant next door had begun to unpack his wares by the time he passed by – scores of meticulously labeled bottles and boxes. An apothecary. He nodded to Keifon as he passed, but Keifon kept moving. He was in no mood to chat, particularly with yet another easterner.

He fetched the lamp and the water barrel from their campsite and set them up in the clinic tent. He opened his valise next to the lamp on the side table and began to take inventory of its contents. They were all there, of course, but doing it gave him somewhere to focus.

"It would be good to have a flame, too," he remarked, mostly to himself. "I'll get a spirit lamp when I can. Do you need anything?"

She pointedly raised her hands, and a faint light played over them. Keifon turned back to his supplies. Yes, it had been a foolish question, but he had tried to be courteous.

"Hello, new medics."

Keifon looked up, and the Nessinian spun around. The apothecary lingered in the doorway. He bowed like a courtier paying tribute. The Nessinian returned it, which earned her an appreciative smirk.

"Edann Fletcher. Apothecary." His accent was different from the Nessinian's, Keifon realized. Achusan, perhaps. He knew little about the country except its widespread atheism, and the fact that it had been the first to discover explosive energy. This one, though, was nonthreatening enough, shorter than Keifon and slender, with bookish glasses. Exactly Kazi's type. Keifon imagined this smarmy young apothecary listening raptly to one of Kazi's fireside whispering campaigns, and felt nostalgia and anger pooling in his chest.

"Agna Despana, second-order healer of the Church of the Divine Balance."

"And you?" They turned to Keifon. His old persona flooded back, the one he had refined as an apprentice, dealing with the buyers who came to trade horses. He smiled at the Achusan as though they shared a private joke.

"Keifon the Medic, of the Yanweian National Army."

A genuine smile melted across the apothecary's face, before he throttled it under an ironic smirk. "Pleasure to meet you." He advanced a few steps into the tent, the tension in his slight frame belying his friendly words. "My shop is next door, so if you or your patients need anything, the business is always appreciated. I intend to refer anyone who might need your help, of course."

"Thank you," Keifon replied.

"Thank you," the Nessinian echoed, and went on in what sounded like her native tongue. Behind his glasses, the apothecary flicked a glance at Keifon and back to her before replying. She went on deliberately, turning a shoulder to Keifon as though to cut him out of the conversation, but the apothecary – Edann – kept Keifon in his line of vision. Keifon felt a flicker of interest, but it died like a wayward spark. Not now, not yet. The thought of striking up a relationship again, even at some indeterminate point in the future, was exhausting.

Edann cleared his throat and replied in Kaveran, as though to rope Keifon into the conversation. "I've been here for three years."

The Nessinian went on ignoring him. "Have you met a friend of mine, by any chance? He looks like an Islander, tall and dark, but he grew up in Nessiny and would sound like a Nessinian. He's a swordmaster – green cloak with a high-quality sword. Rone Sidduji is his name."

"...Doesn't spark anything. Sorry."

"Oh... Thank you, all the same."

"I'd better get back to my post. Good day and good business." Keifon and the Nessinian murmured goodbyes as the apothecary left. The Nessinian lingered at the front of the tent, and Keifon stepped around her when the first patient came in.

"Oh! New healers?"

"Yes, ma'am. How may I help you?"

The patient was a middle-aged woman. He led her to one of the folding chairs with his hand on her arm. She giggled at his jokes. He hadn't thought ahead of time about pulling out his old act. It had fallen onto him like an old cloak, and to his surprise it felt comfortable. It seemed to disarm the Kaverans, making them worry less about his accent and his alien looks. And he could always read those who reacted badly and take a cooler approach.

Keifon ran through a basic examination, listening to her lungs and feeling for unusual lumps and all of the usual mundane checks, as he chatted with her about her health and habits. It was refreshing to deal with a new patient. He had only practiced on the others in his unit during his training, and he knew every detail of their lives already. And he had reached the real purpose of his exile in this country. It was a comfort to finally be useful.

After the woman left, Keifon recorded the details of their transaction in his logbook. The Nessinian pounced on the next patient, a man with two young children.

"A girl healer?"

"Girls can be healers, the fall healer is a lady. Stupid."

"*Hey.* Name-calling. – I guess the Nessinian gentlemen retired, eh?"

"Yes, sir. How can I help you today?"

"Just checking out the little ones for now. *Hey.* Don't touch that."

She persuaded one of the children to sit still long enough to be examined, and another patient ducked into the tent. Keifon swung back into action, leaving the father and children to her, ignoring the clench under his ribs.

A strange light caught Keifon's attention, halfway through the next examination, and he glanced up to see the Nessinian holding out her hands to one of her young patients, letting the child stir her fingers through the pale green light and laugh in delight.

Keifon looked away, half irritated that she would use the divine power for such a trivial purpose, half aching with envy. Both children were about Nachi's age, one younger and one a little older. Keifon wanted to grab their father by the collar and tell him to appreciate what he had.

He returned his attention to his current patient, a man old enough to be his grandfather, who seemed to appreciate his attempts at humor. He unwound the stethoscope from his valise and continued with the routine.

They jockeyed for patients for the rest of the morning, and Keifon ignored her most of the time. When he had patients, he focused on them; between patients he recorded his notes, and tried to recoup his energy for the next round. He tried not to think about her at all.

It wasn't right that a heathen should wield the holy power that way. Only a Tufarian priest, anointed in the service of the gods, could be trusted to channel their power in the mortal world. A heathen with such power over life and death was an unnatural and terrifying thing. What would stop them from maiming and killing, without repercussion? Mortal law, and mortal law was fallible. He was right to be on guard against her.

He reminded himself that she was just a spoiled patrician child. It wasn't his place to criticize, however unnatural her dealings might be. The Benevolent Union had shown poor judgment in setting them to this task side by side. There was no teamwork to be had between a patrician and one such as himself. It was ridiculous on its face. He refused to be her servant, she refused to treat him as human, and they each accepted the impasse that they had reached. The best he could do was to serve his time to the best of his ability, pretending that she didn't exist. He hadn't wanted company anyway.

A food vendor came by, advertising his wares with cries from his apprentice and a wafting smell that roiled Keifon's stomach with hunger and burning pain. The Nessinian leaped to her feet and met the vendor at the door to the clinic tent. Keifon waved off the offer, and the vendor and his assistant moved on. The Nessinian closed the curtain across the door and pulled one of the stools over to the side table.

"You can take a second off," she said archly.

"I'd like to rest," he said. There was no point rallying the act with her. He wouldn't confide in her, but there was no use in putting on a brave front, either. "I'm... not feeling very well right now."

"...Oh. I can check it out if you like." She held out a hand and mimed her energy-scanning gesture.

"No. Thank you." Keifon closed his eyes and folded his hands in Tufar's sign. He repeated the entreaty to the bronze god – not his chosen deity, but relevant in this situation. He wanted to practice the skills that the Army had taught him to the best of his ability. He was helping these people, in his small way. They were strangers and foreigners, but Kavera was under the gods' sight, too. This had to be the reason that they had sent him here. He would atone by serving.

"Are you nervous?"

He looked up at her sudden question. She flustered, crumpling the wrapper from her lunch. "It's natural enough. I mean. I even – I might have felt a little nervous myself. At first. But we're here to help the people. That's the important thing."

"Hm." She was thinking along the same lines, then. Keifon wasn't sure whether to be troubled by that. He passed by her to dip a cup of water from the barrel and drink. She opened the door again, and soon enough, there were patients to distract them.

Keifon's first afternoon patient had a badly healed wound in his arm, a fluke strike with the edge of a sickle, he explained. Scar tissue snarled over the half-healed gash, and Keifon's careful fingers found a small mass under the skin. The patient's fingers barely moved when Keifon prompted him. He might have damaged some of the tendons in his arm, Keifon thought. The man hadn't sought out the local doctors, explaining that they were busy with the road patrol and that most of the townspeople just waited for the caravan doctors. He'd bandaged it himself and went on clearing the rest of his fields for the spring planting.

Keifon had dropped his joking demeanor at once, and slowed his speech so that his instructions would be understood. "This will be complicated. I'll need you to stay calm." He sat with the man to explain that he would have to cut open his arm to take out whatever was making that lump and to try to stitch it together properly. It didn't seem to be infected, however, so it might heal better afterward. The Nessinian handled the next pair of patients, a child of about seven or eight with his pregnant mother.

Keifon helped the man with the sickle wound up to the table. He gave him a heavy dose of knockseed and instructed him to chew it until it was soft. Meanwhile, he dabbed the arm with antiseptic. He handed the patient a cup of water to swallow the medicine when it had begun to activate, and helped him to lie back. He spread a cloth under the injured arm. Injuries were his specialty, after all; the Army's medical training was focused on recovering from battle and monitoring the health of one's fellow soldiers. He knew enough about diagnosing illnesses and chronic conditions, but this was where his expertise lay.

The patient's eyes were glazed and drifting shut, and his breathing had slowed. The Nessinian's young patient hid his eyes, and his mother clucked sympathetically.

The Nessinian spoke as Keifon arranged his scalpels and needles. "I can close the incision, when you're done. You won't need to suture it."

Keifon's jaw tightened. Naturally, she had to undermine him in front of everyone, in the middle of a procedure that he could execute flawlessly. But she was right. If she could heal the incision like a Tufarian priest, the recovery time would drop to nothing. He had no rational reason to refuse her help. "All right," he said at last. "When I'm finished."

35

"Tell me if you need anything," she murmured. Keifon nodded tightly. She turned her attention back to the child and finished her examination. Keifon waited, wanting to spare the child the sight of blood and spare his own patient the extra risk of contamination. He scrubbed his hands as mother and child paid the Nessinian and left. The Nessinian closed the curtain over the door and turned to the side table to write in her logbook.

Keifon tapped the patient's shoulder and touched his injured arm, watching for a reaction. He was unconscious. Keifon lifted his scalpel and cut open the half-healed skin over the foreign mass, carefully teasing the scar tissue and muscle fiber apart to find a chip of something black and inorganic – likely a fleck from the edge of the sickle that had cut him. Keifon pulled it out with tweezers and probed the area for more metal, finding nothing other than excess scarring and damaged tendon. He excised some of the scar tissue, hoping that the Nessinian's healing could make the best of what was left, and rinsed out the cleaned wound with alcohol. At least it wasn't infected. The inexpert first aid, and luck, had done that much.

As he worked, the Nessinian picked up the tools that he had used and washed them. So she knew how to assist in an ordinary procedure, Keifon thought. It was too bad that her attitude was so repellent. He could have used some backup.

"Here." She returned to his side at his terse summons.

Keifon stepped back. She spread her hands on either side of the site, along the inner bend of the patient's elbow and against the palm of his hand. She bent her head in concentration. Keifon held his breath, forgetting his own bloody hands. At first he saw nothing, but then the tendons squirmed and fused. Keifon pressed his wrist against his mouth, willing his stomach acid down. Whether she knew it or not, she was calling on Tufar, he reminded himself. It was the holy power under a false name. He couldn't look away as the cut blood vessels and damaged muscle knitted together, slowing the trickle of blood. Finally the patient's skin scabbed over and then smoothed. The Nessinian lifted her hands and staggered back, dropping into the stool by the side table. She rested her head against the corner of the table. Keifon saw her shoulders heaving with her breath, and his worry subsided.

"God's blood," Keifon whispered. He hurried to gather the rest of his instruments, scrubbed them in water and soap, then rinsed them with alcohol. He scrubbed his hands, pulled the bloody cloth from under the patient's arm, and washed off the sticky antiseptic and flakes of scab tissue. The Nessinian pillowed her head on her crossed arms. Keifon could see antiseptic residue on her fingers, but she did not move to clean up.

"Excuse me?" Another patient, a young woman, peeked around the curtain.

Keifon forced a welcoming smile past his grim thoughts. "Hello there. We have a patient recovering here, but if you don't mind staying quiet, we can see you."

She flicked a glance over at the unconscious man. "Oh, it's Curno. Were you able to do something for his arm?"

"Yes, ma'am. Now, if you'll have a seat over here..."

The new patient was exceptionally susceptible, and he found himself scaling the act back. She had to pay attention and take him seriously, instead of just gazing into his eyes. He listened to her afflicted lungs, prescribed more sleep and twenty minutes a day breathing herb-infused steam, and wrote his recommendations for the apothecary. The Nessinian stepped away to let him use the desk, and paced over to the water barrel to wash up. No one saw that the book he spread over the desk was a dictionary, not a medical reference. The patient didn't know that he had to copy the words individually. The apothecary would have noticed by now, from his recommendation slips, that his handwriting in the Kaveran script was childish and awkward. It was embarrassing. But it couldn't be helped.

As the young woman left, thanking him effusively, the patient on the table stirred and groaned. Keifon jumped to his side. "Sir, please lie still for a little while longer." The man muttered something incoherent. "That's right. We've gotten it out, and your arm will be good as new. Just let the anesthetic wear off." He patted his arm. "You're doing fine."

The Nessinian had recovered enough to make notes in her logbook – which, Keifon reflected, she had the right to do now. She had stolen his patient, and now she could take the credit.

She picked up a new patient soon afterward, and by the time both of them had finished their next set of examinations, the man with the sickle wound began to come around for good. He lifted his arm and stared at it.

Keifon cleared his throat. "Um. She – Agent Despana closed you up after I'd cleaned the wound."

The man flexed his hand, bent his elbow, and touched his fingers to his thumb one by one. "I can go back to work?"

Keifon looked to the Nessinian, and she continued. "I don't see why not. Please rest for a while longer, a day or two. If it starts to swell, please see the local doctor immediately. But your arm should be fine."

He clasped the spot where the wound had been. "Bless you," he said at last. "Bless you both."

"Thank you, sir," Keifon said, as the Nessinian echoed something similar.

He paid them both, despite their polite protests. When he had gone, Keifon lingered by the door, his hand on the curtain. "I'd appreciate it if you wouldn't undermine my expertise in front of the patients."

"...What?"

"I had the situation under control. You didn't need to barge in."

"You couldn't have done what I did, and you know it. I was doing what was best for the patient."

He turned halfway. "If you can handle this clinic on your own, I'll have the Benevolent Union transfer me."

37

She was on her feet, clenching her fists. "Ugh! That's not what I said." She sighed, but Keifon's glacial resentment would not shift. "You took care of taking the metal out. I would have had to do the same thing. But you couldn't close it the way I could, and I knew he would recover faster that way. I did what was best for the situation at hand."

Keifon sized her up. She seemed to believe that. He sank into one of the stools, arms folded, staring at the examination table. She wasn't wrong. A recovery time of some weeks had reduced to no time at all. Still. Was he of any use here? Or was he to be this spoiled child's servant, carrying her things, lining up her patients, while she accomplished healing that was completely out of his reach?

"Fine," he said at last. "But don't do that again. I'll handle my patients, and you handle yours."

"Fine." She turned toward the sound of the food vendor outside. "I'll be back."

She left, and after several minutes Keifon began to try to relax. His stomach knotted. Were it not for the expense, he would have taken some ginger extract from his kit to soothe it. Of course, he hadn't eaten all day, which might also have contributed. But the thought of food made him queasy; if the Nessinian came back with her dinner, he would have to leave.

Rereading his notes helped a little. He made a few notations to clarify the more rushed entries from the late morning. He did not elaborate on the sickle wound cleaning.

The Nessinian returned, empty-handed, saying nothing. Keifon claimed the next patient who came in and left the next two, in quick succession, to her. The flow of traffic picked up outside the tent as evening approached. Many of the townsfolk seemed to be finished with their own work, and had come to the caravan to socialize and shop.

If he'd understood the Benevolent Union's notes, they would be on the road for a few weeks straight, with one-day stops at some villages along the way. The next long stop was far to the east, where they'd stop and trade in the hill country for a full week, over the Feast of Darano, before turning north. It would be four years – four very long years, unless the Nessinian broke her contract first – but dividing it into pieces, concentrating on this stop and that stretch of road, made it feel almost manageable.

At nightfall, the caravan guard circulated and lit torches on the path. The patients had stopped straggling in. Both Keifon and the Nessinian admitted that they would stop for the night. She began to fold the stools and the table. He left her to that minor task and began to untie the tent's side walls. Grumbling, she carried half of the furniture toward the passenger wagon as he continued to break the tent down.

With the tent walls rolled up and tied, Keifon could watch the camp around them as he dismantled the tent's framework. The caravan was swarming with activity, though many of the visitors flowed toward the town. Many of the merchants headed for the center of the camp, and between the other tents he saw glimpses of a bonfire being built.

"Coming?"

Keifon started at the voice. The apothecary stepped off a chair, having untied the awning over his stall. "We get together every night, unless there's rain."

Keifon remembered the evening gatherings of the farmhands, alive with ale and music and loud conversation. The members of his unit in the Army had gathered as well, in smaller groups – the full fifty gathered only at holidays and after training milestones. He'd avoided most of those large gatherings, stealing away with Kazi or seeking out the handful of his fellows who had accepted his limitations. He wet his lips and remembered that he could leave if the tone turned threatening. Or if he couldn't resist temptation. "Thank you for the invitation. I may do that."

The apothecary folded the awning and packed it into one of his cases. He put on a bored expression, but Keifon realized that the apothecary was watching him.

Keifon nearly lost control of the tent poles as he began to disconnect them. The apothecary hauled off his equipment and inventory. The Nessinian reappeared, picked up the rest of the folding tables and chairs and headed toward the passenger wagon. By the time Keifon was finished fuming at her, the tent was down.

The Nessinian had stowed their other gear under one of the seats, and Keifon added the tent to the pile. He made one more trip to the clinic's space to pick up his notebook and valise and plodded toward the camping tent.

She wasn't there when he arrived. Keifon went about building a fire and set a kettle to boil over it. All he wanted was to sleep, or to sit by the bonfire and listen as well as he could, but with the end of the business day his appetite returned. When the kettle boiled, he poured in some of the rice he'd bought in Vertal and put on the lid.

Keifon lay back to rest while it simmered, staring at the sky. His mind churned with medical terms and fragments of conversation in Kaveran. He let it roam for a while. This would become easier in time, just as his Army training had, or his apprenticeship. He believed this theoretically, although the bleary fatigue that enveloped his brain made it difficult to fully accept.

The Nessinian returned to the campsite with a handful of wildflowers. He frowned at her and let it go. She would do what she wished. It was no concern of his.

When the water had boiled off, he dished out a bowlful and ate slowly, not bothering to flavor the rice. The blandness was easier on his stomach. The Nessinian, ignoring him, poured some water into her cup, and placed the flowers in it. She set this by the fire and fetched a flat wooden case and their lamp from the tent. She propped the case on her knees, pulled out a notebook and a pencil, and turned the book to a fresh page. She bent aside to light the lamp, and then set about drawing the bunch of flowers.

This was unexpected. Keifon tried not to react, sipping water along with his dinner. Was art her hobby? Nessiny was full of artists, wasn't it? Artists and opera, and backstabbing nobles. That was all he knew about Nessiny. Wondering about this at least kept his mind off the clinic. Or the apothecary.

Half of the rice was enough for tonight. Keifon sealed the rest in a crock and left it in the larder chest for the next morning. The Nessinian went on ignoring him, absorbed in her work, as he set the teakettle over the fire. Some tea, and then he would join the gathering at the fire. Or he might take his nanbur and find a quiet place to practice. That seemed more appealing at the moment. He could talk to the apothecary when he was less exhausted. Playing for a little while would help him relax, and it would not be mentally taxing.

When the water was ready, he let the tea leaves steep for a while. The Nessinian looked up from her notebook and addressed him for the first time in hours. "Do you mind if I have some tea?"

"Uh... no. Go ahead."

She poured herself a cup as he drank his tea. Her notebook lay on the ground. The drawing was a study of the plant, with insets detailing the leaves and flowers. It looked more like a medical illustration than a painting. Perhaps it was a Kaveran medicinal herb that he hadn't encountered.

He was taking an interest in her actions, Keifon realized. She had crossed his path, like an oddly shaped cloud, and he was curious. That was all.

When the tea was finished, he slipped into the tent to retrieve his nanbur. He'd been away all day, and it was just where he'd left it. He would have to trust in the caravan guard to keep it safe, he'd realized on his first day out. It was a little difficult to accept.

"Oh, are you going to play?" She looked up from her drawing as he emerged.

"Practice, that's all. I'll be back soon." He headed for the edge of the camp before she could respond. She could get angry, be disappointed, bargain with him – he didn't have the patience for any of it.

Outside the camp, a fence ran along the edge of the road, separating it from a pasture. The caravan's stable master had a tent at the nearest edge of the camp, and the pasture owner's farmhouse was visible in the distance. Otherwise, the area was deserted. Most of the caravan's traders had dismantled their stalls and gone to the bonfire, or gone back to their own tents. At most, he would be overheard by a grazing horse.

Keifon pulled out the nanbur before hopping onto the top rail. He took a deep breath, readjusting to the weight of the instrument in his hands. He had practiced on a riverbank last time. It wasn't the same as feeling the grasslands roll out around him, hearing the distant sounds of the herd. But he wasn't a rancher anymore, or a rancher's son.

He plucked the strings one by one. The air was dry enough here not to damage the tuning. He could be thankful for that. A few scales up and down loosened his fingers. It seemed dangerous to play half of the songs he knew – he did not want to play anything nostalgic or patriotic. Not here. He started a love song and abandoned it; too much resentment was creeping into its happy notes. A lament would have to do, one that he had played on the riverbank. It was another love-lost story. Tragic circumstances, implied death, nothing too close to the bone. No anger. No betrayal. Not in this story.

He had brought his nanbur to the inns sometimes, playing with chord patterns and putting phrases together, turning Kazi's political ranting into an anthem. Sometimes he had backed the polemics with fragments of patriotic hymns, pretending not to notice, turning them into something strange and contradictory. Kazi would stop and glare at him, too proud to acknowledge the jest any other way. Keifon would smirk, Kazi would sigh, and they would move on to things other than talking.

Keifon rested the nanbur on his knees and stretched his shoulders. Was this helping? He wanted to do this, to remember everything Kazi had said until it stopped hurting. It had to stop hurting, or at least hurt less. People said that it took time. For him, with Eri, it had taken time, and nearly dying, and joining the Army, and Kazi. And it had hurt a little less. When he'd gone to say goodbye to their daughter, he had tried not to look at Eri.

This wasn't helping. He stretched his hands and started a more neutral song, a harvest song, even though it was the wrong time of year for that. It was brisk, uplifting, and difficult to remember. He hadn't played it for months, and it took concentration to summon the proper progression. It was just a song. Pleasant sounds in the air. A challenge for his hands and his mind. Nothing more. He played until his hands tired. The torches in the camp showed him the way back.

Agna: Loss

The next campsite, in a clearing in the woods outside Prisa, was just like all of the others. A little while after dark, the patients stopped coming. The Yanweian stood and began to pack up his kit. Agna wordlessly did her part, and between them they dismantled the clinic tent and returned to the camp tent. In the field next to the camp, a mulberry tree reached a heavy branch over the fence. Agna paused to pick a sprig of leaves and berries. It would make a good subject. She could even send her sketch to Lina. Her sister would enjoy studying such things, identifying the subtle differences between the plants here and those at home.

Cradling the leafy twig in her hands, Agna returned to the campsite and filled her drinking cup with water. She propped the little sprig in the water, leaning against the side of the larder chest, before fetching her drawing supplies from her trunk and the unlit lamp from the tent floor.

Agna settled in and laid out her pencils, charcoal for shading, and drawing paper. She turned her notebook to a blank page, propped the stationery box on her lap, and sketched out the dominant lines of the composition. It would strain her eyes to do fine detail work in this light, but she could at least rough in the beginnings of her drawing.

Look, Mama, I'm finally practicing, she thought wryly. *Too late, though.* The Agna who had gone to art school instead of the Academy lived in another world, in another time. She would have stayed in Murio. She would never have met Esirel or Rone, her best friends. She would never have learned how to speak Kaveran. She would never have discovered how much she loved healing. She would walk an uncomplicated path into her destiny, and she would have her parents' unequivocal support. She would sleep in a real bed, and consort with respectful and like-minded peers... but all the same, Agna felt a little sorry for her.

The Yanweian ignored her, stacked half of their remaining firewood and lit some tinder. He cooked whatever it was he ate, and then left. Agna packed away her drawing supplies and poked through the larder chest to find something halfway edible.

The Yanweian returned in a sleeveless undershirt, his sleeping pants, and socks, carrying his clothes and shoes. He traded his laundry for his lute case, sat cross-legged on the other side of the fire, and plucked some notes.

Agna ate dinner, ignoring him as best she could. She wondered what he had made for dinner, and whether she could learn anything from his technique. She couldn't ask any questions without irritating him, and she hated to admit that he knew more about it than she did. She wondered whether anyone had written books about cooking over fires, and whether the bookseller in the caravan might carry them.

Leaving him to his practice, Agna gathered her kit and left for the baths. It was difficult to soak comfortably in their small tubs, but a good scrub always improved her mood. She would get a good night's sleep and feel better in the morning. The soft, strange melody underlay her thoughts as she lay down to sleep.

■ ■ ■

Agna opened one eye a slit when the Yanweian returned to the tent. He bent and pulled her trunk toward the tent flap, and Agna's blood froze. "Hey, what are y—" She sat up, and the Yanweian stood, and it was not him at all. It was a stranger, taller than the Yanweian.

"Shit."

Agna screamed. From outside she heard a choked cry. The tent was empty apart from herself and the burglar. She found the Kaveran word at last. "*Guards! G*—"

The stranger clapped a gloved hand over her mouth, cinching an arm around her neck. Two more strangers erupted into the tent, one tripping over her trunk and swearing. Where was he? Where were the guards? One of the strangers hauled her trunk backward through the tent flap, while another grabbed her wrists and pinned them behind her back. The two of them dragged her, stumbling, from the tent.

Two more burglars – bandits? Kidnappers? – held the Yanweian up and muzzled him while a third punched him in the stomach. Blood dripped between the bandit's fingers and down the Yanweian's chin. Agna yelled against the glove over her mouth, and got an elbow in her side in return. She gasped and choked. She tried to catch the Yanweian's eye, to find the closest thing she had to an ally. He didn't see her; his gaze was empty and glazed.

Agna struggled against the hold on her arms. The bandit behind her twisted her arms harder. She relented as her joints reached their limit. Panic danced through her blood. This couldn't happen. They were on a mission for the Benevolent Union, a peaceful organization known for its good works. They were healers. No one would dare. Didn't they know? Didn't the Yanweian tell them who they were?

"It's locked." One of them kicked her trunk.

"It's heavy. There's got to be money."

"I got this." One of them held up the Yanweian's valise.

"Tch. Take it if you want."

One of them grabbed the Yanweian's discarded lute, and the pinioned medic revived, struggling against his captors. The bandit covering his mouth let go so that another one could backhand him in the face.

"Not that." His voice cut through the ongoing muttering about how to open the trunk. "Not that. Please." His lip was split and bleeding. The blood soaking into his shirt had sheeted from a long diagonal cut along his neck. From this distance and in this light Agna couldn't see it very well, but she hoped it wasn't deep. He wouldn't be standing if it were, she told herself.

Agna twisted, trying to get her mouth free, and the thief allowed her to speak. "I have the key. To the trunk. Take it. Leave his lute."

"*Nanbur*," the Yanweian corrected tonelessly.

"Isn't that sweet," one of them sneered. "The foreign girl says she has the key, Boss."

"It's around my neck. Just take it. I don't care, just – take it." It was a lie, a desperate lie. She cared. Her life depended on that trunk. But if they hit the Yanweian any more they might kill him, and she could not watch her partner die in front of her. She half-hated him, and her daydreams of violence against him boiled in her gut now – but she could not bear this. Not in reality.

She could not beg them to leave him alone, because if she begged she would break. If she begged, she would remember that they had all the power. She would remember that there was nothing she could do to make them listen to her.

Someone pawed her neck, the rough leather scraping hard against her skin. The hand entangled the chain and yanked it hard to snap it. Her mother had given it to her before she'd left – just a thin, plain gold chain from her collection. If they just took the trunk and the key and let them go – most of her money was in the trunk, and her books, and the letters from her sister and from Rone. But they would live.

The thieves opened the trunk to rifle through her belongings. Their attention was focused on the money box that they had found. They hadn't muzzled her again. Agna took a deep breath. "*Guards!*"

"Shut up," one of them growled, and twisted her arm fiercely. Something cracked, and her world went white. She cried out, and through the worst pain she'd ever felt, she remembered. She had trained for this, three tense weeks every year that the healers never told their friends about. The swordmastery students and the priesthood students assumed that the healers went through some kind of midterm testing, a traditional and convenient fiction.

She had sat frozen to her seat with her fellows in a civilized practice room, listening to their trusted professors calmly explaining how to violate every precept they'd ever learned.

Our power is life, and it is also death. You know the human body and all that drives it. It is our responsibility to use this knowledge to heal. But in our defense, and only in our defense, we can also use it to harm.

Moving her right arm almost blinded her, but she forced her terror and sickness and panic through her skin and into the hands of the bandits that held her. The energy connected with theirs, jangling, unwelcome, reverberating back into her like a strike of metal on metal, but she shifted it through their arms and clenched it like fists around their tracheas. They choked and dropped her, whistling and gasping.

Agna dropped to one knee. The bandits holding the Yanweian had turned, watching her. Not watching him. She dragged herself to her feet, tears leaking from her eyes, and shoved her spread hand in the face of the bandit on the Yanweian's right side. Her shoulder felt like an infinite well of pain, a sun lit by despair. She forced her rage through his skin and set fire to the nerves behind his eyes. He dropped the medic's arm and staggered back, clutching at his face.

As Agna wavered and fell, the Yanweian snapped back to alertness and grabbed a knife from the incapacitated bandit's belt. He slashed at the bandit on his other side, quick and efficient. Agna's vision was blurring. Someone grabbed her by the throat. She couldn't find the Yanweian among the flashes of steel in the torchlight; she couldn't see how many bandits surrounded her; the guards hadn't come. Her fingers scrabbled against his wrist. She paralyzed every muscle around his lungs until he went away.

It was too much. She had spent too much forcing her will through their resistance. Though her shoulder felt like an infinite well of pain, the rest of her body was finite. She collapsed from the ground up.

Keifon: The Long Night

We are the right hand of Darano, the shield of the motherland. We strike for gods and country.

We are the right hand of Darano, the shield of the motherland. We strike for gods and country.

We are the right hand of Darano, the shield of the motherland. We strike for gods and country.

Keifon was a disembodied force. It was not his knife in his hand. He wasn't sure it was his hand. But the strikes were as true as he could make them. He was bleeding and dizzy, and everything hurt. The night thundered with booted footsteps and Kaveran shouts. A warning shot cracked over their heads. Some of the bandits had scattered. They had taken his valise and the Nessinian's money and they might have choked her to death right in front of him. He hadn't been able to push past in time. Keifon had kept everyone else away from her body, but he would not check her until they were all gone. It was cowardice, doing this. It was easier to fight, to risk dying, than to turn over her lifeless form.

I don't have any money.

How about in the tent, you lying northern bastard? – Search it.

We're with the Benevolent Union. We're a charity. Don't—

She'd screamed, and he'd tried to call to her to run. They'd taken the knife away from his throat and muzzled him instead. They'd dragged her from the tent, and his days and nights of rage and resentment became meaningless. She didn't deserve this. Even heathens deserved better than this. Keifon was a disembodied force. He was vengeance. He was fear.

We are the right hand of Darano, the shield of the motherland...

The caravan guard pounded into their clearing, stomping through the ashes of the fire, training their muskets on the bandits, wrestling them to the ground. The bandit nearest him turned and fled. The knife slipped from Keifon's hand. The dam holding the terror back shivered. He focused on the pale shape at his feet. She might not be dead. Keifon was the medic. The medic shored up the wall.

The Nessinian had collapsed face-down in the dirt. He knelt by her side, shaking her shoulder, praying that he wouldn't make it worse. "Agent. Agent Despana – Agna. *Hey.* Can you hear me? Agna?"

She cried out. He let go and pushed his arm over his eyes. Alive. Wounded, but alive. "I'm sorry – can you move?"

46

She lifted her head, convulsed, and crashed over onto her back, clutching her right shoulder. He found enough space between her fingers to press gently against the bone, to determine that it hadn't been dislocated or broken. Sprained or torn, more likely. She kicked and sobbed out loud, and he shushed her, closing her spasming fingers in his. Keifon was the medic, and the medic saw her as another patient. Not his partner, not a member of his squad, not his responsibility. Only a broken human being that he had to mend.

His soothing had some effect, or maybe her system couldn't register all the pain at once. She took a couple of deep breaths and opened her eyes. He focused, because she did not. Almost immediately she began to slip out of consciousness. A stab of panic pierced the medic's calm. Head injury. "Hey. Stay with me. *Hey.*"

She fought back out of the fog, looking cross with him. Her accent was slippery, thicker than usual; he could hardly follow. "Stop it. You – are all right?"

"I'm fine. Did they hit you in the head? Look at me."

"Stop. Didn't. I just... you aren't..." She slipped under again, and he squeezed her uninjured hand.

"Hey. Come back. Talk to me."

"...s'posed to the power too much – use – the power like that... too much. Tired."

Keifon made himself back off. He knew first aid; he was a soldier. He was not a Tufarian priest, and he did not know about energy healing. "All right. If you say so. You should get inside, though." He looked around. The guards inspected her ransacked trunk and surveyed the tent, their silhouettes cast against the wall. Torchlight had engulfed their section of the camp. A string of guards had encircled the area, keeping a few onlookers out. "...I'll help you. Come on."

The Nessinian pushed herself up on her left elbow and struggled to her feet. Keifon arranged his arms for a proper one-man support, but she didn't know how to accept it, and the two of them stumbled toward the tent. Two guardsmen looked up when they shouldered through the tent flap. One muttered an oath under her breath.

"She needs to sleep. Please go."

"Yes, sir." They vanished. The Nessinian collapsed on her bedroll, panting for breath, but before long she had lost consciousness again. She was breathing, at least. She was alive. That was the important thing. They were alive. He had been there this time. They had stopped it. Keifon wiped his arm across his eyes. He couldn't rest yet. If he rested, it would catch up with him.

He dragged himself back out of the tent. The bandits – or the guards – someone had kicked over their water barrel, diluting a spatter of blood in the dirt. His brain laboriously traced the process to get more water. Down to the stream. Back. Light a fire. Boil the water. But out there it was dark, and the bandits were out there. The part of him that could remember how to get water chided him for the thick surge of terror in his throat, but it could not make him go.

One of the guards approached him, and he jumped. She glanced back and forth along his line of sight. "Oh – can we get you some water, medic? You're to wait here for the guard captain. He should be here in a minute."

Too many thoughts, at once. He stared, putting everything together. She had offered to do him a favor. "Yes. Thank you."

"Why don't you sit down? We'll get you patched up, too. We're not medics, but we can do that." She smiled, and he thought he should acknowledge it, but something got lost on the way. He sat down, and she picked up their overturned water barrel and went. There were plenty of other guards, though, armored and not. Keifon knew many of them by sight, and knew some of their names. He rested his head on his knees. The guard captain would be there soon, and the other guard would help him clean up and get bandaged. The medic was there, fading, reminding him that he was in pain and half-soaked in blood.

The guard returned with their water barrel. He had seen her in the clinic for a checkup. Nita was her name. She was a few years younger than Keifon. She was reserved, compared to most of the other guards. He didn't know much else about her. She set the barrel back where it belonged and placed a small box by the fireside, then looked around. "Do you have cups?"

"Um. In the chest, there."

The bandits had opened it and knocked it over. That had been the second thing they'd done, after grabbing him. Nita set it upright, fished a cup out of the interior, and dipped out some water. She held it out to him. Keifon stared at it before taking it. "Go ahead," she said. "It's from our tank, not from the stream. It's safe."

Keifon couldn't figure out how to apologize. He hadn't been thinking about that; he wouldn't assume that she would hand him undrinkable water. He hadn't been thinking about anything at all. "Thank you." He drank it, and she nodded. That, at least, was the right thing to do. Nita held her hand out for the cup, and he returned it. She dipped out more and set it on the ground by the box, but a commotion behind her distracted her. Keifon looked over her shoulder, his heart racing. The guards straightened up and saluted. Nita scrambled to her feet and did the same. – Not the bandits, then. The guard captain.

The guard captain was dressed in civilian clothes, but his bearing and the sharpened attention of the other guards left no question about his authority. He turned aside to speak to the knot of guards around the Nessinian's trunk. Keifon stood and waited to be addressed. The guard captain approached him, and Keifon stood straighter, trying not to weave. He was a trained soldier of the Yanweian National Army. He would not disgrace his country.

"Ah yes. At ease, soldier," the guard captain said with a trace of irony. Keifon fell into the proper position. It gave him somewhere to put his hands, a way to stand, things to say when he was addressed. The soldier knew his place, and that made it easier.

"What happened here?"

"Sir. I was sitting there–" he turned to point out the spot next to the fire – "practicing the nanbur. Someone..." He was breaking out into a sweat. "...someone – must have come up behind me and put a knife to my back." He swallowed and clenched his hands behind his back to keep them from shaking. "They asked me if I had any money on me. I said no. They pinned me and hit me." They'd put a knife to his throat, too, but that was too vivid, too detailed. If he felt anything he would crack. "They looked in the tent and brought out Agent Despana. She gave them the key. To her trunk. Then she – did something to hurt them, with her healer's skill, I think. I don't mean to speculate, sir."

"That's all right, medic. Go on."

Keifon nodded. "She freed herself and freed me. I took a knife and fought back. She fainted. The guards arrived. I checked her for injuries and helped her into the tent."

"That'll do. So you didn't see where they came from."

"No, sir."

The guard captain sighed. "Well. Can't be helped. We saw where they headed, and we've got some of our better runners on their tail now. Give Virin a description of any of the culprits that you can remember." The guard captain motioned over another of the guards. "That's all we'll need from you tonight. I'll post a couple of my people here with you till morning. Get some sleep and come to talk to the Captain in the morning. We'll have to keep riding, but she'll want to talk to you."

The morning was an abstract thought, one he couldn't quite believe in. "Yes, sir."

"I hear you fought well. You probably saved both of your lives. Stopped them from getting someone else, too."

"She did it, sir. I couldn't have..." He had to stop. "Thank you, sir."

"Dismissed." The guard captain saluted in his Kaveran fashion, and Keifon returned the Army's salute, a closed fist over his heart. Then he left, and Keifon was neither the soldier nor anyone at all. He sat by the burnt-out fire. The other guard, Virin, talked to him for a while. Keifon recalled glimpses of faces, heights and genders, clothing. No names. Virin took his notes and his sketches and went.

Nita eased up next to him. "Can I help you get cleaned up?"

"Hm?" He touched the cut on his neck and looked at the congealing blood on his fingers, surprised by the pain. "Oh. Yes. Thank you."

She opened the box she'd left by the fireside and unpacked some bandages, a bottle of something clear, and scissors. A first-aid kit, then. Keifon remembered his valise and felt seasick. He could never afford to replace all of that. Most of it – his tools, the first round of medicines, the valise itself – had been given to him in the Army, and the rest he'd bought with his earnings since then. Piecemeal, when he had enough to spare.

Nita dabbed at his face with a wet cloth, and he flinched. "Sorry!" she yelped, pulling back.

"...Sorry. I wasn't paying attention."

She handed him the cloth, and he sponged off. Most of his face was sweaty and dirty, not bloody, though the action broke open the cut on his lip. Nita gave him the water cup, and he rinsed his mouth and spat into the fire pit to no real effect. It felt good to be even a little bit cleaner. Nita poured more water onto the cloth, and Keifon swabbed his neck, wincing. The bleeding seemed to have slowed, as long as he didn't tilt his head the wrong way. He wished he had a mirror, but his was in the tent with everything else, with the sleeping Nessinian.

Nita bit her lip. "...Do you want to get a clean shirt, maybe?"

His hand touched the drying and stiffening shirt front before he could remember why she might ask that. "Hm. Yes, I...guess so." His clothes were in the tent, too. But that was his only choice. Keifon got to his feet. His nanbur lay on the ground at the edge of their campsite. He reached for it, his head reeling. It was unbroken. He resisted the urge to hug it against him, owing to his bloody shirt. The case had been kicked alongside the tent, flapping open. He bent to it and clumsily replaced the instrument in its place, then latched it shut. He could put this away, and get a clean shirt. He could remember two things.

He forgot to warn the Nessinian. She shuddered awake when he entered, scrabbling backward in her bed, crying out as she put her weight on her injured shoulder.

"It's me. It's me – it's me. Ssh. I'm sorry. I'm so sorry."

She whimpered in the dark. His throat hurt. He never wanted to hear that sound from anyone. But her breathing slowed, and she seemed to slump back into bed. "...Keifon?"

She said his name like she didn't want to trust that it was really him. He wasn't sure he'd heard his name in her voice before. Keifon sank to his knees and set his nanbur aside, where he would have slept. "It's me." He cleared his throat and found more of his voice. "Yeah. Just me. I'm sorry I didn't knock."

"...Oh." She said nothing more, and he had to trust that she had fallen asleep. For a little while he wavered, kneeling in the middle of the tent. He wanted her to wake up. It was selfish, but he wanted to talk to her. No one else had seen it and lived through it the way she had.

He imagined talking with her, just the two of them in private. He told her that he was afraid, that he imagined the bandits jumping out at him from every shadow. He thanked her for saving his life and apologized for getting her hurt. And she listened, and told him that she was afraid too. That it wasn't his fault. That she'd had to save him, because it was the right thing to do, because they were partners.

I never really hated you. You know that, don't you? He'd seen her smile like that, in fleeting moments, at other people.

Keifon shook himself, pushing away the comforting daydream before it took him apart. She would never understand, and she would never say that to him. She hated him, not without reason, just as he had tired of the sight and the sound of her half the time. He resented the fact that the Benevolent Union had thrown them together, that the gods had abandoned him here to punish him and left him alone with this spoiled foreign child.

He wanted to cling to her because they were both lost and hurt and alone. But it would never happen that way. He would push her away, and she would push him away, and they would hate one another all the more.

He forced himself to swallow and look up, though there was nothing to see. Whoever he was, he held the wall up. Two things. Put his nanbur away, and get a clean shirt. It was too dark to see, so he took his pack outside.

Nita's eyes were sympathetic. He tried not to look. Not yet, so soon after he had almost given up. He could not cope with her sympathy. She would offer him kind words, and he would crumble. He found another shirt in the pack. He stripped off his bloody shirt and crumpled it. He would wash it as soon as he could.

Nita uncorked one of the bottles, and the alcohol vapors cut into his eyes. She soaked a clean cloth with the contents and hesitated. "I'm sorry," she said in a voice too small for a guard, and pressed it against the cut on his neck. He flinched, and she flinched, and apologized, and continued until his eyes watered. She was not a medic, but she had been a guard long enough to dress a wound. Her hands were sure. She dabbed on some ointment and pressed clean gauze against the cut. He helped her hold it still as she wound a bandage around his neck, asking him again and again whether she'd wrapped it too tight. She hadn't, although it was a tricky thing to bandage a cut like this. He turned and let her clean his back, and bandaged the shallow dig they'd made in his ribs.

"Good technique," he managed to say when she was done, and she smiled nervously as he pulled on a clean shirt.

"Thank you. Is there anything else I can do? Did they get you anywhere else? I don't think there's much we can do for your lip."

"Nn. Just punched me. A lot." He half-smiled on the uninjured side. What was he doing? Responding to her, to her kindness, to the submerged suggestion of comfort. Keifon looked away. "If you have some cold water. To drink, and I think it would be good to get a compress here." He laid his fingers on the edge of his cheekbone, where the bandit's fist had hit him. His stomach hurt, not only the roiling inside but the bruised muscles and tendons that held him up. There wasn't much he could do about that, either. Rest. The one thing he couldn't do.

"The water I got is pretty cold. Here." Nita busied herself with getting more, and Keifon sat by the cold fire pit, not thinking. He would put a compress on his face and... then what? Not sleep. Try not to talk to Nita too much. He drank what she handed him, and accepted the soaked cloth, and pressed it against his face. It was cool enough.

"Would you like the fire lit?"

51

"Nn. It's fine. Just the torches."

"All right..."

Nita didn't talk much. She waited with him. She patrolled the campsite. She made notes in a logbook from her breast pocket. She talked with the guards who passed through. Keifon sat, not thinking, not sleeping. Nita brought him fresh water and offered to get him some food. He took the water and soaked his compress and refused the food. Sometime later, another pair of guards approached. One pulled the Nessinian's trunk along behind him, and the other carried his valise. Keifon scrambled to his feet. "You got it back!" The second guard passed it to him. "Thank you. This is... it's... it's my livelihood. Thank you."

She saluted. "We think some of the bottles in it are broken, though. It's sounding awfully noisy. You'll have to see what's still there and report the losses to the Captain."

"I will." The sight of it revived him. He could be the medic and an agent of the Benevolent Union. He hadn't lost what the Army had given him.

The other guard rolled the trunk to a stop next to their water barrel. "This belongs to the other healer, I hear?"

"Yes."

"She'll have to report her losses to the Captain, too. Let her know."

"All right."

The two newcomers conferred with Nita, and Keifon sat in a spot of torchlight to check his valise. The first bottle he picked up was just a shattered neck, still stoppered. He spread out his blood-soaked shirt and laid out the shards as he went.

Seven broken bottles and jars. Three missing. His scalpels were gone. The bandages were soaked with a lung-shriveling brew of mingled reagents and medicines. At least the bandages were easier to replace than the medicines and scalpels. He swabbed out the inside of the valise with one of the cleaner bandages and left it open to dry in the air. The rest of his supplies were all right. He lined them up to dry. Many of the labels had smeared and bled, splashed with the same chemical mess that had claimed the bandages. He would re-label them when they were dry.

He borrowed Nita's notebook and wrote down every item in categories. *Stolen. Broken. Damaged / reclaimable. Intact.* They couldn't read any of this, but he could translate in the morning, when he had more light and a dictionary.

He returned the notebook and pencil, keeping the pages with his notes. "Thank you."

"No trouble. They said they found it by the roadside, a ways down the road. A team went out there to try and catch the rest of them. They think the bandits just dropped it when they ran. It gave them a clue, at least – they might have turned off the road there." She seemed to read something in his expression, because she stopped abruptly. "Do you need anything? ...Thinking about getting any sleep, sometime?"

"Nn. No. And no. Thank you."

She patrolled, and he sat by the cold hearth. The bottles dried in the air. The Nessinian slept. Finally Nita met another patrolling guard and turned to Keifon, smiling apologetically. "Shift change. Goodnight, Medic. I'm glad you're all right."

"Thank you."

Nita walked into the dark. The new guard looked down at him. This one was older, a man, of an age with the guard captain, or with one of his own superiors in the Army. Keifon nodded, and the guard returned it.

"Evening."

"Good evening."

"Can't sleep?"

"No."

"Suit yourself. I'll be here till we break camp."

"I see. Thank you."

The new guard did not offer his name. He set off to walk his rounds around the campsite. Keifon picked up the compress and soaked it. It woke him up for a while.

It was the slow, grinding part of the night. It was the time that he usually started to think about Kazi, instead of letting him stay as a constant background noise in his head. He imagined curling up on a bed in one of the inns they frequented, the one that scented its sheets with lavender. He imagined Kazi sitting behind him, watching him silently. Finally, as though Keifon were a creature that might turn on him, Kazi laid a hand on his shoulder. The thought of it made him shake, and he pressed the heels of his hands against his eyes, squeezing water out of the compress. Kazi would not give him comforting words, would not take care of him – but even so, Keifon's need for companionship was breaking him.

Not Kazi, then. Anything but that.

Keifon pressed the cloth against his face, because it would help, in some small way. With his free hand he made half of the sign of Darano. He hoped that the god would forgive him for the breach in protocol. He remembered the words, one after another, in their proper order. One prayer after another, for strength, for peace, for justice. When the words blurred into something mindless, he switched hands and made half of the sign of Tufar. He called upon the god for clarity, for sanity, for sureness in his work as a medic. He repeated these and moved onto the next.

The gods had not abandoned him. He apologized to each in turn for thinking that his assignment had been a punishment. They had a plan for him, and a purpose. He didn't understand it yet, and his responsibility lay in figuring out what they wanted from him. But they had not abandoned him. He believed, and the gods never abandoned those who believed.

He said all the prayers he could remember. He prayed for the Nessinian's safe recovery, even though she was a heathen. He prayed for the health and

53

safety of Kazi and Eri and Nachi and his brother. Everything hurt and his mind was fogged, but he would be all right. He had lived, and the gods still loved him. Everything else could be borne.

"Son." Keifon started out of a state that might have been prayer and might have been dozing. It was the Yanweian word, but the standing guard had spoken it. "I think it's time you went to bed."

Keifon leaned back against the ground, getting his balance. "D-did you say..."

"Yeah. I'm from Laketon," he said, as though that explained everything. "'Sides, you speak Kaveran, don't you?"

"Uh..."

"Go along. You have a couple of hours till dawn. Get some sleep."

Keifon considered this. He was dizzy, and he wasn't sure he was experiencing time properly. If it was only a couple of hours, he could only have so many nightmares before morning came. He might even sleep for a while, and forget. He nodded. "All right. Thank you, sir."

The guard offered him a hand up. Keifon left his medical supplies out to dry, under the guard's watch. He picked up his pack. He remembered to tap at the tent flap first, and tell the Nessinian that he was coming. Even if she didn't hear him, he had tried.

Agna: The Patient

"Agent?"

Agna's shoulder screamed when she stirred, confirming that last night's nightmare had been real.

"We're moving in a couple of hours. You'd better get ready."

"Nnghhh."

"I'll be outside."

Agna tried to move, yelped, and lay still until the wave passed. She eased onto her left side and rolled to her knees. She glanced at the other side of the tent. The Yanweian's bedroll was tied to his backpack. The caravan rolled in a couple of hours. Agna cradled her right elbow in her hand. Not enough time. She had to get dressed – if she had any clothes to change into – and wash up and pack whatever she had left and load it all onto the wagon. Who could she hire for this? *Move my trunk* was reasonable, but *pack my laundry* was less so. And she had to get a sling for her shoulder.

She emerged from the tent. The Yanweian sat by the fire, drinking tea. For a moment she was angry with him – how dare he drink tea as though nothing had happened – but she saw the same vacant, disconnected look in his eyes that she'd seen the previous night. His neck was bandaged, and a bruised lump had risen under his eye.

The Yanweian set his teacup aside as he stood. "We need to get your arm in a sling." It wasn't his friendly clinical voice – not for her. It was his campfire self, half-concealed.

"I know that," Agna's mouth said, while her concentration was occupied with keeping tears from her eyes. Her shoulder creaked and groaned like a foundering ship.

His hands were up. He took a step forward. "It won't take long, and it will hurt less afterward."

He was right, and that made it worse. She hated agreeing with him. The morning was sliding by too fast. She had to be stronger than this, and prove that she could do all of these things alone. Agna stood taller, eyes watering, conscious of her bruises and her over-protective stance and her unwashed nightgown.

"I'm going to wash up. And then you can check my shoulder. If you want to." Her voice cracked a little. It was good enough.

The Yanweian nodded his concession. "They brought your trunk back." He motioned. Her trunk was parked by the water barrel. Agna's lip trembled, and she bit it fiercely. He went on, sparing her the need to reply. "The guards said you should figure out what's missing and report it to the Captain."

"Right." They might have overlooked her clothes. She wouldn't have to skulk around Kavera in her nightgown. She knelt by the trunk. The key sat in the lock, without its chain. Agna lifted the lid left-handed and found what she needed. It was all tumbled around, but she found some clothes and her toiletry kit. She gathered what she needed, draping the clothes over her left arm, and headed out.

■ ■ ■

She returned from the baths in the inner layer of her dark red dress, belted by itself, the drawstring barely pulled together at the neck. She felt slovenly, but it had been painful enough to pull her arm through the sleeve. At least she was clean now, and more or less dressed. She found the tent empty, her belongings packed up. The trunk stood in its usual place. She wavered between *how dare you* and *thank goodness*, sank to the floor next to her trunk, and rested her forehead against the lid. What had she left behind when she went out? Her blanket and yesterday's dirty clothes. She hated the thought of the Yanweian touching them, judging them as common and petty. But now she didn't have to pack them herself.

Agna was resting when the Yanweian returned, dressed for travel. "Are you ready?" he asked as he tucked away his kit, reminding Agna that her own kit and nightgown were clutched in her hand. She opened the trunk with her elbow and shoved them inside as the Yanweian fetched his valise. She thought she'd seen the bandits carry that away. Maybe the guards had found it, too. She locked the trunk and shoved the key into the money pouch on her belt. There were a few coins in there, at least.

Agna turned to face the middle of the tent and sat up straight. She concentrated on saying, doing, feeling nothing, despite the fluttering in her stomach. The Yanweian settled cross-legged in front of her and lit the lamp next to them.

"All right," he began. "This will probably hurt, and I'm sorry." He reached out, and she steeled herself. She thought she saw something pained and human flicker in his eyes. Then the clinical mien snapped back into place: not his flirtatious act, but a thoughtful consideration of each symptom. He asked her to raise her arm and guided it forward and back, up and down and circling around. Every movement hurt, and she hated him for it – but he wasn't causing it. He was sparing her all the pain he could. She knew that, and hated herself for that more.

"Can you heal it?" he asked uneasily.

"No. Can't heal yourself. You need to connect your energy to the other person's, and if there's nothing else to connect to, nothing happens."

"I see." He went on, carefully prodding the muscles of her shoulders and arms. The bruises on his face were frightful. And he seemed to be mumbling so as not to split open his lip. Agna remembered the sickening solidity of the force applied to his body.

She wet her lips. "Can I check you, though?"

"Check me?" he echoed. Agna raised her uninjured arm in demonstration, and the Yanweian drew back. "Oh. I...um."

"Just to make sure they didn't rupture anything. And I can't do much for bruises, but I can close those cuts."

"I – no, you don't need to do that."

"It'll only take a second."

"Just – let me set your arm first."

Agna sighed, aggrieved, and relented. He found a sling in his valise, rolled into a tiny bundle, and unfolded it. It was almost the same brown shade as the caravan guards' uniforms. He fastened it over her shoulder and adjusted the placement, speaking no more than a word or two at a time, until it was seated properly. The sling took the weight of her arm off her shoulder. The pain was muted now, as long as she didn't move.

The Yanweian closed the valise and sat back. "It's pretty bad," he said. "You shouldn't move it more than you need to for a few weeks, and see how it feels then."

"I know that," she retorted without thinking.

"...Yes. Of course you do."

"What's that supposed to mean?"

"Nothing." He began to stand. "I'll take the tent down whenever you're ready."

"Hey, wait. Let me check you."

He hesitated, like a cornered cat deciding which way to bolt. "I don't..."

"It doesn't hurt. Look, they could have ruptured something that you wouldn't even know until it killed you two days later. Just let me try." It would make it a little better, being even with him, or as even as they could be. She couldn't lift anything or help with the tent or do much of anything for herself, but she could do this. They couldn't take that from her.

The Yanweian warily sat back in his place across from her. "All right."

Agna almost smiled. She could handle this, even one-handed. She took a deep breath, gathering her focus, and spread her hand over his abdomen to check for internal damage. The energy connected readily, but the tension in his body nearly broke her concentration. His pulse raced, its rhythm stuttering through her reaching currents of energy. Agna tightened the muscles in her arm and held her own irritation back. Letting it flow into him would cause a feedback loop.

57

She reverted to the standard routine to circumvent her own thoughts, checking each organ in turn. The muscles were badly bruised where he'd been hit, but nothing seemed to be broken, and there was no internal bleeding. The lining of his stomach was chewed to pieces, though.

"Your stomach's in pretty bad shape. Are you taking any medicine for that?"

The energy twanged against hers, and Agna flinched, severing the connection. "It's not from last night," he snapped. "Never mind that."

"Fine, fine." As a medic he should know better, and she was trying to do him a favor. If he was going to be difficult, though, that was his problem. She laid her hand along the lump on his cheekbone. It was awkward twisting her wrist backward, her left hand against the left side of his face. Her impression was flipped over, like trying to write by looking in a mirror. She was prepared for the harsh tone of his energy signature this time, and screened out her growing irritation. She was almost finished.

The bone hadn't cracked, and though the swelling would get worse through the day, there wasn't much she could do about that. Bruising injuries were far too complicated, compared to the time they took to heal naturally. And there was little risk of infection. If he could bear it, she would let it be.

The cut on his lip would be easy, at least. Agna cupped his chin in her hand and brushed her thumb over the cut. The Yanweian tensed, blushing, but it was healed before he could pull away.

"I–" He felt the spot as Agna caught her breath. Minor operations, every one. Perhaps she needed to catch up on her rest. She felt a little woozy. "I didn't ask you to do that."

"You're welcome," Agna muttered, trying to get her head together. She'd intended to heal his neck, as well. But he was still ranting.

"That's not right. You shouldn't – you didn't ask. You always ask before you do things to people. I've seen you."

Anger overtook her fatigue. He'd noticed that? He had suddenly decided to notice anything she ever did, only to lecture her on medical ethics? Worse, he was right. She hadn't been thinking. "'Do things to people' like help them?"

"Yes! Do you not have any code of ethics in Nessiny?"

"Of course we do. What do you know?" Her head hurt along with her shoulder, and she wanted to cry again, which fed her fury. "Could you at least try to be grateful?"

"I am! But you..." He trailed off, and got up to leave. "Never mind. To respect my independence, you'd have to think of me as human first. I'll get your things. Go see the Captain. I'll meet you there." He slapped the tent flap aside and was gone.

Crying would let him win. Agna blew out the lantern and charged out of the tent toward the Captain's wagon, leaving the Yanweian and everything else behind.

Agna: Interview

Agna hated meeting the Captain half-dressed and carting her arm in a sling. She looked broken. Weak. But there was nothing to be done for it.

A guard stood outside the Captain's door. She took in Agna's face and the sling; her eyes slid away to the ground. "Healer. Please go in, the Captain is expecting you." She opened the door. Agna clumsily took the step up inside and let her eyes adjust to the light. "The Nessinian healer, ma'am," the guard announced, and continued her watch outside.

In the cabin, the Captain and the captain of the caravan guard faced one another. The master of records sat at a tiny desk with a ledger and pen at the ready, looking miserable.

The slight Kaveran woman offered Agna a little bow. "I apologize, personally and for the Golden Caravan, for last night's attack. The safety of our member merchants and their goods is of primary importance to us."

"I..." The rant that Agna had composed in her head on the way over broke apart. The Captain's words were formal enough. Too formal? Were they sincere? "How could this happen?"

The guard captain blinked. "We're very sorry, miss—"

"Healer. Agent. Despana."

"—Agent Despana. We will increase our patrols in areas of known activity, but there are four hundred merchants in the Caravan and twenty guards."

"Hire more."

The Captain sighed. "This is a very complex decision."

"They could have killed me. An agent of the Benevolent Union *and* a second-order healer of the Church of the Divine Balance *and* a child of the Despanas of Murio. Do you want that on your heads?"

The three caravan officials traded a glance. The Captain spoke for them. "I think you'd better calm down."

"I will not. I could have been *killed*."

The guard captain looked at his folded hands; the master of records twirled his pen in his fingers; the Captain sat down, crossed one knee over the other and waited. Agna wanted to throw the nearest chair at their heads, but she couldn't lift it one-handed. She hadn't had time to inventory what had been stolen from her trunk, and she hadn't had time for breakfast. Her stomach was growling, and her head spun. She couldn't waste time arguing with these Kaveran bureaucrats. They only needed to give her a guarantee that nothing like this would ever happen again. What was so hard about that?

Finally the guard captain cleared his throat. "We'll take measures to forestall such an attack in the future, and increase our night patrols. We do have a record of no more than two incidents a year over the last five years, and most were less severe than this. The Golden Caravan has some of the best security in Kavera. It is unfortunate that you were at the center of this situation, but I assure you that it does not happen frequently."

"So I'll get my arm broken twice a year. That's lovely."

"*Agent.*" The Captain leveled a dark glare at her. "I understand that you're upset, but if you can't converse civilly, our interview will wait until you can."

Agna clenched her jaw and tried to take a deep breath. "...Fine. All right. All right."

The guard captain acknowledged her concession with a nod. The door swung open.

"The Yanweian healer, ma'am."

"Medic," Agna heard him say. She flushed at the sound of his voice, but would not look over at him. She would have to apologize for their argument this morning. Another thing that she had no time to do. The Yanweian addressed the captains. "Thank you for sending the guards to help me load our things. It's much appreciated."

"You're welcome, Agent," the Captain replied. "I was just saying to your companion – the Golden Caravan apologizes, as do I, for the attack last night. Our merchants' safety is very important to us."

"Thank you."

"We're all here, Calli," the Captain called in the direction of the door. The guard outside popped her head back in. "Tell Eytaris we can move when the caravan moves."

"Yes, ma'am."

"You'll ride with me, till our next stop," the Captain explained. "We need to talk for a bit."

"What about our things?" Agna blurted.

The Yanweian, having taken his place next to her, leaned in. "They've loaded them onto the wagon for us, and a guard is staying with them until we go back."

"...Oh."

"Now then," the Captain said. "We've got business to attend to. Have either of you had a chance to inventory what was stolen?"

"I have, ma'am," the Yanweian said. Of course he had. "But I haven't had a chance to translate it. I wrote it in Yanweian. I'm sorry."

"Read it to us, then. Ethi, write it down, will you?"

The master of records waited as the Yanweian unfolded a slip of paper from his pocket and began to read aloud. "Um. Stolen. Three scalpels, various sizes. A bottle of cough medicine. A bottle of disinfecting alcohol. And a bottle of anesthetic compound – mostly purified knockseed."

"That's it?"

"That's all that was stolen, ma'am."

"Anything damaged? We want to be thorough, go on."

The Yanweian proceeded through his inventory. Agna had seen him pack and unpack his medical kit often enough; he had named many of the things in it as either broken or damaged. When the master of records had transcribed the whole list, the Yanweian put his copy away.

"Thank you, Agent. Agent Despana, how about you?"

"...I didn't have time to look." Agna flexed her free hand. "I just got up. I needed to sleep after using the healing power too much last night."

"Understandably so," the Captain replied. "Can you check while we talk here?"

"I – don't think I can get there and back. Not before the caravan sets out." It had taken her long enough just to get bathed and dressed. They'd be halfway to the mountains by the time she finished wrangling all of her remaining possessions one-handed.

"That's fine. Calli?"

"Yes, Captain?" The guard appeared in the door.

"Fetch the healer's luggage, please. A trunk, was it?" she directed at Agna.

"Uh – yes."

"Right away, ma'am." The door closed.

"So. A question for both of you, while we wait. Within reason, how can we help you feel safe in our camp?"

Agna had turned over thoughts like this on the way to the Captain's wagon, some more elaborate and punitive than others. But all came down to one conclusion: *Stop it. Stop it from ever happening again.* "Might I keep my valuables with the guards?"

The guard captain, to his credit, appeared to consider this. "The guards are not guarded themselves, I'm afraid; the off-duty members are generally sleeping. We don't have a particular place that's always under watch."

"Including my wagon," the Captain interjected. "We had Calli posted here as a precaution while we have prisoners on the premises. You were guarded last night for the same reason. When they're handed over to the road patrol, I won't be under watch either."

"But... all of those merchants," Agna reasoned. "Some of them deal all day, every day we make camp. Edann – the apothecary, say. Medicines are expensive. Who guards his money?"

"Most of the merchants carry accounts in the city banks along the way. As do I, and most of the guards. Anyone who doesn't spend or drink her take from one town to the next will keep it somewhere safe. Which, ultimately, means somewhere off the road. No offense," she offered to the guard captain.

"None taken."

"Hold it. Nobody ever told me that."

The Captain hesitated before she answered. The Yanweian spoke up in the silence. "I don't think the Benevolent Union properly prepared Agent Despana for this assignment, ma'am." Agna could have elbowed him in the head or hugged him. She wasn't sure which. As insulting as it sounded, it seemed as though he'd intended to speak in her defense. When no one replied, he went on. "And they didn't target her money. They didn't seem to be targeting anyone. They came up behind me because we were at the edge of the camp, and because I was outside. I think it could have been anyone."

"I see." The Captain considered this, arms crossed. The guard captain laced his fingers on top of the papers on the Captain's desk. The master of records, sitting across from him, stared at the ledger. The Yanweian did not explain further, and Agna imagined how it might have happened. He had been outside, sulking or practicing his lute. They had sneaked up to the edge of camp, found him, and grabbed him simply because he was there. Agna shivered.

But it also countered what the Captain had implied, that Agna had behaved recklessly by keeping too much money on hand. If anyone could be robbed at any moment, it didn't matter how much money one kept. Though, she admitted to herself, if you meant to limit the loss if you were targeted, it would be best to keep your valuables somewhere else.

Still, no one had told her that it was dangerous out here. They had guards, after all. But then, perhaps they had guards because the thieves were out there in the first place. They'd known that bandits could strike at any time. Agna had never envied the Captain's wagon for that reason before. She had thought only of material comfort. Suddenly, the difference between wood and canvas walls meant a great deal indeed. A thief could breach a wagon as easily as a tent, of course, but somehow it made a difference.

"Captain?" The five people inside the wagon turned to the door. The guard, Calli, had reappeared. "We have the trunk. I need some help lifting it, though."

The guard captain made the first move, and helped Calli to hoist the trunk into the wagon. "Thank you, Cal. As you were."

"Yes, sir. And I should tell you that we'll be moving in a minute or—" The starting bell clanged behind her, followed by distant cheers. "—maybe now."

"Go and ride your rounds. I'll defend the Captain if need be." He threw a wry look at the Captain, who did not react.

"Yes, sir." Calli closed the door behind her. The wagon lurched, and its inhabitants steadied themselves on whatever was closest to hand.

The guard captain wheeled Agna's trunk away from the door. "Go ahead and check, Healer. Take your time. Let us know if anything's missing."

Agna knelt by the trunk. She would have to pull out all of her things in front of everyone, it seemed. The Captain sat at her desk, the guard captain took a chair next to her, and the master of records waited with his book and pen. The Yanweian stood between them and Agna, balancing against the wall as the wagon swayed.

"Tell me about the chase," the Captain began. "What did they find?"

Agna tried to block them out as she lifted the lid. She had so few things to begin with. The trunk was large, but she hadn't been able to bring much apart from the money box. And that was gone. What was left of her life was heaped in the resulting space. She pulled out one object at a time, folding the clothes as best she could one-handed, stacking the books. Her writing case was all right. She took a moment to breathe, to realize that she still had all of the letters she'd gotten.

They had taken a mirror, one of her three dresses, two pairs of shoes, her cloak, and all the money she needed to survive for the next two years. No – there was a little money in her money pouch, which had been attached to her belt and overlooked. That was all. Everything she'd brought with her. Everything that her parents had given her. And everything that she'd earned from the clinic, from all of those patients. It wasn't much, but it was gone now, too. And that didn't even belong to her; it belonged to the Benevolent Union. How could they?

She weighed the money bag in her hand. She would have to dump it out and count it the next time they camped. It would be a number. Not anything real. How would she pay for food and baths and books and postage and hiring help around the campsite? Food, especially; how was she supposed to cook with her arm in a sling? The camp cook's meals weren't expensive, but if she bought two or three a day, every day, that would add up – she supposed. She had never added it up before. It would have been unnecessary.

It wasn't unnecessary anymore.

It was so ridiculous. Why would you have to do something so obsessive and silly as figuring out how much money you spent on food in a week? How much water did you drink in a week? How much air did you breathe?

Agna took a deep breath, trying not to think of measuring air. She returned each item to the trunk. It seemed empty without the box that had contained her funds. She supposed that it would at least be easier to lift, and bit her lip to keep from giggling.

The question lurked behind her exhausted panic: should she write home? Her parents would help her out. Of course they would. They would be happy to do it.

It's too dangerous out there, dear. Come home. You shouldn't make your own choices, obviously. You failed. We knew that being a healer was a mistake. But that's all right, come home and we'll help you be who we want you to be.

Never.

Agna clenched her uninjured hand in her lap. One hand mirror, wood backing with mother of pearl inlay. One spring cloak, thin wool. Two pairs of good leather shoes and a green silk dress. Money. A lot of it. All of it.

But she would not give up. Not if she starved, not if she had to calculate the prices of things as though she were solving an arithmetic problem in school. She would figure it out, and prove that she hadn't made a terrible mistake. She might have made a mistake in joining the caravan. But not in coming to Kavera.

Not in being a healer. Not in going to the Academy. She would never allow them that.

She was alive. Her shoulder hurt, but it would heal. She could think, and plan, and organize. She could use her healer's art. Money was just money. She would not trade her dignity for it. She had surrendered her possessions to keep the bandits from causing her and the Yanweian more harm. It had been worthwhile then. It was worthwhile now.

Agna closed her trunk, locked it, and palmed the key. She stood to face the Captains, the master of records, and the Yanweian. She cleared her throat. They looked up, waiting.

"They took some things. My cloak, and a hand mirror. A nice hand mirror," she said, and then felt petty. "Two pairs of shoes. A silk dress that was almost new. And my money. Just about all of it."

"How much?" the master of records asked, writing all of this down at the Captain's desk.

"I don't know. My – I came with enough to sustain me through my assignment. And my earnings from the clinic. They took that, too."

The master of records paused and glanced at the Captain. "Give me an idea, please. Was it in Kaveran coin? Gold unions?"

"Mostly. I mean – mine was. The stuff from the clinic was mostly smaller."

The Yanweian cleared his throat. "You have records, Agent, don't you?"

"Oh – yes. Yes, I do. Of the clinic part." She was so relieved to have gotten an answer to at least one part of the question that she couldn't be irritated with him. She elbowed her trunk open and pulled out her logbook. She pinned the book against her body and ruffled through the pages.

The Yanweian reached for it. "May I?"

Agna flushed, but she let him take it. He paged to the end of her notes and read out the total before handing the book back to her. She stowed it again.

The master of records prompted, "And your personal money – fifty unions? A hundred?"

Agna sighed, aggravated. It was so petty. But she supposed that the caravan had to keep records about theft. She remembered the Yanweian's careful list and resented him for it. – That wasn't helping. She knew what her parents had given her; they'd told her the figure – ten thousand crowns – half a dozen times, as though she should be especially careful, as though she would lose it if she didn't realize how much she had. But that had been in Nessinian currency. She had come to Vertal and stopped at that office at the waterfront, where they'd looked at her strangely, and weighed her money box, and calculated...

It was coming back. She had felt annoyed at the fact that Nessinian coins were worth less than Kaveran. Nessinian coins were smaller, she had rationalized, but it hadn't seemed fair, considering that the Kaveran government was such a rickety thing. Agna pulled her memory back to the numbers. She'd had ten thousand crowns, at that annoying rate – a little over seventy percent?

And then, curse it, she had bought food and camping supplies and... she was back to the beginning.

"Ugh. I had a little more than seven thousand unions when I came here, but I've spent some since then. I don't know how much."

"Seven *thousand* unions?" the guard captain gawked.

Agna moved to cross her arms, and winced at the pain in her shoulder. She cradled her injured elbow in her hand instead. "Well. I was going to be here for two *years*."

The master of records dipped his pen. The captain remarked, "I suppose, unless you've been in the habit of buying jeweled toothpicks, you can't have made much of a dent in it."

"Seven thousand," the guard captain murmured.

"What? You can barely buy a wagon for that much. I asked. And I have to buy food, and everything, and that's not even getting into horses to pull a wagon with."

"That's good enough," the Captain interrupted. "We'll say seven thousand to be on the safe side, I suppose." She smirked a little as she said it, and Agna's mouth tightened.

"Yes, ma'am." The master of records completed his notes and blotted the page.

Agna huffed. "Fine. Is that all you need?"

The Captain gave her a warning look. "That's all I need, Agent. Please have a seat. We'll get you back to the passenger wagon when we stop to switch horses at midday. Would either of you like something to eat?"

"Yes, please," Agna blurted, while the Yanweian said "no, thank you." He would. – Agna remembered the stomach ailment that she'd sensed in the scan and felt guilty. She sat on top of her trunk and squeezed the key into her money pouch.

The Captain sliced some bread and cheese, at home with the gentle rocking of the wagon. She handed over a slice to Agna, and then a cup of water. "Thank you, ma'am."

The Yanweian accepted some water from the Captain. The food eased Agna's gnawing hunger, and cleared her head a little. The caravan officials continued their meeting, discussing the pursuit of the bandits and the plans for the night watches for the next several weeks. Finally they lapsed into a discussion about the guards and the merchants – which new recruits were working out, which weren't, which businesses were doing well and which weren't. Agna snapped awake a few times, and she saw the Yanweian doing the same.

He had woken her up when she'd fainted. Not the caravan guard, and, thankfully, not the bandits. She supposed that it made sense; he was the other medic. It was his job. He hadn't been critical, or sour, or sarcastic. He hadn't understood what was happening, but she supposed that was to be expected from someone so unfamiliar with the Academy's art.

She could qualify it and draw boundaries around it, but he had helped her off the ground and gotten her to safety. And she'd never thanked him. He hadn't exactly thanked her for attacking the bandits first, either. But someone had to take the high road. Not now, of course. When they had some privacy. Whenever they made camp, she would extend her thanks to him for helping her into the tent. She practiced some lines, striking a balance between humble and elegant – but they all ended in bitter rejoinders from the Yanweian.

Meanwhile, the target of her silent speeches dozed off, leaning against the wall. Agna wondered when he'd come into the tent to sleep. Not that it was any of her business.

When the wagon stopped, the Captain stood to face them. "All right, medics, thank you for your time." The Yanweian lurched to his feet. The Captain addressed them as though she hadn't noticed. "I commend you for your bravery. We'll talk again soon about security in the camp. Safe travels."

Agna and the Yanweian stumbled out of the wagon, with the guard captain on their heels. He carried Agna's trunk down the short ladder to the ground. Agna grabbed the strap when he let go. It rolled so easily now, as though it were empty. She supposed it wasn't far from the truth.

"Good day," the guard captain said, and went on his way. The Yanweian gave his salute. He scanned around them, through the tangled dance of the stable master and his apprentices as they brought fresh horses into the crowd.

"Stay here. I'll find the wagon."

"I can see, you know. And walk."

He groaned under his breath. "I know you can. ...Fine. Suit yourself."

Agna pulled the trunk behind her as they weaved through the chaos. The passenger wagon was fairly tall, so Agna looked for its canvas roof over the heads of the humans and horses. She and the Yanweian spotted it at the same time and veered toward it.

A caravan guard turned to see them climbing the ladder and stood to help Agna up to the deck. The Yanweian lifted her trunk after them, and Agna pulled it down the aisle. The guard had been sitting with the rest of their belongings, just as the Yanweian had said. Agna wheeled her trunk to a secure spot between the benches and flopped down to rest. The Yanweian checked his lute and took it with him to the bench behind her. The guard waved and hopped off the wagon.

They were back on their usual track, or were supposed to be. Agna's right arm was all but broken, the Yanweian was barely functioning, and she wasn't sure how she'd keep from starving for the next two years. But the caravan had deposited them back in their place. From now on she had to figure this out herself.

Keifon: Safety

The next stop was a campsite beside some anonymous village. Keifon and the Nessinian, unspeaking, brought their remaining belongings to their assigned place. Keifon assembled the tent. The Nessinian held up poles and tied ropes when she could, and Keifon did not dare to stop her. He needed the help, after all, although he would never admit it.

They gathered their things and went to the baths, though the water was cold. The water's bite kept Keifon awake as he unwound the bandages and washed up. Through the canvas wall he could hear the sloshing of her awkward movements in another stall. He thought he heard a few muttered, foreign curses.

They had left their tent unguarded. Keifon had needed to complete his routine for the night, and lacked the energy to argue with the Nessinian about who would go first. And he might have been a little glad that he hadn't gone alone. It was worrisome to leave his nanbur unguarded. On the other hand, if the bandits returned, perhaps he should take it as a sign from the gods and cancel his contract. It was a ridiculous thought, but somehow comforting.

The water had loosened flakes of dried blood from his marriage torque, and he realized that it had seeped into the joints between the segments. His hand lingered on the back of his neck. It was foolish, but he could not bear to unlatch it. He had left it on after Eri had taken hers off. He had left it on when selling it would have put a roof over his head. He had left it on through... everything else. Through Kazi. He would not take it off now, for something so trivial.

Keifon dipped the scrub brush in water and gently scrubbed the metal, flexing each joint as far as it would bend in order to reach every tiny crack. He poured water down his neck, across his violated skin, washing the blood away.

There was nothing else he could do, so he returned to the tent. The air stung his cut skin. He lit the lamp and re-bandaged his neck and his back as best he could, pulling a shirt on just before the Nessinian returned.

She put her things away, spread out her bedroll, and lay down to sleep. Keifon put away the rest of his bandages and tools and set his valise aside. He didn't want to try to read. He didn't want to be the only one awake. He unpacked his bedroll and blew out the lamp.

She wasn't asleep yet. "Hey."

"Hm?"

"What you did, the other night. Helping me back into the tent, after. I wanted to say thank you."

A rush of gratitude pressed against Keifon's throat. He did not welcome this need to be acknowledged, especially by this spoiled, vicious child. But there it was, uncoiling in his chest, drinking in the civil tone of her voice.

He had been silent for too long. She went on. "And... you had a point, about asking before I heal you. It's fair. I usually do ask," she added, but did not press the point further.

"I know," he found himself saying into the dark. "I know you do." The rest was too big, tangled in thoughts about selfhood and rights and status.

"May I heal the other cut? I meant to, yesterday morning. It's got to be hard to have a bandage around your neck all the time."

Keifon touched the edge of it, as his other hand ran along the bandage across his belly. She wasn't wrong. He would only have to be vulnerable for a moment, every fiber of his body exposed under her hands, and then it would be over. "...All right. The back too, if you don't mind."

"The back?"

"It's... it's smaller than the other one. But deeper. They – they had me at knifepoint in the back first." The Nessinian whispered some oath. Keifon braced his hand against the ground, reminding himself that he was here in the tent and safe, not outside, not surrounded by strangers and steel. "So if you don't mind, that one too. That would be good."

"Of course."

The events unfolded against his will once again. The hot pain in his ribs, the panic clogging his throat, the voices he couldn't always understand through the fear. He curled up on the bedroll, his body distant, in another world from the gloved vice-grips bruising his arms and the stink of sweat and smoke. He thought he might be sick, somewhere in the dream where he was safe inside. He hadn't eaten in half a day, though, and his empty stomach twisted against itself.

She said something, out there in the world of safety. Finally she appeared in their clutches, and Keifon couldn't stop the flood of relief and dread. He wasn't alone. They had her. They were trapped. And then she had fought back.

That piece of the memory dumped him on the shore. His mind cleared slowly. She was speaking to him. "Are you all right?"

Keifon loosened his aching muscles and stretched out. He breathed until he could speak. "Last night. Last night you – you..."

Her voice was small. "It's an application of the healing art. We only use it in self-defense, as a last resort."

"...saved my life, I think." She didn't answer. "And I never – I never said thank you. Thank you." Silence. Keifon settled onto his side to sleep. "That's all."

He heard her before the exhaustion dragged him down. "I had to. But you're welcome."

Agna: The Patient

The next morning was a little better. Agna's shoulder hurt, and she was cramped from not being able to change position as she slept. Still lying in bed, she drew up a little bit of energy. It came as easily as ever. She let it burn off her fingertips as a brief, glowing light and lowered her hand. So that much was all right. It would be hard to get around and live her daily life, but at least she could function in the clinic. She could do what she had been sent here to do.

First, though, she had to get cleaned up and eat some breakfast – she had time for breakfast today, even though the mundane actions of cooking would be difficult. Then she had to heal the Yanweian's injuries. She wondered, putting off the annoyance of getting up, why he was so reluctant to be healed. There were healers in Yanwei, even though their methods and resources did not begin to approach those of the Academy. Was it a personal vendetta? Jealousy? Or did he not trust her abilities? He'd seen her heal plenty of villagers over the last two weeks.

Thinking about his grudge made it easier to dodge the deeper unease below that – she wasn't sure she wanted to heal him. She was eager to use her skill, and eager to pay him back for helping her. But it felt strange to scan into someone that she already knew, someone who dredged up so many warring thoughts about rivalry and resentment and gratitude. The Yanweian was not her patient, even if she had healed him. He wasn't a case study or a collection of symptoms. She couldn't send him on his way after she'd finished. She had to feel every thread of his energy merging with hers, feel his blood and his breath through her hands, and then look him in the eye every day afterward.

Agna sighed and creaked out of bed.

■ ■ ■

The Yanweian was drinking his morning tea when she came back from the baths. He set his cup down. "I've gotten some food. It was about a hundred head." Agna remembered the lesser Kaveran coin, which had a bull's head on one side. "You can pay me back later if you want to."

"All right. I'm not sure what I have left. I still have to count it."

He nodded. Agna returned to the tent to pack her bath kit and nightgown. The trunk was so empty. It almost seemed a waste to haul it along, with nothing to put in it. She supposed that her bedroll would squash inside now.

Stretching her neck, Agna returned to the campfire and picked through the larder chest. The Yanweian had picked a sensible, if plain, assortment of the sorts of things that they'd been eating so far – bread and eggs and spring onions and cooking herbs. Agna took some bread and a lump of butter, wrapped in waxed paper. On the flat lid of the larder chest, she was able to precariously cut and spread, one-handed. At least tea made itself. She set a cup to steep as she ate. If she had to live on bread and tea until this sling came off, so be it. She had the impression that bread was cheap, as foodstuffs went. That was another advantage.

The Yanweian opened one of his books. Agna tried not to think about him. It would only take a minute to heal him, if the wounds were not infected. It would be a relief to get back to work in the clinic. She would be nearly as useful as she ever was, and she would have a little more money.

Agna washed out her teacup and packed it away, and turned to find the Yanweian standing by the tent. He slowly unfastened the free end of the bandage around his neck, not looking at her as he spoke. "Here, or at the clinic?"

She shrugged asymmetrically. "I don't mind, either way."

"All right. I'd prefer here."

"Suit yourself. I'll wash up. You can go ahead." He entered the tent, and Agna washed her left hand in a bowl of water from the barrel. In her awkwardness she splashed the front of her robe. It would dry, she told herself. It was a minor thing.

When she entered the tent, he had already lit the lamp and taken a seat. The bandage lay in a folded pile next to him. She lifted his chin to inspect the cut in the light. The skin around it didn't seem to be reddening or swelling. That was a good sign. It was beginning to heal cleanly. No problem at all. She considered their positioning and the difficulty of working with one hand. "Can you turn?" She twirled her finger in the air. "All the way around. I can reach it from the back."

The Yanweian complied without comment. Agna took a deep breath, clearing her mind, and cupped her left hand around the left side of his throat. His energy was more muted today, controlled, as though he'd muzzled his loathing toward her. And it was easier to take if she didn't have to make eye contact.

She scanned first, understanding the placement of the tissues and the interrupted flow of energy. His pulse beat against her fingertips. She gathered some of her own energy and infused it into him, encouraging the broken flesh to knit together. His skin smoothed under her hand, and the energy snapped back, releasing the applied influence like a plucked string. She surveyed the finished product, passing her energy through the area again. Everything was back to normal. She ran her fingers over his skin. At most, he would have a thin line of scarring, and even that might fade eventually. Perfect work.

"Hey—" He turned, jerking sideways out of her reach. "What are you..."

"What? It's done."

He was blushing, and she realized why. The thought brought the blood rushing to her own cheeks. *Context.* Yes, if they were different people, in a different place, in a different situation, the way she'd just stroked his neck might have seemed very familiar indeed.

But his hand had risen to the spot now. "...Oh. I... I see. Yes." His hand lingered there, and she allowed him some time to calm down. He had spoiled the atmosphere, anyway. She had to ask him to take off his shirt next, and now she couldn't bring herself to do it. Why did he have to go and ruin everything? She'd been doing well. Who even thinks of something like that in the middle of a healer's work, anyway? There were stories like that, of course, but they were absurd and not at all realistic, and besides –

She had to focus. She could get through this. "And the other one?" Agna prompted. It was as close as she could get to the topic.

"Ah." The Yanweian awkwardly hiked his shirt halfway up, then shucked it off. Agna held the lamp to get a good look at the second cut. It was more ragged than the first, a crooked gouge into his ribs. Luckily, it didn't seem to be infected either. He'd treated it well. – Of course he had.

She set the lamp down. "Ready?"

"Mm. Go ahead."

Agna shifted on the floor, sitting offset to his right. The cut was a few inches above his right kidney. She laid her left hand against his back and repeated the familiar process. She sensed his controlled breathing like a conversation overheard through a wall. His energy was overcharged, tense – even afraid. She had done her best, this time, to work with his misgivings and follow all of the proper procedures. She was sure that she hadn't done anything wrong. She'd done her best. Was he still tense about that little misunderstanding? She was still a bit unsettled herself, but... Agna shoved this aside and threw her concentration into her work.

"All right, you're set."

He touched the healed spot, bowing his head. "Thank you." He hastened to pull his shirt on. "I'm sorry I can't do more for your arm."

"Oh. Well, there's nothing you can do about that." She had never even considered holding that against him. He wasn't a healer, and he had done all that a medic could do. He couldn't help being what he was.

"I'll get the clinic tent set up." He grabbed his valise on the way out. Agna blew out the lamp and followed.

Since he was trying to be helpful, Agna kept her silence as the Yanweian set up the clinic tent. She helped when she could, holding supports as she had done with their camping tent, though he took over most of her usual tasks in the process. At long last, the tent was set up, and she let him rest while she saw to the first patient – though she couldn't stand to wait around and watch any longer, either.

They were camped outside a small village, and only a few patients came by. Between patients, Agna scratched out some rudimentary notes in her logbook, left-handed. She could just about read them afterward. She left empty lines between each entry, so that she might annotate them when she was healed. – If she remembered any of this, so far in the future.

After an initial trickle, no one arrived for the better part of an hour, and so Agna untied the money pouch from her belt and poured it out on the desk. She sorted out the large coins from the small and counted them all. Six unions, thirty-seven head. The exchange between the two was twenty to one, so it totaled just under eight unions. She had brought seven thousand. Agna shoved the pile into her bag and lowered her head to the desk.

She'd earned five and change that morning, though – a small handful of coins stacked separately at the edge of the desk. Two patients, one at their usual rate of three unions, one a little less. She remembered paying a union to the camp cook for dinner and getting some change back. She had earned enough this morning to pay for dinner for nearly a week. Of course, she earned nothing on the days when they were traveling, and she had to eat more than once a day. Agna sighed and lifted her head.

One letter to her parents. Was she being too obstinate? She could put together an argument that might convince them of her fitness to continue on her assignment. She could afford one letter. Postage was three unions to Nessiny, four to Achusa, and one inside Kavera. ...She could afford three letters, then. One each to Esi and her parents and Rone. Of course, that calculation assumed that she could write a letter in the first place.

She turned on the stool. "Could you take dictation for me?"

"Hm?" The Yanweian focused on her, closing his medical text. "Uh..."

"A letter," Agna prompted. "I'd like to tell my family not to expect any letters from me for a few months, while I heal. So that they don't worry." She left the rest implied; she didn't need to say aloud that she could barely write. It was embarrassing enough to have to ask.

The Yanweian glanced away. "I don't think I could do that."

"Why not?" Agna snapped. "Can't you do one nice thing for me? I'd pay you. All right? I don't have enough money left to eat, but I'd—"

"Listen." He sighed. "I can't. I would, but I *can't*."

"Of course not."

"Agent," the Yanweian said, leaning on it in a way that she loathed immediately. That was how the Captain had said it, half-warning, like an adult who is trying not to scold a misbehaving child. "I don't understand Nessinian. And I doubt your family reads Yanweian."

Agna opened her mouth to insult him, and then realized what he'd said. She looked like an idiot. Curse him. She turned back to the desk, staring helplessly at her working hand. So she spoke Kaveran and Nessinian, and he spoke

Kaveran and Yanweian – it was like one of those logic puzzles from the books she'd read as a child, with foxes and chickens and rivers. "Could you take a letter in Kaveran, then? I can write to Rone and ask him to write to my family." Postage inside Kavera was less expensive, besides. It was an elegant solution. She'd figured it out. Everything would be fine.

The Yanweian fidgeted in his seat across the tent. "I can't."

"Ugh. Why not?"

He crossed his arms, but a flush was spreading over his unbruised cheekbone. "I just can't. I'm sorry."

"I'll find someone who will, then," she grumbled. She'd finally lowered herself to asking him for help, and he'd managed to ruin it. Now she'd have to bribe someone else. Her plan would work; it was still a good plan.

One more patient arrived before lunch, and the Yanweian hung back, sulking. Agna gathered her composure and greeted the man, and by lunchtime she had three more unions. When the camp cook came around with his packed lunches, she allowed herself to buy the smallest one. Half a union, ten head. Every little bit was like a bite off of the raft that held her up. It was irritating.

Over lunch, she weighed the likelihood that her parents would order her to come back if she wrote home for money. They wouldn't care about the money itself, of course; money was just money. But they would judge her for making a mistake, for putting herself in danger. If they wrote to the Benevolent Union or to the Academy to demand that she be sent home, that was that. The entire caravan would know, not that it mattered much; she would lose to the Yanweian; and worst of all, Rone would know that she had proven to be a failure and a stupid child.

She wouldn't let that happen. No more of this, then. She had to be strong.

The Yanweian took a patient or two while she finished lunch, and Agna mulled over her possible assistants in this letter-writing venture. Who else did she know in the caravan? The Captain, the guard captain, the master of records – they had to be irked with her, after their interview. The book dealer who set up shop next to them seemed intelligent enough, and he was obviously literate. She had looked through his wares a couple of times. That wasn't much of a relationship. The passenger wagon's driver, whom she barely knew, even though she rode in the woman's cart every other day. The Yanweian, out of the question. And the apothecary.

That had promise. The apothecary was Achusan; he would be able to write Nessinian, even if the Achusan dialect was different from her own. It would be readable enough. After a couple of weeks of sporadic conversations, the Achusan did not strike her as the type to hand out favors lightly. His manner was as detached as the day they'd met, and he always seemed to find a humorous failing in one of their patients or the other merchants. Agna had laughed sometimes, but she always left wondering what he said about her to everyone else. She had no question that he would expect payment for his time.

She would have to write fewer letters, if she had to spend money on dictation. If she wrote to Rone, she could ask him to pass the news along to her parents and Lina, and Lina could tell Esirel. No doubt they wrote one another every day.

Bolstered by her plan, Agna tackled as many patients as she could, adding to her little, growing pile of Benevolent Union money. It took her mind off the Yanweian's stubbornness and the pain in her shoulder, at least for a while.

■ ■ ■

After dinner – more bread and some slices of hard cheese, and handfuls of blackberries, not entirely unsatisfying – she fetched her stationery box and checked her money pouch before striding out of their campsite. The apothecary's wagon was parked a little ways away from their tent. His wagon was half the size of the Captain's, a wooden box on wheels covered with an arched canvas roof. His horse was nowhere to be seen, probably pastured with the caravan's horses. A campfire burned next to the wagon. The apothecary sat at the fireside, with a book in one hand and a ceramic cup in the other. A lantern and a wine bottle flanked him on the ground. Agna cleared her throat, and his gaze swung up.

"May I help you?"

It was a relief to speak in Nessinian for once. "I'd like to hire you for something."

The apothecary blinked. "My business hours are closed for the day."

"It's not medicine. I need to dictate a letter." She tipped her head toward her injured shoulder. "You're the only person I know here who speaks Nessinian."

He took a drink. "I suppose I am." It wasn't an answer, Agna noted.

"I'll pay you." He shrugged. "Ten head." It was more than she'd tipped anyone to carry her luggage, but it seemed like a low bid.

The apothecary drained his cup and filled it. "Amuse me." He set the book down and beckoned for her stationery box. Agna took out the notebook with her friends' addresses in it and handed the box over. Edann found the things he needed, lining them up on the ground. Paper, ink, a sharpened pen, the box of sand. The firelight flashed off his glasses when he looked up. "All right, go."

"All right." She took a deep breath. "Dear Rone–" She spelled it. "It's Furoni."

"Is that in the letter?"

"No. Just explaining."

"I'm sure I don't particularly care."

It was amazing how he could be so dispassionately jackassed, and only make her want to throw the notebook at his head. It was nothing personal, somehow. He didn't seem to hate her the way the Yanweian did. He simply hated everyone – except the Yanweian – and she was included.

Agna started again. "Dear Rone. I'm writing this to you through dictation, because I have injured my shoulder. Please don't worry about me. I'll be fine after a time. But my letters will have to stop for a while." She paused, waiting for him to catch up. He curled his fingers for her to continue. Agna cleared her throat. "There was a bandit attack on the camp. The healing art helped – I was able to fight some of them off." She folded the notebook against her body, the closest she could get to crossing her arms with the sling in the way. She would pay every gold union she made in the clinic for an entire year to see Rone. He would know what to say. She swallowed past the lump in her throat. "I'm glad you're out there, protecting the shrines. I'll have to remember that, so that I won't be afraid."

The apothecary had stopped writing, and Agna's borrowed pen froze above the paper. He didn't have a barbed comeback.

Agna fought back the threat of tears and tucked her hair behind her ear. "One more thing." The apothecary reluctantly began to write. His face was impassive. "I'll only be able to send this one letter. Please tell my parents that I can't write for a little while, and not to worry about me. Our address is Five Greenarch Court, North Bank, Murio. I'll repay you when I can. With all my love, and in communion with all creation. Agna."

The apothecary sanded the page and shoved it at her, spilling sand on the ground. "Take it."

"I need it to be addressed," Agna snapped. "There's sealing wax in the box." He folded the page, found the wax, and melted the end over the campfire. Meanwhile, Agna unlaced her money pouch, fished out a handful of the coins, and sorted ten of them on the ground. She looked up; the wax was cooling. "Rone Sidduji." She spelled it again. "Care of Tenken Grim, 1214 Bastion Street, Eastside, Vertal, Kavera."

The apothecary wrote this, sanded it, and shook off the sand properly this time. He held out the letter, and Agna held out the money. They traded, and he packed away the rest of her things in the box. He handed that over without comment. His silence was unnerving. Agna had spoken to him a dozen times since coming to this godsforsaken country, and he always had a caustic joke about everything. She had turned a corner from a bustling commercial street into a silent alley, and every instinct in her body clamored for her to get this finished and get out before he began to speak after all.

Agna got to her feet and bobbed her head. "Thank you. I won't trouble you further. Good night."

"It's best if you didn't. Good night."

Clutching the hard-won letter, Agna detoured to the master of records' wagon to post it before returning to her own campsite. It had been worth it. Rone would know what had happened, and wouldn't worry. He would tell her parents, and neither Rone nor her parents would know about the theft. She had taken care of everything for a union and a half, between postage and the apothecary's fee. And now she could go back to the tent and read and sleep in peace.

Agna: Nelle

Dear Agna,

I was so sorry to hear of your injury. Please take care of yourself. I pray for your recovery every day. My thoughts are with you, and please know that I will be here for you whenever you need me.

With my love, and in communion with all creation.

Rone

■ ■ ■

He wasn't there for her. He was in Vertal, and he never came.

Agna's shoulder hurt incessantly. She made herself smile at her patients, channeled her energy through her good hand, and explained over and over that she couldn't heal herself. In the evenings the Yanweian ate dinner and disappeared. At first she simply thanked her good fortune for his absence, and cocooned herself in the tent. She couldn't write more letters. She couldn't draw. She began to re-read the books that she had brought, grew to hate even her favorite, and quit.

Agna ventured out one evening, driven to desperation by the constant dull ache and the scratching of unceasing boredom against her brain. Even with her injured arm, she could wander through the camp and feel sorry for herself. The Yanweian's thundercloud face, his eye now underlined with flat purple bruises, passed by between the tents. So he had the same idea. No matter; she could avoid him either way, and she was sick of the tent.

The camp continued its business as though nothing had happened. The guards patrolled. The merchants cooked over campfires and drank and laughed. People washed clothes in tubs outside the bath tent. As she rounded the corner at the edge of the camp, she heard the bleating of goats. Still full of human chaos and dirt and animal stink, still merry and vulgar and alive. She despaired of ever going home.

Next in her path was one of the enclosed wagons, its horses tethered beyond the fence. Below the small windows, painted vines and flowers twined along its side. The back door was open, and its inhabitant, a young woman in a bright blue linen dress, was yelling at someone across the way. "Yeah, like you'd know what to do with it!"

"Get killed, most likely."

"Ha. – Hey, healer." Agna turned, her ears burning. The young woman on the steps of the wagon smiled and waved, and Agna twitched somewhere around her mouth. "Hard luck, what happened with those assholes in Quickwater. They can't be picking on our new people. And our *doctors!* Low. So low."

Agna stopped in her tracks, taken aback by the unexpected sympathy. "Uh... thank you?"

"Need anything? I can set you up. Free. On account of hard luck. First time, anyway."

"Talk about low," the neighbor across the way slung back ironically, and the woman on the steps made a rude gesture.

"Difference between helping and being used." The woman in the blue dress waved off the facetious argument, refastened the dark, curly hair that had escaped from its ribbon, and focused on Agna. Agna, catching up, processed the botanical motif on the wagon, the mortar and pestle in the woman's lap, and the bundles of leaves behind her on the steps. Agna's throat clenched in sudden homesickness. An herbalist.

"So here, for the arm." The herbalist held up a hand for Agna to wait and darted into the wagon. She returned with a small tin and pressed it into Agna's good hand. "Rub that in if you can stand it. It'll help."

"I... thank you. What do I owe you? I don't even..." *I don't even know you.* Agna slipped the tin into her money bag, all the same.

"Tch." The herbalist flipped her hands at the notion and settled on the steps with her mortar and pestle. "You busy? Sit a minute if you want." She tapped a lower step with a bare foot. Agna hesitated, gave in, and sank down on the step. She hadn't had a civil conversation with anyone other than a patient in... she couldn't remember how long. Did the business with the letter and the apothecary count?

"So what's your name?"

"Hm? Oh. Agna Despana."

"Nelle," the herbalist replied. "Swear to you, it isn't usually like this, getting attacked and all. Usually it's great. Best place to be."

A harsh laugh escaped Agna's throat. "Really." It was easy for her to say, sleeping indoors where it was warm and safe, without some backbiting viper glaring at her all the time.

"You'll get used to it. The green ones do, eventually. If not, well, they drop off into some town and we get someone else. Everyone's free to go."

"I'm not. I'm on contract."

"Pff. The Union'd find you somewhere if you really wanted."

Agna flushed at the accusation and said nothing. The herbalist went on crushing leaves in her mortar. The scent tickled the back of Agna's brain, distracting her. She knew this, or something like it. Something in Lina's workroom. Lina had handed her a bottle full of concentrated extract, proud of her new blend, orange oil and night-blooming whitestar and – that was it. Sweetmint.

"...Is that sweetmint?"

"Wintermint. Related." She held out the mortar, and Agna inhaled the scent. "You interested in this stuff?"

"I suppose so. It's good to know, in the course of healing. And my sister is an herbalist. I guess most of what I know is through her."

"Oh, yeah?" Nelle's voice took on new energy. "So you use sweetmint over in – Nessiny, right?"

"Yes. And yes. Mostly for cooking, though. It can unstuff your nose if you make it strong enough. But mostly it just tastes and smells good."

"Yeah, this is just to cover nastiness in something else I'm making. It helps."

"Hmm. ...What are you making?"

■ ■ ■

Agna found her way back to the tent by torchlight, sated with herbal tea, carrying three books under her good arm. She couldn't take notes on Kaveran herbalism to send to Lina along with her sketches. Not yet. But she would remember what she could, and wait.

The Yanweian returned while she sat up reading. She had begun with the novel that Nelle had thrown on the stack, too sleepy to retain much information from the herbalism texts. She saw him studying the title, but ignored him. He set off on his own preparations, and they made it all the way to lights-out without trading more than a dozen words.

He had nightmares again that night, the wordless, beaten whimpers slithering under Agna's skin. She snapped awake, heart pounding in her throat. It had gone this way nearly every night since the attack. She had asked him about it, the first time. She had approached him over breakfast the next morning and asked him whether he were all right. He had snapped back with such viciousness that she had gripped her teacup to keep from throwing it at his head. Since then, she had frozen in the dark, hating her terrified reaction and hating herself for being so inhumane.

She spoke up, that night. The salve might have eased the pain in her shoulder enough to make her patient, or maybe Nelle's hospitality had loosened her mood. "Hey. *Hey.*" He lurched awake, crying out. Agna cleared her rusty throat. "It's all right. Just a dream."

The Yanweian muttered something in his own language, like a handful of sharp-edged stones. "I... yes." She heard him stir, and a sliver of torchlight lit the door as he nudged through it.

You're welcome, Agna thought, but sleep had begun to drag her under.

■ ■ ■

79

"Why don't you ever come to the bonfires?"

Agna accepted the soaked dress that Nelle held out and fed it into the wringer. "I... don't know. It never interested me, I guess." She cranked it one-handed, pausing to straighten the alignment.

"How do you know if you don't go?" Nelle brushed back a stray wisp of hair with a soapy forearm. "Take your mind off things."

"I'm only in the sling for a few more weeks."

"Yeah, well, other things. Your sour-faced hating-everything-ness," she explained without rancor. Agna piled the wrung dress in her basket.

"That's because of my shoulder."

"Ha, unlikely. Didn't come to the bonfire before the shoulder, did you."

"...Ugh."

"Come and talk. Have a drink. Let people get to know you."

"...I don't know."

"Nothing wrong with reading, yeah, but it's all you do."

"That's not true. I'm here."

"Doing laundry," Nelle laughed.

Agna's lips set in a line. Nelle had been kind enough to help her with her laundry, brushing it off with another offhanded comment. Agna would owe the herbalist so much, once she saved enough money to pay her. But more to the point, she had enjoyed this. More than struggling by herself, at least.

"Anyway, try it."

"I will. Sometime."

Nelle handed over one of Agna's nightgowns, and Agna wrung it through. "So's the rub still working for you?"

"Yes! It helps. Thank you. – I forgot to ask, what did you put in it?" Nelle grinned and launched into a dissertation about topical painkillers, which kept her off the subject of the bonfire for another half-hour.

Even though she had grown up in the caravan and had never studied in a proper school – which had unsettled Agna greatly when she first found out – Nelle was well-educated in her chosen field. She had apprenticed with another herbalist, since retired, and had talked to every fellow practitioner along the circuit's path. She studied and experimented with new mixtures when she wasn't hanging around the bonfire or humoring injured Nessinian healers. She was nothing like Lina at all, and yet...

Agna couldn't imagine her sister traveling in the caravan, peddling medicine and perfume and cooking extracts to backwoods foreigners. She could hardly imagine Lina working in the herbalist's shop in Murio, and that arrangement had gone on for years. But Nelle's eyes lit and her voice took on new life when she talked about her craft, the same way Lina's had. Perhaps Lina would be happy working in the shop, after all, if their parents would allow it.

Nelle's parents had been a carpenter and a guard. They had left her the wagon when they decided to live on solid ground, and let her decide what to do with it. Agna almost envied the simplicity of that arrangement.

"So what are you doing for dinner? You cooking, or buying from Masa?"

"I don't know. Buying, I guess."

"Save it. I'll make us something good."

Agna sighed. "I don't... I can't pay you back for all of this. You need to stop."

"You need to stop being so stupid, city girl."

Agna flushed. "What am I supposed to do? I don't *have* any money. They *took it.*"

"Supposed to do? Supposed to let me help you, till your shoulder is better. They raise you in a box back in Nessiny?" Nelle fished the last sock out of the tub and tossed it in the air. Agna snatched for it and snagged it with the tips of her fingers. To avoid answering, she ran it through the wringer as though it demanded all of her attention.

Why was Nelle even doing this? Because she felt sorry for Agna? Because Agna was so pathetic as to be amusing? Because she thought the guards or the road patrol would eventually find Agna's stolen goods and make her worthwhile again? Because... because. Because it was the right thing to do.

Damn it.

Nelle carried one handle of Agna's borrowed basket back to the tent, and helped her hang her clothes on the line. Because it was the right thing to do. Because they were beginning to become friends.

Keifon: The Game

In the evenings he walked, to get away from the tent and to keep his body moving in the only way it could. The back of his brain shouted at him to hone his combat skills so that he could hold off the rest of humanity at knifepoint, but the bruising along his abdomen made training out of the question.

The camp went about its business as though nothing had happened. Some of the merchants gave him weak, sympathetic smiles as he passed. Some of the guards gave him knowing nods. Most ignored him, chatting and sweeping and counting inventory and washing clothes with no mind to the ghost among them.

At the edges of the camp, whenever space allowed, a loose confederation of guards and merchants gathered to play a ball game. The third time he passed this assembly, Keifon stopped to watch for a while. The teams identified themselves by color, red and blue, with scraps of fabric tied on as headbands or armbands. A few used them to tie their hair back. The rules seemed akin to ma-sei, one of the games that they had played in the Army on their days off. Violations of the rules were debated with some vigor by players and spectators alike, and usually settled by starting over. After an hour or two, Keifon thought he had figured out the differences between this game and ma-sei well enough to follow along. He clapped for both sides and tried to blend in.

At the end of the game, Nita stripped her blue headband off and flashed him an embarrassed smile as she left the makeshift pitch. "You should play next time, Medic. Come by after the shops close. All right?"

Keifon realized that he hadn't spoken to her since the night of the attack, and that she didn't seem to hold it against him. "A-all right. Thanks."

She was gone, melted into the churn of players and spectators. The night shift came around to light the torches.

■ ■ ■

Sometimes the red team picked him, sometimes the blue. Sometimes he stepped in late, replacing someone who had to go on shift or got tired out or had chores to finish. Nita often caught up with him during breaks or at the end of the game. He always knew where she was in relation to himself, his senses heightened to her presence like an animal's before a thunderstorm. When she passed him the ball or foiled one of his plays – depending on their temporary alliances – he didn't have to remember to smile at her. It became a reflex. Nita's returning smile completed the cycle, pouring calm over his skittering nerves.

They almost-talked in glancing blows, hardly more, at first, than he offered to any of the other guards or the merchants. *Good game. How have you been? How are your bruises healing?* They talked more as the caravan advanced slowly out of the forest, lingering in the pitch after everyone else had left. Keifon learned the name and location of Nita's hometown and the length of her service in the Golden Caravan's guard. He learned that she guarded her solitude as much as she could while living in a mobile barracks with nineteen of her fellows. He learned that she had a deep passion for Kaveran military history, and that she loved music, but was too embarrassed to dance. He stopped short of playing the nanbur for her.

Her questions angled carefully toward his past. She stole glances at the chain around his neck until the phrase *my ex-wife* fit into a conversation in a way that he could bear. He did not admit to the more recent partner who had left him in shreds. Nita seemed to sense his reluctance. She did not pry too hard. She moved very slowly along a trajectory that he could trace in his sleep. She was perceptive and thoughtful, and she was trying to get to know him.

Keifon wanted to cry in her arms, or to flee until the land under his feet gave out. He was utterly alone here, abandoned with his own personal Benevolent Union-assigned demon, and there were no other allies to be found. Nita offered him kindness and attention and, somewhere down the line, when they were ready, a more tactile comfort.

She was the only lifeline he'd seen in all of these long months. His nerves were ragged. Every trip past the bonfire, with its laughter and its freely passed cider, made him ache. He could resist for an indeterminate length of time. Another distraction, another obsession to which he could apply himself, would fill the empty spaces when he could not bring himself to pray.

And Nita could, with her perception and thoughtfulness, pick him apart thread by thread. She would spend more time with him – a walk here, a trip into town there. She would give him space and not push too hard. She would keep asking careful questions. And soon enough she would see that he was hollow, that she had been courting an empty shell.

He still longed for Kazi when he tried in vain to fall asleep. She would, given time, know that. He feared the cold and isolation and murderers and coming home to find that his daughter no longer knew him. He was a patchwork creature, broken and rebroken until no glue in the world could hide the seams. She would know that, too, and realize that her time had been wasted. Nita wanted a companion; he read it between her words and in the careful positioning of her body relative to his. She did not need a broken toy.

■ ■ ■

The apothecary watched.

He never played the game; he was small and slender enough that no one would expect it of him, nor risk breaking his expensive glasses. He turned up in the crowd, dividing Keifon's awareness between two opposing poles, and disappeared before the players left the pitch. In the clinic, his foreign cadence and his sharp laugh caught Keifon's ear through the canvas wall. When Keifon stopped by his stall, Edann always had a greeting or a witty comment about the Nessinian or a foolish patient. Keifon laughed, and felt like a co-conspirator, lucky to be included in a circle.

The rest was in Edann's eyes, and in certain sentences left unfinished. The invitation was open and unequivocal. *Come if you will. I won't wait for you.*

He always seemed to have a bottle at hand outside business hours, at the bonfire or at his own campsite. Keifon never got close enough to smell it when he chanced to pass by, but the memory burned in his throat. He had not backslid since he'd come to Kavera, and the danger was greater now than it had ever been. The thought of tasting it on the apothecary's lips made his heart race and his chest tighten.

Edann's comments about the others – everyone, it seemed – were perceptive, cutting, intelligent and vicious. He seemed to think himself surrounded by idiots of the highest caliber, and Keifon was not quite sure whether he was truly exempted from this assessment. Edann's cynicism grated on his conscience sometimes. Followers of Lundra needed compassion above all else, and he had enough trouble focusing on those prayers lately. And Keifon wondered whether he might be exempted from Edann's judgment only as long as the apothecary found him interesting.

The apothecary did find him interesting, for now.

And he did not ask questions.

Edann: Weakness

In the hours after closing time, Edann's errands led him past the field on the edge of the camp, where the guards and those who fancied themselves to be active types tossed a ball at each other. The shouting stabbed into his temples, but he did not react, carrying his sack of supplies back to his wagon.

After each item was fit into its proper place, he hefted the water buckets and headed for the stream. He strayed to the edge of the camp again on the way back, pausing at the edge of the little crowd that sat along the fence to watch. The buckets were heavy. He needed to rest his arms. The players wore scraps of red and blue fabric to mark their teams, tied around their wrists or bare arms, and a few, with whimsy that could make him sick, around their foreheads.

Of course the new medic was playing. Of course he noticed. In the chaos of a dozen flailing bodies of every shade from wheat to oak, he picked out the medic first. Coincidence. When the medic glanced at the crowd and just as quickly swiveled back toward the game, that was a coincidence, too.

The buckets weren't really too heavy to carry. The wagon wasn't far. He did not have infinite time to waste watching a pointless game. And yet.

It was absurd. The last Nessinians had left at the new year, and Edann was the only Achusan in the caravan. He'd intended to escape, and instead set up a perfect situation to embarrass himself – surrounded by guileless foreign rustics, so quick to smile, so quick to trust him. Those who cast looks his way didn't seem to care that he was an outsider. Some even seemed to like it. *My white tiger,* one guard had called him by candlelight. Edann had burned with outrage and attraction in equal proportion. They were no better than him, he consoled himself, if they consorted with foreigners so readily. At least he knew that he ought to be ashamed of his weakness.

He knew damned well that the medic brought it out in him, that there was a perfectly good reason that the medic's voice sometimes reached him from the next tent despite the background noise. The medic was a stone in his shoe, impossible to catch and toss aside. The Yanweian, Edann reminded himself – just as foreign as all of these Kaverans. Just as foreign as the others.

An outcry in the crowd startled him back to the game. One of the guards pumped a fist in the air and was slapped on the back by her teammates. Blue. The Yanweian was blue, too. Perhaps they were winning. He was smiling, for one thing. His cheekbone was shadowed by greenish-brown now, a faint discoloration against his dark-golden skin. Edann wondered whether it still hurt. He had been plagued by daydreams about recommending that salve that he'd bought in Vertal. He kept imagining the cool, slippery salve between his fingers and the Yanweian's bruised cheek, a lingering, a pause, a natural progression to lifting his other hand to the Yanweian's other cheek and leaning in.

Now the Yanweian was drinking from a flask on the other side of the pitch. Water, probably. Edann had heard that he avoided anything alcoholic, that he was a religious fanatic, that his spouse in the home country was a woman – all things that should have broken the spell, and had not. In some ways it only made the problem worse. That torque, for instance; that was part of the problem. For months, Edann had wanted to see it glinting silver against his dark skin in the candlelight. He would make him leave it on.

The players fanned out and launched into motion. Edann shifted his weight and wondered which would be worse: getting caught sneaking away, or slinking away unnoticed?

That water looks heavy. Mind if I carry it for you? Ugh. Edann heaved a bucket in each hand and edged away from the crowd. He had things to do, and he could just as easily wallow in these unhelpful daydreams alone. It was unwise, or distasteful – he wasn't sure which – to stand around drinking in the sights. Or to think of them as sights at all.

The heat of the campfire made his head swim. Edann dumped the water into the pot to boil and retreated to a cooler distance with a book and a lantern. Dusk was beginning to fall, just dark enough to strain his eyes as he read.

An outbreak of cheering pulled him away from the page. The players, sweating, jubilant, red and blue alike, tromped through the aisles – back to their tents and wagons and toward the bonfire. Edann plotted the path from the field to the medic's tent; it did not pass by his own campsite.

The water was boiling, and it needed to be put away. He moved it one dipper at a time, kettle to barrel. His hands were not shaking. He was not a benighted fool or a slumming joyrider. He would ignore this one, the Yanweian. Just this once.

The barrel filled until Edann could heave the kettle and pour the rest of the water in. He sealed the lid, put the ladle and pot away, and slid the water barrel to its place. He turned around and started. The firelight flickered in orange pools on the planes of the Yanweian's face.

"Hey."

Edann swallowed and adjusted his glasses. "Did you win?"

A flicker of a smile. "Yeah. You should've seen it." He crossed his arms. The firelight shimmered over the sheen on his skin. Edann's heart thudded embarrassingly. "Anyway… I, uh. Thanks for stopping by to watch."

"It was on my way," Edann muttered.

"And, um. Because we won…" His dark eyes flicked toward the ground. "I think that's why I was brave enough to come over and talk to you."

"About…" He left it hanging, a noncommittal, neutral prompt. Everything but his voice was busy screaming *Shut up and get inside, you stupid, beautiful beast.* He had wanted this alien cipher for every moment of the last four months, and here he was, delivered on a platter. It was a bad idea. This one was smarter than the others. He would see Edann for what he was.

"Well." The tilt of the Yanweian's head was artful, but his voice stuttered. The little move he made to bite his lip was somewhere in between. "I, ah… I wondered whether you were busy."

Edann breathed. He could still do that.

"Later, maybe," the Yanweian went on. "I should get cleaned up."

Edann opened his mouth first, but it took a moment for his voice to vault over his better judgment. "No. …Stay." The Yanweian blushed, which only goaded Edann's impulsive nature. Edann nodded toward the back of the wagon, enclosed in its canopy. "Care to step inside?"

The Yanweian was speechless, staring at the campfire at his feet and groping for words. Edann stared him down. He would not rescind the offer, like a stammering youth. He needed a bottle of wine. The Yanweian had blindsided him. But he had gone over the line, and he would not go back.

The Yanweian rubbed his neck and stretched his spine. "…Yeah. Privacy is good."

Edann smirked and motioned for his guest to go first. The Yanweian passed by him, flashing him a tiny smile, and mounted the ladder to the wagon bed. Edann watched him climb over the edge. The Yanweian's body was all planes and lines, not much mass – not his usual type. He wasn't attractive, not really. His features were too strange, too Yanweian, the contours of his face unmistakably foreign. And yet. A little shiver of anticipation shuddered through Edann's insides, tempered with self-loathing. He couldn't outrun his weakness for the strange and the stupid, even though this one was smarter than the usual guards and shepherds. Edann knew this abstractly – the Yanweian was somewhere on the road to being a doctor, after all – but he didn't like to be reminded of it.

He suspected that before long, the Yanweian would begin to talk too much. The more he talked, the more dangerous he could be. Especially since Edann had to see him in passing every day. Especially since – his mind shied away from this, from the thought that he saw an echo of himself there, twisted and remote. Abstainer, worshipper, foreigner; Keifon was nothing like him. Nothing.

He dropped the back curtain. In the enclosed space the smell of the Yanweian's overworked body was intoxicating. Edann leaned in and nuzzled under his ear, where his hair lay damp against his neck. The Yanweian let out a yelping noise and scrambled backward, toward the center of the wagon, scooting onto the bed accidentally.

Edann chuckled under his breath, and sat back against his trunk of clothes. "Too forward?"

"Nn – I – s-sudden, that's all. I didn't expect..."

Edann allowed himself an open eye roll. "Then I apparently wasn't flirting hard enough." It was irritating to drag this out. Edann wondered whether the Yanweian would bolt if he opened the wine.

"Well... I mean... I wondered if you were interested, but I..." He gathered his knees toward his chest, restlessly. Edann had rattled him, it seemed. "I thought we would talk for a while," the Yanweian finished.

Edann leaned his head back against the lid of the trunk, rolling his neck. "I'm not in the market for a boyfriend, so I don't really see the point."

"I... I see." He hesitated, and then sat on his heels at the foot of the mattress. "I'm all right with that. It's-it's good to be honest about it."

"Right."

Edann knelt next to him and leaned in. Just a kiss or three, slow, measured, proper. – Well, as properly as one could kiss a foreign stranger after two minutes of conversation. The Yanweian – Keifon, Edann reminded himself that the medic had a name – froze for one or two kisses before responding hungrily. His hands were quick and restless, finding Edann's face and his back and finally resting on his waist. Edann's glasses dug into the bruised cheekbone, and Keifon shied away. He lifted the glasses carefully from Edann's face and looked around as if scouting for a safe place to put them. Edann plucked them away, folded them one-handed, and returned them to the box next to the bed. It didn't matter if he could see, now. The canopies reduced the light to nearly nothing, and he didn't intend to move any further away.

Agna: Nemesis

What happened to your arm?
Can't you, y'know, fix it?
So what happened?
Guess I shouldn't let you try to heal me, look what might happen, heh heh.
Why's your arm in a cast?
Doesn't your healing work?
Is it going to backfire on me?
Guess the country was too much for a fancy Eastern girl.
What got hold of you, huh?
Why don't you smile?
Hey, what's going on with the other guy?
What did he do to Nita? 'Cause we won't stand for that.
Is it true? I mean, your guy and the Achusan?

They didn't listen. The patients, the merchants, and the guards stared at her with dumb smiles, or clucked their tongues without offering real help, or slid away without speaking. They did not understand her pinched explanations about energy connections and the impossibility of healing oneself. They did not understand why she batted away questions about the dratted Yanweian, her own personal millstone.

In the clinic, their only words were directed at the patients. At the camp there were no words at all. Agna visited Nelle when she wasn't feeling too peevish, where she could at least get a little company. There she hung around, staring into nowhere while Nelle tied up bundles of herbs or cooked new mixtures. The medicine she'd bought from the Achusan apothecary made Agna logy, but it dulled the pain in her shoulder, and it had cost too much of her remaining funds to throw away. This realization had lodged queasily in her belly. If she needed another kind of medicine, she could get it only if she did not buy food. The patients in the clinic continued to pay their tiny fees, but her savings were not enough. She felt as though she were suffocating every time she opened her money pouch.

The Yanweian disappeared more often than not, which suited her just fine. He came back late, prayed through his cycle of gods, and went to sleep. His timeframe shifted later and later, until he slipped in after she was asleep. After the first few startled awakenings, she was able to throttle her panic reaction. She lay motionless and opened one eye a slit, her heart galloping without her permission, until she was able to identify him.

One morning she'd passed by Edann's stall, said hello, and received the chilliest greeting she'd ever heard as a reply. He had never been particularly outgoing, true, but after a few such interactions she began to suspect that the gossips were on the right track. The medic was spending the evenings at the apothecary's camp.

It was none of her business, of course. But everyone could see his marriage torque. It wasn't as though the Yanweian hid it, like a villain in an opera who wore gloves to hide his wedding rings. He was right out in the open as a cheating cad. Which, she supposed, made the apothecary partly at fault; he wasn't being tricked. Still, the burden of responsibility fell on the married person. The Church of Lundra had the same view on that as the Church of the Balance. She had read that in school herself. And the Yanweian was supposed to be a man of faith! He was such a hypocrite.

Perhaps he had an arrangement with his spouse, while he was out of the country – but Agna brushed that thought aside. He was untrustworthy and dishonest, and it was easy enough to believe that he had no such permission. Besides, his spouse was not here to speak up. He was a near-stranger, but Agna could not stand by and watch him violate his sacred vow. It simply wasn't right.

She had been in the sling for four weeks when she woke one morning to find the tent empty. The camp outside was lively with the jingle of tack and the heave and crash of equipment being loaded onto wagons. She sat up and cast around. Everything was as the Yanweian had left it last night; his bedroll was lashed to his backpack. She scrambled to stand, her head reeling, and began to pack. He would be back in time to take down the tent, wouldn't he? At least the clinic tent was already packed. What difference did it make? She couldn't dismantle this thing single-handed.

Agna was dressed and packed in record time, and carried the other luggage to the passenger wagon one at a time, even the stupid Yanweian's stupid backpack. She returned to the campsite, where only the tent remained. She pulled the spikes from the support ropes and levered the poles out from the corners of the tent. It collapsed on itself. She stared at it and tossed the poles aside.

She knew the process; it was second nature by now. It was not second nature to complete it alone with one nearly-broken arm. She could not afford to hire anyone to help. She could ask Nelle, and Nelle would help. But she felt a lump press against her throat even thinking about it. If she ran to Nelle crying for help, she would lose her nerve. Everything would come rushing out, the money and the brain-fogging medicine and her aching shoulder and her regret at ever having come here. And then she would have to go and bludgeon the Yanweian with these tent poles, and the Captain would lecture her.

Agna forced herself to breathe evenly. She coiled the ropes into awkward skeins. She dragged the corners of the tent into sloppy folds. She rolled up the canvas and pinned it with her right elbow, panting with the resultant pain, until she could tie it up. It was good enough to get it onto the wagon. She knelt next to the bundle for a little while, pressing the tears from her eyes and waiting for that morning's dose of painkiller to take effect.

She would do it in spite of him. She would get through this and show all of them.

When she could scrape her composure together, she slung the tent over her good shoulder and headed for the wagon. Halfway there, her path crossed with the Yanweian's. She noticed a few things through the bright red fury. Unshaven, red-eyed, half-asleep. She hoped he was suffering.

He stammered something half-formed and reached for the tent. She spun aside. "I got it. Happy?"

"I – I just overslept."

"Yeah. Under Edann. Everyone knows. Cheater."

She registered horror on his face. Good. Agna shouldered past him toward the wagon.

"I'm not cheating, not that it's any of your business," he called behind her. He was following. She increased her speed. He caught up with a few loping strides – damn him for being taller, too – and touched her shoulder. "Look, I'm—"

"Get your hands off me."

He let go immediately and backed off a step. They had reached the foot of the wagon, and Agna slung the tent onto the deck. "I don't want to hear excuses from you. You got what you wanted. I had to carry everything by myself. It was hard. It hurt. A lot. Sorry you missed watching it."

He fell back another step, the horror on his face closing off into something harder. "That wasn't my intention. How dare you even suggest that."

Agna ignored him and mounted the ladder to the wagon deck. She left the tent in the last row and strode down the aisle to the first row. His footsteps followed her, and she heard him slide into the seat behind her. His voice was low and clenched in her ear, his accent bending the words nearly beyond comprehension. "It was an honest mistake. I overslept. You know I don't sleep well."

"I'm sure you're sleeping much better now. And with such a clear conscience."

The bell rang out for the caravan to move, and the wagon's floorboards vibrated with the steps of the rest of the passengers.

She did not turn to face him – she would not give him the satisfaction – but she glanced sideways to see his hand gripping the back of the bench. "What do you know about my conscience? You – thoughtless child." He flung himself back in his seat, muttering, "What do you know, anyway."

"Thoughtless?" Agna snapped, not sure she'd heard correctly. She'd thought a good sight more than he had.

"*Godless*," the Yanweian growled. "You think you can tell me I'm wrong, when you turn your back on the source of rightness itself. You know nothing about me, or my life, or morality."

"Is that the morality that condones running off to cheat on your spouse while you leave an injured person to carry your luggage?"

The Yanweian flung himself to his feet. "You don't know me. You don't know anything." He stomped across the wagon to take a seat at the back. Agna imagined the acid burn of his glare on the back of her head, and stoked her own fury.

The wagon lurched into motion with the habitual round of applause. Agna braced herself on the seat, feeling the jolt of every rut and puddle in her shoulder. The medicine's effects had begun to fog her head, luring her toward a sleep she would never be able to find. She had to put up with this for the better part of a year. She'd begun to feel safe enough at night, jumping at unexpected sounds much less often. She'd taken for granted that if someone else were there, she wouldn't be murdered in her sleep. But who even knew if that were true? His supposed sense of ethics was a lie. What else would she have to witness?

Some part of her wondered whether she were being unreasonable, which only soured her mood further. She could not stop feeling angry, which was more irritating yet. She did not want to be driven to lose her composure by this silver-tongued liar. Everyone in the camp liked him more than they liked her, after all. They were all fooling themselves, or maybe they were just as bad as he.

This was where she had to stay for the better part of a year.

Godless child.

She didn't care to argue with *godless*; it only proved his narrow-mindedness. *Child* was more difficult. She wasn't sure she could argue with that.

Agna: The Feast of Darano

Agna knocked on the door of the wagon. "Nelle?"

"Just a minute," Nelle called from inside. Agna turned to lean against the wall, crossing her arms because she could. She rolled her shoulder and kneaded it with what she still thought of as her good hand. She had never been in peak physical form in the first place, but her right arm felt wobbly and underpowered compared to the left, and it ached sometimes. But at least she could write and cook and do her own laundry, and didn't have to depend on Nelle for everything. And Nelle had asked her to go to the festival today. Agna wouldn't question her good fortune right now.

"All right!" Nelle bounded from the door and twirled around to lock it. She tucked the key into one of the pouches at her belt. "Ready. Ready?"

"Uh..." Agna felt a trace of a flush across her cheekbones. She was woefully underdressed. Nelle's hair had been pinned up here and there with ribbons, and her dress flamed a deep coral-crimson. She grabbed Agna's good arm to hurry her along with a rush of excited chatter about the fun they'd have at the festival.

Agna had dressed in what she wore on her days off: one of her remaining dresses, which was serviceable enough, though it was several months old and probably out of fashion back home. She could lace her corset and bodice properly now, at least, so she didn't have to traipse through the festival half-dressed. But she still looked like Nelle's governess.

"Was I supposed to dress up?"

"Huh? If you want to, that's all."

Agna let the worry slide off as Nelle propelled her along the road from the camp toward the fairground. From what she had gathered from Nelle and the other merchants, the Feast of the Resurrection of Darano was the Church of the Four's version of Midsummer – a bit earlier, but similarly light-hearted and given to outdoor merrymaking. It was a strange development for what her studies had painted as a somber sect. Darano was the god of war, after all, and the feast marked his return from the dead. Hardly merrymaking subject matter. But in the end, she supposed that the common folk would take any opportunity to throw a party.

The noise of the fairground reached her first – clashing music, laughing and cheering, the metallic clunk of some carnival game. The air smelled of sawdust and mud, fried dough, perfume, spilled beer, and a whiff of barnyard. The fairground was arranged like any fairground back home, or the Golden Caravan market stalls – tents and tables set up in aisles, with the revelers milling around in all directions.

Nelle turned to Agna, her eyes bright. "How about a look around first before we pick a spot?"

Agna shrugged her assent at this plan, and Nelle started them on a loop around the fairground. The stalls featured food and drink, quaint local handicrafts for sale, and games of chance. Not much of this appealed to Agna, but at least she would have company. Wandering around and talking with a friend was a pleasant enough way to spend a day off, no matter what the backdrop might be. Agna kept mostly silent, absorbing the sights. Nelle waved to the caravan merchants that they passed, as well as some people that Agna didn't recognize.

They completed their path through the festival, and Nelle began on a second round. "Anything looking good to you?" she asked Agna.

"Eh, not particularly. Anything is fine."

"All right, then. That one about halfway down this side, I think... yes!" She turned aside into an open-sided tent full of tables, her skirt whirling. Agna followed. She wasn't hungry yet, but a rest would give them a chance to talk.

Nelle picked a spot near the corner of the tent, next to a table full of young men. Agna sank into a seat across from her. Her back tightened as a few of the young men turned around, and Nelle leaned back in her chair to greet them. Looking over her shoulder, they would have quite an impressive view indeed. Agna hung onto the edge of the table. Nelle wasn't listening right now. It would be rude to break into their conversation and try to get her attention. Nelle laughed at something that one of the young men had said. One of them had begun to lean on the back of her chair.

A host approached, hefting a tray full of beer mugs and copper coins. "Two, ladies?"

"Yes, ma'am," Nelle chirped, depositing some coins on the tray.

"Um..." Agna began, and did not know how to finish. The host plunked a mug in front of each of them and bustled on to distribute drinks to the party at the next table.

This isn't my kind of thing.

Did you come here to spend time with me, or to pick up boys?

Is this fun to you?

She couldn't say anything that would pull Nelle's attention back to her side of the table. Worse, Agna saw a couple of the young men glancing her way. No, no, no, never in a thousand years. Not here, not now, not ever. Nelle could have them all. Agna had left all of that behind at the Academy – the growing amusement, the snide comments, the underhanded tricks, and finally the willful blindness to her existence. She was done with boys.

"Nelle – hey – I'm sorry." Agna stumbled to her feet, kicking her chair over onto the packed dirt. She ducked to right it and backed away from the table.

"Have fun. I don't really – I'll see you later." She left her friend to her admirers and fled into the mob of strangers outside.

Nelle hadn't abandoned her. Agna could have joined in, could have tried to make conversation with those boys. She didn't even have to drink if she didn't want to; she just had to join in. It wasn't Nelle's fault. Agna knew this, and tried to convince her heart that it was true.

She could come halfway around the world, join a new organization, call herself a full-fledged healer, venture out on her own, and even lose the travel funds that her parents had sent with her – and she had never quite left the Academy behind. Not the good parts, for which she was thankful: her learning, her dedication to her craft, even the echoes of the faith that the Academy espoused. And not the other parts – the gossip, the unspoken but crucially important social rules, and the sense that for some amorphous and unchangeable reason, she simply did not belong here.

Agna passed the food and drink stalls, including more open-air beer gardens like the one that Nelle had colonized. She poked at a few of the handicrafts stalls, finding nothing that appealed to her and painfully aware that she could not spare the funds to buy anything anyway. She convinced herself that every shopkeeper knew how low she had sunk.

Agna ducked out of yet another stall full of woven bags and hats into the flow of foot traffic, heading back toward the camp. The crowd shifted to reveal a figure in a deep red uniform with tall black boots, striding through the festival. Agna stopped short, and he halted in front of her. The Yanweian inclined his head coolly.

He had fastened his quartered shield pin onto his jacket, along with other insignias in gold – numbers, Yanweian script characters, the crossed lines of the medical aid symbol, and the sword-and-shield of the Daranite church. He wore his knife at his hip, on a dark leather belt with a polished buckle. Agna closed her mouth, since she had nothing to say. He stood with a poise that she had never seen in him before. She had seen this uniform before; it was as familiar as any uniform of a foreign army, something from paintings and in history books. She had never seen it on him before. It was something alien, something adult, something that invested him with a new power. And she had been intimidated by some ruffian boys from a nowhere town in the mountains.

She groped after words, any words, forgetting to lift her eyes from the buttons over his chest. "I, uh. I thought your army wore those wheat-colored uniforms."

"Mmn. That's the combat uniform, and for drills. This is the formal one, for ceremonies."

"Ceremonies?"

"At the church, for the Resurrection." He couldn't conceal the pride in his voice. The army and its patron god represented both his profession and his religion, after all. It was an important day for him. He belonged here, more than anyone else, although his uniform was as foreign here as it would have been in Murio.

She thought about going with him. It would be comforting to be with someone she knew, albeit someone whom she could barely stand. But she wouldn't be welcome there, either. She was an unbeliever and a foreigner twice over, and the Yanweian hated her. She wanted to ask him what the ceremony was like and what his insignias meant. She knew a bit about the Daranite faith – just enough to make him snap at her and tell her how ignorant she was. He didn't respect her enough to help her understand. He never would, because she wasn't like him.

The words were out before she'd decided to speak. "Well. If you need to kill anyone in your ceremony, I'm sure it'll do."

"...What?"

"Darano is a death god, isn't he?" she found herself saying, heart racing, before she had a chance to stop herself.

"No. He is not." His voice had gone cold. She knew this tone. She understood this tone. She understood it more than her dawning curiosity and her desperate need for companionship. "He is the god of power and justice, and—"

"War," Agna interrupted. "What do you do in war other than kill?"

"Darano is not only a war god," the Yanweian insisted. "That's a gross oversimplification—"

Agna crossed her arms tight across her chest. "Right. Think about what you worship some time."

"I do," he snapped. "Something beyond myself." He stormed past her and was gone in the crowd. She could see him receding, his deep red coat flashing between the milling bodies, cutting through the fairground toward the center of the town.

Agna wandered around the festival for a little while longer, and ignored Nelle when she called out from her gang of merrymakers. She drifted away from the fairground, slinking back to the quiet camp in defeat. She had already written to everyone who cared about her, and all of them were far away. She found chores and attacked them until every meager thing she owned was clean and organized. Her arm ached. She ignored the Yanweian when he slunk in that night. She didn't apologize. There was no point.

Laris: Agna

While the herds were out in the pasture, Artal gave Laris a few hours free to go to the summer caravan market. Tuca had already gone with some head of cattle to sell, so the ranch's business with the market was covered. Artal's son Gawin, along with the dogs, was left to oversee Laris's section of the herds. Gawin perched on a fence, swinging his feet as Laris left the ranch behind him.

Laris turned toward home when he reached the Square. He couldn't help but wash up a little and change. Caravan market days were some of his favorite times of year. There were so many people from distant places and so many new things to see. He'd been out in the sun all day, and it wouldn't do to go out to the market smelling like mud and sweat. They could make fun of him when he went back; he didn't care. He wasn't dressing up, anyway, no matter what they said – just changing into clean clothes. Properly outfitted, Laris filled his money pouch with enough coin for a checkup at the Benevolent Union clinic and a few books.

When he poked his head into the Benevolent Union tent, two new healers were attending to Laketoners – Feldon's mother, who worked in the Northfield dairy, and Yuta's youngest sister, who had to be about fourteen by now. The healers turned, and Laris waved a little. "I'm sorry. I can come back later—"

"I'll be done in a few minutes, no need." It was the man who spoke, in a Yanweian accent. It was a little different from most of the accents Laris knew from the Yanweian families on the west end of town. Maybe he was newly immigrated.

The other healer smiled and turned to Yuta's younger sister. She was a girl, also young – Laris's age, or something close to it. She wore the same brown robes as the other healers he knew, Solei in the winter and Faran and Linn, who had been the summer healers for half his lifetime. She was as pale as they were, too. And although he wasn't trying to eavesdrop, he could tell when she spoke to Yuta's sister that her accent was Nessinian. Laris hadn't met a Nessinian healer his own age before. They said that Wildern had more Nessinian healers now, owing to the new Benevolent Union base, but Laris hadn't been to Wildern in a few years.

He wondered what it was like to come here from so far away, to travel around the country with the caravan, meeting new people every day. Probably exciting, and probably a little bit terrifying. And the healers were all so knowledgeable, about all sorts of things besides medicine. He'd always thought that it came from being older and well-traveled, and it made him feel a little strange to think about a girl his own age who had learned all of those things.

Feldon's mother stood and thanked the Yanweian healer, and they talked about payment for a bit. The Nessinian healer, glancing over her shoulder, looked into Laris's eyes for a second. Laris froze, his heart thumping. She looked away. There might have been a faint pink blush across her cheek. She sat in profile to him, so it was hard to tell.

She was cute, Laris thought, and wished that he could un-notice that. She could tell him all kinds of fascinating things.

"Ready?" Laris jumped. The Yanweian healer had turned to him. Feldon's mother was gone. In just a moment's time, in which Laris scrambled for words, the Yanweian healer looked him over. Looked back at the Nessinian healer, who ignored him. And the friendly, almost flirting tone clicked into something else, like the tumblers of a lock falling home. "Or you can wait."

"N-no, I'm sorry." Laris dove into the seat on the Yanweian healer's side. From here he could see the Nessinian healer's face clearly, and tried and tried and tried not to stare. She did not look back at him. Not at all.

Hopeless. Hopeless. Hopeless. Yuta's sister giggled. The Yanweian healer listened to Laris's lungs and heart while he tried to get a hold of himself.

"Relax," the Yanweian healer said, with a rueful smile.

"I'm sorry."

Yuta's sister got up and gave a little bow. "Thank you, ma'am."

The Nessinian healer smiled, pushing her hair behind one ear. The Yanweian healer was asking Laris questions about his health now, and he tried to answer. The Nessinian healer discussed payment with Yuta's sister, standing near the door. She wasn't very tall. Laris wanted to talk with her. That was all. All right, maybe his imagination was suggesting other things – but mostly he just wanted to ask about her travels and about the Academy where she'd learned healing. *Hopeless.* And, listening to him stumble and flail, she'd narrow her eyes at him, or laugh, and then –

And then the caravan would move on.

Laris got control of his breathing, at least, as the Yanweian healer felt his stomach and limbs and asked him more questions. Laris watched over his head as the Nessinian healer wrote something in a little book and rose, lingering. Laris smiled at her, feeling as though he might drown. He knew she was watching. She could hate him if she wanted to.

She blushed deeper, he saw it. Then, hesitantly, she smiled back.

"I'm done here," the Yanweian healer said. "May I have your name?"

"Um. Laris. Laris Sona."

He wrote it in another little book. "Keifon the Medic, by the way." He made the greeting wave, and Laris remembered to return it. Without meaning to, Laris looked back to the Nessinian healer.

"Agna Despana," she said. "Second-order healer of the Church of the Divine Balance." And so she had a name.

The Yanwean healer, Keifon, told him the cost for the checkup, and Laris dug into his money pouch for the fee. He had more than enough for a few books, but that wasn't much on his mind at the moment.

Elsa, the weaver's apprentice, poked her head into the tent. "Oh, hi, Laris."

"Hi, Elsa."

The Yanwean healer whirled around to greet her, warm and welcoming once again. "May I help you?"

Laris got up from the examination chair. The Nessinian healer – Agna – hung back, near the desk on the other side of the tent. He could say hello to her now, and ask her something. If he weren't so hopeless and dull, he could charmingly ask her to spin tales of her adventures. He could ask her out for a drink or to dinner.

She cocked her head. "Can I help you with something?"

"Um. I-I just." Her head only reached his chest. He felt ungainly and thick. "You're new to the caravan, aren't you?"

"Oh. Yes, I – we started in Vertal in the spring."

"Mm. Um, you're from Nessiny? How do you like Kavera?"

She might have stiffened just a little. Here it came. She would be annoyed with him for asking so many questions. Laris thought he might be sick. "Well. I came here to carry out the Benevolent Union's mission. That's the important thing."

"Oh." That didn't give him much to talk about. He needed to think of something. "How – how did you learn healing? Did you go to that school in Nessiny?" She almost turned away, half looking toward the desk and her notebook. "I'm sorry. If I'm interrupting you, I can go."

She turned back to him, regaining her dignified air. "It's all right. I – did go to the Academy, yes. It's the best place in the world to train as an energy healer."

"Oh. I thought so. That's where the last set of summer healers said they learned. And the one winter healer. She's like you—" He held his hands out, the way the healers did – "but she's, um, kind of old and-and not very cute." Panic rose in his nerves as he realized what he'd said. "Not that – I mean, she's nice. And everything."

"...I see." She was quiet and still. He didn't mean to disparage Solei, who had always been kind to him; and he didn't mean to say...that yet. "I never met the other healers on the circuit," she said. "The Benevolent Union just sent us to replace the last pair."

"Oh. Well." She hadn't taken offense after all. "I-I'm glad they did."

She watched him for a second. "Thank you," she said.

"You're welcome. Um." He didn't mean to laugh, but it came out anyway, and he knew that he was blushing. But she hadn't told him to go, and although she seemed a little – suspicious, maybe – she was listening. "So, what – um – what other things do you like to do?"

Her politeness wavered into confusion. "Err...me?"

"Well, yeah."

"I... well, I like reading," she said slowly, "and philosophy, and I've been studying Kaveran plants since I came here. And drawing them. My sister is an herbalist, so I promised to send notes back home."

Laris wanted to ask her to come with him to the bookseller's stall. But that would be too forward, too clumsy. "That's – I – um. I, uh. That's really interesting. I mean, I know you're really smart, you'd have to be to go to the Academy, I mean–" *I want to know what you've seen, I want to –* Laris swallowed. And before he knew it, it was out. "I'm – I'm going over to the bookseller's next, would you – be interested in – um, coming with me? If you want to."

Agna blinked, and took a fraction of a step back. And then all at once her face closed up and her eyes went distant. "I'm sorry, I can't. I have to stay here."

"All right. That's all right, I didn't mean to – um. I should – I should go. Will you be here tomorrow?" He knew it wasn't the last market day. It was a stupid question.

A puzzled little frown crossed her face. "Yes, we'll be here."

"A-all right." He managed a smile, and her expression softened. "Maybe I'll see you later."

"I suppose so."

He bowed his head, she nodded, and Laris left the tent. For the rest of his break he looked through books and knickknacks, cooking implements and hunting knives and carpets that he didn't want or couldn't afford yet, and through all of it he couldn't stop thinking about her. They teased him when he got back to work, but it wasn't about his clothes.

Agna: Laris

When they were about to close on the second day, the local boy, Laris, reappeared. Agna looked up from her logbook. "Hello, again. Can I help you with something?"

"N-no, not especially." He lingered in the door, as though uncertain whether he could come in at closing time.

"Oh. ...All right." She finished the last entry for the day, blotted the page, and packed up her pen and ink. Behind her, the medic shuffled bottles and vials around his medical kit. The tiny glass clinks broke the silence.

"Uh... did you have a good day?"

A vague unease settled in Agna's heart. Where was this going? What sorts of tricks did boys play here? Laris didn't seem the type, based on their brief introduction. Did he want to be friends? They'd be on the road in another day. Agna glanced at the Yanweian, who paid no attention. It was up to her to answer, then. "I suppose so. There haven't been many major problems, which is good. And we're glad to meet people from this area."

"Mm." Laris fidgeted with the doorway, running his thumb along the edge of the canvas. "I'm – I'm glad I could meet you, too."

She tried to smile at Laris and tried to figure out when the ax would fall. He had no composure at all. Whenever he did eventually start insulting her, it wouldn't sting as much. Agna fought hard against the impulse to step a little closer and ask what he had bought at the bookseller's yesterday; in turn, that impulse fought against the urge to shake him and demand that he stop this game he was playing.

"...Thank you, Laris."

He almost laughed, as though relieved. She wished that they could have a seat, maybe by the fire. She wanted to stop his fidgeting. She wanted to ask him about what he liked, what people did out here in the back of beyond, apart from – apart from elaborate mind-games with passing foreigners.

"I can finish packing up here if you'd like to go," the medic offered quietly.

"No, that's fine. I'm in no hurry," she said. Laris made a slight sound – surprised, or disappointed. She couldn't decide to walk out of there, because Laris might walk beside her and talk. He might finally spring the trap, or he might – or she might – *stop being ridiculous, just stop.* She had plenty of practice in ignoring her racing heart.

"She may be smart, but she can be dense sometimes."

She spun around on the Yanweian. "What?"

"I'm not good at this." Laris hung his head, his arms bridging the edges of the door. "I've never been good with girls. I'm messing this up. I'm sorry."

"Oh." She stared at his embarrassed frustration. Either he had come to ask for something that would make him more attractive to girls, or – or he was messing this up, now, with her, as though he meant to charm her. As though he had meant to ask her out on a date.

The two potentialities crashed into one another, and the impossible one shattered. "I'm sorry, but my ability doesn't work that way. I can't make you taller or faster or better in conversation. Nothing like that."

"I know, I...I didn't mean that."

The Yanweian muttered into the thickening silence, "I'll see you at camp." He grabbed his valise and his still-drying logbook on his way out. He flew past Agna, who looked away before she could think of an excuse to stop him, and Laris, who stepped aside to let him go.

Laris took a step inside the tent, and Agna felt her chest tighten. They were alone. That was important. He stopped halfway across the tent. Agna couldn't explain why she needed so much space between herself and this confused Kaveran boy, who was merely staring at the floor. She couldn't explain why she wanted to take his hand, either, when he would so obviously laugh at her for it.

Laris rested his hands on the edge of the examination table. "I'm sorry that I'm so bad at saying it. I think – I think you seem really interesting, and I, um. I- I wish I could get to know you better. That's all."

Backing away from him didn't stop the tears from coming. Laris froze, fumbling for something to say. "I'm sorry – I didn't mean to – I'm sorry. What's wrong?" He stepped toward her, she backed away, and the hurt in his eyes made her cry harder.

"Who put you up to this? What do they want?"

"I don't – what?"

"Who put you up to it? Was it a dare? Did they make you do it?"

"I didn't – nobody did. I mean, I – yesterday they – everybody said I should go and see you again because I – at the – at the pub last night I was... you know, talking about you a lot, I guess, I mean, good things – and they said I should go and-and talk to you."

She still wanted to shake him, to demand that he say something less sweet and impossible. Something she deserved. "That's not true, don't say that."

"I...what?"

"You shouldn't do that. Whoever thinks that's funny, they're wrong. You always think it's so funny to tease the homely girl."

"It's not like that! I'm sorry. Please don't cry." Another step and his hand would be on her arm, to comfort her. Her whole body cried out for it. It could not be true.

"Get out."

Laris fled. She held up long enough to lose sight of him.

■ ■ ■

A dark figure stepped into the tent. He stood a little distance away until she had a chance to dry her face on her sleeve.

"Are you all right? What happened?"

Agna sniffled, unflatteringly. "He was being obnoxious. Saying things."

"Mmn." The Yanweian seemed to relax. "I'm sorry to hear that."

"He was—" She sighed, unwilling to lay out her shame. "He was saying things to make fun of me. I guess someone put him up to it."

"Oh. ...That's childish of him. He should have grown out of the 'make fun of the girl you like' phase by now."

"Ugh, stop it! What's wrong with all of you? You think that's so funny."

"I don't think it's funny. I don't understand."

"He didn't *like me*. How stupid."

"I see." It was just a quiet remark – not a defense, not an answer. "I made enough dinner for two. You're welcome to have some."

"Oh. All right." He was in the door before she could add, "Thank you."

The medic was silent long enough for another thought to pass: he wasn't being cold to her now. "You're welcome."

■ ■ ■

"I know it's none of my business."

Agna couldn't snap back. Not when she could hardly think except to feel wretched. Not when he had been kind enough to make her dinner, or at least to make enough for both of them. A passive favor was more than she'd expected from him. Even if she'd had the will to retort, it would be ungrateful.

The medic went on. "I do think he liked you. I think you should talk to him. – No, listen," he insisted. Agna sighed and let go of the argument. She didn't have the energy to launch it, anyway. "You don't have to. I just think you might regret it if you don't. That's all."

Agna crossed her arms over her knees. "I was going to go out to the shrine. I don't have time to do both before it gets too dark."

"I'll go with you to the shrine, if you don't want to go alone."

She straightened to look past the campfire at him. He was staring into the flames, his expression level and uncritical, one hand toying with the torque around his neck. He was offering her a favor, for whatever reasons he might have. "Thank you," she said at last.

"If you do want to go and see him, come back and get me before you head out to the shrine."

103

"All right." Agna rubbed her eyes. It wouldn't prove anything. But the Yanweian was right: she would regret what she'd said. She already regretted it. She wanted to tell Laris that she didn't blame him completely. She believed that he was good at heart, in the end. She wanted to tell him not to be so easily manipulated into cruelty. "I need to change," she said, and scrubbed her plate off.

In the tent, picking through her limited choices, she reflected on what to say, and how to keep herself from flying into an unbecoming tantrum. She would just say what she had to say and go as quickly as possible, she thought, choosing the dark red dress from her trunk and checking the tent flaps before she loosened the belt of her healer's robe.

Agna brushed her hair out, wondering after the fact why she bothered. But at least this dress was cooler than her summer robe. She found some shoes in the trunk – they didn't quite match the dress, but her sandals were wrong for this type of outfit. Why was she even thinking about this? She'd go to the nearest pub and ask, and either no one would know what she was talking about, or someone would point her at Laris's house. He might not even be home.

Agna took a deep breath and left the tent. The medic looked up from the campfire, the poker loose in his hand. His mouth twitched as though he had tried and failed to smile. He said nothing, and silently she thanked him for that.

"I'll be back."

"Good luck."

"Thanks."

She'd look frivolous and cowardly if she backed out now. Agna set out on the road into town, trying not to look as though she were shivering.

Near the edge of town, she found a tavern that looked well-lit and cozy. Chatter and laughter spilled out of the open doors. No one paid her any mind as she entered. Feeling obvious nonetheless, Agna stepped up to the bar.

"I wonder if you might help me. I'm looking for a boy named Laris who lives in town. Can you tell me where I might find him?"

The young man to her right stared and then snickered into his ale. Agna glared at him. "Excuse me?"

"You're the new summer healer, aren't you."

"Yes. Is that a problem?"

He hid another round of giggling behind his hand, and the bartender shook her head and took over the conversation. "Laris Sona. About this tall, can't get a word out."

"Yes, that sounds like him."

The patron pounded on the bar, out of breath. The bartender gave him an exasperated look. "Quiet, you." She turned back to Agna. "He's probably at home now. Down at the end of the block, turn right, third house down. Small place. He's on the bottom floor."

The patron recovered enough to gasp, "But really. Who put you up to this, because I am buying them a drink right now."

"Oh, stop it," the bartender chided.

"I mean, he would not shut *up* about the summer healer girl last night."

"Ras, I don't think the young lady is playing a trick." The bartender was only a year or two older than Agna was, but Agna hardly noticed that behind the rising veil of fury.

"Why is that funny to you?" She resisted shoving him off his bar stool. This random townsboy had taken on every speck of blame for what Laris had said earlier. And behind that, her mind whirled through what he had just said. It matched Laris's story.

The grin fell from the young man's face. "Oh. You...actually do want to go." He turned toward the bar, ducking his head. "I thought – sorry."

The bartender took his mug and pointed toward the door. "Go and show her where Laris lives. That's what you'll pay for that comment. I'll keep your seat."

"All right, all right." He slid from his bar stool and slunk toward the door.

"Thank you, ma'am." Agna slipped a few coins onto the bar and followed the townsboy before anyone noticed.

Outside, her guide ran his hand through his hair. "I'm sorry. I just – you know. He's kind of a clod. Not stupid, just hopeless. So I thought. You know."

"You sound a little bit like him right now," Agna said darkly.

The boy laughed, breaking his chagrined slouch. "I guess so. Ahh, I shouldn't bust on him in front of strangers. I've known him forever. You don't even think about it after a while. He knows he's one of us no matter what we say. Makes a bad impression if you don't know that, though." He paused, looking over at her pensively. Agna broke from his gaze and feigned concentration on the cobblestones. "Did he go and see you again like we told him to?"

Agna wished she had asked for some water at the tavern. She could hardly swallow. "He did."

"And I guess he did all right."

"I... don't know what to say to that."

"Heh. Fair enough. – We're there." He nodded to one of the houses, standing back. "I'd better go before you knock. He'll think it's a joke after all if he sees me."

"Oh. ...Thank you."

"Yep." The boy turned back the way they'd come, and Agna stood before the door, stranded. A lamp glowed through the curtains. She only had to knock. She could apologize for what she'd said, and be on her way. Just as soon as she knocked.

It felt like a very long time before she knocked.

Laris opened the door and froze. "Agna?" A flush rose into his cheeks as he stared.

"May I come in?"

"Um – oh. Yes, yes, sorry." He let her pass in front of him into the house, and Agna slipped out of her shoes in the entryway. Laris closed the door and hung back. Agna was fairly sure that he should lead her in – she had no idea where to go – but she gave up on the finer points of protocol and stepped out of the entryway. She found herself in a tiny room, with an unlit fireplace on one side. The rest of the room was outfitted with some thick woven rugs and some chairs around a table. A stove and water pump formed a kitchen area in the far corner. Apart from a couple of doors into other rooms, that was all. It was too small for a family. Laris very likely lived here alone.

"I – wait a minute." Laris lifted a pair of chairs from the table over to the fireside and fussed over the teakettle on the stove. "Can I get you some tea?"

There was no reason not to stay for a little while, and have some tea and a civilized talk. "Yes, thank you. – And some water, if you don't mind."

"Yes. Sure." He filled a cup from the pitcher on the side table and crossed the room to hand it to her. Agna tried very hard to ignore the jolt that shot through her body when their fingers brushed. Also, Laris didn't let go. That made it more difficult. She couldn't look him in the eye when she spoke, staring at their overlapping hands. She had meant to ask him how he could let himself be tricked into saying something so horrible, how he could possibly – and she could say none of that.

"I'm sorry about what I said today. It was rude and unfair."

"Oh. Um." He was quiet for the space of a few breaths, and the water's surface quivered. "I forgive you. I just – I want you to know that I wasn't teasing you."

Agna swallowed, and her throat ached. She tugged on the cup of water. Laris surrendered it at last. She drank it all before she could answer, and held the empty cup. "I believe you. I only..." Her grip tightened. She didn't want to say it, not to him, not to anyone, even though they all obviously knew. "No one has ever said anything like that to me. I didn't know what to think."

Laris made a small, sympathetic sound, not even a word. He pried the cup back from her and set it on the table, and before she could guess what he was doing, he had folded her into his arms.

Agna fought the sudden rush of tears, hiccupping. Laris's embrace tightened, and she felt his heartbeat racing against her forehead. She found the presence of mind to free her arms and hug him back. It felt awkward and strange and every nerve in her body was buzzing and she had never been this close to a boy before and she did not want to think about that.

It couldn't be impossible when she could feel his arms around her. His warmth and his solidity and all of his fumbling words were real. He was interested in her; it was not a trick. She allowed herself to remember that little flutter when she'd seen him come into the tent: yet another stranger, all long bones and faltering, polite words. She allowed herself to remember, to acknowledge, that surge of heat and panic when he'd asked her to come out with him to the bookseller's. It wasn't the first time she had felt it. Just the first time that anyone had cared.

When the urge to cry passed, Agna wiped her eyes on her sleeve. Laris stepped back, his hands on her arms, as though he didn't quite know what to do with them. Finally he remembered the teakettle and fled to tend to it.

Agna clasped her hands behind her back and took a deep breath as she looked around the room. On the mantelpiece was a carved wooden box and a small vase with a couple of wildflowers in it – dayflower, they called it in this country, a common hedgerow plant with some efficacy against colds. Next to the fireplace, a small shelf was mounted into the wall. Its contents drew Agna closer. Laris began to sputter about the provenance of his collection as she squinted at the titles in the low light. Adventure novels, history, economics, and animal husbandry. The last seemed a little incongruous. Perhaps he worked on one of the farms outside town.

"...whenever I have some money. And Wayron and Rock from the caravans will buy them back, so I only keep a few. My favorites, I guess."

They were all in Kaveran, and Agna had read one, *Travels in Ysmar* – one of Esirel's favorites. This was a translation, of course.

"Have you read *The Wanderer*?" she asked, turning to find him close behind her, looking at the shelves over her shoulder. She hadn't heard him approach, and forgot how to form words for a moment. "It's, um. It's Nessinian. But it's been translated into Kaveran, too."

"Oh, uh. Yes, a few years ago. But I'd borrowed it, and I had to give it back." He retreated to the stove.

"Just wondering. It's one of my favorites. One of the books that I brought with me from home. I have it in Nessinian, though."

She heard him laying out cups and pouring the tea behind her. "I can only read Kaveran," he admitted. "Hardly anyone around here speaks Nessinian except at the shrine. Lots of people who speak Yanweian and Alhara, that's all." He came back with a cup and saucer.

"Thank you." Agna breathed in the steam as the tea steeped. Laris took the other chair, gripping his own teacup as though he might drop it.

"Um. So... did you learn Kaveran at the Academy?"

"Yes. I knew I wanted to come here, so I learned as much as I could." She stared into her cup, avoiding his eyes. He would think of it as courageous, or noble.

But he didn't congratulate her on her selflessness, or ask why she'd come. Worse than that. "I'm... I'm glad you came."

"To Kavera?" she blurted, and Laris laughed nervously.

"Yeah, and – well, here, too. Thank you."

"Oh. ...You're welcome. I'm glad I came here, too."

The conversation ran into a wall, and they sipped their tea. Agna thought about his lineup of books and her conjecture about his occupation. She wasn't sure how to approach that. It might sound patronizing. She hoped that her curiosity was enough. "So," she said. "What do you do for a living?"

"I work for Artal at the Shoreline cattle ranch. I was apprenticed there, so I just stayed on." He shrugged. "It's all right. It's a good living for someone my age. Next season I get to drive a herd to market in Vertal. If I'm any good at that, I might do some more drives too."

"Is that what you want to do? Traveling?"

"Not all the time. Sometimes. A couple of drives a year, maybe. I don't know that I'd want to travel all the time. I'd get homesick. And I'd like to—" He shut up suddenly, and focused on his tea.

Agna let him take the escape route. "I didn't expect to travel when I came here. It, well. It took some adjustment. A lot of the merchants wouldn't have it any other way, though."

"Some people like it. It's a personality thing."

"Right."

He sipped some tea. "I think I'd like to try it, that's all. See some more of the country."

"Have you always lived in Laketon?" It was an obvious question, Agna thought after the fact. Laris seemed not to have noticed.

"Yeah. My folks have an eighth share in the exchange, and they own a ranch up north a bit." Part of that was incomprehensible to Agna, but she tried not to show it. "They'd hire me if I asked, but I wanted to get some more outside experience. Besides, I like living in town."

The entirety of Laketon, surrounding farms excepted, would fit in the space between Silver Road and the Academy. Agna couldn't help but feel a little sorry for him. Some travel would expand his horizons a bit.

Laris was speaking more easily now. He had even stopped clutching his teacup for dear life. Sometimes when she looked he was already watching her talk, and he would look away, or set his teacup down only to pick it up later. Eventually he poured fresh cups. They made their way through the first pot of the tea and then the second.

She told him about the Academy, about the journey to Kavera, and about the Benevolent Union base in Vertal. He talked about his work, the friends he'd made, and how happy he felt being out in the sun. Despite his awkwardness, he knew a lot of people in town. He hung around the pub some nights with his old schoolmates, when he wasn't at home reading. One thing was missing, and she did not want to ask him about it. He didn't have a girlfriend. Laris never brought this up, but Agna pieced it together, outlining the negative space. He was happy with his life, as a whole, except for wanting to see more of the world – and one other thing.

She never heard him say anything dismissive about any of the other townsfolk, and when he asked about her traveling partner, the cynicism of her reply made him fidget and stammer. Agna apologized, embarrassed. It had been a difficult few months. She should try to have more patience with people. Laris seemed the type to give people the benefit of the doubt. Rone was like that too, she thought, remembering him for the first time in hours.

"I should go," she admitted. "I wanted to visit the shrine today."

Laris nodded, looking down at his folded hands. They had drunk their fill of tea and set the cups aside. They stood, stretching. That was when he kissed her.

It was obvious what was coming. He stepped close to her, cradled her face in one hand, and bent down to meet her. Laris kissed too hard, as though it might be his last chance. His mouth was hot, and his hand was gentle on her cheek. His other arm circled around her back and hesitated there. Agna had no idea where to put her hands, so she didn't move.

She broke off, trying not to breathe too heavily. "I... I'm leaving town tomorrow."

"I know." The second time was a little better. In the back of her head was a furious noise: what was wrong with him, this wasn't right, no one liked girls like her. It was hard to hear over the light clanging through her. Her hands rose to his hips, rested there, and stopped on his back. That seemed all right.

Finally, Laris drew away. He held onto her hands, looking past her at the floor, chewing on his lip. "That was too forward. I'm sorry."

"It's all right." She was dizzy with things that she had only read in novels, that she never thought she'd want to do. Never her, not even in her own thoughts. These were things that other people could have. She wanted to discover every inch of his body with her hands, with her mouth, and he would want her to do it, and she was terrified by the prospect. She hardly knew him. Such things were not for her to want. They were two logical reasons, and they meant nothing to her thundering pulse and the tingling in her skin.

"I'm sorry that you have to go."

Agna laughed, relieved to divert the torrent of her thoughts. "I am, too. I would have liked to spend more time with you. But I want to visit the Balance shrine before it gets too late."

He squeezed her hands. "I'll be here."

She smiled at him, the way she had wanted to from the start, warm and unafraid. His returning smile stirred something deeper, something slower than the clamoring need to throw him down in front of the fireplace. She wanted to know him and understand him, as well as... other things. This slow dance would take months and years, but it would be worth the time.

By force of will, she stepped away. "I have to go. And..." ...and if she stayed she'd be tempted to overrun her common sense. "Well. That's all."

"All right." He let her hands go. "I wanted to tell you. You look pretty in that dress. I mean. I think you'd look pretty in anything. But I like it."

"Oh, that's—" She bit off her instinctive dismissal. "Th-thank you." She was blushing to match the dress. She kept talking, like an idiot, feeling as though the compliment should be returned. "I liked the shirt you wore to the clinic. It... ah... fit you well."

Laris chuckled nervously. "Thank you. I had to go back to work, so I changed." They stared past one another. "I'll walk with you over to the shrine," he said. "If you want to. You don't have to go all that way alone."

"Oh... thank you." She bit her lip. "At least to the camp. Is that all right?"

"Sure. Of course." He didn't move, and after the silence stretched into awkwardness, Agna took a step toward the door. Laris followed, laughing at himself.

In the entryway, Agna slipped into her shoes, then stepped aside as Laris put on his own and lifted a key from a hook by the door. He paused before the closed door. She heard him take a breath. "Thank you. For coming today. Even if you have to go. Thank you."

"You're welcome. Thank you for coming by earlier. Even though I was an idiot about it."

"No, no. It's all right. In the end it was all right."

"Yes."

Eventually Laris turned the door handle.

Keifon: Perspective

"You're..." Edann chose his words carefully. "...high-spirited today."

Keifon stretched and folded his arms behind his head. Edann did not always deign to let him linger, and Keifon basked in the privilege while it lasted. Edann's feather mattress was heaven compared to his own bedroll.

"Suppose so." He stared at the arched canvas ceiling, debating whether to explain. He knew the embarrassing source of his enthusiasm, and suspected that Edann would not react well. Lacking any other confidant, Keifon found himself shaping the words anyway. "She – Agna – picked up a suitor. A patient. And..." He shrugged with a rustle of feathers. "They're... sweet. I just – I got to remembering what it was like to be like that."

"What, cow-faced and stupid?"

Keifon ignored the uninspired jab. "Young. What's the word? Infatuated."

"So just stupid."

Keifon glanced over; Edann had huddled on his side, and picked sourly at a loose thread in the pillowcase. Keifon caught his hand and laced their fingers together. His fingertips flexed against the faint dent in Edann's middle finger. There was one on each hand, as though Edann had worn rings for a long time and then stopped. They were invisible, revealed only to touch, and so part of him was intrigued by the discovery. Keifon hadn't asked about it yet, wondering about guild sigils or Achusan fashion. One more thing that he might find out someday. The apothecary was an uncharted country, and he did not give up his ground easily.

Keifon smiled despite himself. "Yeah. Stupid."

"I'm not infatuated with you," Edann grumbled, but his breathing quickened.

Nor I you, Keifon did not answer.

Edann tasted like mint and honey. It had taken a bitter argument and some creative bribery to convince him to wash his mouth out between wine and kissing. It had been worthwhile. Now that he was sated and comfortable, Keifon thought that it had all been worthwhile.

"No – listen," Edann insisted, when he could steal breaths. "Don't get – stupid. I won't put up with – sentimentalism."

Keifon rolled back and sighed. Edann could build up and break down his good mood in a matter of hours. Though most of the building had happened beforehand, watching the young Nessinian and Kaveran orbit one another in fascination.

The healer was young. He wasn't sure how young, but she was several years younger than Keifon, and she was sheltered for her age. Because of this, she was short on common sense and knew little about life in the world, as he'd found to his irritation many times over. It also meant that when she encountered infatuation, it hit her like a thunderbolt.

And though Keifon was a foreigner here, he knew the Kaveran's world. He knew the feeling of working in the fields and catching his breath at the sight of a glance across the room in the evening. He knew how the rush of excitement could sweep away the bone-tired fatigue. He knew how a new face, a new voice, could carry with it all the promise of faraway worlds.

The Nessinian and the Kaveran felt that way now. This sudden connection between the spoiled patrician child and Keifon's younger self left him staring at Edann's ceiling. He remembered, and let the feeling fill him until he could name it.

Empathy.

The Nessinian – Agna – was not his punishment, sent by the gods to plague him. She was just another traveler, far from home. She had her own fears and dreams and hopes, and she could fall in love, because she was human too.

And yet this realization brought him a sinking feeling in his midsection. He didn't know what to say to her when – if – she came back. He hadn't always thought of her as fully human, rounding her down to a symbol, a stand-in for his own fears. No true follower of the gods would do that to another person, even an unbeliever.

Keifon began to see the underlying shape of his cowardice. A punishment was easier to shut out than a real person. If he didn't see her as a real person, he didn't have to explain his own dismissive behavior, or apologize when he lost his temper, or open up to her about Kazi. If she was human, then Keifon wasn't alone. He owed her civility and consideration.

Edann leaned his cheek against Keifon's shoulder. Keifon focused back into the present and licked his lips. "…I should go. I said I'd – I should go."

"Fine," Edann whispered. He plucked his glasses from their hiding place and unfolded them. Keifon watched him slip them on. The muscles of Edann's back tightened, and despite their physical closeness, Keifon might have been no more than a customer, a mark passing by Edann's apothecary stall.

Edann never spoke about himself, so Keifon had pieced together what he could, reading sideways, decoding him like an ancient text. That little gesture of leaning on him had been Edann's attempt at an apology, for chilling Keifon's mood. Keifon's apparent rebuff had stung him, and his hurt feelings came to light as pure ice. It was no use apologizing now, because Edann would never admit to being hurt.

Edann stood, shrugging off Keifon's conciliatory hand on his shoulder. He dressed as though he were already alone. Keifon had little choice but to do the same.

. . .

Keifon's book had been opened to the same page for at least half an hour. He was lost in memory, reliving those stifling, desperate summers ten years ago. He had been just as foolish and ecstatic as the Nessinian and the Kaveran. He had watched from the edges of the crowd and mapped out the network of alliances and rivalries until he could edge closer to the one who burned brightest in his heart in that instant.

Three half-strangers had enthralled him, obsessed him, when he had needed obsessions most of all. One had smiled apologetically at him and kissed his forehead. One had met him in secret, just once, then disappeared to appease a jealous lover. One had stayed with him for a little while, finding what happiness they could, before departing to a distant apprenticeship. Then, when he was almost seventeen, Keifon had met Eri.

At first it hadn't been any different; he hadn't told himself *I'm going to marry her, and we're going to try to be happy, and then I'll ruin everything.* At first it hadn't been any more complicated than his other fancies. It ended at her smile, her laugh, and the absolute necessity that he know her, that he learn the soul behind her keen eyes and the skin under her understated, stylish clothes. That was all, at first.

He had been a different person when he'd met Kazi, no longer young, no longer breathless with the sense of endless possibility. He had found that later, in the inverse of his younger fancies. He had met Kazi as a disillusioned shell and left as a disillusioned shell, and in between he had been whole, at least for a time.

And now... Keifon set the book aside. Edann seemed determined not to trust him, which seemed easier, more comfortable, than the alternative. Keifon was beginning to hope that he would turn a corner soon, that this armored silence would begin to lift. Edann's endless cynicism seemed to suggest that he might accept Keifon's brokenness as the price of being human. They might reach a strange kind of equilibrium, in time.

Keifon laughed under his breath as he realized that the healer had been gone for more than three hours. He wondered again whether she would come back at all. Whether she did or not, he needed to sort out his thoughts. He had gone astray, and he needed to learn from what he had done.

He gathered his body into a seated position, his hands arranged for a prayer to Lundra. He knew prayers for guidance, for thanks, and for forgiveness. He needed all three.

. . .

Keifon looked up at the sound of a soft tap on the tent flap.
"Are you there?"

He unwound from the floor and lifted the flap. The healer was outside; the Kaveran boy lingered behind her, by the unlit fire pit. A nearby torch turned him into a silhouette. Keifon fought a sudden, alien tendril of thought: *You'd better have treated her well.* She didn't need his protection. She wouldn't want it.

The healer fidgeted, her fingers twisting together. "May I come in?"

Keifon shook off the thought. "Of course." He ducked back into the tent, and the healer followed. She unlocked her trunk and rifled through it to pull out a sheet of paper and a pencil.

"I'm just going to get Laris's address, and then I'll be ready to head out to the shrine. Is that all right?"

"That's fine." Perhaps they were going to write to one another. If so, that meant she wouldn't stay behind after all.

"Thanks." She dashed back outside.

Keifon tucked his book into his backpack, waiting for the young lovers to finish their farewell. It was too bad that she had to keep moving. It wouldn't be the first relationship carried out through the post, but he had heard that such things were difficult. They would miss one another, of course. He didn't envy them that hardship.

After a respectable interval, Keifon lifted the tent flap. Agna and Laris held one another in the clearing in front of the tent. Keifon looked away, privately holding onto the sight of them. He didn't want to pry, but some part of him needed to know that such good things existed in the world. Keifon could thank them for that in his prayers.

"Safe travels," Laris said.

"Goodbye. Thank you." Her voice was low but clear.

And then the young Kaveran turned, with one more little wave to his new love, and set off through the camp. Agna watched him go. Keifon watched her, and watched the Kaveran's retreating form. If she cried, he should comfort her. He wasn't sure how, because she would turn on him. She wouldn't want his sympathy. But he had to offer it if she needed it.

Keifon realized that she held the paper with Laris's address. And so, in case comforting her would embarrass her, he cleared his throat and avoided the subject. "If you want to put that paper away first..."

The healer turned. Her eyes were dry. She did not snap at him. Keifon let her pass him into the tent, and she stashed the paper in her box of stationery. She addressed him quietly. "Are you ready?"

"Yeah. If you are."

"Yeah." She leaned over to blow out the lantern, and the two of them left the tent.

She walked beside him on the road between the campsite and the lake, folding her arms across her body. She didn't speak, and Keifon considered and discarded one possible approach after another. He didn't know where to start. He didn't know whether to offer condolences or congratulations. He didn't know whether either of them would offend her, because everything he did offended her, and he didn't understand what was proper in her world.

Their meeting seemed to have gone well, at least. They had looked happy in those last moments.

The healer spoke, startling him out of his worry. "Look, you may as well say it."

"I didn't mean to eavesdrop," Keifon said without thinking.

Before he could babble an explanation, she said, "That's not what I meant."

"I don't – I don't understand. I am sorry for overhearing."

She sighed, aggravated, and closed her fists at her sides. Keifon watched her face in the intermittent light from the lampposts, reading her dark, narrowed eyes and the tension in her brows. Was she angry with Laris, with him, with life itself? Keifon knew he would be frustrated, at the very least, if he'd had to leave a new lover behind. She didn't explain, lapsing into silence beside him, crossing her arms.

The lake murmured beside them, beyond a narrow lakeshore park – a stripe of cropped grass and trees punctuated by stone benches. Keifon thought about waiting there while she made her visit to her shrine. It would be nice to sit and think for a while.

He had to say something, though, before she got to the shrine. He wanted her to know that he wanted things to change, even if she had more pressing issues to handle. It might even ease her mind to know that she had an ally.

"He seems like a nice boy," Keifon offered.

"What's that supposed to mean?" she snapped.

Keifon turned in the near-dark. "What?"

"Is he too nice for me, or something?"

It was the usual swiftness to attack, the usual defensiveness. Keifon recognized his own impulse to lash at her and carefully relaxed the muscles in his shoulders. *It doesn't have to be this way*, he reminded himself. He cleared his throat. "No, not at all. Just as I said. He seems like a nice boy. I'm – I'm sorry for your sake that we have to keep moving."

"How unfortunate for you that I'm staying," she grumbled.

"Hn." Keifon looked out over the lake, and they continued in silence. He could try to go on like this, offering peace and being rebuffed. For a little while. His patience would wear out soon enough, and they would be back to the usual.

If you need to kill someone in your ceremony... She had hurt him before. He could remember that, and take back the forgiveness that he struggled to find now. Cruelty was easy. It kept everyone away.

The healer's voice was quiet. "I think he likes me."

Warm hope rekindled in Keifon's chest, drawing him away from his memories. "Yes. I'm sure he does."

"He can't, though. It's ridiculous. Impossible."

"He came to talk to you today," Keifon reminded her. "And you seemed – very close when you came back just now. I didn't mean to see that, and I'm sorry, but..."

"It doesn't make any sense, though." She kicked a stone on the footpath. "I don't understand it."

Keifon sighed. "It's not that complicated. You two have _ chemistry, compatibility, something. It seems mutual. That's not so hard to understand."

"If you put it that way, of course it makes sense. If it happened to *someone else*."

Keifon's head tilted. "Are you not allowed to take lovers? Is it a religious issue?" Or her family would object to Laris's ancestry or class. Or she was betrothed to someone else, though she would probably say so if she were.

She flapped her hands in a pale blur. "No – no, no. Healers can – do whatever they want. So can priests and swordmasters. Same as your Church. It's not that. I mean, don't you see it? You know how men think."

Keifon looked away, over the lake. She wanted advice. She wanted explanations. From him, of all people. She had questionable taste in mentors. "I know what I think," he said. "Sometimes. I can't speak for all men."

"But you *know*," she insisted. "You know what they like. You know what I mean."

What men like? Keifon felt himself flushing and shook off the thought of Kazi, of Eri, of an underhanded smile. He thought of the light that lit the zealot from inside, and his own deep longing to tend the home fires, to anchor an eagle in flight. What men like, indeed. "I don't think everyone likes the same kinds of men and women that I do. I don't think I could handle the competition if they did."

"...Oh." She seemed to consider this. "Um. I-I mean I'm not much to look at."

Keifon stretched his neck, suddenly tired. She was so young, after all. "If you want to know why he likes you, ask him. I can't answer for him. I really can't."

"No, I..." She sighed. "I don't know where I'm going with this anymore."

Keifon traced her tangled line of logic. He could be helpful to her if he could find something to say that would put her mind at ease. She was confused and lost, and although it was more proper to seek guidance from her priests at the shrine, she seemed to want some kind of wisdom from Keifon. She seemed to think that his age or experience would give him insight. It wasn't quite respect, but his heart responded hungrily all the same. He wanted to have answers for her.

He retraced what she'd said so far. "You don't think he should care for you."

She was quiet before she answered. "I suppose so."

"I don't think you get to decide that for him. You can only decide whether to return it."

"That's from Lundran scripture, isn't it," she replied.

Keifon tensed, gauging her expression. How did an unbeliever recognize Lundran scripture? And what cruel dismissal was she about to launch? But she said nothing, and Keifon reminded himself that she had not criticized his words or his faith. She had only acknowledged the source. He swallowed and made himself relax. "Yes. It is from Lundran scripture."

The healer tilted her head back as she walked, watching the emerging stars. "Lundran scripture was the hardest for me to understand. I mean, nothing like that would ever apply to me."

She had read Lundran scripture? Keifon knew abstractly that there were followers of the gods in the East, but she was not one of them. Why would she read the scriptures? And if she had read them, why had she said such hateful things about the Daranites? Yet she wasn't saying these things now. She was only reflecting on having read the scriptures, and trying to apply them to her own life.

She probably couldn't relate because she was so resistant to the idea of falling in love, or the idea of being loved. She might have read the scriptures, but she didn't seem to understand them. She was getting caught up in the idea of romantic love and missing the rest. It was a common enough mistake. Keifon aimed toward that thought, fleeing the sadness that began to gather on her behalf. "The Lady oversees all human connections. Not just romantic love."

"I know. Still." As she lapsed into thought, Keifon noticed the lights of the shrine in the distance. The healer went on. "I don't understand it. And that's why I'd like to go to the shrine and think for a while. See if anyone can give me some advice. No offense. Your advice is fine."

Keifon chuckled, a short bark without mirth. "Don't listen to me. I don't know what I'm talking about."

"Well, you're married, aren't you? You know something."

He found his fingers sliding along the torque. The metal was smooth and warm against his skin. "Not exactly. I know what not to do."

"What do you mean, 'not exactly'?"

There was the other face of it, the risk that came with the reward. If he were to treat her as a companion instead of as an adversary, he had to face his own failings. He had to know what to tell her about himself. But he wasn't ready yet, and she had her own problems to untangle. Keifon dropped his hand. "I'd rather not talk about it right now."

The healer looked away. "I'm sorry. I shouldn't pry."

They drew close enough to see the pantheist shrine in full. It was a small building, no larger than a country church, dwarfed by the old trees around it. It was built out of wood with a stone foundation and front steps. Heavy wooden columns supported the corners of the roof. It was finely made, but strangely ordinary.

A low stone wall, like one that might separate one property from the next, surrounded the shrine and enclosed a small meeting ground. The wall supported the ring of lanterns that they had glimpsed from a distance. It was clearly not meant for defense. Besides, the gate was open.

Keifon hesitated at the gate, and the healer pulled ahead of him by a few steps. She turned back. "You don't have to come in if you don't want to."

His hand rested on the gate inadvertently, and he pulled it back. "Isn't this your sacred ground?"

"Yes, but you can come in. It would be against their core principles to exclude anyone, don't you think?"

"I wouldn't know."

"Oh. Well, yes. You can come in. They'll have a vestibule in the front; you don't have to go all the way into the sanctuary. But you don't have to wait out in the dark."

He had looked forward to sitting by the lake, but it was kind of her to offer. "Hm. Thank you." He followed her when she continued toward the door.

The two of them climbed the front steps and passed into a warmly lit entryway, lined with benches. A tall Nessinian man in a cloak rose from one of the benches, and Keifon's heart raced as he glimpsed a sword at his hip. His hand twitched, but he hadn't worn his combat knife. Of course. There would be no reason to wear it out on a friendly walk. He hadn't counted on being slain by a temple guard.

The healer greeted the guard in her own language, laying her hands over her heart. The guard replied, making the same salute, and glanced at Keifon before going on in Kaveran. "So, have we got a new priest? Or a new healer?"

"Oh – I'm a healer, but I'm not assigned here. I'm with the caravan. Through the Benevolent Union. This is Keifon, a medic from the Yanweian army."

Keifon's heart hammered as their attention shifted to him. She didn't have to go ahead and announce his presence. His origin was clear enough, of course. But he had seen Yanweians in the clinic over the last few days; he might have passed as an immigrant. He hoped they'd give him a chance to leave quietly.

"Really, now," the guard said. "Suppose Linn and Faran went off the road after all. I'll leave you to your visit. Pleasure to meet you." He sat down and picked up a book.

The healer was turning as if to enter the shrine proper, and Keifon leaned in to mutter in her ear. "Are you sure it's safe for me to be in here?"

She stifled a snicker. "Are you here to loot the shrine? Of course it's safe."

"Hm." She didn't have to make light of it, but she didn't seem to mean it as a real insult, either. She simply didn't see anything wrong with being accosted by a man with a sword upon entering a foreign church.

Keifon watched as she stepped up to a marble font by the inner doorway, washed her hands, and folded her hands in prayer. She looked back at him. "It's all right if you want to wait here. Just take a seat."

Keifon nodded and sat on the bench closest to the door. The healer passed through the inner doors into the shrine. Keifon became keenly aware of his isolation, cut off from even a partial ally, alone with an armed foreigner who had half a foot of height on him.

The guard turned a page. Keifon focused on the book. *Escape to the Frontier,* the spine read in Kaveran. The vestibule was silent apart from the occasional whisk of a page turning and Keifon's own breathing, which seemed too loud. Keifon heard low voices inside the shrine; the healer had found a priest to talk to.

"So," the guard said in Yanweian, "you from around here?"

Keifon blinked. The guard had spoken in Keifon's own language, filtered through some mongrel combination of Nessinian and Kaveran accents. But it was clear enough. Was he being sarcastic? Keifon looked nothing like a Kaveran. But then he remembered some of the patients today, Yanweians who had moved over the border to work in Kaveran ranches. And their spouses. And their children, some of them half-Kaveran or half-Furoni.

Perhaps the guard wasn't being sarcastic. Perhaps he was trying to be friendly.

"Uh, no," Keifon managed after an awkward interval. "Northeast Yanwei. Eastwater."

"Eastwater, don't know it. Northeast, though – ranch country, right? You know Lendu?"

"Yes, of course." It was a city, not far from Eastwater. Keifon had gone sometimes on festival days when he was young.

"Got some in-laws out in Lendu. Never been, myself."

Keifon's mind stampeded after the proper response. If he had in-laws in Lendu, that meant that he was married to one of those Yanweian immigrants. What kind of person would marry a foreigner twice over, a foreigner in a foreign land? Someone who had no other prospects at all? Keifon nearly shuddered, and remembered not to react. It wouldn't be polite to suggest that the guard's spouse must be a terrible person to have had to resort to marrying him. He would never say such a thing to any of his patients, Keifon reminded himself. Even when he had treated some of those half-immigrant families in the clinic, he hadn't thought ill of them. He had focused on their treatment. A small, hidden part of him might even have been envious. Most of them had looked happy.

Before Keifon could come up with something civilized to say, the guard went on. "First time south, then?"

"Well... first time in Kavera. I had an apprenticeship in southern Yanwei for a while. On a horse ranch. Before I went into medicine."

"You don't say. And here you are."

"...Yeah." It was almost a conversation. Keifon wondered how the guard had met his mysterious spouse, and whether that was why he'd stayed in the country. The thought made him flush, ashamed of his earlier aspersions.

It was the same as with Agna. This stranger was no different from anyone else, either. Yet Keifon kept reacting defensively, as though he were constantly under attack. As the healer had said, he wasn't here to loot the shrine. The guard wasn't even particularly on alert, considering the fact that he was reading on shift.

Despite its foreign construction and the font by the door and the pale, green-cloaked guard, the heathen shrine seemed much like a small country church. Keifon imagined an Eytran church instead, with open windows and rushes on the floor and priests in green cloaks. It was probably blasphemous to make the comparison. He deserved to be struck down for being here in the first place, let alone equating this unbelievers' shrine to an Eytran church. But somehow, it made sense.

Eytran churches didn't have guards, though. Only the Daranite churches did, and that was largely symbolic. There had to be a reason why this lonely little building on the edge of a quiet city was guarded. His impression had been that these guards were a common thing, that every shrine had them. He couldn't imagine why.

"So," he began carefully, "what exactly do you do here?"

"This and that. Stand watch. Take turns keeping up the place. Cooking for festivals – you ought to come back for the fall festival sometime! We all pitch in everywhere. We're small time, out here. Only nine of us on staff, so we do what we can."

"Hm." It had answered the question in an entirely unhelpful manner. "But you... swordfight, too, don't you? That's why they call you swordmasters."

"Oh, that. Of course. The other two and I practice. Can't say we've had a real situation since I've been here. It's tradition. Got to have swordmasters, after all."

"I wouldn't know," Keifon said quietly. He didn't understand a thing about this place or the people in it.

But he could understand if he dared to try. He didn't have to agree. He didn't have to be converted. He could merely ask and learn. And if he learned about this place and its people, someday he could come to understand the healer better.

Keifon took a breath and looked around the wooden vestibule. Not that different from the Eytrans, he reminded himself. Maybe the guards weren't entirely different from the Daranites. Maybe it would make sense if he listened.

"I've never been in one of your shrines before," he began. "And I don't know much about your religion. But... I'm curious."

He waited to be thrown out, or laughed at. Instead the guard hmmed thoughtfully and held out his hands as if holding a sphere. "Say this is the whole world, and everything in it, and all the people that ever were..."

Agna: Lakeside

In the vestibule, the medic had moved to the other end of the bench, next to the old swordmaster. He broke off midsentence and stood as Agna emerged from the sanctuary. His eyes searched her face, dismayed. Agna wiped at her eyes. The medic searched his pockets and held out a folded handkerchief. Agna took it, feeling idiotic for having forgotten hers. "Thank you."

The medic turned to shake hands with the swordmaster in Kaveran fashion and traded a few polite words, then met her by the door. "Are you all right?"

She rubbed at her eyes. "I'm fine now. I think. I'd like to go."

"Of course." He followed her out of the shrine, catching up to walk beside her after they passed through the gate. Agna tucked the damp handkerchief under her belt and clutched the ends of her sleeves as she walked. The moon had risen, casting shimmering reflections over the lake. A line of lampposts outlined the footpath through the park. The caravan's camp glowed in the distance, a knot of lanterns and torches with the bonfire at the center. It had been a lively and lucrative day at the market, and tonight was a night for celebration.

The medic said nothing for several minutes. There was no challenge in his stance. He didn't seem likely to make fun of her for crying. He could be cruel, but not in that way. He would probably leave for Edann's as soon as they got to the camp, anyway. Some privacy would suit her perfectly tonight.

He stopped without warning, looking out over the lake. "Do you mind if we stop for a bit?"

"Hm? Oh... that's fine." They had reached one of the stone benches at the lakeside. Agna took a seat at one end, and the medic sat beside her, hunched over, resting his forearms on his knees. His presence was strange, too – personal, somehow. She began to notice the motion of his breath and the space his body took up beside her. He was wearing a braided cord around one wrist today, a simple ornamentation that she hadn't noticed until now. Agna swallowed and focused her attention on the lake.

"I talked to the swordmaster for a while," he said. "He told me a lot about... your religion, how it works. There's so much that I didn't know."

"You can always ask me."

"I didn't know to ask. I thought I knew everything there was to know." He took a slow breath, looking out over the water beside her. "Before that. I guess... when I saw you and Laris, I realized that you were – no different from anyone else."

Agna felt her jaw clench. "That's rude."

"Oh – not that way. I'm sorry, I didn't say that well." He breathed out, folding his hands together. "I meant – that you're no different from me, in a lot of ways. Everything I ever knew about foreigners was that they were faithless and – distasteful. Untrustworthy. How could you trust them if you don't know their families? What's enforcing their honor?" He glanced up, reading Agna's blank expression. "I suppose – that's another story. My point is, I didn't think much of – you. Of people like you. But then I saw that you were a talented medic. I couldn't ignore that. And then when I saw you with him, saw that spark between you, I remembered – I remembered what it was like to feel like that." He crossed his arms across his stomach, drawing into himself. "I realized that 'heathens' live their lives and care for one another like anyone else. And of course you do. You're people too. I need to remember that, and I'm ashamed of myself that I didn't."

It was almost certainly the longest thing he'd said to her at one time. "Is that why you came along today? Because you realized that I'm human?"

She could barely see his crooked smile in the backlighting from the lanterns on the path. "I guess it is. I was curious about your shrine. And I felt guilty, and wanted to do something for you." He looked away. "I didn't know whether I'd get a chance to say any of this. I hope I haven't troubled you. I know it's a bad time."

"That's all right." Agna considered everything he'd said, or at least, all of it that she could understand. He'd realized that they were more alike than different. That realization went both ways. Agna swallowed. "I haven't been fair to you, either. I assume I know everything, and I don't."

"I accept that, if you mean it as an apology," he said.

"I do."

"Thank you, then."

She rushed on, feeling as though this might be her only chance. "And your religion isn't stupid. I said things – at the Resurrection festival. It was unfair. And cruel. I'm sorry."

The medic took a long, slow breath. "Thank you for that," he said, so quietly that Agna felt goosebumps shiver along her arms. She was a little flushed, and her joints felt too loose, as though she would fall if she tried to stand. What had she done? She couldn't take any more surprises today.

"Do you hate me?" he asked, and Agna's mind halted.

"What?"

" —I shouldn't have – I shouldn't have said that. Never mind."

"No, I..." She remembered a blur of exasperation, mortification, and resentment. She remembered day after day when she thought she couldn't take another night sleeping on the ground, using outhouses and outdoor baths, being kind to strangers even when she was tired and hungry and homesick. He had been there, disapproving, infuriatingly silent, another stranger – a stranger who wouldn't leave. Everything she did was wrong to him, proving everything she'd ever feared about coming here, about being a healer, about being herself.

Agna held up her hands. "Two parts." She flexed her left hand. "I hated being in Kavera. That wasn't your fault." And the right. "You're... rude to me. Like you're being forced to babysit and you hate me for it." She laced her fingers together. "And I'm sorry about the first part."

"I see." He thought for a little while. "You are right. I didn't expect to have a partner on this assignment, and I didn't want one. But that's not your fault." A tense second passed before he compulsively stood and paced halfway to the water's edge. From the angle of his arm, Agna guessed that he was touching the torque.

He didn't face her as he went on, looking out over the lake. "And I'm... I'm not... a happy person, right now. Before I came to this country, I lost someone who – who meant the world to me." His voice wavered, and he cleared his throat. His hand dropped. "It's not an excuse. It's one reason that I'm unhappy. I shouldn't take it out on you." He turned, watching a spot somewhere near her feet. "And maybe there's a second part for me, too. The way you seem to – to think so little of me. Pointing out how I'm so far beneath you. I am, I know that, but some part of me resents it. It's pride, that's all."

"You're not beneath me – what are you talking about? Money?"

Agna could not understand the gesture he made with a frustrated turn of his hands – a sweep over her with one, a sweep over himself with the other. *Everything?* "You're – you're patrician. Foreign, I mean, but like a patrician. I don't even have a name." She didn't understand the shame in his voice, either, even though the simple human fact of it made her throat clench.

"I'm not noble, if that's what you mean. My family isn't connected to the Families. We just have some money. And we're known in the art world. But we aren't politically powerful or anything like that."

The medic sighed, touching his folded hands to his forehead. He took his seat beside her. "Still. You've seemed to take a lot of enjoyment in treating me like a servant." Agna almost protested about how she couldn't reach the clinic tent ceiling or lift as much as he could, but she held back. That wasn't what he meant.

He wasn't wrong. She had always needed to even the score. He was older and more experienced, the patients liked him more, and the other merchants liked him more. To keep herself afloat, she'd had to drag him down. She knew the name for that. "That's... well, that's pride, too. You've always known what to do when I didn't know. Like camping, and budgeting. It embarrassed me. I thought I was showing you that you didn't know everything. It was childish. But I never thought you were my servant. I..." She looked into her hands in her lap and closed them. His fault, her fault, chasing one another around and around.

They both had to change. He seemed willing to call a truce, and Agna was exhausted by the fighting. But she had to trust him, to trust that he wouldn't retaliate if she stopped attacking. She had to risk being hurt in order to stop.

She decided and spoke. "I'm sorry. I don't think you're beneath me. And I don't hate you."

He made a strange sound, not quite a laugh. "Thank you. I don't hate you, either."

Agna's first impulse was to call him a liar, but she clenched her teeth. She had to stick with this if she wanted it to work. He sounded sincere. And what did he have to gain from lying? But if he didn't hate her, why did he act the way he did? She straightened her cramped fingers. "Explain to me, then."

"Of course, if it will help."

"You're so nice to the patients, and to me you're... cold."

The medic let his breath go through his teeth. "That." He considered his answer. "What I do in the clinic is – it's not an act, not really. I care about them, and I want to help them. But I act that way even when I don't want to. When I'm tired, or when all I can think about is how much I miss Kazi – my partner. Former partner," he corrected. "Because you have to act a little for the patients. It's part of the job. And outside the clinic, you see me when I'm... when I'm my real self. And my real self is usually unhappy. It's not because of you. I see why you might see it that way." He ran a hand through his hair and rested his chin on his hand, hunched over on the bench.

He seemed to know everything about living on the road and living in the world in general, but it wasn't easy, not even for him. She hadn't considered that he was just as tired and sore and dispirited as she was, sometimes.

The medic went on. "And... I didn't trust you. Because I thought you saw me as scum."

Agna focused on him, drawn out of her reinterpreted memories. "I don't see you as scum. I never did."

"I know that now."

"Do you see me as an evil heathen?"

"...No. And I do want to learn more about your religion."

"Well. ...I have to tell you, I'm not as religious as you think I am. My friend – my mentor was. Is. Compared to him, I'm not. It's something I've studied, more than something I believe."

"Still. I would like to learn about it, and about your culture."

He couldn't see her blush in the dark, and she didn't know why it was rising. "I – thank you. I'd like to learn more about Yanwei, too." Agna hesitated. This was the test. If she suggested a truce, he might laugh at her, and fire back some sour remark. It could all go drastically wrong. Or... "Can we start over?"

He did laugh, but it was a laugh of relief, not mockery. "Yes! I would love to start over."

"All right." Agna cleared her throat and turned on the bench to face him, pulling one knee up onto the stone. She made the Kaveran greeting gesture, feeling stupid and relieved. They introduced one another, by name, by title. Agna, healer. Keifon, medic.

They talked, slowly at first, about their medical training. She didn't go into details about how she'd barely made second order in her graduation testing or garland it with her usual justifications about studying history and Kaveran. He asked her about how the healing art interwove with the Church's teachings, figuring out how it differed from the healing art of the Tufarian priests in his homeland.

Following Agna's clumsy questioning, he told her about his studies: three intensive years on top of his Army training. He began proudly, and he held the Army and his instructors in very high regard. But he seemed to waver off, set back by the fact that he had studied for so much less time than she had. Agna wanted to push him into the lake, or jump in herself. This wasn't what she wanted, either. She didn't want to buy her pride at the expense of his. Not anymore; that was the point.

"Well. A lot of people start as apprentices at the same age that I went to the Academy," she offered. "Besides, three years is almost as long as our practicum. And you're so good with the patients. I think you have a gift for it." Her heart was racing, she realized, and she shut herself up. This was stupid. She was talking far too much.

"Thank you. I..." He couldn't finish the thought, and merely nodded. "Thank you." His voice held no cynicism, no shame, and no hidden agendas. He was flattered and touched to hear praise from her, as though he cared about what she thought. It was confusing and terrifying, and part of her wished that he would say something vicious just to get back to a state that she understood. The rest of her caught his quiet happiness, one candle lit from another. It was worth acting like an idiot, after all.

"Can I ask you something?" he said.

"Um — of course."

"Are you going to stay in Laketon?"

"Why would I stay in Laketon?"

He hesitated, as though regretting having asked. "To be with Laris."

"Oh. No, no. I'm not running out for rings already," she laughed nervously. Keifon squinted. "Rings?"

She stared at him for a moment – was he making fun of her, or being obtuse? – and then remembered. Of course. She tapped the base of her throat. "Oh – right. Back home we wear wedding rings, not necklaces." She raised her hands and wiggled her middle fingers by way of illustration. Keifon's face went blank. She rushed on, embarrassed by her weak joke. "But no, I'll write Laris, that's all. I wouldn't forfeit on my contract. Besides... I don't know." She hiked her knee toward her chest, wrapping her arms around it. "I don't think I would want to live in Laketon. I know that's ungrateful."

"Ungrateful?"

"Because he likes me. Anyway," she went on, too tired to explain something that she barely understood herself. "I'll write to him for a while, and then we'll see."

"That's fair." He thought for a minute, and she realized that the toe of her shoe was resting against his knee. It would be too obvious to move away, but – "Your friend is in Vertal, after all, isn't he? You could be assigned there."

Rone, she translated. "I... don't think he'd like that. He keeps writing about how it's good for me to be independent, things like that." She rushed on, embarrassed. "Besides... I don't know whether he's staying. He could be back in Nessiny by the time I get to Vertal. His contract is over, so he can leave any time he wants to. Back home, or to Achusa, maybe. His boyfriend was on assignment there."

"His – Oh. I thought... oh."

She was blushing again, equal parts fury and embarrassment. "It's not like that, all right? Besides. I always liked Bakari. He was smart and-and nice, and they were amazing together." Bakari and Rone were memories that she didn't need tonight. They had been the Academy's Furoni champions, beautiful and devoted – she couldn't think about that now. "Anyway. Someday I'll go and visit them and their perfect kids and we'll reminisce about school."

"So you're going back to Nessiny when your contract is up?"

"I was just speaking hypothetically. I don't know what I'll do. There's a long time to think about that. Besides, there's more need for healers in Kavera than in Nessiny."

"That's charitable of you."

Agna shrugged. "The best use of my skills is to serve the greatest need."

"The man at the shrine told me about that concept." He took a deep breath. "I should have asked you. Instead of assuming."

"Well. We've started over. Remember?" Keifon returned her smile, and her stomach felt very strange. She needed to straighten up, to move away, to get back on the road. She flailed her way to her feet. "Um. Do you mind if we get going? I'm getting tired."

"Of course."

He persisted in walking beside her on the way back. She was too tired to walk faster and stay ahead of him. They'd be on the road tomorrow. She could ask about his beliefs, since he had taken the effort of learning about the Balance church. Or she could ask about life in Yanwei, building on the things she'd learned in her history classes. She looked forward to the next time they set up the clinic, too. They could learn a lot from one another.

Keifon spoke up as they neared the edge of the camp. "You seem happy."

"Heh. I guess I am. Or delirious."

"Oh, young people in love. What's the word I'm looking for. Obnoxious." He was only teasing, and she still wanted to slug him.

"I wasn't even thinking about Laris—" She realized what she'd just said and cut herself off. "Grr. You know, I could push you into the lake."

"Not if you announce it in advance like that. No element of surprise."

She couldn't maintain the repartee, and let him have the last word. It had been a long day. She had spent all evening thinking about – difficult things. She needed a hot soak, preferably with an unchallenging book, and a long night's sleep.

When they reached the tent, Keifon let her go in first. She lit the lantern and found her toiletry kit and towel and one of her books. In the bathhouse she soaked until she was so tired that she risked dropping her book in the water.

The lantern was burning when she returned. Keifon sat by his bedroll. He looked up as she entered, and his hands unfolded from one of the prayer positions.

Agna focused on her armload of clothes. "I drew a fresh bath and told them to hold it for you."

"Mm. That would be nice. Thanks." He rose from his bedroll and gathered some things from his pack. When he'd left she stowed the book at the bottom of her trunk, unpacked her bedroll, and changed clothes. She was half-asleep by the time Keifon returned. Having packed his clothes away and secured the tent flaps, Keifon lay down and blew out the lantern.

His voice was indistinct. "Agna. Hey."

"Hm?"

"I'm glad we talked today."

"So am I. Thank you."

"Goodnight."

"'Night."

He had been praying to Lundra when she'd come back to the tent. She'd recognized the position of his interwoven fingers. The walk had begun and ended in the same place, Agna thought. Lundra was the god of the bonds between people, and between humans and gods. Bonds of all types, Keifon had reminded her. Lundra was the personification of the shining moment of knocking on a near-stranger's door, of a shared cup of tea, of a long talk by a lakeshore. Every one of them was divine.

Part Two

Agna: The Medics

The next morning, they took down the tents and loaded their luggage onto the passenger wagon. Despite the lack of conversation – limited, for the most part, to "can you take this?" and "thank you" – Agna found the experience to be freeing. She checked the habit of wondering what vicious thoughts brewed in his mind, or reading slights into his terse morning demeanor. They packed their belongings and went back on the road, and that was that.

Keifon fell asleep in his seat, and Agna watched the countryside, fanned herself with the Benevolent Union's old logbook, and wondered how they might rebuild their operation. And, as they rolled by the vast cattle ranges outside Laketon, she wondered what Laris was doing.

A couple of hours later, Keifon woke, apologizing and struggling to pull his thoughts together.

"It's fine," she said. "I would like to talk about some things, but there's no hurry."

"Mmgh." He drank some water from his canteen and wetted a handkerchief to wipe his face. Agna looked out past the other wagons. It was good that he could catch up on a little sleep, at least.

Eventually he was composed and coherent. "What do you want to talk about?"

"I was thinking about how we do things in the clinic. Not how you treat the patients – that's fine. How we divide them up and work together."

He nodded. "We don't work together, you mean."

"I think we could."

"We could."

"Well, here's my thought. I think we should assess each of our strengths and match them to the patients' needs. You're great with calming people down, and with diagnosis. I can knit bones and close cuts, all of that. Each of us has our specialties, so we can trade off when the patient needs it. What do you think?"

Keifon considered this for a minute. "Those are all good points. A-and thank you."

Agna raced on, unsure why he was thanking her, and unnerved by the prospect. "What do you think your specialties are?"

Slowly at first, as though he expected an argument, he told her. She silenced the urge to pipe up about approaches that the Academy no longer used or skills that she thought were better listed under her own specialties. They were having a real, constructive conversation about a topic that was central to their presence in Kavera and their mission for the Benevolent Union. She could defend the honor of the Academy later. Or perhaps never. She was no longer convinced that it was of primary importance.

When he was finished, Agna told him what she could do. She kept the commentary to a minimum, as he had, describing the procedures without trying to prove any points. He asked about how she accomplished some of the techniques, how the healing skill worked in this situation or that – and before she knew it, Masa, the food vendor, had pulled alongside the wagon. Agna bought lunch for both of them, and resumed the discussion as they ate.

His questions and comments had raised some questions of her own, so Agna asked him about his training with the Army – how they addressed this condition or that problem. At some point, he pulled out his medical reference book and found some passages that he said he would translate for her later. Agna promised, in return, to translate anything in *Blackhall's Human Anatomy and the Workings Thereof.*

When Masa and his apprentice came around for dinner, Keifon paid, and shushed her protests. "Please. I would like to start off better, and that includes not forcing me into debt, if you would."

"It's not real debt; it's not as though you're buying a homestead. Come on."

He looked at her and then sighed. "Maybe it's different in Nessiny, then. In Yanwei it's – it's shameful to be indebted to someone, especially outside your family. You treat it so casually, I – thought you just liked to debase me."

She was struck silent. "I – hm. A little. That was petty of me. I'm sorry."

He nodded, and found his voice. "Thank you. Apology accepted."

"And it is different in Nessiny. Or... well, maybe it's different for me, too. I don't like to think about people not having enough money. It wasn't something that you were supposed to talk about at home." She pushed her hair behind one ear. "It was strange, being friends with Esirel – my best friend from the Academy. She had almost nothing, and it bothered her so much. I couldn't imagine not having anything I wanted. So I gave her things, and sometimes she was offended. And we never talked about it."

He took a drink of water, turning this over. "You were trying to help her."

"Yes. With you... I don't know. When I saw that you didn't like it, I was glad. I was getting one over on you, because you... you know so much more than me about practical things, and–" She threw her hands up. "I was an ass. That's all."

He shifted uncomfortably in his seat. "I was glad to know more than you, because you were so fond of reminding me that you were better than me."

129

"But we're done with that. Right?"

"Yes. I'm-I'm glad. I think I can learn a lot from you."

His reluctance to say it made her blush harder. "I could learn a lot from you, too." She found the Benevolent Union log, pretending to be overheated, even though dusk was beginning to cool the air. "So – back to the clinic. Whichever one of us is free will ask the patient about their problem. If they don't know, we'll check them out, diagnose and decide who should take on the treatment. Agreed?"

"Agreed." He smiled a little – a genuine smile, not the sarcastic smirk of a point scored against her. Behind her makeshift fan, she smiled back.

Keifon: Gifts

"So, what are you getting Laris for Lundrala?" Keifon took another bite of melon, the only thing he had felt inclined to eat for dinner.

Agna looked up quizzically from her bowl of sliced tomatoes and cheese. The mere thought of the dish made Keifon want to slug ginger extract, but she ate it nearly once a day lately.

"I... suppose I should get something. They celebrate it here, don't they." Several of the merchants had taken to posting signs, subtle and unsubtle, proclaiming their wares' fitness as gifts. Keifon nodded in response to the rhetorical question. Agna bit her lip. "Hmm."

"Has he mentioned anything in his letters that he might like?" He took a drink, finished his slice of melon, and tossed the bare rind onto his plate. He eyed the remaining fruit – less than half left. He cut another wedge as Agna pondered.

"I don't think so. He talks a lot about – well – he's supposed to go on a trip in the spring, for his work, down the canal to Vertal. Driving some cattle to market. He talks about that a lot. It might be a new direction for him, so it's important to him. And... other things. But nothing about gifts," she said hastily. She eyed Keifon. "You're not going to eat an entire melon and nothing else, are you?"

Keifon shrugged. "It's hot." She made a noise halfway between a growl and a gurgle. Keifon decided to ignore this. "Well... what does he do?"

"He reads a lot. Works on the ranch. Makes friends with everyone."

"Writes to you."

"Writes to me."

"Hm. A book?"

"Is that enough? I've never gotten anyone a Lundrala gift. I mean, there are plenty of Church of the Four followers at home, but my family mostly celebrated Balance holidays. Esi just went along. She didn't care much. – She was Church of the Four."

"Ah." He tried to backtrack through her nervous explanation. "I think a book is enough. It doesn't have to be expensive, and you're not supposed to get more than one thing. It's supposed to be... personal. Representing what's between you." She blushed a little, and Keifon turned his attention back to eating. What was between them, indeed. "But you can get whatever you want. I'm sure he'd appreciate it."

"I see." She returned to her dinner, pausing to nibble on her fork meditatively. "Wait, is it just – you know, romantic people, or..."

Keifon chuckled. Romantic people? "People who are connected to you. Friends, family, things like that."

"Oh... oh, damn," she muttered.

"What is it?"

"That's more people."

"Mmhm." Keifon tallied it in his head. He had to mail some gifts for his brother and Nachi soon. Then... he supposed he would get something for Agna, now. They were connected through their assignment, after all. Who else? Something small for a few of the merchants, like Baran and Wayron. Nelle, now that the herbalist seemed to have annexed him as an ally through Agna. Edann was a more complicated case. Keifon stretched out on the ground, munching and pondering.

"Lying down while you eat is bad for your stomach," Agna said in her clinical tone.

"Ngh." A little flicker of reflexive anger flared and died. She wasn't wrong, and she was looking out for his health. Keifon sat up, lounging on his hand. ...Edann was complicated. He was unquestionably one of the central people in Keifon's life right now, but if Keifon were to bring a Lundrala gift, Edann would snap at him. And he wouldn't get Keifon anything in return. In fact, Edann would be doubly insulted by the pressure of having been given an unreciprocated gift. It seemed against the spirit of the holiday, though. It didn't seem right not to acknowledge their... whatever they had. Besides, the only gift Keifon could think of was wine, and that wasn't appropriate.

Agna distracted him from a mental track involving more inappropriate and less tangible gifts by getting up to wash her dish. Keifon cut the remaining melon into two slices and offered her one. She gave him another scolding look – about eating nothing but melon for dinner, he gathered – and accepted it. She meticulously sucked the juice out of each section before biting in.

Two gifts to post, one or two gifts in person, about five token gifts. He could afford all of that. It had been a little less expensive to share food and laundry expenses with Agna, since Laketon. And he hadn't added up the figures yet, but he suspected that they were going through more patients per day now.

Agna slurped one more bit of juice off her rind and tossed it onto the heap on Keifon's plate. She licked her fingers. "Where does it stop, though?"

"Hm?"

"I mean, Laris, and Nelle. And – and you. Is that it? Or everyone in the caravan?"

"Eh...if you talk to them a lot. I'm going to get the same thing for a few of the people in the caravan. Baran and Wayron, people like that. Acquaintances. It's expected that you'll get your acquaintances all the same thing, or types of the same thing. Something small and impersonal, but something that says you're thinking of them."

"Ugh, this is complicated."

"Heh. It's not that bad. You don't have anything like that in Nessiny?"

"Not really. You give people money on their festival. Or flowers. You wrap it up in this little package. The money, not the flowers."

"Their festival?"

"Yeah, when they turn a year older."

"Hm. Odd that you call it a festival."

"Well, it is a festival. Mine's Midsummer."

Keifon's melon-stuffed stomach panged with guilt. Midsummer had passed, and he hadn't known. "I'm sorry I missed it. Um... if you don't mind me asking... how old did you turn?"

"Twenty-one," Agna shrugged. "So when's yours?"

"My birthday? It was, uh, about three weeks ago. But that's all right, I don't need a lot of fuss."

She laughed. "You're Midsummer too, then."

"A ways after Midsummer."

"...Still. ...Unless... you celebrate it down to the day in Yanwei."

"We...do," he said. "They do in Kavera, too. So you...don't? What do you do?"

"You round to the closest festival," she said, as if stating the obvious. "Unless you're a little, little kid. After two years your parents stop counting exactly when you were born. Unless they're trying to be funny."

"That's...hm. So a quarter of everyone turns older at the same time."

"Yeah, more or less." She considered this, crossing her ankles in front of her. "You must never stop celebrating, then. If everyone has a separate day."

"Heh...well... it depends. But you usually just get someone one thing, like Lundrala." He smiled, remembering, and considered whether to tell her. It wouldn't hurt anything, he reminded himself. She wasn't out to hurt him anymore. "My nanbur was a birthday gift. Combination birthday and Lundrala. I was nine."

"That's sweet. Who was it from?"

"All the hands on my parents' ranch. They all pitched in." Shiu had delivered it, though. Shiu had been his favorite, and everyone had known it.

"Oh, what kind of ranch do your parents have?"

"Horses. Did. They're dead now."

Agna rocked back as though she'd been struck. "Oh. I-I'm sorry."

"Murdered," Keifon clarified, though it never helped. "By bandits. Came to steal the horses. I was eleven."

"Heart of the world," she murmured. "I'm so sorry."

He shrugged. Her sympathy was a stone tossed into a chasm that yawned to the center of the world. But it was all she could offer. "Thank you."

Instead, he told her about the day he'd gotten his nanbur. He'd tried to practice on Shiu's nanbur before, and the ranch hands had all decided that he was old enough to get his own. He told her how proud he had been, because he thought they'd all begun to see him as an adult. He'd been desperate to grow up, at nine. He'd been two years away from growing up, and he'd had plenty of time to regret it.

"So you've been playing for – a long time."

Keifon half-smiled. "Sixteen years."

"I wasn't fishing for numbers," she said, putting on a wounded tone. "I meant to compliment you on your dedication."

"Hmn. Thank you. It's difficult, so you have to keep practicing. But I like it."

"You always seem to." She looked away, awkward again. Keifon took the opportunity to excuse himself with his plate full of rinds and walk it to the camp's compost heap. When he came back, Agna was seated by the unlit fire pit, lost in thought.

"How about a swim?"

"Eh." She shrugged. "Maybe when it gets dark."

"Well... leeches. Bugs."

Agna shuddered. "Right... right. ...I guess so."

Something was wrong, something she didn't want to come out and admit. The new moon was a couple of weeks away, so that wasn't it. He sat cross-legged, across the fire pit from her. *When it gets dark...* she had been so self-conscious the first and last time they had taken a swim in the river. It had taken her half an hour to throw off her dressing gown and sprint to the water. "Nobody's looking," he said. "It's all right."

She blushed to the neck of her robes. "Well... everyone looks. All the time."

"Nnn – well – if anyone makes you feel bad, I'll drown them. How about that?"

She laughed painfully. "You're just trying to get a bigger Lundrala gift. Personal assassins have got to jump to the top tier."

"Right behind poison-tasters." He had made her smile, at least. He could do that now.

Agna: Connections

The new Benevolent Union compound in Wildern was built in the style of the other, more historical buildings on Wildern's central streets, with grand timbers and white plaster walls. The bartender's directions had brought them to one side of the building, where a sign over the door displayed the Benevolent Union seal and the medical aid symbol. It seemed strange to see the two devices on a real building; they had become so associated in Agna's mind with their own clinic tent.

She and Keifon scuffed their shoes at the doorway and stepped into a clean, simple waiting room, where several patients, most merely sniffling, waited on wooden benches. Perhaps this was why their business had been slow yesterday. No matter – it was all for the same good. They approached the reception desk, and Agna cleared her throat.

"We're the Benevolent Union healers from the fall caravan," she explained, picking up the name that the people in Wildern used for it. "We were interested in seeing the base."

The agent behind the desk gestured ironically. "You're here. Though you should probably go to the main atrium and start there. Around outside to the right, or I suppose you could go through the back way." He waved toward the opening of a hallway behind him. "Head down this way and look for the blue signs."

Agna gave him a gracious nod. "Thank you."

The wood-floored hallway murmured with voices and distant footsteps. Side hallways led to examination rooms and sickrooms, labeled with tidy green signs. Ahead, the hallway ended at an intersection, also annotated by signs: Offices, in blue; School, in red. Agna and Keifon took the turn toward the offices.

The base in Vertal was an administrative hub and a dispatching center at its heart, housing agents as they came into the country and deciding what to do with the army of hands and minds at the Union's disposal. The Wildern base was a center of at least two of the Benevolent Union's true missions: education and medical aid. The Vertal base thought; the Wildern base acted. It was, Agna admitted, kind of exciting, despite its isolation. And as a building, it was beautiful – well-ordered and modern inside, harmonizing with its surroundings outside.

Wildern was a charming backwater, as far as she'd seen, but the Benevolent Union had begun to revive it into something more promising than Laketon had been. The base had drawn more commerce to the area to support the agents who had moved here to teach and heal. The locals bragged about their tiny storefront library and the new construction at the edges of town. Wildern was small, but it was growing.

The hallway gave onto an atrium, where the receiving staff oversaw the comings and goings of the base. From there, two polished wooden staircases angled up to a second-floor overlook. Keifon drifted toward the central desk, picking up the pamphlets on display. Agna drew closer to the paintings on the walls. She didn't recognize the artists. Most were idealized, fanciful depictions of the northwestern Kaveran countryside, with the unrealistic contrast and intensity of color that had been in fashion in Kavera for the last several years. It was a well-curated collection, fitting the location and function of the building – a flagship project in such a small town could be expected to promote some local pride.

The largest painting, in the angle between the two staircases, was a more typical depiction in oils of a posed crowd of people. Agna perused it in turn. Half a dozen Kaverans were arrayed on one of the same staircases that loomed over her head. Most held tools, or carried them hooked into their belts – hammers and hand saws and so on. The last, leaning casually against the banister, wore a suit of more fashionable cut and a meticulously clipped beard. And beside him –

Agna froze. One was not a Kaveran; his skin was too dark, even for the rest of the sun-browned group. His hair was cut short – he hadn't grown it back out – and his shoulders and arms had filled out with more muscle. He was not wearing the green cloak, though she could see the sword belt slung around his hips. The sword itself was hidden behind the well-dressed man next to him, but she knew what it would have looked like, and she knew its name. *Satri.* "Unity" in Alhara, the language of the Islands.

Someone had approached her. "Are you all right?" Keifon tracked her gaze to the painting. He read the title plaque aloud – something about the dedication of the building.

Agna remembered how to read. A larger plaque below the painting said *Wildern Base Dedication. Aines Shora, Project Head. Construction Lead Team...* She skimmed the unfamiliar names and titles, to the bottom. She reached out for the raised bronze lettering, because she needed to touch something to anchor herself to the world, and her lifelong indoctrination would not allow her to touch a painting on display.

Rone Sidduji.

"It's him," she whispered. "The – the Islander, there, on the right. That's Rone."

"...I see." He did not ask questions, did not ask why a sworn shrine guardian would show up in a painting of a construction team in some Kaveran backwater. She didn't have answers. She could spin theories about collaborations between the Church and the Benevolent Union; she could concoct stories about secret shipments of supplies, attacks from brigands, or evil rival architects. But the truth was that she simply didn't know. She didn't know why Rone had been here, because he wouldn't say.

Keifon cleared his throat. "He's, uh. A nice-looking fellow."

The incongruity broke Agna's trance, and she laughed, stuffing her wrist against her mouth. Keifon half-turned as though making sure that no one had heard them, and his bearing tightened as one of the base's agents approached them.

"That's the team that built this base," the agent said, in a calm, cultured voice, laden with pride. Agna turned, and flicked a look at the painting. He was well-dressed, with gray-frosted hair and a meticulously clipped beard. He was the last agent, standing next to Rone in the painting.

"I know him," Agna blurted. She waved vaguely behind her. "Rone Sidduji. We – we went to the Academy together."

The agent's face softened, smiling with something very much like nostalgia. "Ahhhh, lovely. I admit that he was my favorite of Weston's team." He joined his hands behind his back, gazing into the painting. His smile was almost dreamy. Agna's heart raced. Rone had always gathered admirers behind him, but they had always been other students.

"Remembering our dear princeling has ruined my manners, I'm afraid. Aines Shora, captain of the Wildern base." He made the Kaveran greeting wave with an elegant hand.

"Ag-Agna Despana. Healer of the Church of the Divine Balance. And the Benevolent Union. With the caravan."

"Very good. And?" He turned to Keifon, who had gone so still that Agna had nearly forgotten about him.

Keifon's voice was half-lost, not remotely his charming self from the clinic. "Keifon the Medic, from the Yanweian National Army." He made his usual salute, a closed fist over his heart.

"Welcome to Wildern. A healer... hmm. Oh, yes! Are you one of Rone's young protégés, by any chance? I do seem to recall..."

"Yes! – yes. Agna. The other one was Esirel Relaska. A swordmaster." Her mind pieced this together: he did know Rone. Well enough for Rone to have spoken about his time at the Academy. Well enough for Rone to have mentioned her. And she had no idea why Rone had been here at all. She couldn't ask this agent, either, not out of the blue. Not when Rone had decided – for what reason she couldn't even fathom – not to tell her himself. And as always, she couldn't ask Rone about it. This painting would talk more than he would.

The agent watched the painting more than he looked at her. "So you came to Kavera after all. We're honored."

Agna couldn't tell, through the slow churn of something that began to bend toward anger, whether Agent Shora's tone had been sarcastic or not. She could only say thank you and hope that it sounded polite. Some part of her was unnerved, some part of her was flattered, and some part of her wondered very hard about that look of dreamy nostalgia.

Agent Shora retreated as another agent hovered behind him. "A pleasure to meet you. Do give Rone my regards." He turned, accepting the papers that his underling held out, and trotted up the staircase in his polished shoes.

Agna did not move for several breaths. An admirer, then, that Rone knew – trusted – well enough to talk about his friends and their aspirations. Not an admirer, then. Perhaps a friend. Perhaps not. *I admit that he was my favorite...*

This man was nothing like Bakari, Rone's boyfriend from the Academy. Agna hadn't known Bakari very well. She had stammered out perfunctory greetings when she had crossed his path on campus, intimidated by his upperclassman status, by his easy smile, and by his importance in Rone's world. She wasn't sure that he even remembered her name, though he had always recognized her and greeted her. He had seemed kind and intelligent. He was known around the campus for his dedication to his dual studies of theology and swordsmanship, and, before long, his mutual dedication to Rone. He had been worthy of Rone's love. This agent, though... he might be famous in this backwater, and he was handsome enough, but something about him was staged.

That wasn't like Rone at all.

Keifon waited in her peripheral vision. She couldn't begin to explain this to him. She couldn't even put it into words to herself. She was still chasing her old friend, though she had his mailing address on paper, tucked into her stationery box. He had never really been there, ever since he'd come to Kavera. She got letters back from an absent person.

She tried to speak, got nothing but rust, and tried again. "I'd like to go now."

Keifon nodded. She trailed him through the main doors and out onto a busy street. He bought two paper cones of honey-coated nuts from a street vendor, handed one to her, and walked beside her as they licked their fingers and wandered another unfamiliar town.

The temperature dropped as evening came on. Agna breathed into her hands as she weaved through the market, picking out ingredients with Keifon – a small pumpkin to roast in the coals, a jar of honey, sacks of grain and flour, hard wedges of cheese wrapped in linen.

The prosaic reality of the sights and smells and textures focused her thoughts. She could imagine Rone here, shopping for dinner. That was what bothered her. He didn't belong here; he belonged at the Academy, waving at her and Esirel across the quad, or facing off against that jackass Lunden in the tournament square. He didn't seem to exist outside the Academy the way Esirel did. Esi came home with Agna on breaks, after all; she was in love with Lina; she existed outside and beyond the Academy. Agna wasn't sure how Rone existed outside the Academy. But now she could picture it.

He was real. He was just a person, like these Wildernian shoppers, squeezing the gourds and weighing the cheese. And she had held him up as a shining example, and had followed him to Kavera for no other reason than to catch a little of his reflected light. He hadn't come here for glory, she was sure of it. Agna knew perfectly well now that there was little glory to be had on the road. There were triumphs both small and large, daily challenges and irritations, and an endless stream of new faces and stories. She had not found glory.

She didn't even want glory anymore.

She wanted to meet more of those people, and help them however she could. She wanted to go back to the campsite, let Keifon take his turn to cook, and draw something new. She wanted to push the limits of her healing skill, hone her Kaveran, and learn more about Kaveran art. She did not want to follow Rone's lead.

Agna could trace her own path, find a new assignment or make the best of this one, and learn everything that Kavera could teach her. She had to make the decisions herself.

Keifon: House Calls

Once Agna bought proper winter clothes, things were easier. She had come to Kavera with nothing heavier than a cotton cloak, and after it had been stolen, she had never replaced it. When Keifon had asked about it, concerned that she might not have understood the climate in northern Kavera, she had muttered a vague answer and changed the subject.

Between the infrequent visits from patients, she counted out her earnings from the clinic, wrote page after page of figures and lists, and finally made the rounds of the caravan. Three times she reappeared at the clinic tent to ask him whether he wanted anything, and twice he said no; the third time he asked her for something hot to drink. It was easy enough to cover the clinic alone out here. Hardly anyone made the trek through the snow. The Benevolent Union's notes explained that their predecessors had begun to make more house calls after the snow began, eventually forgoing the clinic tent.

The thought of venturing out there without the shelter of the clinic tent made his heart pound and his head swim. When Agna left, Keifon pulled his cloak around himself more tightly than was normal. It was irrational; he knew that. They would be attending to their patients in their own homes, not out in the cold. But venturing out on foot ran a little too close to a vein of old fear. It had been bricked over in the Army with order and structure and the relative comfort of the barracks, lying dormant until the image of setting out into the snow broke through the wall.

He would not freeze out there. He had shelter, Agna would not let him freeze, and he had the backing of the Yanweian National Army and the Benevolent Union. He was valued as an agent, as a medic, and even as an infantryman. He would not die forgotten in the snow.

Keifon spent much of the afternoon trying not to think about it. If his hands cramped from clenching, he did not think about that either.

At dinnertime Agna returned. She had bought a thick wool coat, fur-lined boots, mittens and a long scarlet scarf, and she beamed as she showed off her purchases. She had also brought the crock of broth from last night, which she had thawed and heated to steaming. Keifon padded the edges of his cloak over his hands and accepted the crock from her. The smell of the broth calmed his stomach, turning the uneasy flutters into growls of hunger.

"More surprises at the camp," she announced as he sipped.

"Thank you for this. – You've been busy."

"It's difficult. There's so much I *could* get and so little we can carry. But I think this will help."

"I'm sure. You look better equipped."

"It's so nice." She pulled the scarf up to warm her cold-flushed cheeks.

"I told you."

Her breath steamed through the scarf. "Yes, yes. Anyway, I apologize in advance for the next time we have to move it all."

Keifon took another sip. "It's worthwhile. And I've been thinking... You've read the old healers' notes, haven't you? About making house calls?"

Agna took a seat on the other stool. "Yeah. I'm willing to try it. What do you think?"

"I think we should." The broth warmed him from the inside out. Her relief was a little bit contagious, too. "People will expect it once the snow sets in."

"I guess so. And it looks like the snow is here to stay."

Keifon nodded and sniffed as the hot broth steamed his sinuses. "We might get another thaw, but not for long. It's time. And if we're going out into the towns, then we won't have to carry this tent out, or any of this furniture. We can leave it on the wagon. So it might not be so bad."

"I see your point." She huffed her breath into her cupped hands. "I promise I won't buy more things to make up the difference."

Keifon smiled. "I'll hold you to that."

"Though if I got a covered wagon..."

He chuckled. "I'd fill mine with books."

"I'd have one giant featherbed," she sighed. "Though books would be good. And a fireplace."

"Great combination. Paper, feathers, and fire in a tiny, moving wooden wagon. The cold has made you delirious."

"Being *warm* for once has made me delirious," Agna retorted. She stripped off her mittens and held them out to him. "Here."

Keifon hesitated. His hands had been warmed by the heated ceramic, and she didn't need to freeze for his sake. But he took the mittens, slipped them on, and left the overthinking for later. The fibers retained her body heat. He cupped his hands around the crock and hastened to drink the rest while it was warm. It was becoming easier to believe that they would be safe out there.

Agna smiled. "Can't wait to show you."

It would do very little good to try to get more details out of her. She was deriving too much pleasure from stringing him along. "The world isn't exactly beating a path to our door right now. Why don't we go back sooner rather than later?"

"You make a good point," she mused. "We can plan tomorrow's house calls."

"Yes. So... it's settled, then."

They left the tent for last, letting it protect them from the outside air as they packed up the furniture. When it was all tied up and packed away in the passenger wagon, they trooped through the mud to the campsite. The fire still smoldered, from when Agna had stopped to reheat the broth, he supposed.

Keifon poked the ashes and began to feed in wood. Agna hovered behind him. He ignored her for now. It would be pleasant to find out what her little folly was, because she had learned better than to hold the expense over his head. As the wood began to catch and throw off raw waves of heat, Keifon reflected that she wouldn't have much money on hand left after this anyway.

By the time the fire was self-sustaining, Agna had shed her boots at the tent door and sealed herself inside; the lit lantern cast her silhouette on the wall. Keifon left her to it and set some water on to boil. They had potatoes and cheese and onions, though it looked as though she had brought him all of the rest of the broth. Tucking Agna's mittens under his belt, he sliced the potatoes and onions into the water and let it heat.

Having settled that matter, he ducked into the tent. Agna had taken off her new coat, and warmed her hands over a small, glowing brazier. She smiled up at him, half gleeful, half guilty.

"Oh." Keifon remembered to fasten the tent flaps to keep the wind from blowing them open. "Um. That – that must have been expensive. Thank you."

"Yeah, but we'll be warm! Whenever we want! Feel it."

"Mm." He warmed his hands with her. "What does it burn? Charcoal?"

"Yeah. We'll just have to remember to keep the vent open in the tent roof, and be careful not to tip it over."

...and buy more charcoal, he thought. "Hm." He remembered her mittens and handed them back. She tossed them onto a pile of clothes in the corner. "Well. I have dinner going out there. It'll be a while."

"Taxman's Rounds?"

"Hn, or sevens. Either one."

"Sevens is shorter. We can play something else after that." She fetched the deck of cards from her trunk and began to shuffle.

Keifon took off his cloak and folded it along the bottom edge of the tent flap, where the draft came in. "I admit, I'm not in the mood for wagering today. Do you mind?" They only wagered for chores, bargaining over who would sweep the snow or build the fires, but even good-natured bickering did not appeal to him at the moment.

She shrugged. "That's all right. I already owe you one for making dinner, anyway."

"Well." He waved at the brazier.

"You're not in debt to me for that. I bought it for both of us."

He watched her cut the cards until he came up with a reply. "Thank you."

Agna shrugged and began to deal. "So, how do you like sevens, anyway? It was the popular game when I was in third or fourth year. I always missed it, later on. Everyone started playing this one called Cross the River instead."

"I like it. It's kind of like Shepherd, but you build your pack up instead of down, and you stop on seven and not one."

"Where'd you play that one?" she asked, and in building his hand he forgot to think about the question.

"Oh, mostly in the barracks. Taxman's Rounds was for when we had a lot of time. They would start drinking at the beginning of the game and forget who was winning somewhere along the way. I didn't stay for a lot of that." He laid down an eight and nine and reordered what was left in his hand. "Go ahead."

She picked a card from his hand, laid down some cards, and reorganized her hand. She held her cards squarely in line with one another, like Dola had, during the unit's games. He hadn't thought of Dola in months, he realized. She'd had such an infectious laugh.

"Hey."

"Hm? Oh." He picked a card from her hand, decided that he couldn't build on anything, and pulled from the deck. "Go ahead. I should check dinner." He set down his hand. In the barracks anyone walking away from a hand of cards was asking to be sabotaged, but it would never be an issue in these games. He shoved his feet into his boots, pulled on his cloak and ventured out.

Some of the water had boiled off, and the vegetables had begun to soften. He stirred the pot, set their bowls by the fire to warm, and filled the teakettle. They were running low on water. One of them would have to venture over to the creek one more time before they broke camp. There wasn't much untrampled snow to melt.

Agna was warming her hands when he returned. Her cards lay in a neat stack. "Fifteen minutes," he reported, and spread his hands across from hers. The unfrozen memories ran too close to the surface. Cold that went on until the end of the world. Unwelcome light, unwelcome dark, emptiness inside him and out. That was a lifetime ago, he reminded himself. It was stupid to feel this way; he had survived, after all. But he had been marked by it. That winter was waiting in him.

He picked up his cards.

"Are you all right?" Agna watched him over her own cards.

Keifon shrugged it off. "I don't like the cold. I'd rather not think about it."

"If you say so." She sorted out her cards and continued the game. Their conversation had lapsed into a neutral silence. Later they would talk about their strategies and the routes they would take through the villages. For now there was only the soft crackle of the brazier's fire and the faint slap of cards as the snow muffled the footsteps and voices outside.

Agna: Caretaker

At first, the house calls proceeded without incident. In each village or town, Agna and Keifon found the local doctor or herbalist, if there was one, and offered their help. Most of the time, everything was well under control. One doctor invited them along on her own rounds, to make quicker work of it; a few pointed them toward houses where the locals could unload their usual minor complaints on fresh ears. In villages without doctors of their own, Agna and Keifon trooped from house to house, asking whether anyone needed medical help or wanted a checkup. Keifon began to carry fewer bits of equipment in his case, and more medicines – painkillers and remedies for upset stomachs and concoctions for coughs. They carried on like this for a few weeks, through one village after another. And then Keifon began coughing two days after a visit to a patient with a high fever, and the next morning he woke shivering.

Agna scooted across the tent to lay her hand on his forehead, shivering in the cold herself. His skin was burning. She pushed him back onto his bedroll. "Oh, no. You're staying here today."

"You need help," he mumbled, curling up on his side, coughing into his cupped hands. "I can't – I can't stay here."

"Yes. You will." Her mind raced, clearing away the last remnants of sleep. She could give him blankets and drinking water, and buy some broth from Masa. They were supposed to camp here for two more days, to sell to the town just over the hill. Two days might be enough for him to recover if he rested. But if he wasn't better by the time they moved on, she could hire one of the guards to help her with the tent, and—

"Agna?"

"Hm?"

"You can't – fix this, can you?"

"No... well. If you have any pain, I can help that. And I might be able to help your throat if it's raw from coughing. But mostly you'll just have to stay warm and get enough to drink and rest."

"Mmn." That set off another cough. "Don't go out on rounds by yourself. All right?"

"I'll be fine. I'll get you some water and something to eat before I go. Here... " Impulsively, Agna pulled her blankets from her bedroll and spread them over him. Keifon pulled them up and huddled in, whispering thanks.

"I'll be back soon. Just rest." She grabbed her clothes, her coat and her bath kit, and remembered to close the tent on her way out. She could handle this; she could come up with a plan that would let her do rounds and allow Keifon to rest. She would have to be resourceful and determined. Behind her worry, she hadn't felt this alive in a long time.

■ ■ ■

By mid-morning, her preparations were complete. Keifon had slept fitfully, shivering under their combined blankets, as she bustled in and out of the tent. She had left the water barrel inside, along with a crock of broth ordered from Masa and two of the vials from Keifon's kit: one to lower fevers, one to calm coughs. She considered waking him up to administer them, but it was best if he was able to sleep. She bundled up in her winter gear and hoisted Keifon's valise. She assumed that he wouldn't mind if she borrowed it, under the circumstances.

They hadn't come into this town for rounds yesterday, having made camp late in the day. But foot traffic had already trampled a thin track of frozen mud into the road between the campground and the town. This town was large and organized enough to have its own cobbled square in the center. Facing the square were several houses, better-appointed than most that she'd passed on the way in; a meeting house; and an Eytran church, if she interpreted the snow-drifted statues correctly. Agna approached the church and knocked on its door. A hooded priest answered, peering into the cold wind, and directed her to the local herbalist's house.

The herbalist was younger than she'd expected, a man not much older than herself. He seemed grateful for the help, and jotted down some directions along the town's few streets. Agna followed the list, remembering the herbalist's name to weave into her introduction – *Hello, I'm the new Benevolent Union healer from the caravan. Rasil the herbalist sent me. How are you feeling today?* She tried to keep her voice bright. She checked on a pregnant woman near delivery. She checked on a few villagers with the same fever that Keifon had, most of whom were being watched over by relatives. Agna returned to the herbalist's house, pulling her scarf over her face as she waited on his stoop.

He returned not long after, trudging through the snow. "Hey there, healer.. Any trouble today? How were they?"

Agna reported as the herbalist led her inside. "All as could be expected. No delivery yet, the fevers at three or four days seem to be breaking, the earlier ones are getting worse." She bit her lip, wanting to tell him about Keifon's sickness, wanting reassurance.

"Ah yes. Four days is what I've seen so far." He unstrapped the case of supplies on his back. "I've seen a few more with the same fever, today. It's been spreading from the north, as far as anyone can tell. With any luck it will be past this area soon."

"I hope it will be," Agna replied. "So... have you found any way to treat it?"

"Ah, no. Not really. Time, rest, all of the usual. Treating the cough if it makes them more comfortable. Oh yes, if you're with the caravan you'll see more of it, I'm sure."

"Yes, that's true..." Agna waved off his offer of tea. "Thank you, but I should be getting back." She took a deep breath. "The other Benevolent Union healer, traveling with me. He has the fever, too. I'm... worried about him."

"Ah, I'm sorry to hear that. I'd wondered, since they always send two people. Will you be here for another day?"

"Yes."

"Then don't worry about us tomorrow. Take care of your partner."

Agna blushed under her scarf, but couldn't protest his choice of words. "All right. Thank you. I should be going now."

"Well, godspeed then, and good luck."

"Thank you. And same to you. Good luck to your town and your people. We'll see you next year."

"Hope so." He opened the door for her, and Agna stepped out into the wintry dark. She followed the frozen track one step at a time. Passing by the last of the houses, she realized that she'd said *we'll see you next year.* Agna hurried her steps up the hill and back down. It was a polite thing to say, no more. Her replacement would return here next year, no doubt. She didn't have time to think about this. She had to get back and make dinner and tend to Keifon. If the fever held on for four days, they would have to break camp, travel and begin their next camp while he was ill. She would need to hire help.

Agna dragged herself back to the camp and gratefully collapsed to the tent floor. Keifon woke as she came in, pushing himself up on one elbow. He was flushed, and when she stripped off one mitten to feel his forehead, his temperature was still high. "Did you get some rest, at least?"

He shifted away from her touch, avoiding her eyes. "Mmhm. Most of the day. I'm sorry. I'm just...I'm tired."

"No need to apologize. We know about being sick. Don't we?"

That got a weak smile out of him. "Yeah. Um... can I ask you a favor?"

"Of course."

"I'm kind of dizzy. Probably need to eat something. The broth was good, but...could I have some more?"

"Oh! Right." She had forgotten about making dinner for herself, too. At least she hadn't taken her boots off. "I'll go get more from Masa."

"I'll pay." He sat up, reaching for his pack, and Agna stopped him with an arm across the chest.

"Oh no, you don't. Back."

He settled down, sighing. Agna fished her own money bag out of her trunk and picked up the empty crock. It had been a long day. It would be nice to buy dinner for herself, as well, and not have to cook. She could afford a day's indulgence. She set off through the trampled snow to Masa's wagon.

146

When she got back, Keifon was awake and coughing weakly. Agna passed the crock to him. Keifon huddled under his blankets to sip the soup that she had bought. "Thank you. I'm so sorry."

"You can't help it." Agna lit the brazier. Now that she was here to keep an eye on it, they could heat the tent safely. That would do him some good, too. She settled in with her own dinner: Masa's roasted root vegetable casserole. "I saw a few patients with this fever, too. The herbalist in this village said it's been around."

"Don't get sick yourself."

"I'm fine."

"But... please rest tomorrow. At least part of the day." Keifon pulled one of the blankets up around his shoulders. "I'd... I'd like the help, too. If you don't mind. It was hard... moving around and things."

"You were supposed to rest."

"I know, but – you know, getting up to drink, and everything. I was so dizzy it was hard to even sit up. I–" He broke into coughing, and set down his soup. "Look, I don't want to impose on you. But I can't..."

"All right, all right," Agna broke in, sparing him from cataloguing all of his hardships. "The herbalist in town said it was all right if I didn't come back tomorrow, anyway. I'll stay. All right?"

"Yeah. ...Thank you." Keifon sipped the soup, and the two of them finished dinner in silence. There was no question of playing cards tonight. Keifon huddled on his bedroll, drowsing. Agna gathered their dishes and returned to the cold to wash them, then took her kit to the privy and the baths to clean up and change for the night. She returned, shivering, in her pajamas and boots and coat. "Do you need anything else, before we're done for tonight?"

"Um. I think I'm going to skip a bath today. If you don't mind. I don't think I can manage it." The shame in his voice twisted in Agna's stomach.

"Don't worry about it."

"All right. Just... just a minute, then." He got to his feet unsteadily and slipped his cloak and boots on. She almost stopped him before she realized that he was headed to the privy. He would rather freeze than have her escort him, even part of the way.

She warmed her hands against the brazier's heat while she waited. It was strange. He was nakedly concerned about her overworking herself or getting sick. But he didn't seem to want to ask for help, even though both of them were adept at treating medical situations. She supposed that she wouldn't want to ask, either. When the bandits had – when she'd twisted her shoulder, it had been irksome to have anyone help her. It seemed as though things should be different now.

Agna helped Keifon out of his cloak when he returned, although he turned away when she moved to help him pull off his boots. He curled up on his bedroll and muffled his coughing in his pillow. Agna had unrolled her own bedroll while he was gone, and spread her coat over it in lieu of the blankets she had lent to him. It would be cold, but she wouldn't freeze.

Keifon focused on her bedroll as she fastened the tent flaps and doused the brazier. "Wait, no. Don't..." He began to pull one of the blankets from his pile.

"I'm fine. You need it more than I do."

"Don't do this. I can't – I can't argue with you. Just don't."

Agna folded her arms, half a show of determination, half an attempt to keep her hands warm. "I'm fine."

He growled under his breath and braced himself against the ground. "Don't argue with me about this," he said again. "Please don't." He wiped his eyes, and Agna realized with horror how upset he was.

"Hey – hey. It's all right." She helped him lie down and tucked the blankets around him. Keifon laid one arm across his eyes. "Look, I just want you to get better."

"I'm sorry, I can't – I'm tired, and I know I'm not making sense," he whispered thickly. "Just please. Take care of yourself."

"I am. I'm fine."

"You're not going without blankets in the middle of winter! I won't let you do that."

Agna sighed. It was upsetting him this much; she could compromise. "All right. Give me my thick one, but keep the spring one. Is that enough?"

Keifon pinched the bridge of his nose, thinking, and then nodded. "But if you get cold, you need to take another one, or light the burner, or something. Promise me."

His fixation on her welfare kindled a wobbling uneasiness in her middle. She could handle the sickness; she could assess symptoms, administer medicines, and advise him to take fluids and sleep more. But she wasn't prepared for his insistence on protecting her, or the half-incoherent vulnerability of his exhaustion.

She clenched her hands in her lap. "I promise. I won't get too cold."

Keifon peeled off the topmost blanket and held it out to her. She scooted across the tent to accept it. A memory rose in her mind, garbled with old fever dreams. When she was small, her parents had banished Lina to a guest room when Agna was sick – how Lina had wailed! And when Agna had woken up in the night, needing water or air or reassurance that she wasn't being chased by some nightmare beast, someone was there. Her mother, or her father, or Tane the housekeeper – someone was there, and had made it better.

A little dizziness spun her off balance as she gathered the blanket and pulled her bedroll across the tent.

"What are you..." Keifon's eyes were shadowed and panicked in the lamplight.

"Taking care of you. Shh." Agna arranged her bedroll an arm's length away, with the blanket and coat laid out on top. She crawled in under them and blew out the lamp.

"You don't have to."

"I know." She propped herself on one elbow to feel his forehead, and her fingers shook just a little. "Just sleep. It'll be all right."

He murmured sleepily. "I'm sorry I'm so – I just –"

"Shh. It's all right. You're not feeling well, that's all. Sleep."

"Mmn." Keifon curled up on his side. "Thank you." They lapsed into silence. She listened to his breath, close and feather-light and deeply human, and eventually she slept.

■ ■ ■

He woke four or five times in the night, muttering in Yanweian, too exhausted or delirious to translate. Once he clung to her hand and called her a name she didn't recognize – *Maya?* – couched in words she didn't understand. Once, from the husk-dry tone of his voice, she figured out that he needed water and held the cup for him. But most of the time, as soon as she murmured some incoherent reassurance or reached out to lay her cautious hand on his arm, he would sigh and relax into calmer dreams. For a while she would lie awake. But something always lulled her back to sleep. It reminded her of being little, of sleeping curled up with Lina during a thunderstorm, with the furry bulk of the housekeeper's dog lying across the doorway.

She woke free of the fever, but Keifon's cough racked him as soon as he woke. He was still in no shape to go out. Agna rubbed the sleep from her eyes and plotted her plan for the day. She could handle this. But the previous night had shaken her, though she would never admit it to Keifon. When she dealt with patients, she put their bodies in order and sent them on their way. She didn't know how to stay there and be needed continually.

It didn't matter; there were things that needed to be done. She checked that the barrel of drinking water wasn't empty yet, gathered her things, headed out to get dressed, lit the campfire and swept the new snow from their little yard. She could catch up on some sleep herself, do some reading, or write some letters. There wasn't much to draw at this time of year, but she might have a chance to sketch a leafless tree or practice her shading.

They were low on food; they'd planned it that way, buying a little at a time. Agna put together an omelet with onions and cheese for herself and considered what was left as it cooked.

She poked her head into the tent. Keifon squinted against the light, so Agna let the tent flap close behind her. "Hey. Do you think you could handle something solid today? We have some oats and barley. I can cook it down into porridge. Would that be all right?" He laid a hand on his stomach, considered, nodded. Agna rubbed her hands together. "Coming right up."

He wanted water more than anything, and drank a few cups before taking the bowl. But it seemed to fortify him, and by the time they had finished with breakfast, he seemed a little steadier. She insisted that he take some of the medicine for coughs, and he acquiesced, swallowing the thick syrup with more water.

"I'm sorry about last night."

"Hm?" Agna turned at the doorway, hands full of dishes. "...Oh. No, nothing to apologize for. You don't feel well, and your mind gets strange when you're feverish." She paused, remembering one of the fragments. She shouldn't bring it up at all, but her curiosity won out. "Though – what does *Maya* mean?"

Keifon froze. "What — was I – talking in my sleep?"

"A little."

"Oh... I, uh... Mya was a childhood friend of mine."

"I see." Agna wished she wouldn't blush. "That's kind of sweet."

"Did I say anything else?"

"It was all in Yanweian," she shrugged. "I'm sure it was nothing."

"Hm."

She hurried out before he could say any more. When she returned, he didn't resume the conversation, and so she left well enough alone. She lit the brazier and the lamp, positioning her trunk to block the direct light from Keifon's eyes, then sat cross-legged on the tent floor to write her letters. Keifon slept, and after a while his coughing fits seemed less frequent.

She mentioned none of this in her letters, at first. There was no need to worry her family and friends, making them think that she might fall ill herself. She told Rone about the western farmland, wondering whether he'd had a chance to see it during another season. She told Lina about the herbalists in the villages.

She told Laris very little, responding to his last letter, and offering nothing about her own situation. She wrote about how she missed him, trying to be upbeat and affectionate rather than desperate and clinging. She wasn't sure where the line lay, and started over from the beginning when she had written half a page. It was safe enough to say *I wish you were here*. She could not deny the truth of that.

She wrote to Esirel about the bitter winter weather in Kavera, about the snow, about peering into the country homes and helping however she could. Eventually she wrote that Keifon had fallen ill, and that she was taking care of him. *It's strange*, she wrote, and had to stop there. She wrote about the book she'd been reading, instead.

Agna carried the letters to the master of records' wagon. No letters had come in for her. She stopped by a few of the other wagons and tents to buy ingredients for dinner, just enough for tonight and tomorrow morning. She bought bread from Masa, because they could at least eat that on the road, by itself or with some of the cheese she bought from Menon the goatherd. It seemed like a reasonable plan. They would be on the road tomorrow and through the next day, and would reach the next camp the following day if the roads were in good enough condition. By then, Keifon would be nearly recovered. She hoped she could keep him warm enough on the wagon. – One thing at a time.

Lugging her goods in a bag over her shoulder, she stopped by the guards' headquarters and explained her situation. The guard captain listened, nodding gravely, and collared a young guardsman on break inside. Agna thanked them and insisted that they take some extra money. For the first time that day, she felt almost accomplished.

A cloudy dusk had begun to fall when she returned to the camp. She checked on her charge one more time – still asleep – and swept the campsite before lighting the fire. She fed it the rest of their firewood and set about making a simple dinner for the two of them: the last of their grains cooked into a porridge for Keifon, and toasted bread layered with cheese and winter greens for herself. The greens had been expensive, but she had to try to eat healthy things, to stay well through the winter. She would insist that Keifon do the same, as soon as he had recovered enough to eat properly. She brought the food inside when it was ready.

She set Keifon's bowl by his bedroll and touched his arm. "Hey. Dinner." He woke with a start, rubbing his eyes. Agna searched his face for signs of improvement, but he just looked tired and disoriented. "How are you feeling?" In reply, Keifon made a gesture she recognized as *so-so*. Agna laid a hand on his forehead. "About the same, I think." His skin was hot and dry; the fever hadn't broken.

He hauled himself to a sitting position and took the bowl. "Thank you."

"Think nothing of it." Agna settled in and munched contentedly.

Keifon set aside the bowl and spoon when he'd finished and sipped a few cups of water. "I'd like to try to get out to the baths this evening. I'll feel better, I think."

"All right. Anything I can do for you, I will."

"Mmn. Thanks. Just... be patient with me."

Agna looked away. "Of course." She scrambled to her feet to gather their dishes. By the time she returned, he had gotten up and gathered his cloak and a change of clothes. "Are you sure..." Agna's mind stuck and skipped a line. She certainly wouldn't offer to help him with this. "...Be safe. I'll be here."

"Thanks."

She changed into her winter nightgown and read while he was gone. She worried all the while. It wasn't as though the camp were dangerous, normally, and at this hour the bathhouse offered hot water. She worried about him walking out in the cold, and navigating when he seemed so unsteady. But he returned, shivering but otherwise unharmed, sometime later. He'd changed into some of his looser everyday clothes and thick wool socks. He seemed grateful to crawl back into bed.

"I don't think I've seen you sleep this much on the entire trip, combined," Agna remarked, intending for it to be a joke. Keifon laughed weakly. "And don't apologize," she added, as he drew a breath. "I'm glad. You need to take care of yourself."

"Hm. ...I've been thinking. I could do a little better. With that. I try to sleep, I mean, but... getting enough to eat, and things like that. And getting exercise."

Agna nodded. He had seemed healthier in the summer, when he'd been able to take walks and play ball with the others. "We need to be kinder to ourselves." Hurriedly, she went on, "In Nessiny we have a saying, 'the sick doctor heals no one.' It means that if you intend to help other people, you need to stay strong yourself. Sacrificing yourself only goes so far, in the long run."

"Hm."

"So. We can promise to do that."

"Yeah."

She hugged her knees. She could keep reading, or she could sleep. And that meant thinking about logistics. She didn't want to take her extra blanket back. She wasn't sure she could ask him whether he wanted her to stay close again. She wasn't sure how to say it, or how to cope with his answer.

"If you don't want to – you know, it's all right. You can go back to your side."

She focused on him; he wasn't looking at her, turned over toward the wall of the tent. "No, that's...hm." It would be a lie to say she hadn't been thinking about that. But it sounded awful to say that she had been worried about repeating last night's sleeping arrangements. She wasn't afraid of catching the fever. She was afraid of the strange, light feeling in the bottom of her stomach when he had calmed at her words or her touch. She had no name for it. "It..." she began, and had no way to finish.

"...it felt good," he murmured, and Agna's head spun with the sudden rush of relief. *Why?* she demanded of herself. *Why do you feel like that? What's wrong with you?* Because it had been good, in an unnerving sort of way, and she thought it had been her imagination?

She had been quiet too long. Keifon went on. "I liked... I liked having you close. I don't mean that in an untoward way."

"I know it's not like that," Agna said, finding the easy thing, the safe thing, among all of the dangers. "That would be revolting." He didn't answer. "—For you! I meant for you." She was shaking, and hated herself for it. "Obviously."

Keifon turned to face the middle of the tent, his hand half-curled by his chin. He did not look her in the eye. "Please don't make it ugly. It was – it was good. Please let it be good."

Agna blinked back a sudden blur. It was truer than anything she'd said in this labyrinth of a conversation. It had been good. It had been trusting. He needed her, and she wanted to help. Was it that simple? But it wasn't. That was the terrifying part. She wouldn't do the same for any merchant in the camp who fell ill. They would get her clinical expertise, but she wouldn't sit with them through the night. She would do that for – for Nelle, and for Keifon. The parallel struck her in the throat. Nelle called her a friend. Would Keifon do the same? Agna realized that she would call Keifon her friend now. It had been that way for months.

What's wrong with me? She shoved the heels of her hands against her eyes to dash the tears away. "...I'm sorry. You're right. It was good."

He nodded, and shifted to lie on his back. "Thank you. For being there."

You've thanked me more in these two days than the rest of this trip combined, too. They were both still. And then she blew out the lantern.

She unrolled her bedroll an arm's length away, with the medicine and water glasses and lantern nearby. On a sudden impulse, she leaned over and smoothed his hair. She wasn't checking his temperature this time. It was only a moment of contact, to let him know that everything was all right. She escaped to her own pillow.

"Good night."

"Mmn. Good night. ...I just... I wanted to explain." He turned over in the dark to face her. "I'm sorry I'm so... strange about the cold." He fell quiet, marshaling something. "I...had a bad winter, a few years ago. After Eri. Before Kazi. I'd lost the ranch, and I was out on the street for a while. I thought I was going to die. Or lose something to frostbite. I almost did, a few times. I was playing the nanbur for money, so I was worried about my fingers." He laughed mirthlessly. "I still think about it a lot, during the winter. So I'm sorry if I'm strange about it."

"It's all right," Agna said, and rushed on, panicking. "I mean, that you're worried. It's all right to be worried. Not what happened to you, that's awful." Her mind whirled through all of this, but failed to piece it together with the other scraps she knew. It was beyond anything she had ever faced. "I'm glad you're out of that situation now."

"Yeah. The Church picked me up. Or I would have frozen to death."

Agna found his hands folded together in the space between their bedrolls and covered them with her own. Keifon lifted their hands to his burning forehead.

"I'm so glad you didn't," she tried to say, but her voice failed her, thinning out to a whisper. "You're safe now. I won't let it happen again."

Keifon pressed his flushed cheek against the back of her hand. His breath hitched, and for one terrible second Agna thought she would cry herself. But his voice was clear when he spoke. "And I won't let it happen to you."

"I know. Sleep, now."

"Yes."

They slept through the second night in fragments. Agna dreamed of dark winter nights full of terrible and strange things. She dreamed of a warm place and kind words, and the sweet inner fire of knowing that she was cared for and safe. When she woke, Keifon lay half off his bedroll, head pillowed on his arm, his fingers tangled in her sleeve. Agna's pulse hammered in her throat, but her panic was superseded by a coughing fit.

Keifon stirred and sat up, alarmed. "No..."

"It's all right." She groped for a cup of water. "I don't think I'm running a fever."

"I didn't at first, either," Keifon fretted. He touched her forehead, brushing her hair away. "I can't tell. I'm too warm, I guess."

"Well. I asked the guards if someone could help us pack up. They're sending Zil this morning. So all we have to do is get dressed and ride."

Keifon squirmed out of his blankets and began to fold them. "Ah. Good. Good thinking."

Agna watched him critically. "How are you feeling?"

He shrugged. "I can't get warm. Not as bad, but not well."

"Well, stay wrapped up. We just have to get you to the wagon, and you can rest till we reach the next camp."

He finished his stack of blankets, keeping the thickest one aside, and rolled up his bedroll. "You need to rest, too."

Agna shoved her bedroll into her trunk. "I will. If you can help me pack, we can make this work."

The two of them got their possessions in order, dressed in the warmest clothes they could find, and made last-minute errands. Zil, the young guardsman, appeared amid the camp-breaking chaos and hauled Agna's trunk to the passenger wagon. Agna and Keifon dismantled the tent, and Zil returned in time to help them pack it up. They bundled themselves in their cloaks and coats and blankets, and hobbled toward their destination. Zil met them on their way; Agna thanked him and pressed another coin into his hand. She didn't have the energy to fight his polite protests. He fled when she began coughing.

The few travelers riding on the wagon gave the pair a wide berth. Keifon propped himself on the bench, wrapped in a blanket. Agna considered this, then slid to the far edge of the bench. "Come on."

"Hm?"

She patted her knee, as though summoning a cat, and darted a sidewise look in time to see Keifon blush. But he folded up on the bench, pulling the blanket over himself and pillowing his head on her lap. Agna considered propping her arm on the back of the bench, and experimentally rested her hand on his shoulder instead. He sighed, and she felt him relax. Perhaps it hadn't been the worst idea in the world, after all.

■ ■ ■

Agna woke from a half-doze, coughing. Keifon sat up. "No... no, no. I'm so sorry. I didn't want you to get sick, too."

"Can't be helped." She looked around; it was midday, at least, and the snow had stopped. "I guess if we're both sick, we'll just have to help each other."

"Mmn." He cleared his throat, fumbled the flask out of its laces on the side of his backpack, and took a drink. "Did you want to lie down for a while?"

"I guess that would be good," Agna admitted. The movement of the wagon made her dizzy. Keifon shifted in his seat, bundling up, and let her lie on the bench with her blanket over her and her head in his lap. It did feel good to lie down, and to feel his hand on her arm. She felt safe. Protected. She could let him handle this for a while.

Keifon: Teamwork

The guard that Agna had hired reappeared when the caravan touched down. Keifon stumbled down the aisle of the wagon to help Zil with the tent, to haul the ropes with shaking arms, to stifle his own cough and try to stay upright. Agna had taken such good care of him. He had to come through for her now, even if he wasn't quite ready for it.

By the time the tent was constructed and Zil vanished, Keifon had run out of energy. He had intended to get some food, and refill their water barrel. He had intended to get a stake and a board to make a sign explaining the closed clinic. He had intended to get Agna anything that she needed. But when Agna rolled out her bedroll and collapsed, fully dressed, Keifon surrendered and did the same.

He woke out of a distressing, nonsensical dream – trying to post the sign for the clinic and feeling it slip through his hands, over and over. There was someone outside the tent. He fumbled at the ties and stuck his head out, squinting against the sunset. Nelle, the herbalist, turned away from their larder chest and gave him a guilty smile. "Hey, you."

Keifon's head reeled, and he inched out of the tent and pulled his body into a sitting position. The ground was too far away. Nelle held out something toward him. He took it, and the next thing she offered, and stared at them. A dark medicine bottle. A cup of water. He drank the water first, then a slug of the medicine; it was sweet and thick, coating his throat. Nelle took the bottle and cup and stowed them in the chest.

"How are you feeling?"

"Nnn. Not good."

"How's she?"

"She's starting to come down with it too. I'm coming out of it, though. I can take care of her."

"Good." She closed the lid of the larder chest. "Brought you some things. Shouldn't have to cook them. Bread and such. If you need anything else, yell. All right?"

"Mmn. – Maybe another blanket or two. For her."

Nelle flashed him a wicked little grin. "For either of you, all right? Be right back."

Keifon curled up where he sat, huddled into his cloak, conserving his energy. He wondered whether Edann had noticed that he was sick. He wouldn't show up anyway; he liked to pretend that Keifon meant nothing to him. Or perhaps he wasn't pretending. Keifon was too tired to think about it.

Nelle brought three woolen blankets, and Keifon swayed to his feet to accept them. "Thank you. You didn't have to..."

"Yeah, I did." She stooped and lifted their water barrel. "Move a little." Keifon shifted out of her way as she carried it into the tent. He reconsidered his notion of carrying their food inside. He could hardly hold himself upright. He heard Nelle's voice inside, hushed and soothing. "Hey, city girl. It's me. Keep sleeping." Keifon smiled to himself. Nelle re-emerged and carried the larder chest inside as well.

"All set. Take care of yourselves. We'll need you soon. You're not the only ones."

"I'm sorry. I... brought it back from one of our patients."

"Tch. Things happen. Rest up." Nelle rounded the cold campfire, tracing her own tracks through the snow. Keifon fled to the relative warmth of the tent and forced his nerveless fingers to fasten the flaps tight.

Keifon unfolded two of the blankets over Agna and the third over his own bedroll, then crawled under the covers and let his body go slack. Agna murmured in her half-sleep, turning over. Something pressed against his throat and around his heart, something thin-skinned and delicate like a newly hatched bird. It wasn't right. It was too right. It fit into a void that wasn't supposed to be there. He fell asleep, dreaming of snow and the bitter taste of herbs, and Agna and Nelle reaching out for his hands.

■ ■ ■

Shivering in the early morning cold, Keifon took a long drink from the barrel. He directed his feet to the bottom of his boots, wrapped his cloak around his body, and tottered out to the privy and back. The camp had begun to stir, but everyone he passed gave him an inordinate amount of space. The cough wasn't so bad today, and from what Agna had heard from the townspeople, his fever should break any day now. But to keep it from spreading, he would be better off sticking to the tent until he was completely well. He could take care of Agna and wait. The thought appealed to him as he trudged along the path to their tent in the gray dawn. He would enjoy the quiet for another day or so. He would have to make the rounds out there soon enough, and survey how far the fever had spread in the camp. He hoped that Nelle wouldn't fall ill after coming to help them.

Agna called from the tent as he reached out to the flap. "Wait a minute!"

"All right." He pulled his cloak closer around his shoulders. "What's wrong?"

"Just getting changed. – All right, come in."

Keifon ducked into the tent as Agna huddled under the covers. She had changed from her traveling clothes into her winter nightgown.

"Thanks for the water," she said as Keifon fastened the flaps.

"Nelle brought it. And some more blankets, and food, and medicine. You should take some." He fumbled in the chest and found the bottle of cough medicine. She grumbled when he helped her sit up, but she swallowed the medicine all the same and dove back under the covers.

"Thanks." Her voice was muffled by the layers of blankets. "You should change. More comfortable."

"Nn. Not making you go out."

"'m not gonna look. Do what you want."

Keifon was tempted by the thought of changing into fresh clothes. "Are you sure?"

Agna pulled the blanket over her head. Keifon stripped off his traveling clothes, shoved his shivering body into clean pajamas, and crawled under his covers.

She emerged. "See? Better."

"...Yeah." He took a deep breath. "Hey. You're sure you're all right with this?"

"Hm?"

"I mean..." Keifon searched for the right words for so long that Agna's breath deepened into sleep. He never found the right way to say it. *I'm honored to get to take care of you. I know you hate being vulnerable, and when you trust me to see you like this, I...*

I feel like I matter to you.

Keifon half-dreamed of the sun-warmed fields, sitting on a fence rail, sharing pilfered apples with his first and dearest friend. She laughed with him, and he trusted her with his life, and he would never see her again. Mya was gone, disappeared into the machinery of apprenticeships and inheritance. She had changed him. And he had kept changing after she had gone. But she would recognize him now, he thought. This part of him was still good.

■ ■ ■

In the morning, Keifon fed Agna and himself with bread that Nelle had given them, spread with a paste that the Kaverans ate on their toast, made of crushed nuts mixed with spices. The texture was strange, but it sated their hunger. They drank cup after cup of water, took doses of Nelle's medicine, and fell insensate. Somewhere between the second and third cycle of sleep and half-wakefulness, he realized that he was drenched in sweat, and that his space under the blankets no longer felt freezing cold. He struggled out from under the tangle of covers and felt the chilled air on his skin, but no longer inside his bones, trying to get out. The fever was passing through him.

He burrowed under the covers, throwing one over onto Agna's pile. Soon he would be able to move around, have a bath and a badly needed shave, make some hot tea, and cook something. If he could stay awake for more than a few minutes, he could light the brazier.

It wasn't a matter of indebtedness, even though Agna had taken care of him uncomplainingly for those first days. He wanted to do this – to watch over her and help her. It was another fragile thing, not ready for light and air. It had threaded deep into his marrow and soaked his dreams. He needed to do this, even though he wasn't sure he deserved the honor. She was only his partner as defined by the Benevolent Union. This new closeness was an anomaly. They did what they had to because of the sickness. When they were both well, they would go back to the routine.

His sleep was deep, and his dreams were as ordered as any dreams. He woke for the last time and got back to work.

Agna: Strategy

They played sevens after dinner, warming their hands over the brazier between turns, careful not to singe the cards. Agna railed about a certain patient and the nerve that might lead one to insult two representatives of the Benevolent Union in their hearing. His views were becoming antiquated, anyway; in the cities everyone accepted that the Benevolent Union employed agents from all countries and all faiths.

Keifon did not return her ire, picking his cards calmly, and before long she ran out of momentum. There were more interesting things to talk about, anyway. She wouldn't let that old fool waste any more of her attention.

"The decorations were nice," she offered at last.

"Mmn. They were."

"Do they decorate like that in Yanwei? The pine boughs seem more fitting for Eytra than Tufar." The Feast of Eytra lined up with New Year's, on the other hand, and by that time of year, there were other plants and flowers to use as decoration.

Keifon rearranged his hand. "We do use pine if we can afford it. It all has to be shipped in from the southwest, though. Usually it's paper chains and things like that for the Golden Anniversary."

"Which is the anniversary of... bringing the idea of writing to mortals?"

"Yes." He was smiling a little. "I think you'd rather like Tufarian scholarship, if you wanted to read any."

"I may, someday. I did read a little in school, but just the basics."

After three rounds, Agna had won two, and Keifon capitulated to the terms of clearing the snow off the campsite for the next two days. The tent had grown cozy, and Agna shed her blanket from her shoulders.

"Do you mind if I practice for a while?" Keifon's hand lay on the lute case.

"Go ahead," Agna shrugged. She basked over the brazier, luxuriating in the warmth at the tips of her fingers. She had the beginnings of a sketch in her case; that would be a pleasant way to pass the rest of the evening. And she could feel her fingers. That always helped.

Agna unpacked her drawing materials as Keifon pulled out the lute. She twiddled a pencil as she looked over the sketch and considered the next steps. Keifon cradled his instrument in his lap, adjusting the screws on the neck. He plucked one string and leaned his ear toward the lute, listening for some change that Agna couldn't hear. Agna was reminded of Lina, squinting at some bit of glassware – or even the Blackhall doctors, with their beloved gadgets.

"Sorry."

"Hm?" Agna looked up from the sketch.

Keifon clicked his tongue fretfully. "It's kind of out of tune. The cold, I think."

"Oh." She wondered why he'd apologized. "That's bad?"

"Nn. Fixable. Not good, over the long term." His hand spread over the belly of the instrument. "Changes in temperature and humidity can warp the wood over time. It can't be helped, right now. I worry. That's all."

"I see."

His attention shifted back to the strings and his careful testing, if that was the proper word for it. Agna doubted it was the right word. Tuning, she thought. He'd said it was out of tune. She strengthened the main lines, warming up her hand. Keifon's repetitive pings began to melt into something flowing and cohesive. Apparently he had fixed the problem.

Agna watched his fingers on the strings, forgetting herself. Keifon paid no attention to her, absorbed in concentration and in the intricate patterns of muscle memory. And expression, she supposed. It was an art. There were no words to this song, and so she didn't know what he meant to say through the music. But his expression and his posture were relaxed.

Agna reset her grip on the pencil, letting the sound flow through her. She tried to relax the muscles in her neck. Would he be offended if he realized how little she understood? She didn't mind that he wasn't interested in art. It was difficult to explain things to him sometimes, but she didn't take it as an affront. Maybe it was the same in this case. She hoped he wouldn't mind if she watched him at his craft. She didn't mind when he watched her draw.

The music stopped, hanging on the air until the piles of blankets soaked it up. Keifon looked up, and Agna was ready with a smile. "That was lovely."

"Thank you. I learned it from Baran at the bonfire a while back. It's a Kaveran lullaby."

Agna imagined the mountainous toymaker crooning a lullaby to Keifon, and hid a smirk in her hand. It was a sweet image, for all that. "You've picked up a lot of Kaveran songs at this point, then?"

"Hmn, a few. Half a dozen that I can remember by rote. I'd like to learn more." He returned to the lute, lacing the quiet with light, sweet notes. Agna sketched some more contours to bring the rock and stream into relief, and outlined the first shadows before reaching for her charcoal. The brazier's heat glowed all along her side. She paused to tuck her blanket around her feet.

It was nice, working in parallel like this. They each had separate pursuits, and each didn't fully understand the other, but Agna felt a sense of camaraderie, of shared creativity. It was a private thing, this space that they had built and shared. She felt welcome here, and calm, and safe.

If it would be like this from now on, it wouldn't be so bad. The ground under her was as hard as it had ever been, the wind was cold outside, and she was sick beyond death of root vegetables and dried mushrooms. She and Keifon got tired and hungry and cold, snapped at one another sometimes, and grumbled about the chores they'd wagered over cards. But they still played, and they did what needed to be done. They shared the burden, and over time, day to day life had ceased to be an uphill battle.

That was why she had decided to renegotiate her contract in Vertal, after all, she recalled. It wasn't the mission, and it wasn't the patients. It was the stupid feud with Keifon, and the everyday slog of chores and cooking and living out of a tent. She had become used to most of that over time. And so there was no reason to stop now.

A little chill, unrelated to the cold, prickled down her back. She didn't have to leave.

She wasn't sure whether this mission represented the greatest need, as the Church of the Divine Balance would define it. But it was an immediate need, and she knew that she was equal to the task. She was of real use on this mission. Her skills and her knowledge were valued and needed. She and Keifon couldn't help everyone in every circumstance. But they were doing good things for the people out there. She had learned more than she ever dreamed, and continued to learn every day. She had met more people than she ever knew existed in the world. She had, after long bouts of stupidity, found a new friend.

And more than that, she thought. A familiar flutter in her middle heralded the memory of Laris. She could visit him again when the caravan came past Laketon. And she could tell him that she'd stuck it out, that she was resourceful and resolute.

What would Rone have done? He would have done what he was told, of course. He would see the need for the Church's help, and do whatever he could. But Agna wasn't Rone, either. She wasn't a true servant of the Church. Rone might accept turnips and lumpy ground and cold feet and ungrateful patients in the service of the Church. Agna would complain, and then rebel.

She had beaten the cold, after all. She had strategized and budgeted, even with the restrictions of her limited income, and now she and Keifon slept warm every night. She could tackle the other things that held her back. And then there would be no question that staying would be worth it.

Sleeping was one thing. She didn't sleep as well as she liked out here. She had gotten used to the bedroll most of the time, but there had to be an alternative. She had seen other arrangements, glimpsed in the doorways of the merchants' tents. Edann had a feather mattress in his cart – that would be too bulky to wrangle as they packed up. Nelle had a bed that folded against the wall, which would only work in an enclosed wagon. Still...

"Looks like it's going well."

Agna's spiral of machinations halted. The tent was quiet. Keifon had leaned over to look at her sketch. She focused; the shading wasn't too bad for having been drawn semi-consciously. "Oh. I guess so. – I was thinking about something else, actually."

"Hm. Must be inspiring."

Agna set her charcoal down, and then set the lap desk aside. "I was thinking. Do you think it would be too difficult to pack up and move those folding cot frames, like Vociel makes? The ones that work kind of like the clinic chairs, with canvas."

"Too difficult for... who? Whom?"

"For us. I'm thinking about getting better equipment. It would be a good investment."

Keifon hesitantly put his lute down. "Uh... I'm not sure I agree. It's only for a few months."

"Oh – well – I was thinking about staying on. So do you think we could pack up and move them?"

"W-wait, wait. Here, with – with the caravan?"

"Yeah. I have another year on my contract."

"...Oh. I... that's... that's great. I didn't know you were considering that." He kneaded the back of his neck – the muscles, not the torque, Agna noticed. "Um, so I don't think that a cot frame would be too heavy. It might be a little – what's the word I mean. Unwieldy. It'd take up a lot of space on the wagon, too. But if you want to, we can make it work."

"Do you think they'd fit under the seats?"

"Hmm. Probably."

"That might work, then." Agna nibbled a fingernail. "I'll talk to Vociel before we head out. Just for a bit. I don't know what she charges for them."

"Mmn."

"And if you don't want to spend the money, that's all right, but I think it would be good for both of us to sleep better. Besides, I'd feel weird if you were still on the ground." Agna laughed unconvincingly, realizing as she did that Keifon wasn't following the conversation. "...What is it?"

Keifon hunched up, hugging his knees. "I just... I have to soak this in for a minute. That's all."

"What..."

He didn't look at her, talking into his crossed arms. "I mean, all this time, I always had to remind myself that you'd be gone soon. Work together, but don't... And I just... we have another chance, now. That's... I don't want to waste that."

Agna was sure that her face was hotter than the burning charcoal in the brazier. "Well... it's worth it," she fumbled. "We're helping people." He hadn't been talking about the mission. He didn't sound like that when he talked about the mission. But it was the one safe path that she could find. Agna ran back toward her original track of thought, before he had detoured into these uncertain thickets. "I was thinking about improving our standard of living for the next year. You see what I mean?"

He unknotted his posture, settling into his relaxed position. "Yes. Bed frames."

"Right. And... maybe cooking. Not that your cooking is bad! Just that I think I could learn some more variety. I just know how to make a few things. And a more varied diet would be good for us."

"Hmm. That's a good point."

"So... I guess I'll ask around, see what everyone else does, get some ideas. Or...oh! Do you think there are books about campfire cooking?"

Keifon returned her smile. "I bet there are."

Agna wiggled in her nest of blankets. "And then it'll hardly be like camping at all. Except for the bugs, and carrying everything we own, and everything else, but still..." Hearing him laugh compounded her excitement. They would work together and make things better. They were good at that, she and Keifon. She was beginning to look forward to the second year.

Keifon: The Tourist

Keifon cut through Prisa's Foreign Quarter and into the neighboring district. A few more questions, posed to street-corner vendors and lounging elders in porchside rocking chairs, led him to the church.

The Church of Darano in the Meadowside neighborhood was as outwardly stolid as a hospital or a school. A series of signs led him through the dim corridors inside to the sanctuary. A small group of men and women gathered with a priest at the front of the sanctuary, discussing scriptures, and a few solitary worshippers were scattered among the rest of the benches. Keifon passed them to make his offering and kneel at the altar.

After a brief prayer, he found a seat and paged through the Kaveran prayer book slotted in the back of the next bench. The words were unfamiliar, the names of the gods spelled in strange letters, but the meanings behind them were the same. The foreign prayers and Kaveran faces on the statues did not change the gods' true natures. They were here, he reminded himself, just as much as they were in Yanwei. They were everywhere, they were all, and they watched over him. They still heard his prayers.

He hadn't visited a Daranite church since the Feast of the Resurrection, the better part of a year ago. He had prayed enough since he'd come to Kavera. Most of the time. It was best to visit churches when he could, though, to hear the priests speak and to stay in touch with other believers. That had been difficult. He had never been much inclined to carry out those obligations back home, either. He had found solace in private prayer. He had studied the scriptures and reflected on them until he understood as well as he could. To face other people was less comforting.

He replaced the book. Yanwei was far away now, despite the glimpses of familiar script in some of the store windows in the Foreign Quarter. He was in Kavera now, as the itinerant medic of the Benevolent Union as well as the infantryman of the Yanweian National Army. He was both of these things, in layers, and whether or not he could return home when it was over, he would carry this time with him. It had begun to change him, to bend his growth. The people of Kavera and the experiences that he'd had here had changed him. Agna had changed him. Edann had changed him. Being away from home had changed him. Kazi had said that this assignment would be good for him. He had been right, in the end.

The thought of Kazi cut through him, but he kept breathing. It was the echo of pain – beginning to be a scar, not a wound. Or a scab, at least. The thought of this sent panic crowding into his throat, and he pulled his hand away from the torque and tightened his fingers in Darano's prayer sign. Kazi was beginning to be a part of his past, not a missing part of his present. Keifon let this thought fill him. He let the fear come, and let it fail to slay him. He wasn't going to see Kazi again. He would never listen to one of Kazi's political harangues in an inn room with the fire blazing behind him. He would never catch Kazi's private smile from across the barracks. Keifon had to live without him. He was beginning to think that he could.

Darano wasn't the proper god to address on the topic of heartbreak, even though Keifon and Kazi were dedicated to Darano's service. Keifon prayed for strength instead, and for the clarity of judgment to find the right course. The gods had sent him here for a reason, and he would trust them to guide him until he found and fulfilled his purpose. He wasn't merely running from Kazi, obeying Kazi's order. He had found too much meaning here to reduce his assignment to that.

Keifon left the church and walked south, at right angles to the campsite. He had a few hours till nightfall. He could visit Edann, though Edann would probably seek out one of the bars in Prisa, and he knew that Keifon would not join him. They had found such understandings in their intricately circumscribed relationship. Keifon wasn't sure he was in the right frame of mind tonight, in any case. He wanted to talk about the upcoming year, and Edann resisted talking about the future or his feelings. He would talk about politics or books or the other people in the caravan, but he would always carve out that circle of silence at their center.

Agna would talk if he wanted to talk. She would listen, and do her best to understand. That was another new aspect of his life. He seemed to have won the respect that he'd craved so badly. He'd won Agna's trust, trading it for his own, though it had terrified him at first to do so.

And now she would stay for another year. He tried not to think of it as staying *with him* for another year. She was re-dedicating herself to the cause. That was all. But the thought warmed him. They worked well together now, and he enjoyed her company, their card games and their conversations. Maybe someday they would grow to be friends. It wasn't a preposterous idea anymore.

On the way through the Foreign Quarter, Keifon browsed through a few book stores and looked over clothes and camping gear. He went back to the campsite empty-handed and at peace.

Agna: Celebration

The Foreign Quarter was rather charming, Agna decided. She had meandered through the bookstores and spice shops and clothiers until her feet ached. Now, stretched out in the tent with the lamp at her head and one of her new books in hand, she could rest and reflect.

Perhaps it was worth examining the fact that Prisa had a Foreign Quarter at all – Murio had plenty of immigrants, but it didn't have one place to put them all. A lot of Islanders lived on Shortrun Road, and what Yanweians they had lived way past the river, but they didn't have to. ...She was probably overthinking it. Surely foreigners didn't have to live in the Foreign Quarter. Still, it was a little worrying, even though it made it convenient to shop for Nessinian spices and books. She hoped that Keifon would find something to his liking there. ·

He came back without having bought anything, disappointing Agna's curiosity, but insisted that he'd had a good day out. "Have you eaten yet?"

Agna shrugged. "Nah. Had lunch out, but not dinner. In a bit, I think."

"Mmn. Hang on." He vanished, and Agna resumed her book on Kaveran history.

Keifon returned with a dark glass bottle and two crocks of food, wrapped in linen napkins. Without comment, he uncorked the bottle, filled their cups, and handed one to her. His mouth was set in a little half-smile, and Agna felt herself echoing it.

"What's..." Agna tasted the drink; it was blackberry juice, not wine. Keifon passed her one of the crocks. She settled it in her lap and pulled the lid off. It was full of one of Masa's specialties, baked rice mixed with vegetables and spices. The food steamed against the air, and her stomach growled. Keifon took his share, made the signs of the gods over it, and fell quiet, smiling to himself. Agna started over. "What's this all about?"

Keifon glanced at her and away, as if embarrassed. "Just a – a celebration." She began to ask why, but he had gone on. "Thank you for this past year. I know it's a week or two early, but... I wanted to mark the occasion."

Agna pinched the corners of her eyes. She wanted to cry, and to punch him, and to hug him. What else was new? She drank some more of the juice, as if thirst would explain the rasp in her voice. "You're welcome. It's worth celebrating. Thank you."

It was good to see him happy. She picked up her fork and savored the first forkful of rice, distracting herself. "This is good. We should get it more often."

She couldn't watch his reaction. She was too close to breaking, one way or the other. But she heard enough in his voice to understand. "Mm. We should."

Agna: Balance

I've only been here once in my life, Agna insisted.

Vertal appeared against the distant line of the sea: church spires and houses and shops and a thicket of ships' masts. Somewhere among them was the world headquarters of the Benevolent Union. The caravan would stay for five days, and the merchants would rush the docks, making deals with the importers and exporters in their warehouses and offices. They would trade cattle for silks, ores for wood, goods for money, money for goods, and promises for promises. Agna remembered passing through the docks, flouncing around the money-changers' office, already impatient with everything Kavera had to offer. It had been a lifetime ago.

Ahead lay another year of this – the patrol station, Prisa, the mining country festival, Laketon, Wildern, and all of the villages and homesteads between them. Another turn of the seasons, through rain and heat and bitter cold. More time to learn, to write letters, to meet the people of this land she'd been sent to help, and to do what she could.

Beside her the Yanweian was calm, his arm cradling the lute case that sat on the bench between them. He caught her glance and smiled fractionally. Another year of this, too.

"So – would you be interested in dinner, after we've settled in? It's a gift," she added.

"Hm. All right."

"Such enthusiasm. I said I'd buy you dinner, not break your arm."

"I have a lot to do in town, that's all," he retorted, but he seemed to have understood that she was joking.

"So do I. We have five days, though. Surely that's enough time to enjoy yourself a little."

"Yes, it should be."

"I can't even imagine sleeping in a real bed again. Maybe I'll just sleep for five days. Or, no – twelve hours of sleep and twelve hours soaking in the baths, five times over. They have hot water *all the time.* – What?"

He stifled his snickering and waved it off. "Nothing."

"So, do you have any plans?"

"Hn. It's time I had a checkup. And I would like to see the cathedrals, at least one or two of them."

"I'm sure they're lovely. I think I'll find a bookstore. Wayron has been a lifesaver, and that history book that I got in Prisa is good, but I'd like to look anyway."

"I see." He was quiet. "If you do find something, could you tell me where? If you don't mind."

"I might. Or I might bring you along. If you don't mind."

"Oh. – Yes, that – thank you."

She rushed on, thrown a little off balance by his flattered reaction. "You can keep me from buying so many books that we can't lift them."

Keifon smirked. "'We'?"

"Yes, well." She fidgeted with the strap on her trunk, curling it around her fingers. "I'm going to take care of my business with the Union first, if you want to visit your cathedrals." Before she'd left Vertal the first time, she had been instructed to turn in her logbook for review so that the administrative agents could settle out her pay. She had barely listened, back then.

When the wagon stopped, Agna felt a strange dizziness, as though the ground had turned to water under her. For so long she had dreamed of returning to Vertal so that she could storm into the Benevolent Union base, demand justice, and claim her right to a more important mission. Now, it was melancholy to think of the caravan moving on without her. If she could have told herself then that she would stay on this assignment for a second year, she would never have believed it. Agna shook the thought off and gathered her luggage.

The home base of the Benevolent Union was still the largest building Agna had seen since setting foot in Kavera. In the entry lounge, the agents clustered around a pair of their fellows, engaged in a chess game.

"Names and affiliations?"

"Agna Despana, Church of the Divine Balance."

"Keifon the Medic, Yanweian National Army."

"Healers from the spring merchants' caravan, correct?" Agna and Keifon chorused their affirmatives. They each accepted a key and their directions from the agent.

"May I turn in my records here?" Agna lifted her logbook.

The receptionist slid the drawer of keys shut and locked it. "You may."

Agna tossed her book onto the receptionist's counter, and Keifon did the same with his. The receptionist whisked them behind the counter. "Thank you. You'll be contacted when the review is complete."

"Thank you," Keifon said. He picked up one end of Agna's trunk, and together they carried it to the second floor.

They followed the directions and their key fobs to their assigned rooms, which were next to one another. Agna wheeled the trunk into her room and parked it at the foot of the bed, then popped back out into the hall. She leaned through the doorframe into Keifon's room as he situated his belongings. "I think I'll have a bath first. No laughing. Meet you back here in an hour?"

"All right. I'll be here. I'm going to lie down for a bit."

"Rest well." She retrieved some clean clothes and her bath kit and ran down the stairs toward the baths. They would have tile floors, not wooden slats over mud. And real walls. It would be warm, even steamy. Agna sighed and looked over the paintings and framed parchment along the walls of the hallway. Illuminated commendations and proclamations jumbled next to engraved plaques and paintings of other bases, other projects, other teams of agents. The memory of Wildern's base chilled her mood, and her gaze dropped to the red wool carpet, worn smooth by foot traffic.

In the baths, Agna basked in the steam as she washed, then soaked in the tile tub with her head pillowed on the edge. Her mind wandered back to the Wildern base. She could make a visit to a certain address in Vertal, during her free time. Maybe. But she had decided to stay for another year, and no one would convince her to change that course. The only thing that might change her mind was if the shrine at Laketon had an opening. But even then, Laris would be out of town for several months on his cattle drive. Agna knocked her head softly against the edge of the tub. She couldn't win. All she could do was hold out, and hope that their paths merged again. The thought made her stomach jitter.

She had relived her meeting with Laris over and over and refined it in retrospect, thinking of a thousand things she should have said and done. She dreamed about turning up on his doorstep the next time the caravan passed Laketon. That imaginary meeting was rather... creative. Agna glanced around the bathhouse to make sure she was alone, embarrassed even in her solitude.

But it was more difficult to imagine living in Laketon. The priests and swordmaster at the Laketon shrine had seemed kind enough; she could almost imagine working for them as a healer. Still, as much as Laris loved his town, she wondered whether her lukewarm acceptance of it would disappoint him. And she couldn't wrap her mind around the concept of Laris in Murio. It simply didn't work.

They had time to work it out, she reminded herself. They were young, and as the Church of the Divine Balance said, the world was full of promise.

■ ■ ■

"You know," Agna mused, "I had a bookcase this size at home, in my room." She marked out the height over their heads and as far as her arms would stretch from side to side against the polished oak shelf. "All for me. And..." She shrugged. "It was just there. And now it's exciting to even think about going from seven to eight books in my collection."

"Hm." Keifon slid a book back onto the shelf. This one was thin, bound in fawn-colored cardboard. "In the barracks, my footlocker was half full of them. I had to keep my valise under my bed, because of that and the nanbur." He smiled a little, remembering.

Agna pulled another book from the shelf. "In my head, I think I was only packing for the crossing to Vertal."

"You didn't know you'd be on the road," he said, scanning along the titles, his fingertips brushing the spines.

"True, but I knew that I wouldn't be home again for a long time." She wasn't seeing anything on the pages of the book in her hands. "Though it's longer for you. I can't complain."

Keifon shrugged. "I sold everything that I couldn't take. I only left people behind. And they all knew that I'd be away for a long time. That was... that was the point of it."

Agna made a vague noise of understanding. He would plunge into melancholy if he kept talking about Kazi, even indirectly. She cleared her throat and shelved the unread book. "Well. It doesn't seem so long to me now. I'm enjoying some of it."

That got a small chuckle. "Some of it. Right."

"I think I'll stick with the history book that I got in Prisa," she remarked. "I have a long way to go with it. I did want to look, though. I hope you don't mind."

"Not at all." He put another book back and scanned along the shelves. Agna thought of offering to buy whatever he chose. That wouldn't go over so well. Besides, he might take it as a sign of impatience, and she didn't want to rush. The masses of paper and leather and cloth seemed to absorb all sound, and she was content to read through the titles and wait for Keifon to finish his search. They'd paused in a section full of politics and economics and sociological studies; behind them was poetry, epic on one end, lyric on the other.

Agna paged through one of the collections of lyric poetry as Keifon reached the end of the political section. Even these unfamiliar writers and their unfamiliar forms recalled her studies at the Academy, practicing for her final presentation in oratory. She remembered reading aloud as Esirel lay on her bunk, eyes closed, listening raptly.

She became aware of Keifon's gaze on her and snapped the book shut. She slid it onto the shelf more roughly than it deserved.

"Do you like that kind of thing?"

She fidgeted, straightening her skirts. "I read a bit at the Academy for my literature classes, and for practice in oratory. I prefer fiction and history, but it's all right sometimes."

"Oratory, really." It seemed to amuse him, not unkindly. He looked over the poetry shelf. "I've played for you. Will you read for me sometime?"

Agna almost tripped over her words. "I – that's – I suppose I could. There's no reason to, but..." He was smiling. Agna crossed her arms and leaned against the political bookcase. She wasn't angry, merely embarrassed, and she couldn't even define why that was so.

Keifon sidled off to a more distant section, and she let him go. Maybe they had adult books here. She didn't want to embarrass him, after all. She wandered in another direction until she heard him settling with the bookseller. Keifon slipped sideways to block her view as she came up behind him. "Do you mind?"

"I just wondered whether you'd gotten something I might want to borrow."

The bookseller finished wrapping his purchase in paper, and Keifon relaxed. "Hm," he said – not an answer – and accepted the package, thanking the proprietor. It was not a very large package, probably a single book. He slipped it under his arm as they left the shop.

The book shop was part of a cozy shopping district; the receptionist at the base had recommended it for dinner as well as for book shopping. "I'm hungry," Agna remarked. "The agent mentioned that place on the right, there, the Three Oaks. What do you think?"

"That's fine. Whatever you like."

"All right, then." She headed for the tavern at the corner, irritated a little by his noncommittal response. At least he kept up with her.

The front wall of the Three Oaks was lined with windows, allowing a clear view from the street. At this hour it was quiet, half filled with diners and drinkers, who seemed to be absorbed in private conversations. Agna turned back to Keifon, who nodded. They went in together.

The host found them a little table in the corner, and brought drinks and a napkin-draped bowl as they decided what to order. Agna peeked under the napkin; it was full of salted crackers. In the taverns in Murio the usual offering had been pickled capers. She tasted one and insisted that Keifon do the same. He obeyed, not answering. He'd set his book on the table at his elbow.

"You're ruining my good mood, you know," she declared. "You owe me nothing for dinner, and I don't want you acting as though you've done me some horrible wrong because of it."

"Hm."

Agna raised her menu between them and drank a little of the punch she'd ordered. Keifon had gotten water, and it seemed awkward to order wine or cider alone – so she had tried some house specialty, a concoction of fruit juice and herbs. It was too strong to drink along with dinner, but it was pleasant enough beforehand. It was almost enough distraction to make her stop thinking about favors, and about the book he'd bought.

The host returned. Agna decided on a rustic but promising baked dish on the menu, since it was difficult to bake anything sufficiently over the campfire. Keifon ordered a savory pie.

"What are you going to do tomorrow?" Keifon asked.

"Take my clothes to a laundry, I think. Have my sandals repaired."

"Mm. Laundry for me, too." He wiped off some condensation from his glass; it ran in runnels from his fingers to the tabletop. "Are you going to meet your friend?"

Nelle? Agna thought, and remembered. Rone. "Oh. – I... don't know. I mean, I – wouldn't want to bother him."

Keifon's brow creased. "Bother him? It sounds like you were close, back in school."

"Yes, but – I don't – look." She closed and opened her hands on the tabletop. "I was stupid. He doesn't need me following along behind him like a–" –*lovesick*, she bit that word off in time – "like a baby duckling." She took a long drink to distract herself. *Besides, I was here for a whole week when I got to Kavera, and he never came to see me*, the back of her mind helpfully suggested.

Keifon laced his fingers together and sighed. "You'd know him better than I would. Of course. I just... I hope you do what's right for you."

Agna folded her arms. "I am," she said uncertainly. And then she'd said it, out loud. It was enough of a reason not to double back. She was an adult now, and she was moving ahead into her own future, not following Rone anymore. She did not need to ask him for help. She could hold to her decisions.

Keifon lifted his glass. "To a successful year."

Agna grabbed hers and clinked it against his. "And more to come." That made him smile, which helped. "Cheers."

■ ■ ■

Agna lay in the dark, on a real mattress – she wondered whether she could tell the difference between straw and feather mattresses anymore, because they all felt heavenly. There were clean sheets on it and a blanket over that, and a thick down pillow. It was a small room in the Benevolent Union's base with a small window that didn't let in much light, but she could see the outlines of the room in the light that remained. It was all hers for the next five days.

Through the wall Keifon was getting ready for bed, or already asleep. She hoped that he would sleep well. It had been strange to say goodnight and close the door behind her. It was a relief, she thought; it was a luxury to have this much privacy, to change into her nightgown and stretch out on the bed and not have to worry about working around someone else's comings and goings. Still, it would be nice to have someone to talk to as she did her laundry tomorrow.

She could hear his lute through the wall as she fell asleep. *I'll read for you*, she thought. *Sometime.*

On the second day she did laundry and had her sandals repaired.

On the third day she toured three cathedrals with Keifon, and he toured two art museums with her.

On the fourth day she read the letters that had arrived from Laris and Lina. Laris missed her; he was looking forward to the trip downriver; he had re-read *The Wanderer*, borrowed from someone at work. He warned her that the mail riders wouldn't be able to find him on the canal, but he would keep writing all the time. He missed her. He loved her.

Lina reported that she had taken a full-time job in the herbalist's and moved into the apartment over the shop. Their cousin Violetta had goaded her on, and she and her boyfriend Marco had helped Lina move. Sometimes Lina was worried or lonely, and worried whether she'd made the wrong decision. She wondered whether Agna ever felt like that. Esi planned to visit next year. Lina hadn't told her about the move.

Agna wrote back to them after lunch. She careened through the streets of Vertal, not appreciating their architecture, thinking about her next move. She sold her trunk and bought a backpack like Keifon's.

That night, she wrote one more letter, to her father. She did not apologize or admit that the trip had been a mistake. She did not mention Lina's news about moving. She asked for one more thing. It was hard to bring herself to write her request, but when she sealed up the letter, she did not regret it.

On the fifth day, the caravan left town.

Agna: Postwar

Agna had learned the source of Fort Unity's name. She knew the names of the generals in the battle that had been fought here. She had read the proclamation of peace. She had learned about the establishment of the road patrol that was quartered here.

She and Keifon set up the clinic tent together and divided the patients, most of whom were spouses and children of the patrol officers, based on the patients' diagnoses and their own strengths. After business closed for the day, Keifon went shopping for dinner, as it was his turn to cook.

Agna stopped at the master of records' wagon to pick up her mail. Four letters waited for her. She knew the handwriting on three of them. She rushed back to the tent and lit the lamp.

Laris was the easiest. Two of the letters were his. Agna slit them open and checked the dates.

First: Their little convoy had left Laketon to drive two hundred head of cattle alongside the canals to market at Vertal. Laris managed the center of the herd with a fellow rancher, Weira, the lender of *The Wanderer*. The other four ranchers were arrayed at the front and back of the pack, with dogs and horses to complete the team. Laris said that he would try to figure out whether their path would cross the Golden Caravan's. He said he thought about her every night.

Second: He talked about camping in the open, listening to the sound of the water. He thought about her every night. He was getting to be good friends with the others on the team, learning more about the trade and the country. Tufari taught him about repairing boats, which they did for extra money along the route. Feldon, the eldest, taught him years of lore about cattle. Atme told stories around their campfire at night. Everyone kept Gawin, the boss's son, in line.

The rest of the letter was about Weira.

Her family was half Yanweian. They didn't have their own ranch. She loved working in the open; she loved the freedom. She and Laris read a lot of the same books.

He'd told her all about Agna. She said Agna sounded amazing. Laris said she was right.

Agna set the first two letters down. Her head swam. That was supposed to be the easy part. She missed Laris like a fist in the gut, but that was hardly anything new.

Two more.

She opened the unfamiliar one. *Dear Agna,* it began, and ended two pages later with *Cordially, Marco Pirci.*

The new contact, from her father's agency. Agna set it down. Dessert. Probably. Face the other one first. Rone's.

What he said was, *I must have upset you, and I want to make it right.*

What he said was, *I'm sorry.*

What he said was, *I miss you.*

What he did not say was, *You're an idiot and you messed up again.* Agna supplied that part, and the rage that came with it, all by herself. She threw the letters aside, curled up on her new wood-framed cot, and soaked her new pillow with angry tears.

■ ■ ■

The tent flap rasped open and shut. Agna covered her head with her arm. Someone sat on the edge of her cot. Agna registered the scent of lilies and herbs. Nelle.

"Kei came and got me," Nelle said softly. "What's wrong?"

Agna sniffled and wiped her face enough to keep the liquids in check. "I'm stupid. That's all."

"Not gonna agree, and not gonna guess."

Agna sighed. "I didn't – in Vertal, I didn't go and see my friend from back home. He's upset. I'm an ass."

"Upset?"

"Sad. Blames himself. Thinks he did something to offend me."

"Did he?"

"Of course not. I just – didn't want to keep on being a stupid little girl who followed him around everywhere."

Nelle folded her arms. "You tell him that?"

"...No."

Nelle waited.

"It was too embarrassing."

"So instead..."

"Ugh. So instead I hurt his feelings *and* I didn't get to see him, and now it's going to be a whole year, or maybe – maybe forever." Obviously forever, because she had tried to do the right thing and had ruined everything. And if she had gone after all, she would have proved that she hadn't learned anything in five years. Every road was wrong.

Nelle gathered her in to sob on her shoulder. The second wave passed more easily. Agna dug out a handkerchief from her belt pouch. Nelle scuffed her feet on the floor and waited for Agna to compose herself.

"Water, hon?"

"Yeah. Thank you."

Nelle slipped out of the tent. Through her sniffling and nose-blowing, Agna heard urgent voices, and then the clunk of the water barrel's lid being replaced. As Nelle lifted the flap, Agna caught a glimpse of Keifon standing outside.

Nelle handed over the cup of water. Agna dipped a corner of her handkerchief to wipe her face, then drank the rest. She took a numbered series of deep breaths.

"Gonna be all right?"

"Yeah. Sorry, I just—"

Nelle held up a hand. "None of that. Now – wanna get away for a little bit? You and me."

Agna collapsed onto the damp pillow. "I guess. Yeah, I guess it would be good for me."

"Tavern in Unity, nice place, has dart boards. Quiet at this hour. Good food."

Not made on a campfire, Agna thought. Her repertoire had begun to expand, but the thought was tempting. And she hadn't gotten around to spending time with Nelle in Vertal, either. "All right."

"Yeah! I'll get some money – it's on me. Just wait here." Nelle dashed off, leaving the tent flaps swaying in her wake. Agna sat up and slowly opened her new backpack to find some clothes.

She had just pulled out a light summer dress when someone tapped on the flap. Agna sighed and rubbed her face. One guess. "Come in."

Keifon stepped in, and Agna read his worry before he'd crossed the threshold.

"Is everything all right?"

She gestured, *so-so.* "I mean, nobody's died. I —" She squeezed it down to the barest explanation with the fewest possible words. "Rone is hurt because I didn't go to see him."

"Mmn." He seemed to decide against further commentary. "Do you want some dinner?"

"Thanks, but Nelle's taking me out to town, I guess."

"Oh. That's good." He lingered, gripping his elbows. "I'm-I'm here if you need anything."

"Thanks." She couldn't force herself to smile for him, and he didn't seem to mind. "I'm gonna get changed and head out. Just tell Nelle to wait for me, please."

"Sure. Have a good time." He tied off the door on his way out.

As she changed, Agna tried to think about shedding her old worry and stepping into a new, clear, well-adjusted, non-backwards mindset. It would have been easier if she'd had any clue what that might look like, or what the right answers were. Fresh clothes helped a little, though.

Before she left the tent, she spotted the letters, discarded next to her cot. She hadn't read the agency contact's letter yet. Impulsively, she scooped up all four letters and stowed them in an inside pocket, lying against her ribs.

■ ■ ■

Nelle ordered bread puffs filled with sausage and greens, and elderberry cordial. As they waited, Agna pulled out the unread letter.

"Hey." Nelle slapped her hand on the paper, pinning it to the table.

"That's a different one," Agna protested.

"No trauma?"

"No trauma." She yanked it out from under Nelle's hand. "It's from an agent in my father's company. I asked him to get me in touch with somebody. Get me up to speed. Build some professional relationships in the art world. That sort of thing."

Nelle nodded and folded her arms. Agna started from the beginning.

The contact, Marco Pirci, was not from her father's agency, as it turned out. He was from her aunt Naire's agency. Agna's father had contacted him through Naire-ceisi to strike up a correspondence with Agna. Marco went on to ask about her assignment and her interests in the art world. He professed an interest in folkloric and literary painting, and chatted for a while about his background: a very prestigious business school in Murio, and then an apprenticeship with Naire's agency. From the timeline he presented, he had to be more or less the same age as Agna, Lina and Violetta.

The letter closed with hopes that they might start a fruitful and mutually beneficial conversation, and offered his mailing address in downtown Murio. Then, *Cordially, Marco Pirci.* Agna's brain turned over that name as she refolded the letter. It was naggingly familiar, as though it had been the name of a character in a book she'd read.

"Well?"

"Well... normal." She slid the letter back into her pocket. "He works for my aunt, not my father. Which is a little unexpected. But she does the same thing, so it's not that important, really."

"So that's good?"

"Could be. I'll get back in touch with the business." She traced the grain of the tabletop with her fingertips. In another way, it could mark the end of her foray into healing. Maybe it was just a youthful distraction in the end.

"Cheers to that." Nelle raised her glass, and Agna gamely clinked hers against it.

The arrival of the food was a welcome interruption. Agna and Nelle applied themselves to its demolition, and Nelle ordered a round of beer. As Agna minutely sipped at the bitter stuff, she re-read Laris's letters. Surely she was being too suspicious about – things. She wanted Laris to live a free and happy

179

life, with as many friends around him as he wanted. She would be hurt if Laris ever cast suspicion on her friendships with Nelle or Keifon, and Laris would never do that.

Was it a friendship, with Keifon? Agna followed the sidetrack. She supposed it was. Not as close as she'd been with Esirel. But as least as close as she was with Nelle, albeit in a different way. She trusted him, and they depended on one another. She enjoyed his company. The book shopping, cathedral touring, and art gallery crawling in Vertal had been lovely, even considering the other disastrous parts of the stop.

Nelle motioned for a passing steward to refill their mugs. At worst, then, she had lost one friend in Rone and gained another in Keifon. But she wanted both! Was she being selfish after all?

"Hey. Second warning." Nelle patted Agna's head, and Agna realized that she had slumped her chin down to her crossed arms on the tabletop. She pulled herself up.

Nelle finished her mug. "Darts?"

"I've never played darts."

"Not an answer."

"All right, all right." She allowed Nelle to hustle her over to one of the boards at the back of the tavern. Nelle pulled several darts from the board and turned a handful over to Agna.

Agna listened to the rules twice. She was getting sleepy, frosted over with a red fuzz of irritability. Her first dart bounced flat off the wall. Nelle dove for it. "Forward, straight forward." Then, "Less shoulder, more elbow."

"I'll give you more elbow," Agna grumbled.

"So yeah, how about getting that aggression out? Darts tradition."

Her next dart buried itself in the wall halfway between the target and the floor.

Nelle hesitated. "Better."

It didn't mean anything that Laris talked about this other girl like – like – *thunk* – like she was the greatest thing to grace the world.

It wasn't the end of Rone-and-his-little-sisters. She would find the right things to say, damn it – *thunk* – and things would be all right.

They played round after lopsided round. Nelle stopped keeping score. Agna's fatigue melted; her irritability galvanized into a strange righteous fury. She improved her throws hardly at all.

"I'm not jealous. I don't get jealous. All right?"

"Uh-huh."

"My best friend's marrying my sister, and it's great. See? And Bakari is the biggest sweetheart."

"Who in all gods' names is Bakari?"

"Rone's boyfriend. Priest. Islander. Everybody loves them. 'Cept jealous people. And I'm not."

"Uh-huh."

"People being happy is good. I mean, look at Keifon and Edann. Edann is a horse's ass and everybody knows it, but Keifon's happy, so it's all right. Even if he probably isn't over his Kazi and they should never have even started, it doesn't *matter*, because they love each other and that's good."

"Uh…"

"If Edann can love anything that isn't his own reflection, 'cause I don't know. Keifon loves him, though. You can see it."

"Uh-huh."

"And my sister is moving into some, I don't know, hole in the wall, but *she's* happy, so it's all right. And Letta won't let her get murdered. So it's up to me to listen to our parents yelling about it for the rest of our lives like I have anything to do with it."

The next mug Nelle handed her was full of water.

"I keep seeing Marco's name in Lina's handwriting. That's what."

"No idea what you're talking about. Move over, it's my turn."

▪ ▪ ▪

"What did I do wrong? Why does everyone hate me, Nelle?"

"Tides, babe. Star positions. And you're kind of drunk."

"I don't drink."

"Yeah, well. Fine for now."

"You know, Keifon doesn't either. Ever, ever. You think he had a family member drank too much? That's what I think."

"I think your boys are driving you crazy, city girl. Which is why a little drunk is all right."

"They are. They *are*. All of them. I miss Esirel. And Lina. I miss you. We should do more things."

"Sounds fine. Let's do that. Like let's play darts."

"I'm terrible at darts."

"Yep."

Keifon: Counterpoint

Shaken by worry and driven to surround himself with company, Keifon took his nanbur to the bonfire and settled on a log bench. He warmed up and ran through some scales, then started in on "Rise, Children of the Land," a quick, agitated melody that he hoped would absorb this churn of anxiety.

Nelle would take care of Agna. Agna would find a way to apologize or explain to her old friend, and everything would be fine. What bothered Keifon more was the despair that echoed in him. He could not bear to see her hurting. He'd been cowardly, running to Nelle instead of helping Agna himself, because he didn't trust himself not to panic. He didn't know what to make of this, or whether he should make anything of it at all. The answers would come in time, he told himself. He would pray on it tonight. Until then, he only wanted a corner of the crowd and something to occupy his hands.

The merchants arrived and took their accustomed spots in the circle. The day's take was compared to others' takes, to last week's, and to the last ten years. Well-worn arguments broke out over the interpretation of the tidal rise and fall of the price of goods. The news from Fort Unity was repeated, dissected, and summarized. Expectations for the next stop at Quickwater Crossing were floated. A few glints of firelight caught the eyes that turned Keifon's way. The attack. He held onto the notes, though they grew clipped.

The conversation turned back to Fort Unity. Keifon shifted into one of the Kaveran songs he'd learned, something about a valley. He hadn't gotten the words down. He didn't want to talk about much of anything right now, least of all Quickwater Crossing, so the more popular song choice stood as his thanks.

A familiar hand slipped over his shoulder and kneaded his neck. "God's balls, you're tense."

"Don't," he muttered, even as a grateful shiver rose up his back. He meant the cursing, not the massage, and Edann knew that perfectly well. Edann bent over the log to plant his wine bottle and his book in front of the log, leaned against Keifon's back and set both hands to the task. Keifon struggled to keep the melody for another half verse before giving up. A few facetious boos rose from the crowd.

Keifon managed to lift a hand. "In a minute." He set the nanbur safely at his feet and leaned into Edann's touch.

"It's not fair," one of the others jibed. "Everyone gets to hear the music, not everyone gets a neck rub."

"Not unless you've got dangly bits and a pulse," someone chuckled.

"And be one of the third, I suppose."

"I'd cross over to the fellows for a good neck rub."

"Not so much since the medic domesticated him, though."

"Oh yeah."

Keifon felt Edann's grip tighten in a manner unrelated to working the knots out of his muscles. "You get to watch," Edann offered sarcastically, garnering a few snickers. He leaned into Keifon's back a little more, and snugged his cheek against Keifon's hair. The gesture was empty of any real affection. Keifon's muscles tensed against Edann's efforts.

Kazi had shown him off once. It had been early on, when Kazi had claimed that he couldn't get attached. Keifon had heard him across the common room of the inn, proselytizing – *helping the cause of the downtrodden – my friend there, he was unjustly thrown out of his family...* Their first argument had raged half the night in the room they'd rented.

It wasn't worth the effort to fight with Edann. Keifon's energy was too sapped from worrying about Agna to dive into a trench of Edannspeak. Edann never argued straightforwardly; he never admitted mistakes; his world was hemmed in by elaborate fences and walls that shifted daily; he warped ideas into twisted remnants of themselves. Keifon let his showboating go on. It didn't matter, in the end. Edann was himself, and nothing Keifon said or did could change that.

All the same, he was showing affection in public, which seemed like progress. After Edann had proved whatever point he intended to make to the crowd, he lounged on the log bench, taking up his book. He snugged his head in Keifon's lap. Keifon felt his insides warming. This was what hooked him. Edann could ignore him for days and then give him a little affection, and Keifon would devour it as though he were starving.

Keifon felt like a traitor against himself. But it was enough. He couldn't ask for much more than this, after all he'd done.

He picked up his nanbur and warmed up his fingers. After he'd played a few scales, he bent down to murmur to Edann, "I know I haven't domesticated you."

Edann's smirk was intoxicating even upside-down. "I know you haven't."

Keifon began another song.

■ ■ ■

Agna and Nelle spoke in hushed voices, but Keifon heard them. He set down the book he'd bought in Vertal just as Agna ducked inside. The smell of beer clinging to her clothes made the acid rise in his throat, and he pressed a hand against his mouth.

His mind stampeded. Not her. Not now. Not here. Not where he was safe. Agna smiled. Her steps were steady as she crossed the tent. She did not weave. Keifon forced his thoughts to slow down. She drank so rarely, and she didn't seem too drunk now. She and Nelle had probably gone out to a tavern and had a little, just a little, because some people, most people, could do that. Nelle wouldn't let anything happen to her.

"Hey, how's it going?"

The smell roiled his stomach with a sickening combination of longing and revulsion. "Um – can you – can you clean up before you turn in tonight? I just – your clothes – they smell like beer, and I can't – can you please?"

"Oh. Sorry. Yeah, of course."

Keifon lay back in his cot and breathed until his head stopped spinning. He dimly heard her approach, and opened his eyes just as she picked up the book.

"*Immigration Patterns in Kavera*?"

"I – it – hey." He grabbed the other end of the book, and she let go. Keifon stuffed the book under his pillow. "I didn't mean for you to—"

"Is that from Wayron's cart?"

"Uh – n-no. It's what I bought in Vertal."

"Ohhh. The secret one."

"...Yeah."

"Hm. Well, I'll go clean up. I'll hang my clothes outside, is that all right?"

"Y-yeah. Thank you."

He stowed the book under his cot and turned over to sleep. She smelled like soap when she returned. Nothing more.

Agna: Vigil

Keifon and Agna grew quiet as Quickwater Crossing drew near. The trees closed in overhead, no different in species or habitat from any of the other trees they'd passed along the route, but under their canopy the air seemed sinister.

Agna's hands shook as they set up the tent in their designated spot – in the same spot. She ran through one scenario after another in the back of her mind. She could ask Nelle if the two of them could stay over, and pitch it as a little private party. But it was unlikely that either she or Keifon would be able to playact for long. The guard captain wouldn't allow them to hire a personal guard for the night, as it would wreak havoc with their schedules. It was too late to flee back to Prisa. She was out of ideas. Stay up all night, and keep the lantern burning. That was all.

She felt a little better about having sold the trunk in Vertal. Every changed detail reminded her that this year was not last year. They unpacked their backpacks, set up their cots – another change, that was good – and took refuge in the clinic tent. As long as the patients needed her to be calm and competent, she could be calm and competent.

Keifon did not speak about last year. They talked as much as was necessary to handle their cases and take care of business. Otherwise, he had glazed over. He wasn't angry; she could read that much in his posture and the tone of his voice. He was simply far away. She remembered how glassy-eyed and distant he had been during the attack. At the time, Agna had taken it as incompetence in soldiering. She understood now that it had something to do with his parents' death, connecting the two events in his mind.

The patients stopped coming soon after dark. Keifon looked up at her and planted his hands on the examination table as he stood. But Agna found herself speaking first.

"Are you all right?"

He blinked, and the mask dropped. He sat down, his hands hanging between his knees. "I... hm." There was no point in asking what she meant. It hung in the air, in the gathering dark. She had only pointed it out.

Agna fidgeted, straightening her belt. "Because I was thinking about what we could do, you know, instead, and I didn't come up with anything."

"Instead?"

"Of, uh, waiting. Around. Tonight. In the tent."

"They're not coming back," Keifon said. She wasn't sure that he believed it.

"Yeah, but I still feel weird. I know it's stupid, but I do."

He was quiet. "...Yeah. Me, too."

A shiver of relief displaced a little of Agna's worry. It felt better just to say it, to know that she wasn't alone, to know that they were looking out for one another. "So... I guess we can go back. We have to pack this up anyway."

"Yeah."

They set about dismantling the tent together. When the clinic had been packed and hauled off, they walked across the camp to their tent. The bonfire was beginning to glow in the middle of the camp.

"Bonfire?" she asked, as Keifon picked through the larder chest.

"Ennh. If you want to go, I'll go."

"Not especially." She sighed and flopped on her heels at the fireside. "Could you hand me the flint box?"

Keifon passed it over and continued to assemble ingredients for dinner as Agna built the fire. He arranged their new pan on its stand while the flames were low. Agna offered to help, and together they washed and cut the vegetables that he had bought that afternoon. When the fire had caught on enough to heat the pan, he added some oil.

Agna surveyed the operation; he seemed to have a plan in place. "How long will this take, do you think?"

"Mmn, twenty minutes. Thirty at most."

"Do you mind if I..."

"Sure. I won't start without you."

She packed up for the baths, leaving him to the cooking. Upon returning to the tent, she realized the flaw in her plan; she would have to either get dressed or eat dinner in her dressing gown. Sighing to herself, she wrapped up in her nightshift and dressing gown and tried not to worry about it. It was a stupid thing to worry about, anyway. Keifon didn't comment when she re-emerged. And, she thought as she settled into her spot by the fire, it was comfortable. Keifon passed her a cup of water and a bowl of spring greens, delicate green peapods, and oil dressing.

"My, my. I feel spoiled. Thank you." She tasted a forkful; the dressing was spiked with vinegar and herbs. Her appreciative noises made him chuckle.

"You're welcome. Well, we said we wanted to branch out. The vinegar is from Nelle's shop. Infused with... things." He waved a hand.

"That sounds ominous."

"Garlic, and herbs and things."

"That sounds delicious and ominous."

Keifon stirred the vegetables in the frying pan as they finished the salad, and dished it out into their empty bowls. He had put together something that seemed Yanweian, though she couldn't name it – spring onions and vegetables cooked in a salty sauce.

"I'm sorry that we don't have rice or meat or anything. I couldn't... I didn't want anything too heavy today. I hope that's all right."

"That's fine. It's very good." She wondered whether his stomach might be bothering him. Last year she had detected some ulcerous damage, but she hadn't brought it up again. Maybe he would let her check, now that things were different.

Agna forgot about the indecency of her wardrobe for a while, and almost forgot about the bandits. Afterward, they scrubbed the dishes and put them away. Agna put water on for tea, and Keifon excused himself for a bath.

Agna sat on her heels by the fire, poking it more often than it needed, aligning every unpredictable log and ember. It might be all right. They were doing well. She felt better having eaten, and Keifon seemed calmer. They could play cards for a while, and then... not sleep. Maybe they could play cards for a long while. And read. She had borrowed a book of Kaveran poetry from Wayron, having passed up the volumes in the shop in Vertal. It was far enough out of her usual habits to distract her for a while.

But not long enough.

She had to sleep eventually; she couldn't stay up all night and nap on the wagon. She'd be a wreck for days afterward. She had to stop thinking about staying up all night. It was unreasonable.

The teakettle had heated by the time Keifon returned, and Agna sipped meditatively on some herbal tea of Nelle's devising. She looked up and felt her breath stick in her chest. Keifon sat cross-legged on the other side of the fire and reached for the kettle.

"Is everything all right?" He shook some leaves into his cup and poured water over them.

Agna set her cup down. It was what he always wore at night, when it wasn't too cold. He'd worn the same thing last night. But last night she hadn't thought about what those clothes had looked like covered in blood.

"Just..." She shook her head. "I still don't... feel quite right."

He almost smiled. "I never feel quite right."

Agna felt a little guilty for letting her mood lighten, even a fraction, but it worked. "We'll be shivering wrecks together, then."

"Mmn. I appreciate that." He sipped his tea as Agna finished hers. At least she wasn't alone this time.

She hadn't been alone that time, either, she reminded herself. No matter what she'd insisted. The signs had been there, even then. She had risked reprisal from the bandits to help him, charging them with her healer's art. He had all but carried her into the tent afterward. He had put her arm in a sling, and she had healed some of his injuries. They had tried to help one another, in their own hostile, clumsy fashion. She had seen his overtures as a threat, and rewrote his help into an insult to explain her own hostility.

She couldn't speak to Keifon's mental state at the time, but he certainly hadn't taken kindly to her healing. And, Agna realized, she had never offered again. She would offer soon. Some time when she had less anxiety weighing on her mind, and fewer distractions.

Without speaking they completed their routine and retired to the tent. Agna reread Laris' letters until she came to the end. She couldn't write him back. Worrying about that wouldn't wipe out the worry about their safety; it would only compound the problem. She put the letters away and picked up a book.

Keifon put down his own book and sat up. "Do you mind if I practice inside?"

"No, go ahead."

"Thanks." He busied himself with unpacking and tuning his lute, and Agna turned her attention back to the page. Wayron had assured her that this book was a classic. The syntax was different enough from prose Kaveran to absorb her attention, untangling the inverted clauses and looking up words in the dictionary that she'd all but abandoned. Keifon's lute plinked. He didn't seem to be practicing any song in particular, and he seemed restless and distracted.

"Hey."

Agna looked up from "The Maiden's Journey on a Summer Day". "Hm?"

"What are you reading?"

"Poetry. Kaveran. Got it from Wayron."

"Ah. So you do like that kind of thing."

"Sometimes," she said, leaning on it mock-defensively.

Keifon's fingers soundlessly picked out a figure on the neck of his lute as he thought. "I was thinking... what we talked about in the bookstore, back in Vertal. I think that would be good tonight."

"A reading?" She scanned the page. She could do a fair job of this type of thing, even though she hadn't done readings in Kaveran in school. And it would be distracting.

"Not so formal. Just..." He chewed on his lip. "If you don't want to, that's all right."

"I didn't say no." Agna sat up in her cot and flipped through the preceding pages for a likely candidate. "What would you like?"

Keifon shrugged. "Anything. Your choice."

Agna let a flash of irritation flare and sputter out. He had asked for it, after all, and now he was being indecisive. ...No, that wasn't what he meant. The point wasn't to explore the literary works of their host country. The point was to hear a friendly human voice on a dark night.

She paged back to the first poem in the book, took a sip of water by the cup at her bedside, and began to read the heroic account of the Charge at Creek Bend. As the company formed and began to march, Keifon picked up his lute.

Agna lowered the book. "Too dull?"

"No, no. Go on."

Agna narrowed her eyes at him, but went on about the rhythm of the march and the flashing banners and all the rest. Keifon's lute picked up a soft, percussive strumming, underlying Agna's voice. When the rival army appeared over the ridge, with appropriate dramatic tension – she was beginning to get into this, a little – Keifon went silent for a few lines, then eased into a louder melody.

It was probably an artful addition, Agna reflected. Setting the mood, and augmenting her reading. It was good that Keifon could participate. It felt more like a collaboration and less like performing for an audience.

They kept up the counterpoint of words and music through the trumpets, the speeches, and the final doomed charge. After the smoke cleared over the battlefield, Agna closed the book. Keifon set down his lute. They didn't speak for a little while.

"Thank you," Keifon said.

Agna sketched a seated bow. "Thank you for your accompaniment."

He shrugged, embarrassed and flattered; she recognized the way he looked slantwise, and the hesitation in his voice. "It's just... a thing I do. Used to do. Sometimes." He bent to put the lute back in his case, and ducked out of the tent. Agna rubbed her eyes, and looked up to find him offering her a cup of water. She thanked him and drank. Keifon curled up on his new cot.

"Ready for sleep?" Agna tried not to sound as though she dreaded it. It was late, and her head swam a little, but she could imagine the dark trees outside and what lurked among them.

"Mmn, no. Not yet." He huddled under his blanket. Agna reached for the book of poetry and had half-lifted it when he spoke. "Actually... would you read something from one of your books from home?"

Agna frowned. "They're all in Nessinian."

"I know. I mean, I'd assumed they were." He adjusted the position of his pillow against his neck. "I just wanted to hear what it sounded like. It's... kind of like music, if you don't understand the words. Tones and sounds and inflections."

"...Huh."

"If you don't want to, that's all right."

"I don't mind. Let me see..." She considered her collection. A copy of *The Dialogues*; philosophy would put her to sleep at this hour. Her medical reference, *Blackhall's*, which was hardly a bedtime story either. Two novels. One she would be too embarrassed to read aloud, even if her audience didn't understand the language. The only remaining choice was the right one after all.

She found it in her new backpack and turned the cover toward his curious look. Keifon nodded. "I've seen you reading that one."

"It's an old favorite of mine."

He smiled. "I wish I could read it."

"Well, it's been translated into Kaveran. Laris said he's read it before."

"I'll have to look for it, then."

Agna tucked her hair behind her ear. "All right, so... *The Wanderer* is more or less a fantasy story. It's about a girl who was chosen by her village to go out and find truth. It's allegorical, really. And you're never quite sure what it's an allegory about. But – that's later on. This is the beginning."

Agna settled into her blankets, lifting the book toward the light. "Chapter One. A Village." The sounds of her native language felt strange in her mouth, as though she were speaking in a dream. She hadn't bothered to speak Nessinian to Edann in several months, and she hadn't gone to Rone's house in Vertal, after all. But the familiar words drew her in, step by step along the path.

She had read *The Wanderer* first when she was eleven, right before she'd gone to the Academy. It had stayed with her through her life in the dormitories, through meeting Esirel and Rone and choosing her course of study as a healer and all of the heartbreak and infighting and triumph that had come after. The world in the story was always the same, and always changing, and always a mirror to Agna's world, held up at an angle that she couldn't quite see.

Keifon listened to her voice. She understood why, or thought she did. It didn't really matter what the story was, and perhaps he could draw some kind of musical interpretation from the sound. But her voice was a sign of safety on a night when they needed such things.

Near the end of the first chapter, she glanced up to find him asleep. She let a private smile slide across her face as the heroine prepared for her journey. The Wanderer wasn't alone in her world, either. Not for long.

At the end of the chapter, Agna softly closed the book and set it down. Her arms felt light and free without its weight. She could sleep as long as she needed to. She moistened her lips, and spoke in words he wouldn't know. "I still don't understand you. But I'm glad we're here."

She blew out the light.

Keifon: Favor

"Keifon?"

Someone touched his arm. He thought he said something, though it probably came out as incoherent mumbling. His neck was stiff. Sitting on her heels by his bedside was the friend whose voice had lulled him to sleep. Keifon's fogged brain reconstructed the facts and deduced that it was, indeed, morning. He heaved up onto one elbow and stretched his neck.

"Mmgh. G'morning."

"Good morning. I hate to wake you, but we need to get moving pretty soon."

"Mmhm. Thanks."

Agna edged back, giving him enough room to sit on the edge of his cot and rub some life into his face. He noticed eventually that her cot was gone. Conflicting reactions swirled sluggishly through him: she had packed it up; he had slept right through it; he envied her energy at this hour.

The nanbur case by the foot of his cot reminded him of his strangeness last night, and the requests he'd made to keep himself from panicking. "Hey – I'm sorry about last night. I know it was weird. Thank you for humoring me."

She executed a maneuver that was becoming intensely familiar: an oblique dip of her head, a sudden flurry of motion in her hands. "It wasn't weird. And I offered in the first place. The important thing is that we're here, and safe."

"Yeah. We are." Keifon stretched as he stood, rotating the stiffness from his joints. Yawning, he pulled some clothes from his pack, set them aside, and folded his blankets. Agna sat silently, not watching him. Perhaps his request had bothered her after all. Or she was worried about Laris, or regretted not having met her friend in Vertal. Keifon had to figure out how to ask without hurting her.

"Hey," she said, as he headed for the door.

Keifon turned. "Hm?"

"I was thinking. About – last year, sort of, and your stomach, and how I never helped you. With that. I wondered whether I could, sometime. It wouldn't take long."

Last year, after the attack. That morning when he'd been unable to do anything but bind her torn shoulder and hate himself for wanting to help her more. She'd closed the knife wounds in his back and his neck and healed his split lip without even thinking about it. She had noticed that something was wrong with his stomach, and he had brushed her off, embarrassed by his weakness. She remembered that. And she wanted to help.

Agna's nervous stammer was familiar now, too. "I mean, if you want to. I don't mean to intrude—"

Keifon sank to the floor next to her and let go of the bundle of clothes. Agna's monologue snapped off.

"You don't have to," he said, and regretted it. "That's – that's not what I want to say. I mean, thank you. I just don't know if it would help. I don't know whether it would just come back afterward. I'd hate for you to waste the effort. But thank you."

"It's not wasted effort," she insisted. "If it starts hurting again, I'll heal you. That's all."

That's all. She assumed that she would be here, and that she would be willing to heal him. She thought nothing of it. It wasn't that easy; nothing ever was. Even so, it meant something that she had offered. Even if his flawed and mistreated body undid the good she'd done for him, he wanted to accept her offer.

Keifon smiled, and the growing worry in Agna's eyes melted. That was a reward in itself. "Thank you. I appreciate it."

■ ■ ■

It didn't take long, after all.

The healing process had taken just a few minutes last time, Keifon reasoned. It had only seemed longer. His dread and confusion and resentment had piled onto her simple act of kindness until it took on monumental proportions in his head.

They cleared out the tent. Agna sat on the floor and explained in her clinician's tone that he might be more comfortable lying down. Keifon stretched out on his back, feeling not very comfortable at all. Agna explained that it would help to make clear contact with his skin, and when he indicated that he understood, she slipped her hands under his shirt. Her hands were warm, one under his ribs, one over. Keifon tried to control his breathing.

A trace of a smile quirked Agna's mouth. "Relax."

"I'm sorry."

He watched her to distract himself from his nervousness. She focused her concentration; he'd seen that inward glaze hundreds of times as she'd treated their patients. She would go somewhere inside herself and then – He felt her energy connect to his, with a warm, humming sensation where their skin met. Agna's smile widened. "See? Not so bad."

He couldn't bring himself to speak while she was connected to him like this. It was too – intimate, somehow. He could feel calm radiating from her, and suspected that she could already feel his nervousness, with her more attuned senses. He was suddenly too shy to put words to it.

As a reply, he made himself relax, willing himself not to resist. Agna seemed to sense it, and her energy flowed through him like warm honey through water. She shifted inward, bearing toward the bleeding wreck of his stomach. The warm glow wrapped around it and numbed all sensation except the faint warm tingling of the healing art. Keifon sighed, realizing how much he took the background pain for granted. It was so lovely not to hurt.

Agna glanced at him, gauging his reaction. Her hands repositioned slightly, and he felt subtle shifts in her energy as she worked through the damage, little by little. Keifon concentrated on breathing evenly, and found himself hovering near the edge of sleep. He wasn't worried anymore; he wasn't sure what he had been worried about. Agna would not hurt him, or shame him for having ignored his condition for so long.

"Not much longer," Agna murmured. Keifon opened his eyes, and looked away from her sad little smile. "It'll feel so much better, I promise you. I didn't realize it was this bad. I'm so sorry."

He shook his head minutely. Not her fault, of course. It had been this way since he was thirteen or fourteen; at his worst the ulcers had fought against his alcohol consumption, leaving him vomiting blood into the gutter on more than one occasion. In Kavera he'd ignored it, taking for granted that he was always going to hurt a little, that keeping his body fueled was always going to be a hassle. He had never even considered that Agna could take it away, even temporarily. But of course she could, and of course she would. That was the sort of thing she did.

The warm thrumming slowly rolled away like water on a beach, until it centered under Agna's hands. Agna held onto the connection for a little while longer. The healing energy washed through him again, one more tidal flow before nightfall. Agna had referred to this as merely checking her progress, making sure that everything had been set to rights. It didn't do justice to the sensation at all.

Finally Agna sat back, lifting her hands from his skin, and sighed deeply.

Keifon waited. Nothing hurt. He couldn't even feel the queasy acid burn of his system waking up.

"There." Agna got to her feet and offered him a hand. "Ready to go?"

Keifon looked up, formulating thanks that could never even the balance, and took her hand.

Keifon: The Feast of Darano

She came with him this time. That was what made all the difference.

As Agna finished her breakfast, Keifon dressed for the ceremony. He brushed off the jacket and trousers he'd hung up overnight and gave his boots a final polish. Memory and pride lay thick in his chest. The rest of his unit was out there, still a family tighter than blood. A single leaf had blown from the tree and whirled into another land alone.

He was pinning on the insignias when she called. "Can I come in yet?"

Maybe not entirely alone.

"Yes, come in."

She lifted the flap over her head and stopped short. Keifon took an instinctive step backward, sensing her intimidation in the pit of his stomach. The uniform was unfamiliar to her. To her, he looked like a foreign aggressor, like a one-man invasion force. Was that it? She wouldn't look at his face. She was – she was blushing, a little. ...*Oh*.

The realization twanged through his nerves. It didn't mean anything, of course. Keifon was familiar with every thread of the Army's uniform, and even he had to catch his breath when he saw some of his unit mates in full dress. It transformed them. It lent them dignity and authority. It brought out confidence and pride.

Keifon swallowed and smiled, motioning with a twitch of his fingers for her to look up. She finally did, shedding the moment of wordless awkwardness, as she tucked her hair behind her ear. A fleeting response to his smile came and went on her lips. "Hi."

"Hey."

"That's, uh... you look, ah... pretty impressive."

"Umn. ...Thank you. It's just me, though."

She laughed, half to herself. "Well. – I'm ready, I guess. I should see what Nelle's doing. Have a good ceremony? Is that inappropriate? Blessed Resurrection, I mean." She sketched an abbreviated but accurate Daranite prayer gesture and a bow.

Keifon returned the prayer gesture, unable to find suitable words to reply. For Agna to salute him like that and to wish him well on a holiday that she didn't even celebrate meant more to him than she realized. It meant that she respected his faith. She didn't believe, and he had come to accept that – but it was enough, somehow, that she respected him.

He wanted her to be there when he was done with the ceremony. He wanted to share this day with her. But he couldn't demand such a thing. She wouldn't want to wait around for him. She would want to go out and enjoy the festival with Nelle.

As he imagined the scene, Agna spoke up. "I was thinking... I've never seen a Daranite ceremony. Would it be allowed for an outsider to watch?" Keifon stared at her, struck silent by the granting of a wish that he hadn't allowed himself to have. Agna flapped her hands and blundered ahead. "I was just curious. If that's sacrilegious, I'm sorry. I didn't mean any disrespect."

"N-no, I... it's... it's allowed. If you're sure. I..." He forced himself to swallow, to steady his voice. "Thank you. I would be honored." Before he could stop himself, he had gone on. "Afterward, would you – did you want to take a look around the festival?"

"Oh – if it's not too frivolous. I thought I might. I didn't really have a good time last year." She sighed, shaking off that track of thought. "Might be better this time."

Keifon couldn't help but smile. "Yeah. I think it might." He squeezed the remaining sigil pin in his hand, remembering that he wasn't quite ready. "I just need a minute. Actually – is this on straight?" He turned so that she could see the unit tab on his collar.

"Hmm, it looks like it is."

"Thanks." He unlatched the medic's pin and attached it to the other side. "How about that?"

"Looks good."

"Good." He straightened his coat and took a deep breath.

Agna stood at attention. "Ready?"

"Yeah. – Thank you again."

She shrugged, embarrassed. "I just... thought I should try to understand. The way you did."

Keifon remembered that conversation with the shrine guard – the swordmaster – in Laketon. The swordmaster had simplified the precepts of his faith without judging Keifon's own, and had answered Keifon's defensive questions. It had been the first step.

He had thanked Agna over and over already. All he could do now was to go out with her into the morning light, feeling her confidence rise with his own as she walked beside him. An infantryman in full dress reds and a foreign healer in civilian clothes – they made a ridiculous pair. The merchants who watched them pass with smirks or whispered commentary weren't unjustified. Still. It was more than that to Keifon. He believed that it meant more than that to Agna, too.

Agna led him to Nelle's wagon first, to explain to the groggy herbalist that they would meet her later at the festival. Nelle seemed more than willing to catch up with them sometime that afternoon. They left her to her rest and walked toward the fairground.

It was early enough that the crowd was still thin; he had gotten a more timely start this year. Some of the festival booths were half-built. Keifon led the way through the fairground and beyond, into the town proper. The town wasn't any larger than many of the others they served along the circuit, but the Daranite church took it as a point of pride to host the biggest Resurrection festival in this part of Kavera. It seemed that the holiday and the caravan had built on one another to create the fair as a whole. Villagers came from all over the eastern mining region to pay their respects and to do business. Keifon had gathered all of this last year, listening, not talking, and feeling miserable and betrayed. He had asked Edann to come with him to the festival, and Edann had laughed at him. He hadn't asked this year.

It wasn't the same as last year, Keifon reminded himself. The Nessinian woman walking next to him now was proof of that. She caught him looking over at her and smiled, a little puzzled. Keifon turned his eyes toward the church steeple. He hoped that she would understand even a little of the ceremony, and that it would not bore her or offend her pantheist sensibilities. He hoped that she would ask him about it later. There was still so much to say.

The priest at the door greeted him with folded hands. "Blessed Resurrection."

"And to you." Keifon made the Army's salute in return. Agna bobbed her head. The priest waved them through into the interior.

The church dripped with flowers and banners in crimson and white, pinned with silver ornaments – the Daranite colors representing blood, holy raiment and steel. Every undraped surface blazed with candles. A few worshippers had found places on the benches. Keifon headed up the aisle, his boots ticking on the flagstones. He felt Agna trailing him, and a few of the Kaverans' heads turned, but this was beyond them. This was between Keifon and the god who had claimed him.

He knelt at the altar and pulled the offering that he had prepared from the pouch at his belt – a handful of coins wrapped in white and red fabric. It landed on the others in the collection plate with a muted clink. Keifon folded his hands and prayed, with the words of the benediction in his mind and pure wordless gratitude in his heart. He had been given so much, every day, even when he did not understand or appreciate the gift. He had been given every day of his life, every breath he drew, by Darano's grace. His life had been traded to Darano's service in return, and even then he would never repay the gift. Every morning he saw, every patient that he could mend, every smile he traded with his new friend – every one of these was a drop in the river that led back to one moment: a priest in ceremonial armor under a heavy cloak, extending a hand to a man who would otherwise be dead.

It was more than that, even then. Keifon stood from the altar and led his companion to a seat on the benches to wait for the ceremony. He folded his hands and closed his eyes. The priests had saved his life, yes, and taught him how to live as he never had lived before. But that was just a transaction. A transaction could be summed up and repaid, expressed in numbers or words. He had come to know meaning through his studies of Darano's word. He had come to know purpose, justice, and at long last, forgiveness. The studies of the other gods' teachings had helped, of course. Each flowed into the other. But he was chosen by the crimson god, and Darano had led him to seek to understand more every day.

When he opened his eyes, Agna was reading the order of ceremonies on one of the slips of paper that had been distributed along the benches. She gave him a cautious, polite smile. Keifon relaxed his fingers and his posture, retaining the poise appropriate to the uniform. She half-watched him as though she wanted to ask him something.

Keifon cleared his throat. "What is it?"

She pursed her lips, plotting out her next thought. "I mean no disrespect. But I was wondering – you're a medic. Why not Tufar? He's the patron of medicine, isn't he?"

"Mmn. Well... it's complicated."

"I guess it should be. I just wondered."

Keifon composed his answer. "For one thing... I was a soldier before I was a medic. I specialized in medicine after I'd sworn my service to the Army."

"I see."

"And... the easiest answer is that the Daranite church saved me. I – there was a time when – when things were bad for me. So bad that I can't... I don't think I can tell you about them. Yet," he added under his breath. She lifted a hand, as though to ask a question. He motioned for her to go on.

Agna pitched her voice so that no one could overhear, although the seats around them were empty. "Like you talked about in the winter? With... being out in the street."

"Yeah. That time. There was more to it, too. But then. They... the priests found me, and took me out of there, and – I would have died, if they hadn't. Frozen, or starved. I wouldn't have made it to the spring. The Tufarians healed my body, where I needed it. The Daranites did more than that." He drew a shaky breath, clasping his hands together to draw strength from wherever he could find it. "They started to heal my soul. They gave me... purpose, and dignity. My humanity. I'd lost it. They showed me – showed me how to take it back."

He felt her hand rest on his arm, lingering there to tell him what she couldn't voice. He remembered what she'd said in the dark as the fever ravaged his body. She had said that she was glad he'd lived. He held those words cupped in his heart like an ember.

Keifon covered her hand with his own, all he could bring himself to do in acknowledgement, and after a little while she pulled away. "Thank you for your answer," she murmured.

"Thank you for asking."

They did not speak to one another again, but Keifon felt her presence near him through the ceremony, through the sermons and the prayers and the hymns. She might not fully understand, but she respected his need to come here. She was willing to ask questions and to seek to understand.

It would offend her if he told her about the murky hope swirling deep inside him – the half-formed thought that the gods had brought them together. She would not understand that he saw it as an honor. She would see it as denying her free will. She would talk about chance or the pantheist idea of the will of the universe.

Someday she might begin to understand, and he took comfort in that. The idea itself was terrifying sometimes. But it was the one thing that began to explain why he felt that her presence here with him was not only right, but needed. She was an unbeliever, she was a foreigner both to him and to the priests and worshippers in this church, but she belonged here.

When the service ended, Keifon and Agna left the church and lingered in the churchyard. Agna linked her hands behind her back. "Thank you for that."

"Nn. Thank you for coming. It means a lot to me." He looked away, realizing that Agna's dark red dress harmonized with his uniform. Had she dressed to honor the festival, or was he reading too much into it? Keifon shoved off that thought and offered her a smile. "Ready to see the festival?"

"Sure."

They walked side by side through the fairground, and as they remarked to one another about the sights, Keifon felt the weight on him easing. It was important that he pay his respects, and he was deeply moved by what she'd done, even if she didn't understand why. But he was ready to take some joy in the day and spend some time with his friend.

They browsed through stalls selling reed baskets and woven blankets, not intending to buy anything in particular, appreciating the local handiwork. They bought bottles of water and crepes filled with berries and salty goat's milk cheese, a Resurrection tradition in this area – something about the colors, white and red. They sipped and munched as they walked. Agna's mouth stained red, and she fretted half-seriously about Keifon's uniform. He'd been careful, though, and hadn't spilled a crumb.

At the games of chance and skill the barkers homed in on him, calling him out because of his uniform and because he was walking with a companion. Keifon waved them off, blushing nearly as crimson as his jacket when one made a comment about impressing one's lady friend.

"That was rude," Agna muttered as they hurried down the aisle to another booth. "You'd think they wouldn't be so cruel, trying to get customers. Unless they wanted to make you angry, to prove them wrong."

"I'm not angry, I'm just embarrassed. I don't like being the center of attention." Agna motioned at his clothes as if to explain an obvious point, and he squirmed. "Yes, but... it's different. I dressed up today in honor of the holiday. I'm not doing it to get attention."

She had gotten off the topic of their apparent appearance to outsiders, at least. He gravitated toward another booth, and she turned her attention to that.

At the next games booth, Agna stepped in front of him and tossed down the copper coins to play. The barker glanced over her shoulder at Keifon and his look of horror, but did not goad him into joining. Agna threw her allotted handful of darts at the target, and clipped the edge of one target, sending the dart bouncing into the straw. She bought another round of chances, and the last dart hung trembling at the edge of the target. She threw her hands in the air, cheering.

"Very good," he said as they walked away in triumph.

"Someday I'll get better," she sighed.

In the middle of the fairground a band began to tune up, and Keifon drifted toward it. He was curious about the instrumentation in the mountain country and the songs they played for the Resurrection, but given the jovial atmosphere in the crowd, it seemed that they would play summer festival songs. Agna took her place beside him, and as the sun swung overhead she retreated to the pool of shade under a tree. Keifon followed, realizing that he was beginning to sweat under his wool. For a while he lost himself in the harmonics and the buoyant mood and the blend of percussion that seemed to be unique to this area. He nearly forgot the holiday and his formality and everything else but the pleasure of a sweet summer day with good music and good company. When the band took a break, he apologized to Agna for keeping them there.

"No need," she insisted. "I know it's something that interests you. I don't mind."

"We can move on now, though. What would you like to see?"

She bought just one thing, in the end – a bookmark woven in a fine pattern of bright colors. She bought one for each of them and shoved one in a pocket of his jacket, shushing his protests. It was a souvenir, she insisted. He acquiesced and carried it in his pocket.

They looped past one of the beer gardens, and Agna spotted Nelle, surrounded by revelers. The herbalist raised her glass, beaming. Agna waved. Keifon realized that she didn't intend to stop, and waved as well. "You can sit with Nelle if you want to. I wouldn't mind changing. It's getting warm."

"Eh, it's all right. She's having fun. I'd rather..." She trailed off, and cleared her throat. "Ready for a break? I do love a nap on a hot afternoon. Am I getting old, for saying that?"

Keifon laughed. They returned to the campsite, which was lazy and quiet, half-emptied into the fairground. The sky had clouded over, pressing the heavy air against the ground. Keifon unbuttoned his jacket and unpinned the sigils on his collar, grateful for the cooler air against his soaked undershirt.

"What does that one mean?"

He paused, embarrassed that she was still in the tent. Modesty had never been an issue in the Army, and he had fallen into old habits. "Um." He looked down at the pin in his hand. "Oh – this is for my unit. And this is for my specialty."

"And the one you usually wear is for the Army in general."

"Right." He slipped them into his pocket, trading them for the bookmark. Unsure what to do with it, he held it as he stripped out of his jacket and pulled off his boots. Agna grew restless and came up with a garbled excuse to leave the tent. She closed the tent flaps after her. Keifon stood in solitude, letting the day wash through him. It wasn't over yet, but it had been good so far.

He changed into lighter clothes and slipped the bookmark into his logbook, where he would see it when they reopened the clinic. When Agna returned, she stretched out on her cot and dozed off. Keifon waited until she was fully asleep and found his new book in his backpack. He stretched out near the open tent flaps to read by daylight.

Agna had thought that he'd bought something private, something salacious, in the shop in Vertal. It was not remotely salacious, but he had kept it private for as long as he could.

Immigration Patterns in Kavera. Chapter Three. Yanweian settlement in Northern Kavera.

He had read about the original settlement of Kavera in antiquity. He had read about the Nessinian political refugees who came in waves whenever Nessiny's leaders shifted their loyalties. And now, as the faint breeze stirred over his face, he read about the ranchers who came south to establish homesteads around Laketon. They had mingled across the border for hundreds of years. The native Laketoners were used to Yanweians in their midst. They all knew how to say hello and goodbye, please and thank you, in Keifon's native language, and many were passingly fluent. A few of them even intermarried, like the Nessinian shrine guard, with his in-laws in Lendu. Keifon was not the only one of his countrymen in this land. He was not the only one who thought about the possibility of staying.

He paused at the end of the chapter to rest his neck. Agna slept. She was going back home, he reminded himself. As lovely as today had been, he had to remember that their time together was finite. They could work together and make the best of their arrangement here, but that was all.

Not entirely all. Keifon rested his head on his crossed arms, over the open pages. He had to acknowledge what was happening. He'd been happier today, going to the fair with her, than he had been for a long time. He had been so proud to walk next to her, to wander aimlessly through the crowds and talk.

When the carnival barkers had called them out as lovers, it had stung. Not because he wanted it to be true, necessarily. He sorted through this, now that the moment had passed. He did not envy Agna and Laris because of their love for one another, specifically, but because they had found love at all. He was happy for her, even as he worried about their separation and the difficulty of carrying on a relationship at a distance. He wished he someone he could trust and care for the way that Agna and Laris cared for one another. Edann would not allow such sentimentality.

Keifon couldn't approach the idea of caring for Agna that way. It was too bright, too loud, too heated; he cut wide around it. In the meantime, Keifon was sure that his growing love for her – he could name it that now – was different from Laris's, and did not preclude it.

Keifon remembered someone else, from very long ago. When he'd been a rancher's son, he'd ranged through the fields and climbed the neighbors' fences with Mya, a girl from a few farms over, the daughter of vegetable farmers. They had shared all of the best fishing streams and hiding places. At his parents' funeral, Mya had slipped through the crowd to hold his hand, standing resolutely beside him. His brother had clung to him on the other side. The three of them, Kei and Mya and Jafi, had been alone, three children in a sea of Keifon's distant relatives.

He hadn't seen her again after the funeral. She'd gone away to her own apprenticeship, somewhere. By now she had to be married. He'd loved her, and being with her made him happy. That was all he knew.

Agna was not Mya; she would never climb a water tower or throw apples at his head. ...Perhaps she would, at that. But he recognized this feeling.

Agna would not believe him if he told her that he loved her. She would find excuses. But he could share his fishing streams and his hiding places. He would stand by her when she needed him. She would understand that.

A sudden summer storm swept over the land, pelting the ground with rain. Raindrops pattered in through the open tent flaps, and Keifon put the book away. He leaned back against his backpack to watch and listen. The rain sluiced the mountains and the fields, and in the morning the campground and the fairground alike would be paved with sucking mud. But for now, the rain brought cool air and quiet relief. Agna slept through it, trusting him to keep watch.

Laris: Confessions

Dear Agna,

I am so sorry.

I didn't want to do this to you, and I am so sorry.

I didn't mean for anything to happen.

But it did.

I told Weira I had a sweetheart, she said that's all right, and we haven't done anything but talk. But in my heart I think – I haven't stopped being in love with you, I promise you. You're the most interesting person I think I've ever met, and I still want to crawl inside your head and live there. But I have to be honest with you. I'm in love with her too. When I'm with her, I'm just home. I don't know how to even describe it to you.

I am so sorry. Weira and I had a long talk last night. I decided that I had to tell you. I guess the Lundrans would say that being in love doesn't make me a scoundrel, but covering it up would. I don't know, I've always been more of an Eytran if anything. But I knew that you have to have the truth.

I don't know what you want to do. I would wait for you if this hadn't happened. Now I don't know what to do. I really don't.

It looks like we're going to be coming pretty close to the summer caravan between Deeproot Valley and Tirington. I'd love to see you, if you want to come. If not, I understand.

Love,

Laris.

■ ■ ■

Agna came.

She rode in the saddle of a tall chestnut, looking like a princess from another land in a dark purple dress, her hair windblown. Her eyes were puffy, and she stumbled a little as she dismounted. Laris' heart pounded in his chest and in his throat. It was like a half-awake dream, seeing her here in the real world. She was lovely. All of the things she'd said, all of the things that he'd dreamed were caught up in his head. He couldn't look at her without hearing her words in his mind.

She held onto the horse's reins. Laris hugged her, and the reins tugged around behind him when she hugged him back. "I-I didn't think you'd come.

Because of what I said. You know." It was still a little hard to say Weira's name out loud. It was like an incantation, a magic spell.

"Yeah... well. I had to see you." Agna pulled back and knotted the horse's reins around a fence post. She patted its neck. She wasn't carrying anything with her. She didn't mean to stay long, Laris realized with a growing panic. He'd ruined it after all. Maybe he wouldn't ever see her again.

Agna smoothed her hair and tucked it behind her ears. "How have you been? Otherwise. Sounds like the drive is going well."

"Yeah. Yeah. It's going great. I mean, I don't know that I'd want to do this all the time. I'm homesick sometimes. But we're getting to see the country." He shut himself up. She was listening, but her eyes were drifting somewhere near his elbow. "I'm rambling. I'm sorry."

"I'm glad you're happy," she said, and swallowed hard. "I'm happy for you. And Weira."

A sharp little pain spiked in the back of his eyes. "I'm sorry. I'm so sorry, Agna. I never wanted to hurt you, never."

"I know." She sounded so tired. He held out his arms to hug her, and she sighed and let him. Something had gone, though. The lightning, the energy, was gone. He felt the same excitement, like he was the luckiest man in the world to have convinced this person to somehow pay attention to him. But she wasn't there anymore. She hugged him like a distant relative. "I'm not mad at you, if you were wondering," she said into his chest.

Laris laughed uneasily. "I guess I was, a little."

"I... won't say I'm not sad. I'll miss you." Her voice was just barely loud enough for him to hear. Laris's throat began to close up. She couldn't be saying this now, and he had known all along that she would. Both of these things were true at the same time, somehow. "I want you to be happy with Weira. So you can give her all of your attention, and be there for her. Because she can be there for you. ...Thank you for all of your letters." Her voice dropped to a whisper. "Thank you for everything."

She must have felt his stomach quivering, or heard his breath get uneven. She rubbed his back and shushed him, like a child, which made it worse. And then her own breath hitched in a little hiccup, and Laris lost it entirely. He couldn't make her cry. She had come across the ocean and studied ancient arts and traveled around the world and talked to everyone in Kavera and read every book and some stupid farm boy couldn't make her cry. But he had. It wasn't right. It wasn't how the world was supposed to work.

"Don't cry," Agna got out between her own gasping breaths. "Please don't. It's good. I'm glad you found someone who can be with you properly. I don't think I was ever all right with you waiting for me."

"I would have waited," Laris insisted. "I wanted to. I just..."

"It's all right. It was supposed to happen. Right? Don't you believe that sort of thing?"

"I don't know," he said helplessly. "I don't know. I love you."

"I love you, too."

She got control first, leaning her forehead against his chest. His tears dripped down his chin into her hair. He wiped his face on his sleeve, letting go for a second.

"You're kind, and honest," she was saying, her breathy voice winding deep into his body, "and strong, a-and – and adorable, and I want you to be happy."

"I want you to," he said, swallowing the last of the lump. "Be happy. I do."

"I will. I think I will." She hung onto his shirt for a second longer. *Now*, Laris thought. It wasn't for the future; the future was far away, another unmapped country. It was for every letter he'd read until the pages got ragged at the edges, for every night he'd fallen asleep wondering where she was and whether she missed him. They had outlined what they wanted, filling in the spaces around it without quite saying it. *I miss you. I wish you were here with me. I wish I could...*

He kissed her like an animal scenting the first breeze of spring, ready to bolt. She gasped against his mouth, then leaned up on her toes. It was back, whatever it was; she wasn't hugging him like a distant relation. She was there with him, one more time.

Laris didn't bolt.

■ ■ ■

Agna got on her tall horse and rode down the road between Deeproot Valley and Tirington. Laris stood in the road and watched her go. Weira didn't come, not yet. She would, soon enough. She would be there for him. But for a little while, he had to share his love and his grief with the fences and the water and the sky.

Part Three

Keifon: The Long Season

Keifon tried not to count each passing week against those that remained in the summer. The season between New Year's and Lundrala was long, and normally it was taken up with foaling and training and listening to neighbors' complaints about plowing and planting. Now, in what his life had become, it was taken up with worrying about Agna.

She was quiet. He couldn't define it more than that, or name all of the symptoms of her grief. She didn't let him catch her crying, though he saw her swollen eyes afterward. She didn't talk about Laris, instead stopping herself and changing the subject, or getting up to leave. But he felt her tidal sadness under their feet, under their skin, all the time.

The air had been heavy and damp all week, and Keifon and Agna pinned up the clinic tent walls and waited for patients and breezes. It was Midsummer tomorrow – at least they called it that in Kavera. Back home it was just the beginning of summer, the longest day of the year. He remembered that odd conversation last summer about birthdays. Agna's was on Midsummer, by her culture's reckoning. Keifon could have kicked himself for forgetting it until now, though they had both been preoccupied.

He didn't have any gifts for her, and any gift he gave would be useless against her pain. Money and flowers, she'd said, so long ago. That was what they gave for birthdays in her country. He had little enough money, though he wasn't opposed to giving her what he could. Flowers were more difficult. They were available, and some were inexpensive. But too much of him was back home, and saw a gift of flowers as inappropriate for a birthday. Maybe Nelle would have some ideas; she knew a lot about plants.

Keifon cleared his throat. "It's Midsummer tomorrow, isn't it?"

Agna did not look up from her logbook, where she doodled in the margins. "Yes – I suppose it is."

"Would you want to celebrate it at all? I don't... I don't have a gift. But we could do something. If you want to," he added.

Agna bit her lip, thinking. "Well," she said at last. "It's your festival too."

His birthday was over a month away, a point he didn't correct. She remembered. If she chose to recast it as something she understood, he didn't mind. Or maybe she wanted to deflect attention away from herself. Or maybe she wanted to share it with him, some incorrigible part of his mind suggested.

Agna's voice quickened a little. "I guess we could do something. That might be nice. Nothing fancy. There isn't much in this town, I don't think. Unless you'd want to go to their town... singing... thing. Caroling?"

"No, we can skip that."

"Hm." She twirled her pen in her fingers, the feather's tip blurring in the heavy air. "I know you're not much for wine," she remarked absently. "How about a nice dinner? Pick out things that we both like. It isn't much, but I'd like that."

Part of him heard her. A small part, a single scout over a distant hill. That small part kept track of her musings while the rest of him sank.

You're not much for wine. As though it weren't important. As though it were a simple preference. *You don't like sweets, or songs in reduced eighth key, or wine. That's all.* As though he didn't wake up some nights with the imaginary taste of bile and cheap liquor in the back of his throat.

He'd never told her. He'd forgotten, sometimes, that he had never told her. She never asked, and sometimes he told himself that she had figured it out and didn't mind. He told himself that he didn't have to go through with telling her after all.

"Are you all right?"

Keifon surfaced from his thoughts. "Mmn. Sorry."

She studied him, and he saw her decide not to pursue. Not yet. She would catch up with him later. "All right. What do you think, though? A nice dinner? And maybe go to the bonfire for a little bit. It's been a while."

"All right," he said, able to echo her words, but not much more.

"Are you all right? Is it something I said?"

"No – well – not now. I need to think."

Agna's lips thinned. "Do you ever stop?"

His mouth twitched, the closest he could get to a smile. Agna let the subject drop, and the two of them waited.

■ ■ ■

Flowers and money. He had counted out the latter, folded the coins in paper, and enclosed them in an envelope. Thinking about courting and weddings and funerals, he knocked on Nelle's open doorframe. A sharp green smell drifted from the interior of her wagon.

"Hey there." Nelle turned, tucking a stray curl into the mass tied at the back of her neck. "What's the occasion?"

"Midsummer," Keifon replied. "Agna's – in Nessiny she said they give people flowers for their birthdays, and hers is on Midsummer. Kind of. What kind should I give her, do you think? I thought you might know." He gestured vaguely at the bundles of herbs and the cooking concoction inside.

"Well, I'm not a florist." Nelle paced barefoot to the door and sat on the stoop.

"Yeah, but – I thought she might like something medicinal instead. Or cooking herbs. Something – you know, something pretty and useful."

A grin exposed Nelle's eyeteeth. "Pretty and useful, huh?"

"I just thought she'd like that." He didn't like the level of defensiveness in his voice, but he didn't have the energy to spar with her. Flowers and money wouldn't make up for what he was about to tell Agna. They were the only ideas he had.

"Hmm." Nelle gazed toward the tree line beyond the campsite. "Yeah, give me a minute and come along. Can gather some nice things. Won't be far."

"Thank you." He sank onto her steps as she climbed back in to clatter some pots on her stove.

It wouldn't be enough. But it mattered as a final gesture, if nothing else. He could sleep on the wagon easily enough; many of the temporary passengers did. And Edann would let him stay over some of the time. Agna would be professional enough to continue their working relationship in some form, although of course she would never trust him again. Keifon's stomach clenched, and he leaned against Nelle's doorframe. It had been good, in the end. Going to the Resurrection festival with her was still the best day he'd had since he came to Kavera. He could remember that, and be grateful.

"You all right?" Nelle prodded his thigh with a sandaled foot.

"Mmgh." Keifon unfolded from the steps. Nelle gave him a look, but turned without comment and led him across the campsite.

Keifon followed her over the edge of the rise that delineated this campsite. Among the long grasses the air seemed to move a little more freely, and Keifon let his steps lengthen. Nelle parted the whippy branches at the edge of the wood until he could catch them. The two of them burrowed through a wall of broad-leaved undergrowth and emerged under the trees, wading in feathery ferns up to their shins.

He caught his breath, uneasy in this terrain, as Nelle looked around to orient herself. They were alone. At most, he could spot a few birds and a squirrel. No one was going to leap at them.

"So. What's the problem?"

"Huh?" Keifon snapped back from thoughts of knives and blood.

"You fighting or something?" Nelle hiked northeast through the ferns.

"No – well."

She laid her hand on a sapling as they passed. "Not yet?"

"Maybe." He sighed. It was cooler in the shade, which counteracted his urge to run back to camp. Besides, he would have to face Agna there.

Nelle let him keep his peace. She stooped to pick a sprig of frothy blue flowers and handed it over to Keifon. "That's not all," Nelle commented. "Got ideas. Just hang on and we'll put it together."

"Yes, ma'am," Keifon murmured, and accepted the fern fronds that she passed him. She stalked off through the brush, and Keifon followed, cradling their finds. She added three or four more plants to their growing bouquet; he recognized two of them from the preparations he'd bought for the clinic. It looked nice, he thought. Agna would appreciate the gesture.

They crossed a rill, stepping bank to bank. Nelle turned to follow it downstream. Watching her back as they walked, Keifon wondered whether Nelle knew how Agna would react. He wondered whether it would accomplish anything to ask. She would offer her opinion of any camp gossip that came her way – loudly – but she wouldn't repeat anything said to her in confidence. Not that it would matter for much longer. He just didn't want Agna to find out before he could tell her.

"I, uh. I have to talk to Agna about something."

"Just be a minute." Nelle waved a hand at him.

"No, I mean – that's what's wrong. It's-it's something I've been hiding from her."

Nelle turned. Her dark eyes regarded him levelly. He knew where her loyalties lay, if he ever dared drive a wedge between them.

Keifon's fingers tightened around the bundle of flowers and herbs. "I shouldn't have. I know. And my conscience is catching up with me. So I'm going to tell her." There was no wind to move the leaves over their heads. "It's bad," he said at last, giving up. "It's really bad. I think this is it for us."

Nelle let go a long, slow breath. She spread her hands. "Kill somebody?"

"—What?" The back of his brain, already primed to disaster, felt the strange knife in his hands and the blood sheeting his neck. They had been trying to kill him and Agna. And it was never clear whether he'd struck a death blow to any of them. "No, that—"

"Rapist?"

His hands dropped to his sides. She was guessing his secret, facetiously. "Gods, no."

"Does Menon need to watch his goats?"

He set his jaw. "Now you're just being an ass."

"Yep." She stretched her arms over her head. "And everyone knows you're with Lord Crankypants. That's hardly a secret."

The blood rushed to his face, though he could not name it either anger or shame. *I'm not "with" him. He wouldn't have it. He wouldn't have me. I don't know. I'm not sure I care anymore.* "That's not it, anyway."

"Well then. Whatever it is, be honest with her. She'll get over it." Nelle turned to follow the stream. "She respects honesty. You know that."

Keifon's legs would not let him follow. It was all they could do to keep him upright. The distance stretched, eight, a dozen paces. "I... I was a drunkard, back home."

Nelle turned.

His fingers found the torque, cooling in the shade, merely as warm as his skin. "That's why my wife left. I was – I was a waste."

"You and everyone's uncle, farm boy," Nelle said softly. She looked up into the canopy of leaves. "Must have it managed, then."

"I'm trying."

Keifon's stomach churned, waiting for the sentence, waiting for the truth. Nelle gave a little philosophical shrug. "What should I do? Faint?"

He swallowed hard. *Yes. Or denounce me. Something. Something I deserve.* The absence of what he expected hurt like a pulled tooth. Nelle only smiled – not the wicked grin that bothered him for reasons he didn't want to examine, but something clear and kind. "Talk to her. It'll be all right. Matters that you're trying now. Not so much what happened then."

He closed his eyes for a breath, switched the flowers to his other hand, and sighed. "Yeah."

He could follow her now, and she led him back to the edge of the meadow. Keifon looked down at the bundle in his hand. Nelle fished in her pocket for a string, and he held it up so that she could bind it together.

"It's nice," he said. "Thank you."

Nelle sketched a bow. "Maybe I'm in the wrong business after all."

■ ■ ■

Agna licked honey from her fingers, and Keifon stared over the peaked tents and scrolled wagon roofs. He felt heavy and sleepy, full of Masa's rice casserole and ripe peaches. Agna had followed that with a little oat cake soaked in honey, and now they lounged by the fire pit, too lazy to move.

They had been able to chat amiably all through dinner. They had talked about the towns they'd passed lately, the traveling musicians who were visiting the camp, and the last novel that Keifon had read and then passed to Agna. She didn't seem to notice that he was playacting everything, that he was counting down to the end. Keifon noticed that she wasn't entirely herself, either. Her melancholy over Laris could not be erased with one evening of companionship.

His news would not make her happy, and neither would his paltry gift. But it was all he had. Keifon cleared his throat. "I have something for you."

"What? No!" Agna's sadness was dashed away by panic. "I don't – well... ugh! This is too sudden."

"It's not much. Really. Don't worry about it." Escaping her confusing reaction, he fetched the flowers and envelope from where he'd stashed them behind the tent. The stems, soaked in his water glass, dripped on her skirt as she took them.

Agna pressed the back of her hand against her mouth, and he saw her eyes water. His heart sank. The wrong thing? The wrong time? "I – you – you said flowers and money. I'm sorry."

She dropped the envelope into her lap and fumbled in her belt pouch for a handkerchief. "No, I'm sorry. I guess I'm getting homesick, all of a sudden. This is so sweet of you."

"Um... Nelle helped me pick them," he said, realizing that he was overstating the case. Nelle had picked them, and he had carried them. "They're all medicinal, or edible. We thought you'd like that." *We.* He was digging himself deeper, not that it mattered.

She carefully set the bouquet aside, then lifted the clinking envelope and shook it. A half-smile ghosted across her face.

"I didn't know how much was customary," Keifon forced past his dry throat. Agna tapped the coins into her hand. Keifon blushed, suddenly embarrassed by the paucity and sentimentality of his choice. "It's, um. Fifteen head. Which is, you know, not much of anything, but uh..." He saw her forehead crease, working out the meaning of the number. He swallowed. "For the last fifteen months. That's all." The reckoning included the first few months, but even that had been part of their travels together.

"Fifteen...oh." She closed the copper coins in her hand. "...Oh." Her smile turned strange, and Keifon nearly lunged to take the money back and apologize. But she shook it off. "Thank you. That's lovely."

Keifon bit his tongue over more babbling apologies. She liked the gift. He had made her homesick, but that was a sweet kind of hurt.

"I guess – I have something for you," Agna said, setting the envelope next to the flowers. "I was saving it for Lundrala, but – it'd be nice to have more time. Hang on." She disappeared into the tent. Keifon drank some more water, which did little for the dryness of his throat, and waited.

She emerged with two books, cradling them nervously against her body. "It's better for a Lundrala gift, really. And maybe it's a stupid idea, but–"

Keifon frowned, trying to work out some inkling of what she meant, until she held out one of the books to him. He accepted it. It was a heavy leather-bound volume, as thick as a dictionary. He turned it to read the spine, and his breath stopped. *Introductory Nessinian*, written out in his own language. His fingers traced the embossed title.

"You don't have to if you don't want to," Agna was saying. Keifon opened the book to an early page. *Greetings and Conversation, part 2.*

His throat closed as he realized what the book's mate might be. Agna held it up in reply to his questioning look. The Eastern script on the cover looked much the same as Kaveran writing. He didn't know one word, but the other looked like *Yanweian*, the way it was spelled in Kaveran. Nessinian to Yanweian, the other way around. He closed the book and pressed his fingers against his eyes, willing his breathing to even out.

She wanted to learn. She wanted to communicate with him. She wanted them to keep learning about one another's lives, even though they had less than a year left. Keifon imagined writing her letters that she could read and getting letters from her that came right from her heart, without translation. She wanted to keep in touch with him even after she had gone.

He remembered Nelle's smile, dappled with shadow. *What matters is what you do now, not what you did then.* He could believe it, if only for an instant. He could believe it long enough to tell Agna what she deserved to hear, and know that she would be with him afterward.

He forced himself out of his spiral. Agna stood uneasily, her arms crossed over the *Introductory Yanweian* book, held like a breastplate over her chest. Keifon swallowed and lifted his head. "I'm sorry. It's – I love it. Thank you so much."

Agna's relief washed off her like the first light of morning. "Oh, good." She sat next to him. "I'd like to read them together, if you don't mind. I looked at mine and didn't understand the pronunciation at all."

"Yeah, they say it's hard if you're a for—if you're learning it as an adult. It might help to hear it out loud."

They leafed through the books as Keifon gathered his courage. At least Nessinian script was similar to Kaveran – the same, as far as he could tell, except for a number of little extra marks that differed from one to the other. Teaching Agna how to read Yanweian script might take as long as everything else put together. Maybe they should focus on spoken words first.

Thinking about this, vaulting over the roadblock that lay directly ahead, evened out his fear. He didn't want to spoil their Midsummer, but the longer he waited, the more he risked losing his nerve. It didn't have to ruin everything. He had to believe that.

"Agna?"

"Hm?" She looked up from her page, and slowly closed the book as he went on.

"I wanted to talk to you about something. Something you said earlier – you didn't do anything wrong, but you reminded me of something I have to talk to you about." He set his book aside, frustrated that he'd made a complete circle. "Some bad things. In the past. But not only in the past. That's the important thing. I know I – I dwell, and I'm trying not to."

Agna nodded. "Go on."

He took a deep breath, stopped himself from touching the torque, and watched the ground. "You said I don't like wine. I don't, now. I'm trying not to drink it now because I used to drink too much, back home." He found that he could breathe, and though he didn't look up, Agna hadn't stormed away yet. "Far too much. I couldn't control it. It was why – why Eri left. And why I lost the ranch. I couldn't keep it together." His voice wavered. He cleared his throat, and in that silence Agna spoke.

"I'm so sorry," she murmured. "Sometimes I wondered, the way you kind of tense up when – anyway, it doesn't matter. Can I give you a hug?"

He was shaking a little. It was embarrassing. But he nodded, and she came to him. Her arms were solid and warm around him, and he hugged her back fiercely. His breath shuddered in his chest.

Of course she wouldn't leave. It was only his own fear, his own decision that he didn't deserve for her to stay, that told him she would. Faced with Agna now, with the living weight of her body and the smell of her skin, he couldn't imagine her casting aspersions on him and bolting. It didn't make sense. That wasn't something she would do.

"I'm so sorry you went through that. I can't stand to think of you suffering." Her hand moved in slow, soothing circles on his back. Keifon closed his eyes and held on. "But I know you're doing your best. Was that in the Army, when you stopped? Like you told me at the Resurrection festival?"

He nodded against her shoulder. His voice was tight and wavering. "Before. The Church got me off the street. Helped me quit. Then got me into the Army."

Agna squeezed him tighter. "I'm proud of you."

His breath let go in something between a laugh and a sob. He pulled away before he lost it completely, and Agna dabbed her eyes with her handkerchief.

"Thank you," he said. It was all he could think of.

"Thank you, for trusting me with that."

Keifon's hand landed on the Nessinian book, and he opened it and leafed through the first few pages for what he needed. *"E-emelo la. – Le? Emelo le."* *Thank you.*

Agna chuckled, biting her lip, and rifled through the Yanweian book. *"Eisaru,"* she read, her voice ironing out the tones like a stereotypical foreigner in a slapstick play. *Thank you.* Despite her clumsiness, the sound of her voice in his own tongue grabbed him in the gut. She was trying. She was trying to meet him halfway. She was still here. That was all that mattered.

Agna: Aspirations

The traveling musicians put down their instruments to a round of applause. Performing near the fire had left all of them perspiring in rivers. They took seats in the circle, setting their instruments aside, fanning themselves and picking up the passed bottles.

Agna clapped politely and glanced aside at her companion. The music had helped his mood a little. He caught her eye and even smiled faintly. Agna couldn't ignore the fear lurking in the back of her mind. She'd known for a long time that he could fall prey to his melancholy at any moment. Knowing how far his melancholy went and the weapons with which it armed itself only added color and detail to her nightmare. But for now, sitting by the bonfire despite the lingering summer heat, surrounded by the other merchants, they would be all right.

"The northwest canal spur is going to fail," announced one of the merchants, a spare man who dealt in odds and ends.

Vociel, the carpenter, waved him off. "It's been what, four years?"

"Three," someone corrected.

"Three, fine. It's lasted three years. Wildern has been shipping lumber down to Vertal twice as fast as they used to send it around the coast, and it's in better shape when it gets there. Ten times as fast as going overland. The mills and the builders are churning out profits on both ends. Where's the failure in that?"

"In depending too much on the influence of *one company* in the entire Northwest."

Agna detected a marked increase in the number of people pretending not to watch her and Keifon. The Benevolent Union, then? She'd heard a few passing remarks against the Benevolent Union, which struck her as strange. It was hard to imagine what they held against hospitals and schools.

The dealer continued. "As the Bennies go, so goes Wildern now. That's just not wise."

Several other voices rose. "The Benevolent Union is just about as likely to fold as the damn Council, and you know it."

"Less. The Bennies can't go to war."

"Oh, can't they."

"I didn't say fold, I said where they *go*. If they decide one day to pack up all their money and go back south, where does that leave everyone else?"

"Logging like they always did," Vociel remarked sourly. "Except now they have a canal."

"No, no, they've built up too far. If half the town is empty—"

A livestock dealer blew a stream of smoke toward the fire. "The Benevolents aren't half the town anymore, and besides, people've started shipping trade over the border."

"To the—" The speaker stumbled nervously, darting a glance toward Keifon. "To the Yanweians?"

Another passed a bottle of wine around the circle. "Through the blasted *mountains?*"

"I'm telling you, it's happening. Not much, yet. But bring all that Union money up to the border and somebody starts thinking of how to multiply it. They have routes—"

"Six months out of a year."

"You wait. They'll find a way. Get some earthbreakers up there…"

"Earthbreakers can't move an entire mountain, just crack it. You still need an army of people to haul it away."

Keifon had leaned back and crossed his arms over his chest, listening. Agna tilted her head toward the debate. "What do you think?"

He spoke quietly, only to her. "Hm. Wildern and Ceien aren't really that far apart, mapwise. If they cut out a decent road through the mountains, it could turn into a good trade route."

"Ceien," Agna mused. "That's… where your daughter lives, isn't it?"

"Mmhm. And Eri's family." He chewed his lip. Agna left well enough alone; he seemed calm.

She ignored the discussion and watched the movement of light, the shadows it cast on skin and fabric, and the shifting contours of a gesturing arm or a grimacing jaw. Life drawing had never been her forte. It was a shame; she could have done so many sketches tonight. Of course, she had never considered herself any good at drawing plants, either.

Your lines are sound, dear, you just need practice. She remembered her mother pacing through the library. It was her idea to send Agna to art school. Her father had, in the end, thrown his vote in with Agna's dream of the Academy.

She'd never intended to make art. And what she drew and sent to Lina wasn't the same sort of thing as the art that her father sought for his clients. – What she would seek for her own clients, soon enough. Less than a year, now. Had she learned anything that mattered? She and Marco wrote back and forth about Kaveran art, and the fact that most artists here were amateurs. She'd heard that in Vertal and Prisa the market was robust enough to support professional painters, but not any further north.

She was still learning, she reminded herself. She was learning about healing and art, and about how to fit them together. She wasn't done yet.

"Are you glad you came here?" she asked, watching the fire.

Keifon looked up from the flames. "Hm. ...I am. Except for being away from Nachi for so long. Otherwise... I am. It's..." He trailed off, shifting his position on the log seat, hunching forward meditatively.

"It's gotten better," Agna offered.

"Yeah. ...Are you glad you came? I mean, I guess not. You've said that."

"No, I'm..." Agna sighed. If she'd stayed at home and found a placement at a hospital or a country shrine, she wouldn't have this intermittent pain in her back or need to know as much about water-borne diseases or know so many moderately insulting words for foreigners in Kaveran. She would be surrounded by family and peers who understood her and respected her talents. She would achieve more, gain recognition, and be appreciated for her hard work and her natural skill. She could secure a position on the board of a hospital, or open a gallery on the side as she completed her obligation to the Academy. She wouldn't waste any time before continuing her life's goals.

Still.

Her patients respected her talents as much as any patients in Nessiny would. She could just as easily be surrounded by rivals or bullies or layabouts who expected her to pick up their slack. If the Academy had harbored all of those, she could find them anywhere. She had been lucky, in the end, when it came to colleagues.

She had learned things about Kaveran art that she would never have learned at home – things that no one might have considered before, because no one with her particular background had come here. Few of the healers and swordmasters that the Academy sent were affiliated with the art world, after all. She had been uniquely placed, despite her original intentions.

Keifon waited for her answer. Agna took in the circle of merchants, the camp beyond, and all of the sleeping villages and half-familiar cities beyond that. Even when – if? – she went back, she would be changed by her time here. She would carry it with her.

"I am glad I came," she said at last. "Some things more than others. You and Nelle and Laris, absolutely. I would be a different person without you. Even though things didn't work out—" She cut herself off before she could choke up fully. She hadn't intended to fall through that trapdoor this time. She cleared her throat, and knew that he would not think less of her for the waver in her voice. "Even then."

Keifon squeezed her shoulder gently. "I'm glad you found some good in it. Even if it's hard."

Agna nodded, not quite trusting her voice yet.

Half a year had passed since her decision to stay, when she had vowed to improve her situation on the road and make the most of her assignment. There was more work to be done. She and Marco slowly circled something in their letters, drawing closer to undiscovered shores. She only had to keep moving and keep an open mind.

And what about her companion? He was so resigned to everything hopeless and ruined in his life, but she would not let him succumb. If she could find a way, so could he. She couldn't solve his problems for him, but a solution had to exist for him if he would only stop refusing to look.

If she insisted, he would resist. She had to approach it sidelong, even if her ruse became obvious afterward.

She kept her eyes on the flames. "I think that if I could practice healing, be involved in art somehow, and travel sometimes, I'd have everything I wanted." A fourth goal hit her in the chest, and she crossed her arms. "And, well. Have some friends around. That's important."

Keifon nodded. "Hm. You can do all of those things."

"How about you?"

She saw the temptation flash through his eyes to duck the question, to turn it into a weak joke. But he looked into the bonfire's embers and gathered his thoughts.

Keifon counted his goals one by one on his fingers. "I want to see Nachi. Even if it isn't all of the time. I want to get married and have some more children. Not a lot. Two or three. And I want to be a better medic. Or even study to be a doctor, with a permanent practice. Someday." He looked at the three fingers he'd extended and slowly added a fourth. "Stay sober. Stay healthy. And—like you said." He opened his hand, but did not name the fifth thought.

"You can do all of that, too," Agna said.

He shrugged. "I think I'd need to leave the Army to study. I've learned everything they need a medic to know."

"Will they let you leave?"

"Hn. Under certain circumstances." He shifted, sitting cross-legged on the log. "I can petition to have my contract with the Benevolent Union extended to match my obligation to the Army. The Union would own me then, instead. But there are more options with them."

"Like... going to the University in Prisa?"

"I can't afford that. And it's too far from Nachi."

Agna sighed. He seemed determined to refuse any path she found. "Is there somewhere to study in Ceien?"

Keifon considered this. "Apprenticing with a medical practice. It's slow, but I could afford it." He leaned on his hand, slanting away from her. "But I'd rather not live in Ceien. I know it's wrong of me to say that. Even though Nachi is there. It's – it's complicated."

"Kazi," Agna said softly. "I know." She shoved down her vicarious anger at this man that she had never met and would never meet. Keifon was trying to make things right, and he still let Kazi's ghost chain him down.

Keifon opened and closed his hands. He seemed about to jump up and pace. "And – other things. Not just him. I don't think. It's – my old life, too. Going back and being the person I was at home."

Agna remembered the cold-eyed stranger who had once shared her tent. "I think you've changed."

Keifon laughed quietly, looking away. She recognized his standard reaction to flattery. "Thank you. I mean... thank you." He cleared his throat. "Still. I don't want to go back to my old life."

"So... how about somewhere in between? How about the new trade route? Would that make it easier to visit?"

Keifon fell silent, chewing on his lip. "Wildern."

"Yeah. Or Laketon – you liked Laketon, didn't you?"

"Yeah. ...But Wildern is closer." He fell silent, thinking. Agna drew patterns in the dust with her toe. What was she doing? Solving his problems, fine, but Wildern? She had been the one with the foolish fondness for Wildern. It wouldn't accomplish anything to push him to move there in her stead.

"Well," she said, breaking their bubble of silence amid the camp's chatter. "Maybe you can visit Ceien when we're out near Wildern. See how the trip goes, back and forth."

"I couldn't do that to you, make you keep up the clinic by yourself."

Agna rolled her neck, growling under her breath. "I *could*, though. Let me decide that. How long would it be?"

Keifon made a complicated motion with his fingers that seemed to help him calculate the distance. He blew out a breath. "Six days' ride from Wildern to Ceien, in good weather, on the new road."

"Well, it isn't that snowy when we reach Wildern. Right?"

"No, it isn't."

Agna caught her breath as he thought over her suggestion. There was an odd, shivery, warm feeling somewhere under her ribs, and she could feel a flush high on her cheeks. This was a real plan that could do so much good for him, if he would only take her offer. He could see his daughter again, after he'd given up on seeing her for years. This was real, Agna thought. It was adult and huge and terrifying. Taking the tiniest chip away from that mountain made her feel invincible.

"I think it could be done," Keifon said at last. "If I left early. So I could get north and then back before it snows."

Agna danced in her seat, and Keifon looked over at her and cracked a nervous smile. "I'll have to write to Eri first, too," he said. "To make sure it's all right with her."

"Fine, fine, but—!" Agna leaped up, unable to sit anymore, and Keifon followed her. Silhouetted against the fire, he stood and watched. She spun into the dark, toward home, toward nowhere. It didn't matter.

"Thank you," he said. "I don't think you understand how..."

She pulled him along. "I do. I know."

217

Keifon: Waiting

Keifon waited until dark to approach Edann's campsite. The rest of the caravan had known about them – had come up with working theories about them, at least – for nearly a year, but Edann preferred meeting after dark. The wine, or his eyesight, or secrecy; Keifon wasn't sure. It was a small concession to make.

"Hey."

Edann looked up from his book. A guarded fatigue lurked behind his eyes, and his movements as he stood were slow and loose. More tired than drunk, though. Keifon calculated his mental state as Edann gained his feet. That was important. He only had the beginning of his speech, his opening argument, plotted out in his head. The rest depended on Edann's reaction and his own ability to hold onto his temper. If Edann had turned out more drunk than tired, he would have given up.

"Evening. Not long; I'd like some sleep."

"Mmn. Actually... I'd like to talk."

"Tch." Leaving the bottle and taking the book, Edann climbed to the bed of the wagon. Keifon followed, and dropped the curtains as Edann lit a lamp. The canvas enclosed them in a slab of stuffy air, but Keifon was thankful for what little privacy they could claim.

Edann put his book away and flicked his fingers at Keifon, *go ahead.*

"I've been thinking. About my plans, about what I'm doing after this." His muscles tensed; he needed to pace, an impossibility in the precise puzzle that was Edann's living space. "I'm thinking about transferring to Wildern, to the Benevolent Union base. Serving out my contract there."

Edann did not vary his careful pose of slightly impatient forbearance. The urge to give up and kiss that look off his face flared in Keifon's gut, but he forced it back down. Not now. If this went badly, not again. Edann's favor was not as fragile a thing as he liked to make it seem. He had stayed with Keifon for a year, after all, complaining about his sentimentality and his religiosity and his upbringing all the way. Still, he had stayed. So far. Keifon suspected that he approached Edann's limit now.

The silence soured between them. "And?" Edann prompted.

"A-and I wondered – I thought you should know."

Edann rolled his eyes. Fighting attraction and irritation in equal measure, Keifon flexed his jaw and took a seat on top of a crate of inventory. "Don't you ever think about leaving the circuit?"

The apothecary drew a long sigh as he unbuttoned his shirt cuffs. "And this is what, a heartfelt declaration of our intentions? Since when is that part of the deal? Because it *isn't*." His voice hardened, and Keifon felt a spike of ice slide under his heart. "I've been perfectly clear about the terms. You aren't going to change them unilaterally. I don't do heartfelt declarations, and I don't do happily ever after."

Keifon's fingers clenched on his knees. "I'm not changing anything. I just wanted to know what your thoughts were."

"I don't see how that's your business," Edann grumbled.

An old, old wash of hot rage swept through Keifon's heart, as familiar as his own name. He was on his feet, towering over Edann's lounging form. "Do I mean anything to you?" he cried, knowing that his Kaveran was harder to understand when he was upset, knowing that he would lose the words entirely before long. Not that it mattered, because no one was listening. "Do I mean anything to you at all, after a whole year?"

Edann slowly straightened, his back flat against a packing crate. His face was set, his pale eyes cold as the moon. "You're an excellent distraction."

A wordless cry tore from Keifon's throat, half laugh, half sob. "Fuck you."

"I told you at the outset," Edann stated. Keifon thought he heard something behind it, but that might have been his own despair. "The first night. I told you the terms. I'm not the one who got all sentimental."

Keifon spun futilely, denied the space to pace. The boards creaked under his feet. "Treated you like a person, you mean. Like a human being with a soul. Yeah. I'm trying to."

Edann's voice quickened. "Your decision. Your problem. Don't throw this on me like it's my fault."

"I'm not throwing anything," Keifon retorted, and realized that he was shouting. He growled and unclenched his fists, willing himself to relax, to change course. This would lead nowhere. Edann was hurting him, but Edann was good at that. It was how he countered being hurt himself. He liked to pretend that no one knew, that Keifon had never figured it out. The thought of Edann being hurt evaporated his anger. As infuriating as his lover could be, Keifon did not want to hurt him.

Keifon sat on the crate, facing Edann across the wagon bed. "I'm asking you what you want. That's all."

"Why?" Edann retorted, arms folded.

"Because I *care*," Keifon spat, and reined his temper in. "Because I'm thinking. About my future. And I want to know about yours."

Edann shifted his hips to sit on top of the crate, on Keifon's level, before refolding his defensive posture. "And your future is what, now? House in the country, packed full of kids? Church in town, wedding chains, all of that?"

"Yeah. Actually."

Edann's eyes narrowed. "It's a lie, and you're an idiot."

Insult balanced against empathy, and Keifon waited for the insult to wane. Edann had never respected the things that were most important to him – his faith, his family, his attempts to better himself. That was what kept him at his own arm's reach, even as Edann pushed him away. He had hoped, vainly, that someday Edann would wear down, that he would see that the world wasn't out to stab him in the back. But Keifon couldn't wait that long. The thought settled in him like a cold stone.

He was ready, or would be soon, for Wildern, for the house, for a family. Edann wasn't. He had been hurt deeply, and he had refused to heal, despite Keifon's efforts. Keifon couldn't force him. Edann had to come of his own will or not at all.

The wagon bed was narrow enough that Keifon could lean forward and take Edann's hands without leaving his seat. His thumbs found the faint dents around each middle finger. He knew what they meant now, and his heart ached.

"Whoever hurt you... I'm sorry."

Edann yanked his hands away. "Fuck *you* and your condescension."

"I'm not—" Keifon sighed. It wouldn't do any good to argue. Offering Edann empathy was like trying to feed a wild animal; he would just keep snapping.

Edann stood and paced the two steps between Keifon and the back of the wagon. His slight frame hummed with tension, as though he might snap in half at any moment. "I should have known this would happen. I kept you on too long. It's – you're – you're good at what you do, but I should have seen that you'd get – attached. Damn it."

Keifon lowered his head to his hands, waiting for the tirade to stop. Edann's dismissal fit so neatly into the spaces inside him that he accepted it out of hand. Of course it was pointless for Edann to get mixed up with him. He had destroyed everything he'd ever loved. Being rejected now only made sense. – And yet some part of him felt... relief. He already missed Edann's wit and incisive commentary and encyclopedic knowledge of what exactly would drive him over the brink in the most deliriously efficient fashion. He did not miss the sense of throwing himself at the gates of a city that would never open.

I know you're in there. I want in. I want you to trust me. But I can't make you, and I can't wait anymore.

Edann had stopped talking and stood staring at the curtain. Keifon licked his lips. "This isn't – this isn't what I want anymore," he said, and gave up trying to guess what was going to come out of his stupid mouth. Edann wouldn't have him back anyway. He may as well be honest and have done with it. "This. Us. It was – it – it's been good for what it is. Was. I don't know anymore." He dragged in a breath. Edann waited, motionless. "But I need more. I need someone I can talk to, and trust."

Edann half turned, not looking at him. "Your Nessinian girl," he said quietly.

Keifon felt an angry flush start up his neck. Edann was baiting him again. He knew exactly what would set Keifon off, and pulled his strings like a master puppeteer. He wouldn't take the bait. "Well... someone I can trust the way I trust her," he allowed. "Like that. Yes."

Edann gagged. "Yeah. You go and bury yourself in *that*. You'll be begging me to take you back."

Keifon closed his fists, counted to six, and opened them. Strings. Pulling. His voice came out dry. "If you were ready to be honest with me, then I would. You're – you're smarter than anyone I know, and you make me laugh, and I used to think that I couldn't be attracted to foreigners, but – well – you proved me wrong. Over and over." He caught his breath, thinking about all of those nights, wasted. Not wasted. True to what they were, at the time. "If you would stop shutting me out, I'd be thrilled to be with you. But not like this. I can't – I can't take this anymore."

It lay between them, like a dead thing that Keifon had heaved onto the floor. Edann's eyes were distant. The muscles of his jaw flexed. He was thinking about what Keifon had said, though; Keifon read it in the subtle signs he'd learned from a year of never talking about anything that mattered. In the spaces between their words he had learned how to read this person who wouldn't allow him close enough to love, and in that code he read: *I hear you. I can't ever admit it. My pride won't allow it. But I hear you.*

Perhaps someday he would be ready. He wasn't ready now.

"You've gone soft," Edann muttered at last.

Keifon stood and crossed the endless distance between them. "Yeah. I guess I have." He kissed Edann's temple as Edann turned away, and his mouth as he turned back. Edann tasted like wine. "The ground has to be soft for things to grow," Keifon murmured in his ear. He found Edann's hand, hanging empty by his side, gave it one more squeeze, and dropped away. "Thank you. For everything."

The silence pushed him out of the wagon, away from the campsite, and into the empty fields beyond. The sliver of moon kept him hidden for as long as he needed.

Agna: Love and Money

Food for the week, drawing paper, postage, a little aside in case she found a villager who would trim her hair, her share of the lamp oil, laundry and bathhouse fees... Agna drew a decisive line under the list and calculated a quick sum. – Enough. Despite the unexpected shift in her gift-giving timetable, she would have enough. She set down her pen confidently.

She looked over the columns, adding up the weeks and averaging them out. She made enough at the clinic to cover expenses and to pay the Benevolent Union their share when the time came. If she kept all the same clothes through this year instead of buying new ones and borrowed books instead of buying them, she might have a little left over when she – possibly, she hedged – relocated to Wildern. Not enough, however, to open a gallery, or anything of the sort. It occurred to her that she would first need to buy a house, or rent a room, as Lina was doing now. The thought seemed vaguely wicked. More to the point, such an investment would take some capital. Despite the swiftly mending bridges between herself and the Despana empire, she would not beg her parents for money.

Agna resisted picking up her pen, leaving the figures exactly as they were. She would find a way. She could even continue to work for the Benevolent Union, in their new base. She could get over the lurking mystery of what Rone had to do with it and whether she might just be following him once again. It was a matter of expediency, no more. A healer could draw a reasonable salary in their hospital, she was sure. She made a note at the bottom of her ledger: *Write BU, hosp salary??*

Abandoning her pen, she escaped the stuffy tent to see a man about some unseasonable wool.

Agna returned from her errand to find Keifon sprawled on a blanket, studying the Nessinian book. It seemed like an improvement, an observation Agna kept to herself. She was at a loss what to say to him, and her continued silence grew more frustrating every day. He had been so helpful, giving her the space she needed after – after Deeproot Valley. She wasn't sure whether space was what he needed now. She didn't know why his relationship with Edann had collapsed, and so she couldn't decide between commiseration or forgiveness or a sense of fraternity against the cruel vagaries of chance. Studying grammar, however, was comprehensible.

Keifon looked up and squinted against the sun as she approached. "Hey."

"Hi. Don't you want some shade? It's beastly out here." The talk of wool and yardage had not cooled her, either.

He waved a hand lazily. "Ennh. It's worse inside, I think."

Agna ducked through the open door to find, as predicted, a box of damp and stagnant air. The humidity by the canal counteracted the benefits of shade. "Ugh."

"Told you."

"Bleah. I don't want to sleep in this!"

Keifon turned and propped his body on one elbow. "We could camp outside. More outside, I mean."

Agna plopped to the tent floor to stew. Plenty of the other merchants had taken to sleeping bags or bedrolls outside their tents, or on top of the larger wagons. The guards made jokes about stepping carefully at night. But outside, where anyone could see you? All night? Agna ran her hands up her arms at the imaginary chill. "I'll... think about it."

"Mmn." He returned to the book, and after a proper sulking interval, Agna located her Yanweian book and joined him next to the fire pit. She propped the book open on her lap and craned to read his book upside-down.

Keifon's fingers steepled under a line. "*Ente... le. Alaste?* I don't know that I really understand this. The difference."

Agna closed her book gladly. She struggled to understand Yanweian words, able to distinguish only two of the six tones. She had secretly decided to tell *sing* from *love* from the first half of *violet* based on context. It was ten times harder than learning Kaveran. The line between frustrating and challenging shifted every day.

"I guess Yanweian lumps them all together, then, like Kaveran does."

"I... guess so." He chewed his lip.

"Well, in Kaveran you say 'I love you' the same way to your kids, and your spouse, and your friends, and your gods, and everything. It's all the same word."

Keifon rolled aside to prop his head on his hand. "Yeah, but they have synonyms. You wouldn't tell your friends that – well, that you adore them, or something. Maybe you would, but it wouldn't be serious."

"True, but there's one word that covers everything. We just don't have that. It's always different. I guess we think about them differently because of it."

"And so you always know what you're talking about."

"Well. They overlap. And you can use them metaphorically, or ironically, like anything else. Or, you know, not admit to how you feel. But you know where you are to start with. You just...know. You learn it when you learn the language. Like you know your tones. Though really little kids sometimes say *alaste* everything, because that's what their parents say to them, and so it's what they know."

"*Alaste...*"

"Familial love. *Nicolina alaste la*. And-and good friends. The kind you'd trust with your life. – Esirel is *alaste* to me," she said hurriedly, by way of explanation, or deflection. "Devotion, I guess, in Kaveran. Or loyalty."

"Hmm. *Alaste... alaste Nachi*."

"*-Le*," she corrected. "And reverse it."

"Yes, right. *Nachi alaste le*." His accent was the same in Nessinian as in Kaveran, bending the new words in the same directions. It seemed like the strangest thing, somehow. She had heard Yanweians speak the language before, though not often. His voice threw her back to those few isolated students in the Academy, though simultaneously it seemed like something that belonged only to him. It was nice to hear him say these things. She liked to hear him try.

"*Ente* is just... like?" he guessed in Kaveran. "I like... things."

"Yeah. Things and people. *Ente* is for... your friends, your pets, books, abstract concepts, peach pie, sunsets. It's the most common."

Her list made him crack a smile. "I like you as much as peach pie? Touching."

"Well. You have to start somewhere."

He turned a page. "*Amane* I think I get," he muttered. "Now that you explain the others."

Agna looked away, letting him gloss over it. *Amane* was for Eri and Kazi and Edann, and for everything that hurt him in the end. It was for the way she had loved Laris and still failed. It was a bad time for *amane*. He did not practice it.

"And – *inire* is something religious?" he guessed, drawing Agna back from her thoughts. "I think I don't get that one."

She took a deep breath, grateful for the digression. "I guess it helps to go to the Church of the Balance on that one. It's the word they use for the love of humanity. Compassion, I guess. The respect you feel for someone as a fellow part of Creation. Though the Church of the Four uses it all the time, too. They use it for the gods' love for mortals and vice versa. Not really worship, not really respect – a little bit of both."

"Hm. ...*Darano inire le*, then?"

"I guess so, yeah." Her smile was apologetic. "I'm not the one to ask. But I think you're right. – And, say, Golden Caravan *inire la*, as..." She drew a circle in the air. "As a group. Because you'd say *Murio inire la* – or I would, I mean – so it would work for this too. Meaning the city, or the group, as a whole. That's..." She tapered off, registering confusion in his eyes. "That's more like the love of humanity thing."

"Hmm. I think I see that."

"So does that help?"

"It does. Thank you."

She set the Yanweian book aside and stretched out on her back to watch the sky. She did not know which of the words fit him, and she did not try to make them fit. She did not trust her assessment anymore. She had been wrong with Laris – or she had been right, and things had gone wrong. She had been wrong with Rone, lavishing a god's worship on a mortal boy. And-and more, she thought, her cheeks warming at the thought. Half a country away from Vertal and a year and a half removed from the Academy, she could almost admit to it. She had been stupid in so many ways.

She was not the one to ask on the topic.

Keifon squeezed her shoulder. He had left off reading. "You looked... unhappy."

She shrugged against the ground. "What else is new, nowadays."

He thought for a moment, his chin resting on his stacked fists. "Want to go into town? Just to look around? Something to do."

Agna sighed. "Suppose so. – Though... Nelle told me that there was an artist in this village I should talk to. If that's not too boring for you."

He was already gaining his feet. "Not at all."

Agna did not attempt even a half-hearted *You don't have to go.*

■ ■ ■

Nelle had described the artist's house: built of stone with blue shutters and window boxes, guarded by an enormous dog. The village was small enough that wandering up and down the roads seemed like a reasonable way of navigating. The angle of the sun cast a shadow from a hedgerow over one side of one of the roads, so Agna and Keifon walked in the shade for as long as they could. Agna even stopped fanning herself. Keifon watched the clear sky as they walked, and slowed his pace enough that Agna was tempted to push him along.

She caught him smiling when he thought she wasn't looking. Maybe this village reminded him of home. Maybe getting away from the camp took Edann off his mind. Whatever the reason, Agna was glad of it, and she realized that the shade and the fresh air and the chance to meet a new artist had lifted her spirits as well. Some part of her wished that Laris were there, holding her hand as they rambled and telling the story behind every cow and pasture wall. But he was happy out there somewhere, and on an afternoon like this, she could believe that she could be happy, too.

The artist's house appeared just as expected, surrounded by a dense flower garden. The air swam with lazy bees. Agna shifted her grip on her notebook and pulled the metal bell handle mounted on the gatepost. A rumbling bark answered the jingle, followed by a mass of fur that galloped around the corner. It reared up and planted its paws on the gate, bringing its head well over the top rail. Agna backed up a step while Keifon held out a hand for the dog to sniff. He clucked at it under his breath in Yanweian, with words that Agna couldn't quite catch. The dog allowed him to scratch its ear and lolled out its tongue in approval. Uneasy that the owner had not yet appeared, Agna jingled the bell again.

"Go find your person, huh?" Keifon ruffled the dog's head. Its collar clanked. Agna reached out and got in a couple of ear scratches before the creak of the front door sent the dog whirling away.

"Visitors, Bear?" The dog romped at the feet of the woman who appeared in the doorway. She was tall and wiry, dressed in a beaded vest and loose trousers, her white hair rolled into a knot at the back of her neck.

"Good afternoon, ma'am," Agna called. "My name is Agna Despana. I'd heard about your artwork from a friend, and I wondered if you might have a moment to talk."

"About the art? Oh yes, any time." She'd reached the gate, and surveyed the two of them. Keifon bowed his head. "You've come a long way," she observed.

"Yes, ma'am. I'm from Murio, in Nessiny. I'm traveling with the Golden Caravan as a healer. I heard about your work from Nelle, the summer caravan's herbalist. This is my friend, Keifon the Medic. He's also with the caravan."

"Pleasure to meet you, ma'am," Keifon chimed in.

"Dara Nesh. And you're – art connoisseurs?" A trace of wryness twisted her voice.

"Well – yes," Agna replied. The artist swung the gate open; Agna and Keifon stepped through as Bear the dog bumped against their legs. "Actually, I come from a family of art dealers. And my mother is a painter. I'm not in business yet, but I'd like to learn as much about Kaveran art as I can."

"Is that so. You've been to the museum in Prisa, then?"

"Not yet. I have been to the two in Vertal."

"Eh." Dara shrugged and ushered them into the house. Agna remembered to take off her shoes in the entryway. "Historical, of course. They have all of our wartime painters and the old masters. But Prisa has everything new."

"I see. I'll be sure to visit." Agna scribbled a note, *Prisa museum – new*, hoping that it would be legible; she was still sun-blinded.

"Water, either of you? Tea?"

"Water, please," Agna replied.

"The same, please," Keifon echoed.

Agna's sight began to adjust to the interior light, and she forgot what she'd intended to ask next. She turned to take in the paintings on the walls, which were interspersed with candle sconces and bundles of flowers hanging up to dry. Every wall had at least one work. Many were unframed canvases, simply tacked onto stretchers and mounted on the wall. A few were watercolors on paper, glued to board backing. A vast oil painting of a group of people had pride of place across from the front door. Agna tiptoed closer, fighting an uneasy feeling of déjà vu. Of course not, she chided herself. That would be ridiculous.

The people in the painting were all Kaveran, it seemed, and Agna tried not to sigh with relief.

A splash broke her concentration, and Agna turned. The kitchen took up one end of the front room, and Keifon had hurried to help haul up a rope-and-pulley cold box. Water sheeted off the platform and dripped into the underground storage chamber below. Dara set the brake and selected a sealed jug from the cluster on the platform. Agna glanced around the rest of the room; the house was fairly large by the village's scale, a stone cottage built out in wings, likely over a period of many years.

Keifon handed Agna a glass of cold water and peered at the painting.

"Thank you. – Thank you very much," Agna tossed across the room.

Dara dried her hands on a kitchen towel and joined them in front of the group painting. "Four generations," she announced. "That's me, third from the left in the second row. Of course, I finished that part later. Actually, I only made the initial sketch at the reunion, and spent a year going around to fill the others in. Not a museum piece, of course. Great sentimental value."

"I can see why," Agna marveled. "Though the detail is amazing."

Dara laughed. "Well, that comes from taking your time. You have that luxury when you only paint five people out of forty at a time. Though I lugged that canvas up and down the east road so many times that it didn't feel like any kind of luxury."

Agna turned to the next piece, a watercolor of a field and farmhouse. "You work in oil and watercolor, then?"

"A bit. I studied in oils in Prisa, many years ago. But you have to try new things or you get stale." As they made their way around to each painting, she explained that she'd spent a lifetime painting during off hours as a midwife. "Working on a sketch is quiet if you're waiting up, and the more people and places you see, the more it benefits your work."

Agna was fully enthralled, and spent the next half hour asking about the interplay between art and medicine. Dara offered them supper, which Agna resisted with a great deal of inner conflict. She didn't mean to impose on Dara's hospitality, but she hadn't even seen her work space yet, and Dara would have so much more to tell.

Keifon looked up from his seat on the floor and gave her a little go-ahead wave. Bear snuffled his knee, investigating this unauthorized lapse in belly-rubs.

"Aren't you the charmer, Bear." Dara bent to add a scratch of her own, sending the plumy tail lashing.

Agna gave Keifon a wry smile and mouthed *You, too.* He put on a dignified face and returned to his duties as he spoke up.

"Is there anything we can do to help? We don't mean to impose."

"Not so much, young man. I'm happy to talk shop for a while; there aren't many others out here. Tell me about Nessiny, then, while I get this together. There's a dear."

Keifon jumped up to wash his hands and pitch in. The three of them assembled a light meal of green salad, bread and currant jam. Agna chattered about the Murian art market, her father's agency, and Marco, her contact in the business. She and Marco had corresponded about the art scene in Kavera, she explained, and though she hadn't spent much time in Vertal or Prisa, it was fascinating to meet people along their caravan route who were involved in art.

They sat at the wooden slab table in the kitchen to eat. Bear propped his head in Keifon's lap until Dara chased him away, chiding him about his manners.

She settled at the head of the table. "What are you thinking to do with all of this information, then? Buy up art for your galleries in Nessiny?"

Agna flushed and swallowed a bite of bread and jam. Keifon met her guilty glance. "It's-it's complicated," Agna stammered. "I'm not sure yet. That's one thing I'm trying to figure out with Marco, what the market back home might take to."

"Hmm. You're their agent in the field, huh?"

"I suppose so. Unofficially."

"Well, I haven't spoken to a Nessinian art dealer since I finished university, unofficial or not, so I'd say you've got a unique business model here."

"Thank you, ma'am."

Keifon nudged her knee under the table, and Agna glared at him. He beamed at her with unmitigated pride. She nudged him back and took another forkful of salad.

After dinner, Dara set Keifon to harvesting berries from the side yard under Bear's supervision, freeing herself and Agna to tour the workroom. Agna's notes grew to five pages as Dara pulled one work after another from a storage closet, telling stories about the subjects and her influences and her years at the university in Prisa. Agna noted Kaveran makers of paints and canvas, other artists' names and addresses, and everything Dara could tell her about the art world in Kavera for the last fifty years. The excitement simmering in the back of Agna's mind threatened to boil over. She had enough leads to keep her on the run for the rest of the year, if not longer.

As Dara slotted a canvas back into the closet, Agna glanced around to make sure that Keifon and Bear were still outside. "Actually... I have been giving some thought to dealing art here. I haven't decided yet, so I haven't told Keifon about it. Or my father," she added, and regretted it. She sounded so childish. "But Marco and I have written about the possibility. And that's one reason why I want to learn as much as I can."

Dara turned from the closet, a smile sneaking across her face. "I see. And what are your other reasons?"

"Well... I love it. That's all. It's fascinating." She spread her hands, notebook in one, pencil in the other. "I learned all about history and the Nessinian movements, and I've grown up around artists all my life, but I never went out and talked to people like this."

"Good answer," Dara replied. "Though you'll find plenty of artists only want to put food on the table – or line their pockets – and some guard their process like dragons. They aren't all nice old ladies."

"Oh, I know. Still."

"Another good answer. Well, child, you and your friend had best get moving before it's dark." She closed the closet door. Agna despaired to think that there might be more that she hadn't seen. "You're welcome back any time."

Agna did not demur that her contract would expire by the time the Golden Caravan came this way again. "Thank you so much for your time, and your hospitality. It was a true honor meeting you."

"My pleasure. – Oop, here they come now." Bear rampaged through the front door as Agna and Dara emerged from the studio. Keifon followed, balancing a colander heaped with berries. Dara took it off his hands and sent them home with another round of thanks.

Dusk was falling as Agna and Keifon returned to the lane, aiming for the rise in the distance where the bonfire glowed. The air was heavy, but the sun had set low enough that shade was no longer in short supply. They shifted to the middle of the lane, where the dirt was hard-packed. Agna clutched her notebook and twirled as she walked. The early stars wheeled overhead.

Keifon chuckled. "That was amazing. I'm so glad you could come here."

"Thanks for coming with me." Agna considered all the things that it would be ludicrous to say, like *I hope that wasn't too boring for you*. She hadn't seen him so relaxed in weeks.

"My pleasure." He sighed happily. "Do you think she'd adopt me?"

"Her dog already has."

Nightfall had brought some relief from the heat, but Keifon and Agna set up their cots next to the fire pit, under the clear sky. Agna watched the stars with names and dates and colors swirling through her head until they spun her into sleep.

Keifon: Freedom

The Laketon shopping district dissolved into rows of houses, and Keifon hesitated, turning back. He was sure that he had passed a jeweler's shop half a block ago. He stood for a minute, feeling sick, on the edge of something too large to comprehend. It was time. It didn't matter what he did next. He could stay in Kavera or go back to Yanwei or fly to the moon. He could find someone and get married and settle down on a farm and have six children, or he could stay alone for the rest of his life. It was all immaterial to this decision.

The bells on the door jangled as he pulled it open, shattering his concentration. The guard by the door looked him over and let him pass.

"Can I help you, sir?" The jeweler was Kaveran, after all, not that it mattered. She spoke Yanweian readily.

Keifon swallowed. "I'd... like to sell this."

"Speak up, please?"

He stepped up to the glass counter. The jeweler waited as he fumbled with the clasp. The stiff pivots and joints loosened, and the segments slithered into his hands. Keifon closed his eyes, taking deep breaths to fight the clench in his throat.

In one swift second, he was unchained from his home and everything that had happened there and everything he had been – and at the same time, it was just lifeless metal, and nothing had changed at all. He had always been free. The land where he was born still soaked in the sun, in another family's name. Eri, his wife, his love, the owner of this torque's match, had left him starving in the night. But day by day, she had taken another role in his pantheon. She was no longer his wife or his lover, or even his friend. She had kept their little girl safe – safe from him, in the beginning – and raised her into a thing of wonder. He would honor both Eri and Nachi by giving up the past.

The torque had never belonged to Kazi. Kazi was gone, and no metal working could ever change that. Keifon had hungered for some tangible sign from Kazi, but Kazi had given him nothing: no letters, no tokens, no marriage contract. No evidence. Nothing but his time, his trust, his body, his love. Keifon's memories would have to suffice.

Edann had claimed that the institution itself was a lie, that no one could be trusted, that Keifon had been a fool to commit himself to any of them. Keifon did not believe that, even in his darkest hours. Yet clinging to the vestiges of a dead love would not prove Edann wrong. Moving ahead would.

Keifon could not chain any of them to him by wearing this earthly thing. Neither could he wear it to remind himself any further of the mistakes he'd made, because his mistakes were the river that had borne him to this point. He had washed up in this land, had made new mistakes, had tried again even when he wished for nothing more than escape. He had persisted in living, and in being himself, even after every course plotted out for him had failed.

The torque was warm in his hand. He cleared his throat and spread the chain of metal and stone across the jeweler's counter. The sinuous clicking broke the staring silence of the jeweler, the guard, the jeweler's apprentice, and the one other customer in the shop. "I'd like to sell this, please."

"Sir..."

"It's desanctified. I was divorced four and a half years ago."

The jeweler turned over the uncoupled ends in her slender fingers and inspected the back of the torque through a magnifying glass. Keifon laid his hands on the counter, having nothing else to do with them. The torque hadn't been outside his reach since the first time he'd taken it in the church in his hometown. As the jeweler consulted a reference book and studied several other details, Keifon's sickness subsided. The jeweler treated it with careful respect. She would weigh it, measure it, determine its value, and translate its workmanship and its rarity into coin. It was only an object.

"Where and when did you buy this? Can you tell me the maker's name?" Her tone was pleasant and balanced. She was skilled at not sounding as though she were checking for thievery. It was not a personal slight.

"It was eight years ago, in Yanwei, in Eastwater. It's in ranch country, in the northeast. There was just the one jeweler in Eastwater. Um." He searched his memory, slipping past Eri and the priests at their wedding, Jafi standing in for his dead parents, the scent of flowers filling his head, and the joyful, spinning music. The jeweler's name. In Eastwater. "Uh, Zara. Zara Medri was the head of the shop at the time."

The Kaveran jeweler could not buy the memories of Eri, her fingers gliding over the gold on its velvet tray. Keifon could not trade away the memory of taking the chain in the church or the little tremor in Eri's voice as she spoke the vows. He would keep all of that. It was a part of him.

"Hm. That checks out. Thank you." The jeweler lifted the chain and weighed it on a scale, juggling tiny lead weights onto the opposite side. The scales swung into balance. Tucking her fine brown hair behind her ears, the jeweler made notes on a slip of paper. "Now. We can offer you forty unions for it."

It was the opening move of a complex game which Keifon had no intention of playing. He made a token effort to argue it up to forty-eight, and the jeweler capitulated.

"I won't keep you, sir." She made another note and copied it on another page, then passed the slip to her apprentice. "Thank you very much."

"Thank you." He wandered after the apprentice to the other side of the shop. After more pleasantries and exchanges of paper and words, Keifon walked back onto the street with the weight of his dead marriage lying against his hip in Kaveran coins. He stopped to breathe, one hand clasped against his naked throat.

He had punished himself for as long as he could, and it had not stopped him from living, nor from trusting again, however slowly. He was still alive. He remembered those whom he had loved. He shivered at the absence of the torque's weight and the brush of his clothes against his uncovered skin. He had the rest of his life to adjust to the feeling.

Agna: Second Chances

"Hey."

Agna turned as Keifon took a seat next to her on the bench. "Hey. – *Oh.*" She saw that his skin was bare under his collar. The exposed line of his collarbone seemed obscene. "You actually did it."

"Yeah." His hand rested against the back of his neck, a familiar gesture with new meaning. "It's... weird."

"It's a big step. Are you all right?"

He glanced at her, as if to gauge her sincerity. "I think so. I've been walking around the city since then. Thinking."

"Yeah. I've been out here thinking."

Keifon lowered his hand. "Good day for thinking, I guess."

"Who knew."

"Thinking about Laris?"

Agna blew out a breath. "Among other things. It never stops being complicated. I wish things were easy."

He laughed quietly. "That would be nice. Why aren't things easy?"

"According to *your* religion, it's because we have free will."

"Ugh. Right. And yours... hm..." He tangled his fingers together, illustrating. "...because all things in the world have conflicting needs, even if they're all part of the greater whole. Something like that. Right?"

"Yeah. Pretty good."

They watched the water of the lake as it sparkled copper in the sunset. "I can learn a lot in a year," Keifon murmured.

Agna remembered that night in the dark, seething with misdirected anger and panic over Laris. They'd started over that night. "I can learn a lot in a year, too."

"You have. I'm so proud of you."

"Oh – stop it." Agna pulled one foot onto the bench and locked her fingers around her knee. She leaned back, the halves of her body counterbalanced against one another. The sky was clear this evening. If she looked up, she didn't have to look at him. "I'm proud of you, too."

They listened to the water and the distant call of birds. Agna rocked idly in her seat. "So how was town?"

"It was interesting. It's not as... cohesive as the Foreign Quarter in Prisa. There's no Yanweian town square. But there are a lot of my people, and shops and things like that."

"Did you get anything good?"

"Mmn. Some tea, and some spices. A Lundrala gift for *some*body we know. And some books."

Agna sat up, her interest piqued. "Yeah?" She covered her mouth when he hesitated. "Oh – oh. If they're racy books or something, then never mind. I mean. Uh..."

"No. Well... one is just a novel that looked interesting. And I got – not much of a book. A pamphlet, really. About immigration. Not a history." He swallowed, the movement highlighted by his naked throat. "This one is, um. A guide."

Agna felt something rising in her chest like a soap bubble. "A guide to immigrating? So you are thinking about moving here after all?"

"Maybe. I'll see what the trip to Ceien is like. I might... I mean, it's just an idea."

"Yeah, of course, but..."

"I've been thinking about that plan. Moving to Wildern, and getting some more training. I think... I think I could do it." His unease was transforming, warming into trust and pride. Agna clenched a fist against her mouth, willing herself not to shout for joy. Keifon was smiling now; it was hard to resist. "And when Nachi gets older, she can visit me."

She could no longer contain the fizzing excitement. Agna's squeal drew an alarmed look from Keifon. "I'm so happy for you," she explained.

Even her embarrassment could not quench the buzzing under her skin. She wanted to walk back to camp right now, or run, or dance; she couldn't sit still. She slipped her shoes off and picked her way down the shore to the edge of the lake, to let the water lap against her bare feet. The lake bottom was pebbly and slick with algae, but the water was cool.

"How is it?" Keifon called.

"Slimy."

He waded in, passing her by a pace or two. He'd rolled up his pant legs.

"Show-off," Agna sighed.

"You don't have to wear those long skirts all the time."

Agna huffed good-naturedly. Gathering her skirts under one arm, she waded in a few more steps. The water was deliciously cool in contrast to the warm night air. Tiny insects skimmed over the water's surface. Most of the canoes cut back to the docks, leaving a handful of reluctant stragglers and fishing boats.

Laketon would not be home to her. She could have tried; she could have made the best of it. But it would not be the end of her road now. She wasn't sure that Wildern would be right, either. Perhaps she would fail and flee back to

Murio after all, to take her place as her father's and Marco's shadow. But first she had to try.

Keifon spoke, looking out over the lake. His back faced her, arms folded, unreadable. "Do you think it could work?"

"What, moving to Wildern?"

"Yeah."

"I do think it could work. I know you want it to work, and I know you can make it happen." Agna stooped to cup the lake water in her free hand. She let it drain through her fingers. She wanted to ask him whether her scheme would work, but to admit that would be to admit that she was trailing behind him instead of behind her father and Marco. She would have to admit that she hadn't learned a thing from her foolish decision to run after Rone. Keifon would forgive her for that. But she could not face disappointing him. That was its own kind of weakness.

"If I go somewhere that I know somebody… is that weak, do you think?"

That made him turn. "What do you mean? If you didn't go back to Murio?" His voice absorbed her pronunciation of her hometown and reflected it through his own accent, making violet out of red and blue. "Do you have family in another city?"

She hesitated between truth and pride. "Something like that."

He tilted his head, looking past her into the future, or the lakeshore, or some version of Nessiny based on books and her own descriptions. She saw the muscles in his calves flex as he curled his toes among the stones. "I think it's brave to strike out and establish a new branch of the company in a new city. And if your family can support you while you do, that's not weak. That's what family is for." The faint crack in his voice broke Agna's heart.

She sighed, half a step closer to truth. "What if it's a friend?"

Keifon half-smiled with a lazy shrug. "That's what friends are for, too."

Damn him. "But – is it…" She kicked the stones under her feet. "When I came here, I was stupid. I was a stupid, blinkered girl, and I made bad decisions that I will never be able to take back. I will have to live the rest of my life knowing how idiotic I was. And I never want to do that again." She risked a glance up to find him staring at her, his hands hanging empty. She dropped her gaze away from the pain in his eyes. When he spoke, she covered her face in her free hand, as if to shield herself from the quiet words.

"You… you think it was a mistake to come here?"

Agna lunged toward the shore, slipping on the pebbles and regaining her balance. Keifon called after her and followed, splashing behind her to the bench. She paced barefoot, her hands coiled into fists.

"No. That's not it. I don't regret *being* here. That's not what I meant. I'm glad I'm here now. I'm glad I met you. All of that."

Keifon slowly took his seat on the bench, seemingly satisfied that she wasn't going to escape. He listened as she continued to pace.

"What I mean is, the decision that brought me here was based on stupid reasons. One doesn't justify the other. You didn't want to break up with Kazi, but that's what brought you here. Do you see what I mean?"

Keifon looked at his steepled fingers, leaning over his knees. "I see what you mean."

Agna collapsed into the seat next to him. Her furor was spent for now. She didn't have the energy left to be angry, only dully irritated with herself. She tucked her skirts up to let her feet dry.

The lights were coming on in the distant town. Streetlights traced the streets one speck of light at a time, and the windows of the homes were warm with firelight. Someday, would one of those firesides be hers? Would she make tea for a visitor and talk about books and hopes for the future? It seemed impossible sometimes. But the world was strange. She now sat on a park bench with a dear friend whom she had once hated. That was another thing that Rone's religion believed: the world was immense, and you could never predict it all.

"I know you don't believe in the gods," Keifon began slowly. Agna's spine prickled at the echo of her own thoughts. Keifon kept his eyes on the opposite shore. "You don't have to believe. That's not for me to say. I just – I mean to speak to what I believe. That's all." He paused, as if gathering courage. "And I – I think that the gods brought us here. So that we could learn from it, and find purpose in it. Even if we had to suffer to get here. It's – it was worth it."

She didn't believe. She doubted she ever would. But through countless hours of watching him pray to his gods, reading his books, talking into the night, she never doubted that his faith brought him strength. She didn't have to believe to see how much it meant to him. "So... the good outweighs the bad."

He glanced at her. His anxious posture settled. "Yes."

"That's how the Balance faith would see it, too. The good doesn't unmake the bad, but it's outweighed, and that's the important thing."

"That's... that's how I feel about this. About the things that brought us here." He seemed about to speak, but nodded and quieted.

"I see." Agna considered this. It seemed like cheating to let herself go unpunished for her immaturity, for her embarrassing decision to follow Rone like a puppy. But even if she had made the wrong decision, it had turned into something else over time. She had planted weeds and managed to grow a garden.

"It was worth it," she agreed at last. "And it's past. I understand."

Keifon nodded. "And even if you doubt your decision now, it isn't the end. You can make the best out of it. However it starts."

"But... I don't want to make the same mistake again. The *same one*. That would mean that I'm not learning."

He shrugged. "Only if you don't make anything of it. Only if you stop there." He watched her coolly in the dim light. "Did... did Rone decide to move back, then?"

"What? No. Not that I know of. – Oh." She flapped her hands, wishing she hadn't left all the clues scattered for anyone with half a brain to assemble. "Never mind that. It's complicated. Some other time."

"Mmn." Keifon leaned back on his hands. Agna looked away from the line of his arms and stomach, from the way that her shadow fell across his body. "You won't stop," he murmured. "I know you won't. Not until you get what you want." The shadows around his throat shifted as he swallowed. Keifon shook his head, looking away. "I admire that. That's all."

"I don't think you'll give up, either," Agna replied, keen to turn the subject away from herself. "You've been through so much, and you just keep going."

Keifon almost laughed, grimly. "I created most of what I went through."

"Still." Agna fluffed her skirts back over her legs and hugged her knees. The edge of the stone bench was cool against her feet. "It isn't over. Not for you, not for me."

"Eight months," Keifon remarked softly.

Agna calculated. The spring festival, or New Year's. – Oh. Until she was supposed to go back home. That wasn't what she'd meant. Was it really only eight more months? It had been a whole year since they'd been here last, since they'd sat on a bench in this park and laid their weapons down.

She didn't want to think about New Year's. She didn't want to lose herself in last year, either. "We don't have to start over, this time," she said, turning toward him and pulling one knee up on the bench. "So let's just keep going, and making everything better."

Keifon turned toward her, and she saw his hand shake a little through the Kaveran greeting wave. "Keifon the Medic," he said. "...Reji Keifon. I will."

Agna smiled and echoed his gesture. "Agna Despana. So will I."

He shifted a little on the bench, and his hand rose toward her arm. In stages, as if he hadn't quite convinced himself, he laid a hand on her arm, leaned in toward her, and looped his other arm around her back. "Can I – can I do this?" His pulse hammered in his throat, alongside her own.

Agna hugged him. "Always."

He tightened his other arm around her. Tears spiked in her eyes. If he would let her in this close, like Esirel had, she would have to tell him. She couldn't hold it back for long.

Agna swallowed hard against the lump in her throat. Her voice was weak, but it didn't have to travel far. "Can I tell you something? It's... kind of weird."

"Yeah," Keifon said, so softly that the skin on the back of Agna's neck prickled.

She took a deep breath. It would be all right. She had to believe that. The weight of his arms convinced her that he would forgive her for anything. "A-alaste la. Do you remember what that means?" *I love you like one of my own. Like my family.*

Keifon's breath hitched. Agna felt something hot spill along her neck. "I don't—I don't deserve that," he forced out. "I don't..."

"Ssh." She cradled the back of his head, unthinking, and he stilled. The short hair at the nape of his neck tickled her wrist. Agna kept her voice low. "You don't get to decide for me. You told me that."

He snugged his face into her shoulder. "...Yes. I did. You're right." After another breath he straightened, and wiped his sleeve across his eyes. "*Alaste le.* Is that right?"

A ghost of a smile curled Agna's lips. "Perfect."

"*Alaste le,*" he repeated, and said it again in Kaveran. "I love you. *En da si.*" The words bent and slid with his language's music, the way she could never quite master.

"*En da si.*"

Keifon chuckled, and wiped across his cheekbone with the heel of his hand. "That's 'I sing you.' – It's all right. We can keep practicing."

Agna gave him one more squeeze, burning off her nervous energy. She felt the tension leave his body as though he were a part of her. He was doomed now. He'd have to fight her away.

She pulled back, smiling. They found their places on the bench, side by side. The water breathed against the shore, and cicadas and crickets droned in the distance. The heat of the day rose slowly away from the lake. The air was sweetened with nothing more than grass and lake water, but every breath was joyful in her lungs. She had said it. They would go on together, and work in the clinic and play cards and talk till all hours. She would tell him about her plan someday. Not yet, but someday.

"Reji Keifon?" Agna asked quietly. She had noticed the name he'd used during their facetious introduction. He had never used it before. He had called himself "Keifon the Medic" to her, and their patients, and everyone else in the Golden Caravan. She had heard him call himself *Kei* in passing – *Kei, pay attention* – but this was new.

"I shouldn't have said that."

"Is that your family name?"

"Yes. In this country they'd say Keifon Reji. Either way, I don't have the right to use the family name anymore."

Some strangers she'd never seen had passed judgment on him and found him guilty of failing to live up to their standard. She knew he had done wrong, and had made bad decisions. She had gathered, one scrap at a time, that the family business had failed on his watch. Still, it seemed particularly cruel to strip him of his own name.

"Reji Keifon," she echoed, taking his culture's order.

He rubbed the back of his neck. "It's... strange. It almost seems like another person's name, now."

"And when you went into the Army, they named you the Medic?"

"After a while. They had another name for me. Mocking. *Zinfan,*" he said. "In Kaveran it would be... something like 'Doomcrow.' Keifon Doomcrow. Kazi liked the name Kazi Eagle-eye, so..." He gestured, joining his hands like two halves of the same thing.

"Because you were... gloomy." *Are*, she thought, without malice. *Not all the time.*

"Miserable. But..." He watched the emerging stars. "They weren't wrong. I just hated that they'd named me that. Because it felt like that's all I could be."

"I'm sorry. I know it isn't all you can be."

"Mmn. Thank you." Keifon did not look at her, but she could read his slight smile. She had learned this over the time they'd spent together. Her words reached him, and they mattered. Agna wanted to thank him in return, but he wouldn't understand why.

"And now you're Keifon the Medic. And if you want to be Keifon Ruler of the World, you can."

He laughed, at least. "And if you want to be a healer and world traveler and art collector..."

Agna's heart lurched. She could tell him about her plan. It would be all right. Or maybe he would chide her for being childish and unoriginal. – Not yet. "Yep," she said, faking bravado. "Official art dealer to the ruler of the world."

Keifon bent to roll down his pant legs. For a while he lounged on the bench beside her, watching the lamplight glitter off the edges of the lake. Crickets and frogs sang in the dark, throwing shards of sound into the hushed night.

She scooped up her shoes at the base of the bench. "I'm ready to go back now, if you are."

"Mmn. Sure." Keifon pulled on his socks and shoes as Agna slipped her shoes on and leaped off the bench. Keifon rounded the bench, and they started down the path to camp, side by side.

"Kei?"

"Hm?"

"Is it all right if I call you that?"

She saw him smile, though he did not look up. "Yeah. I'd like that."

"How about some cards, when we get back? Nothing for wagers, just for fun."

"I'd like that too."

"Good." She might have bounced a little as she walked, out of sheer relief. It was better than twirling around laughing, which was her first impulse.

"You seem happy," he said. "I'm glad."

"Thank you. I think I am."

The light from each streetlight passed over and behind them, one by one. Keifon's hand found her arm in the shadows, squeezed, and dropped away. They walked away from the lake in silence together. The edge of the camp drew nearer, ringed in fences and torches. The sparks from the bonfire leaped into the sky. Agna and Keifon found their way back to the tent and played cards by lamplight. It was good to be home.

Keifon: Forethought

Lundrala began as a web of errands, as merchants and guards crisscrossed the camp to deliver their gifts and tokens. Menon delivered small crocks of cheese; Baran brought hand-carved wooden buttons; Agna traded packets of fine writing paper that she had hoarded and bundled with ribbon; Keifon distributed ink that he had mixed in reused medicine bottles. Keifon and Agna's gifts to one another were kept secret by a mutual, unspoken pact, saved for the last hours before that night's celebration. Their patients, fewer in number than usual, were in high spirits for the most part. A few even brought gifts and thanks for last year's procedures.

Even the shower that passed through that afternoon could not dampen the camp's level of enthusiasm. The bonfire's firewood had been safely tarped over, and the rain washed some of the humidity from the air. Between patients, Keifon and Agna lingered near the door of the clinic to catch the breezes. Occasionally they tossed questions at one another, testing their respective vocabularies. *Rain. Gift. Boredom. Happiness.*

The grammar books had been meant as Lundrala gifts, Keifon recalled. His blunder at Midsummer had bought him six weeks of poring over declensions and discussing traditions after lights-out. From Agna's sly, gleeful hints, it was clear that she'd bought him another gift for Lundrala, but part of him didn't want anything else. Only for this to continue.

Behind the vocabulary quizzes and the occasional patients, Keifon's mind turned over Agna's enigmatic question about following her friend. She had said very little lately about her friend in Vertal. Keifon had a vague notion that her sister lived in their home city. Perhaps Agna meant to settle near her art agency contact, Marco. Keifon was not sure whether this person lived near Agna's family. He was, on the whole, a mysterious figure. Still, Agna spoke of him with such enthusiasm that the idea seemed likely. The two of them might colonize a new Nessinian city with their business and found a new generation of art dealers.

Colonize. Generation. Keifon cleared his throat. His mind leaned in telling directions.

The bustle outside suggested an early end to business. Agna caught his eye. "Well?"

"I'm ready to pack it in if you are."

They packed up their logbooks and supplies, leaving the tent for the second day of the two-day stop. Agna built a fire and shaped the dough that she had prepared that morning. They would bring the bread to the bonfire as their contribution to the festivities. Agna covered it to bake and clapped her hands at Keifon. "Ready?"

He held his elbow out to her, and she laid her hand on his arm. They swanned along like a duchess and her consort, an effect that was lessened by her outcry upon crossing the threshold. "Eeegh!"

"What? – Oh." The tent floor was damp. Agna danced around the puddle to dry ground as Keifon inspected the walls. Tracing the moisture with his fingers led to a worn-through spot at the corner of the roof. "Leak. Right here."

"Grr. So who fixes tents? Tem?"

"I don't think that's necessary. Looks like the pole just wore through. I don't think it's any more complicated than fixing clothes. We'd just have to waterproof it afterward."

Agna made an empty-handed gesture. Keifon stopped short.

"You've mended your things before, right?"

"By... taking them to a tailor, yeah."

Keifon closed his mouth. "Oh. Hm. ...Well, uh, have you done surgery? Hands-on, I mean."

"Yeah, back at Blackhall. Years ago. No practice since then."

"Um... well, I'll fix it, then."

Agna slumped on her cot. "I'm sorry. This is one of those things, isn't it. That I'm supposed to know, and don't."

"It's all right. I can teach you if you want. We can practice on something easier."

"Yeah." Her body straightened, regaining some of her holiday enthusiasm. "Thanks."

Keifon surveyed the leak as Agna went about lighting the lamp. A sizeable puddle had formed on Agna's side of the tent and trickled toward the door, but her backpack and cot had escaped the rain.

"Well," Agna said, "presents?"

"Yeah. Of course."

She bounced on her toes and dove for her overstuffed backpack. Keifon let her go first, savoring the anticipatory flutter under his ribs. Agna turned back with an armful of dark cloth. "It isn't a good time, I know, but..." She held it out to him, and he weighed it in his hands. Wool, it seemed, which explained her comment. He let the bundle unfold.

"For your trip," she said. "I know it's cold in the mountains."

Keifon righted the garment and slipped it on. It was, indeed, the wrong season for a long wool coat with quilted lining. It was, indeed, cold in the mountains. It was all he could do not to hug himself. Instead he took the coat off and folded it carefully. "Thank you. That's so thoughtful."

"Does it fit all right?"

"Perfectly." He draped it over the end of his cot and knelt to unbutton an inner pocket in his backpack. He kept his back turned, gathering his thoughts. "I asked at the shop, and they said if you're traveling, this is the way to go." He turned and passed the flat metal case to Agna.

She cracked the lid and squealed. "Thank you, thank you!"

Keifon breathed again as Agna settled by the lamp to admire the pastel crayons' colors. She explained how the effect differed from that of oil paint, its nearest analogue, and how she might apply this new medium to her next drawing. Keifon basked in her excitement. She resisted the urge to try them out and packed them in her stationery case. The two of them gathered their steaming bread, their gifts for Nelle, and the favors that had not yet been distributed.

As the bonfire's orange light enveloped them, Keifon offered silent thanks. Lundrala was the time to celebrate the people you loved. The day wasn't long enough to finish his thanks.

Agna: Conspiracy

Agna convinced Keifon to come with her and mend the tent roof on the riverbank. He had protested at first, saying that he needed the campfire to finish the weatherproofing with melted wax. She reminded him how nice it would feel to get into the cool water. Finally she set out, trusting him to follow, and found a spot separated from the other bathers by a stretch of open water and a patch of tall brush at the shoreline.

She slipped behind the scrim of plants and slipped her dressing gown off. It was a little easier this year. Not enough to go swimming in front of the whole camp, but she was comfortable with Keifon. She slipped into the deeper water and felt her swimming clothes saturate and cool against her skin.

Keifon's head appeared over the edge of the bank. She waved. That hadn't taken long. He had brought the tent and his mending kit with him, and sat at the edge of the bank where the ground was dry. He arranged the folds of the tent in his lap, centering the worn spot in the roof where he could reach it. Agna lay back in the water, soaking the sweat from her hair. She envied Keifon's short cut, and wondered whether it might be worth the hassle of having it trimmed every few weeks. Her mother would be apoplectic. – Of course, that wasn't a mature reason to do it.

Keifon wiped his face with his forearm and pulled a length of string over a block of beeswax. His eyes wandered to the river. Agna pointedly held up a handful of water and let it drain.

"In a minute. I haven't even started."

"Suit yourself." She dove under, squeezing her eyes shut. The cool water pulled the heat from her skin. It couldn't pull away her exhausted frustration, of course. Not technically. But it helped. She surfaced and floated, kicking lazily to counteract the current.

"How are your parents?" Keifon asked. He was setting stitches now, attaching the patch with surgical precision.

"Fine. Same as always. Though..." Agna ran through their last letter in her mind – her father's letter, primarily. She slid closer to land, sitting on the pebbly shore where the water was just deep enough to riffle over her body. The air was sullen and hot against her face and shoulders, but it was worth it to carry on a conversation without shouting. "They seemed a little too interested in Marco. What we've been talking about, and what I... think of him." She twisted her

243

shoulders uneasily. "It's strange. I feel like they're getting at something, like they have ulterior motives, but I can't imagine what."

The thread drew through the canvas with a quiet whisking sound, just over the hush of the water. "Does Marco work for your father?"

"No, he works for my aunt – my father's sister. She runs the other half of the agency. The two of them split it up years ago."

Keifon turned the section of tent and fanned himself with a loose corner. "They're in competition, then?"

"Only technically. They don't make a show of it, but most of the time they collaborate. You should come in, it's much cooler down here."

"Mmn. You're the heir to your father's side, right? Who's the heir to your aunt's side?"

"My cousin Violetta, but she doesn't want it. She just wants to paint. They'll probably give it to..." She sluiced water over her exposed skin, considering. "Someone like Marco, I guess. An employee who shows promise." She shrugged. "Especially since he and Letta seem to be, you know. Together. If he marries her, he'll get the agency for sure."

"Ah." Keifon was quiet for a little while, except for the tug of the needle through the canvas. "What if he doesn't?"

"What, marry Letta?"

"Yeah."

"...Then he probably still gets the agency. Letta's an only child, and even if she has kids, they won't be old enough to take it over when her mom wants to hand over the reins. Marco's pretty well placed."

"Would that be a problem for your family? Losing it to an outsider?"

Agna slid down the bank so that she could submerge up to her neck, and crossed her arms behind her head. If Naire-ceisi lost her agency to Marco and Agna stayed in Kavera, what then? It would be the end of the Despana dynasty in the Murian art market. Agna's goosebumps had little to do with the temperature of the water. A two-year assignment could swerve the course of one hundred and seventy years. It didn't seem right, somehow. She couldn't tell Keifon that, twofold – she couldn't admit her dreams about Wildern and opening her own gallery, and she couldn't tell him that she stood on the verge of collapsing her family's legacy. He would cry. And then he would tie her to the mast of the next ship bound for Nessiny.

"I suppose it would be a blow to the Despanas, yes. They would be well-regarded for having built the agency, but it would be in someone else's name. We would become a footnote eventually."

She tipped her head back to watch him. He tied the thread and snipped it with the tiny scissors from his kit, then folded up the tent. He would have to finish it back at camp, as he'd complained. He stripped off his shirt and dropped it next to the tent, then kicked off his shoes.

Keifon settled next to her on the bank, stretching his legs in the current, and splashed handfuls of water on his face. His sigh was half groan. "Better."

"Told you."

"What I'm thinking is... your family would have an investment in having Marco marry in, wouldn't they. If they think he's a good heir, it's better to have him be a son-in-law than an employee."

Agna slid a look sideways at him. "You're too good at this."

Keifon shrugged, his dark eyes darting away. "It's how I was raised. Everything in Yanwei works that way."

"How exhausting. – Well, I guess they would have an investment in it, sure. Lina seems to think that the family is behind him and Letta. But it's too early to say for sure."

"And..." He fidgeted, shifting toward the stream, and finally pushed off to tread water. He didn't look at her as he spoke. "She isn't the only eligible heir."

Agna kicked lazily underwater. "Oh yes, she is. At least for him. Lina doesn't date men."

Keifon cleared his throat. The water riffled, reflecting the late-afternoon sun around him in a fractured blaze of light. He didn't speak, and slowly Agna realized that this was intentional.

"...What?"

He half-turned toward her. She hardly heard him over the stream. "Well. You do."

"I do what?"

"...Date men."

Men. As though it were plural. Ha. Agna backed up to piece together his fragmentary comments. *She isn't the only eligible heir.* She darted past him into the deeper water, diving under and surfacing somewhere else. Her teeth chattered. "It's – that's ridiculous. What, marry Marco off to *me*?"

"Then... your father steals the promising employee. Or... if they want to merge the branches... if Marco has one branch and you have the other..."

"Ugh." She windmilled her hands, splashing in a radius that didn't quite hit him. She wished she could crawl out of her skin and leave it on the river bottom.

He wasn't wrong, though. Merging the agencies through marrying their heirs would let them consolidate without appearing to convey a lack of confidence in either branch. It would be devious, but effective. And her father was strangely interested in how she was getting along with Marco. "Ugh!"

"I'm sorry."

"No – it's not your fault, it's just – Marco would never fall for that. He's too smart to be used as a pawn."

"But he'd end up with both branches, in the end. And it's not as though you'd agree to a straightforward marriage arrangement."

She splashed him.

He shook the drops out of his eyes. His arms, flung out for balance, seemed fragile against the deep water. "And, well. Maybe he'd actually fall in love with you."

Agna pounced at him and grabbed his slippery shoulders to dunk him underwater. She felt the resistance leave his muscles, letting her shove him down. Silvery bubbles rose under her chin. An irrational stab of panic clawed at her stomach, and she clutched his arm to haul him back up. He could swim as well as she could, if not better. But seeing his body through that murky water touched an atavistic fear. Keifon breached the surface, his hair plastered against his head. He was fine. Of course he was fine.

"I'm sorry – I'm sorry," she stammered. "That was stupid."

"It's all right." He wiped the water out of his eyes and flashed half of a smile. "I know it's just how you show affection."

Agna blushed, but she could not be diverted. "He wouldn't," she insisted. "Marco. He wouldn't do that. I wouldn't allow it."

His laugh was voiceless. "You don't get to decide that for him. We've been over this."

"What I mean is, I'd tell him. That he should stay with Letta. That I'm..." *That I didn't even measure up to a backwoods farmhand. Even if he was smart and sweet and wonderful and she loved him and they were probably perfect together.* Her stomach clenched.

"Don't." Keifon's hand was warm on her cheek, and anchored her to the world. "I would tell him that you're twice as wonderful as you say you are."

She swam out of arm's reach. "You don't speak enough Nessinian for that yet."

"I'd learn."

She smiled, brittle but real. "You would."

Keifon slowly rolled over on his back and floated, letting her calm down. Agna considered doing the same. The sky was too bright right now. She treaded water near him and watched the smooth rocks and the darting fish in the shallows. She imagined the water pulling away her tension and paranoia. She imagined floating here forever.

"Your parents want you to be happy," Keifon said quietly. "If they're pushing too hard about Marco, I'm sure it's out of love for you."

"I can be happy without getting married," Agna protested.

"Of course you can. But..." He closed his eyes to the sky. "When someone experiences something good, they want to share it. I'm sure they want you to be as happy as they've been."

The skin across Keifon's collarbone was a shade lighter than the rest, a faint halo where the torque had blocked the sun for so long. Agna sensed that he missed being married, not only to Eri but to anyone. It was part of the life he wanted and part of the person he wanted to be. It was true that she could be happy without being married. She wasn't sure he could be. And there was a little envy in his voice, in considering that her parents wanted something good for her. Agna regretted the vehemence of her outburst, if not the words themselves.

"I know they mean well," she admitted at last. "It's just... it's such a bad time, after... after Laris."

Keifon rolled into the vertical, treading water with long, smooth strokes. "They don't know that, though."

"I know." She sighed, ducked her head to feel the cool water on her face, and slicked her hair back. "What now?" It wasn't a question, and he waited for her to answer herself. "I want to ignore all of this matchmaking nonsense and talk to Marco about art. That's what."

Keifon smiled. "Do that, then."

"I think I will."

Agna: The Home Front

Agna looked up from her copy of *Blackhall's*, letting it dip into her lap as she realized that Keifon was reading his ex-wife's letter again.

"How much longer?" she asked, though she knew.

"Four days." He folded the letter and slid it into its envelope. It was made of cream-colored paper, addressed twice in black ink: once in Kaveran, once in Yanweian.

"Are you nervous about seeing Nachi, or...?"

Keifon landed on his back, arms crossed behind his head. "I'm not sure. All of it, maybe. Going home." He sighed, and Agna watched his chest rise and fall. "Do you ever get nervous about going home?"

"Oh, I don't know." She marked her place with her woven bookmark from the festival and leaned on her hand. "It's a long way off."

"Not really," Keifon said quietly. "Seven months."

"That's more than half a year," Agna retorted, unnerved that he had it figured out so precisely, and then felt foolish for having stated the obvious. "But I do feel nervous sometimes. Because of the agency, and my parents. Things like that. I don't have – you know, situations like yours. Kids and exes and things."

He laughed bloodlessly. "One kid, one ex."

"...Two," she said softly.

"He's not a factor anymore."

"Yeah, but... I thought you might worry anyway. It's an excuse to worry." He turned his head to glare at her, half-seriously, and Agna smiled. "I know you."

Keifon's eyes softened. "...yeah. You do."

The leaves were beginning to turn. Agna balanced her vicarious excitement against her nervousness. He would take a safe path, and he knew how to defend himself. And she would be fine, of course. The solitude would be calming, for a change.

■ ■ ■

On the last day, a dozen people appeared at their campsite just after dawn. Agna shook Keifon awake and stuck her head out of the tent to plead with them to wait a few minutes. By the time she had thrown a few more layers over her nightdress and slipped out to let him get ready, Nelle had lit their campfire. Agna thanked her and filled the kettle with water.

Keifon emerged, unshaven, yawning, embarrassed at all of the attention. Nelle grabbed him and hugged until Agna was sure his back would break, and slipped a vial into his pocket. Baran pressed a wrapped parcel into his hands, making him promise not to open it until he got home. Masa brought him a packed lunch, free of charge. Everyone wished him safe travels and congratulated Agna on her dedication and promised to help her out whenever she needed it. And one by one they drifted away, back to their own tents and their own businesses. Nelle was the last to go. Edann never came. And eventually it was just Agna and Keifon at the fire.

They ate bread and cheese and drank tea, commenting on what the others had said and done. Nelle's gift had turned out to be an aromatic mixture that made Agna's head swim when she leaned too close. For sleep, Keifon read from the label. The scent was supposed to be soothing.

They finished breakfast. Agna swallowed the uneasy tension that had risen into her throat. She couldn't cry. It would be silly. Keifon went off to shave and change; Agna sat by the fire and took deep breaths of the chilly morning air. She changed in the tent while he was gone. It would be her space alone, for a while. She could stretch out as much as she liked.

She heard his footsteps before he came back into the tent. She hadn't gone out to meet him, just in case her treacherous eyes couldn't be trusted after all. Keifon packed away his clothes and stood facing her, empty-handed.

"I... I'll miss you," he said, his voice turning harsh and whispering. He cleared his throat. "Thank you so much for this."

Agna tried to think of something breezy and flippant. When nothing would come, he closed the distance between them and took her into his arms instead. And that was the end of that. She sniffled, trying to muffle her hiccuping sobs against his shoulder, but Keifon swayed with her as though rocking a child.

"Ssshh. Not for me. Please."

Agna struggled out of his grip and shoved him in the shoulder. "Of course for you. Stupid. I'm going to miss you, too." She took a pair of frustrated, spinning steps around the tent, as if to find a way out. "I know you're coming back, I know it's stupid. I can't–" She wiped her sleeves across her eyes, furious with herself for having ruined his farewell.

He hugged her. Agna calmed despite herself. Keifon kept her steady as he spoke. "Thank you for – for missing me back. I don't think you know what that means to me."

She had been awake for barely an hour, and she was already dizzy as though she'd been up all night. "Not fair," she murmured. "Trump card. Hugging is a trump card." She could feel a chuckle knock around his ribcage.

"You can play it, too," he said, and drew away a little. Agna sniffled. Keifon leaned in to kiss her forehead, and darted off to grab his backpack and lute case.

She didn't say goodbye as he flew from the tent. She called "Safe travels!", and he turned to wave. And that was all.

■ ■ ■

During the day, she managed the clinic, one patient after another. The first day left her exhausted, her concentration sputtering out by day's end, her head crowded with other people's energy signatures. She apologized and closed the clinic early. On the second day she took Keifon's medical kit with her and used his tools when she could. She had trained in medical tools at Blackhall, but it had been some time since she'd listened to a heartbeat through a stethoscope instead of through her hands. The patients didn't comment. She began to get used to switching back and forth, using her art when the situation called for it, conserving her energy. It began to feel natural.

Lines began to form in the clinic, despite her best efforts. Even conserving her energy wouldn't let her treat two doctors' worth of patients at once. She learned to stop tensing up when there were people waiting, because they arrived at the front of the line as tense as she was, more often than not. And then their energy, when she connected, was jangling and harsh. Agna worried and castigated herself for this, because Keifon would have been better at it. He would have put them all at ease, or even made them enjoy waiting. But eventually it got easier.

Agna imposed order. The first person in line took this spot, and the next, and progressed in a certain direction around the wall of the clinic. She borrowed some extra books from Wayron and stacked them on a spare stool by the door, along with some wooden toys from Baran. Agna began to greet the patients cheerfully, striking up conversations as though this were only a trivial setback. The patients often started conversations among one another. She listened to their interconnecting stories, lost in a swirl of narratives that flowed one into the other, as their neighbors chimed in with tangents and sequels.

She noticed that if she had been talking to one of the patients, it was easier to read them and find their currents. She knew the theory; she had always known the theory. It was why it had been so difficult to help Keifon, so long ago. Their energy carried their baggage, good or bad. But it was a help to her now.

On days off, she and Nelle fell back into doing their laundry together. They talked about the plants that ripened this time of year, the gossip around the camp, and the plans that Agna had begun to formulate for this year's fall festival. As their laundry dried, they suited up in leathers to hike through the underbrush and collect berries and roots. Agna brushed the burrs out of her hair, kneeling on the tent floor. She experimented with painting with berry juice and making plant-based ink.

She got one short note: Keifon had reached his destination. He said *thank you* again. He didn't say much else. Lina's and Marco's letters continued. Rone wrote her with a new address. He had moved to Prisa. He didn't explain why.

She became more conscious of the sounds of the camp at night, falling asleep listening to creaking and coughing and the pitchy crackle of the torches.

■ ■ ■

Masa agreed to make Nessinian food for the fall festival, an exotic holiday to the rest of the caravan. Fox, his apprentice, popped over to the clinic tent now and then to ask questions about ingredients or traditions. He was ravenous for new information, having learned Kaveran cuisine inside and out. Agna told him what she knew as she packed up the tent, and he helped her dismantle it before the caravan moved on.

The merchants gathered for the fall festival at a campsite outside Wildern. Agna ate a little bit of everything that Masa and Fox had made, listening to the others as they talked, argued, opined and proclaimed. She slipped away from the table to find the cooks and to compliment them on their skill. Fox grinned. Masa put her to work carrying more platters out to the tables.

Nelle reached a precise titration of tipsiness. When most of the others had disbanded, leaving the survivors in quiet clumps around the bonfire, she leaned on Agna's shoulder. "In Wildern, we should go out. You and me. All right?"

"Yeah, we should." Agna had wanted to explore the city and get some real information to bolster her dreams of relocating, but it would be a more pleasant trip with some company. There were theaters in town, and a library; there would be things to do.

Nelle drifted around the bonfire, talking with each of the remaining clusters in turn. Agna watched the flickering firelight against her back. It was strange that the two of them should stick together like this. But then, they were close to the same age, and shared a few interests... maybe it wasn't so strange. Agna had to put aside the thought that she could only be truly connected to people from Murio and the Academy. It wasn't true anymore, if it ever had been.

Rone's religion said that everyone was connected. They believed that just being human made them fellow travelers in life, to a certain extent. That was a bit of a stretch, Agna thought. But maybe being alive was one drop, and being part of the caravan was another, and every experience they shared was one drop and the next, and so the cup was filled. Nelle had become her friend somehow, and Edann had become Keifon's, for a while. And Keifon... Agna watched the fire on her own for a while.

Somewhere on the other side of the mountains, he was back together with his little girl. The thought tied a knot in her throat. Her knowledge of Kaveran art was more specialized, and her healing work was more laudable in the grand scheme of things. But she was proud of having made the reunion possible, too.

■ ■ ■

Wildern had already had a tiny storefront library when the Benevolent Union base had been built, but now it had a grand two-story building with a central atrium, crammed with books. There were two theaters and a singing company that performed outdoors in good weather. There were clothiers whose wares made Agna's chest constrict with homesickness as she passed outside their windows. She didn't know what was fashionable anymore, but she longed for silk and fresh linen all the same. She was saving her money, just in case. In case of what, she wasn't sure. She had become used to doing so.

Nelle loved the idea of a library afternoon and a theater evening. She bent over herbalism texts, spread out over the tables, as Agna wandered through the stacks. Agna inhaled the air and watched the dust motes in the sunbeams. She found a librarian and introduced herself in hushed, polite tones. The librarian found another, who found a historian, who swept Agna into her office and shut the door.

Two hours later, Agna floated back to the center of the library to find Nelle. Her brain was packed, her throat was raw, and her blood was full of lightning. Under her arm she gripped a folder full of notes, names, ideas. Dreams. Potential.

Nelle closed her array of books and grabbed her by the arms. Her eyes lit up with the promise of conspiracy.

"Later. Dinner," Agna whispered. "Starving."

They found a restaurant, where, before the entrees arrived, Agna laid out her notes on the tabletop.

Wildern was growing, and with it grew its cultural offerings. The library, the theaters, and the Benevolent Union school were a solid foundation, but talk had begun of museums, trade schools, and more churches beyond the old Eytran church.

The historian, Jaeti, was a specialist in northwestern Kaveran history, and had been looking into the possibility of opening a history museum. She had found a few available spaces – most were storefronts left behind as their tenants moved into newer, larger buildings – but nothing quite suited her plan. She had also found little enthusiasm in funding a history museum in a city that seemed so poised for the future. But with an art gallery linked to the history museum, both might have a greater chance of survival.

After dinner, Agna dragged Nelle past one of the vacant buildings and fogged the windows with their breath. She would write to Wildern every day for the rest of her assignment if she had to. She would grovel to investors, live above a storefront, and invest everything she made on the road. She would spend every bit of goodwill she could raise as a scion of the Despana family. It would take teamwork and long, thankless hours. But she could make this real.

She walked away for now, returning to the theaters with Nelle. They read the flyers posted outside, their breath steaming in the air. Agna buried her chin in her scarf and hugged the folder against her side. They had a brief, unserious debate and settled on the play that started earlier. Nelle spun through the cold night on the way home, lobbing back Agna's incoherent, gleeful chatter.

Agna composed a letter in her head that night as she fell asleep, an invisible companion to her regular letters to Rone and Esi and Lina and Marco. *Things are good. I miss you. I hope you're doing well.*

Keifon: Past and Future

Eri rested a hip against the doorframe. "You look better."

Keifon tried to stifle a yawn. "Joke?"

"No. You looked terrible last time, that's all." But she moved aside into the warmth and light of her parents' house and let him come in. Her parents' eyes fixed on him. He inclined his head, determined not to rise to their bait, determined to prove that he didn't deserve their continuing resentment.

Ignoring all of them, Eri sauntered toward the back of the house. "Can I get you something?" Keifon lowered his backpack and his nanbur case to the floor by the door, shed his new coat and soaked boots, and scrambled to catch up. He shivered on the kitchen's slate floor. Eri was already pumping water into a teakettle.

"I-it's good to see you," he chattered, rubbing his hands.

"Nachi's asleep," she said. "We could wake her, but she wouldn't go back to sleep, and she has school tomorrow."

"I understand." He couldn't even resent the decision. He could hurt for a while longer, more keenly, now that his girl was just a couple of doors away. But school was important, and they'd have more time later. Not enough. But a little more.

She leaned against the scarred wooden counter, crossing her legs at the ankle. Her eyes softened. "You're really all right."

Half a laugh escaped his cold-tightened throat. "Yeah. I'm – I'm good." He caught the half-dozen layers of meaning in her voice and in her posture. He could read her like a measure of music, tones over tones. *Are you drinking again? No.*

"You stopped wearing it." Her long hand touched the hollow of her throat, swathed in the neck of a soft wool sweater.

"...Yeah. Actually... wait a minute." Sniffing, Keifon darted past the elder Sans and knelt by his luggage. The bag of money sat cradled in clothes in the center of his backpack. He extracted it and carried it to her, feeling like a child who had caught a frog. "It's from – selling my torque. And some of what I made this past year. It isn't much. I'm sorry."

Eri set it on the table. The coins settled against one another. The stove crackled behind her. "You're sure you're all right."

"*Yes!* Damn it. – Yes." He reined in the old snappishness and quickness to anger. Too much time had passed. He couldn't slide back. "I'm sorry. I'm – I'm cold, and exhausted, and–" hungry, it seemed pathetic to heap that on top of everything else – "and I know I deserve it, but I'm too tired to cope with your parents right now. I'm fine. It's going well in Kavera. Really well." Once he had started, he couldn't stop. He breathed on his hands. The blood was returning to them now, and his clothes were drying out. "I'm getting experience in the trade. I – I've been working well with the – the person that the Benevolents assigned to me. I miss home, I miss Nachi. But it's been good." He looked into her eyes, to prove his sincerity and to see her relent. "I'm getting better. I promise."

Eri puffed out a scoffing sigh. "All right. I'm not your godsforsaken jailer." She turned to lift the kettle from the stove and poured him a cup over loose black leaves. "Are you hungry?"

"Umn, yes. But you don't have to—"

"I know I don't." Muffling her movements, she opened a cabinet and busied herself with plates and knives. Keifon wrapped his hands around the scorching cup and basked in the steam. Even if it blistered the skin off his fingers, he wouldn't care. He hoped the rain would stop before tomorrow. He hoped he would be back tomorrow.

"Eri?" Her mother peeked in the door, surveyed the layout of the room, and was apparently satisfied with what she found. "We're going to bed, kitten."

Eri set down her arsenal and rounded the table to give her mother a kiss on the cheek. "Goodnight, Ara."

Eri's parents' steps creaked up the stairs as Eri finished her task. She slid a plate loaded with two sandwiches toward Keifon on the table and wiped her hands on a towel. Keifon felt his ears burning. "...Thank you."

"If you want to talk, we can go out by the fire." Her voice had softened, too. Keifon knew this voice, with its quiet drawl. It tightened in his chest. He cleared his throat.

"Mmn. Sounds nice."

She took the teakettle; he took his plate and cup. They left the money bag on the table. Keifon glanced at it as they passed out of the kitchen. She hadn't counted it, so the amount wasn't in question. Did she think that he was buying her approval? He'd brought money before. It was for Nachi, that was all. It was the least he could do.

Eri sat on one of the chairs by the fire, tucking her feet under her. It was a little easier to take her mannerisms as time went on. It hurt a little less. She was more Nachi's mother than his own former partner now. The balance shifted more every time he visited. Time kept moving. Keifon sank into the other chair with the plate and cup balanced in either hand. His stomach growled, but he had to drink her in, to convince himself that she was really there. She was back to cutting her hair short, fringing softly around her face. She was still careless with her limbs, like she had just woken up. She was still lovely, but he could appreciate that more distantly now. He had to.

"...You look good, too."

She smiled ruefully. "Thanks."

Keifon bent aside to set the teacup on an end table and tried not to inhale the sandwiches. The last stretch into the city had been interminable; the cart had bogged down four times in the mud. Keifon had agonized about the rain getting into his nanbur case, and arriving too late to see Nachi. But, he reminded himself, he had made it here. He was at Eri's fireside, and she was listening.

The firelight warmed the planes of her cheek, outlining the border between light and shadow. She didn't look at him as she spoke. "I should mention, before it gets too late – one of my cousins had a room for rent. It's not far, and it's a reasonable rate. I'll take you there when you're ready."

The warmth spread from inside him, meeting the fire's glow. "Oh... thank you." He took a sip of tea and started on the second sandwich. "Is it... is something wrong with the money? It's for her. That's all."

"I know," Eri sighed. She folded her arms and rested her chin on them. She looked so young curled up on the chair. "But it's a lot. Isn't it?"

"Nn. I guess. Forty thousand, thereabouts."

"God's blood."

"It's what I can do." He didn't trust himself to speak without resentment or bitterness tainting the words. *This is all I can do. I can't be here.* "Please take it for her."

She rolled her neck, and he saw the real fatigue in her movements for the first time. "Some of it. Keep some for yourself. We're all right, and she'd be devastated if you starved to death for her sake."

Keifon smiled despite himself. "I'm not going to starve to death."

"What *are* you going to do? Stay in Kavera?"

Trust Eri to strike right where he was weakest. "I... I don't know." He took a couple more bites to stall, to formulate an answer that made sense, an answer that would convince himself as well as Eri. "I love my work, even though traveling is... it's difficult, sometimes. But it's worth it. I'm doing good for those people, and learning, like I said. I think..." He swallowed and set the empty plate aside, then propped one heel on the edge of the seat and leaned on his thigh, echoing her posture. "The Army would let me go honorably if I kept working for the Benevolent Union. There's... in Wildern, right over the border, the Benevolents just built a new hospital. I think I could... I could apprentice there. And study, and someday be a full-fledged doctor."

"Then what?"

"Stay there, I think. I can't... I can't risk coming back for good."

"Ugh. Because of that asshole."

Keifon tightened his jaw against the words that crowded his head. *He was there for me when you weren't. Until he wasn't. You have that in common.* But then... she was defending him, wasn't she, in her own way. Defending him against Kazi. Keifon rested his forehead on his folded hands. "Because of Kazi, yes. Partly."

"Are you still talking to him? Writing, or anything?"

"No. Not since I left. He wouldn't have it."

She let out a breath and relaxed her shoulders. "That's one thing." Her gaze leveled at him. Shaken by the turn of the conversation, he hoped that she would find something worth honoring. He had come so far, whether she realized it or not, and he wanted her to know that he had.

"I think... I think I'm over him. More or less." He found a way to take another breath. "I haven't found anyone else yet. Friends. People who have been good for me. But I'm not seeing anyone. Not exactly."

"Not exactly?"

His heart raced. He hadn't meant to say that. "Well, for a while I kind of saw someone. It didn't work out."

"Already," Eri sighed. "Oh, Kei. Another self-obsessed maniac?"

"No. But – he wasn't good for me. He's... he drinks too much, he's moody, he's never quite honest with me..."

"He's you."

Keifon looked away. "...I guess so."

"At least you know that's bad for you. That's progress."

"And I have friends who are better influences," Keifon went on, wanting to escape as far as he could from the topic of Edann. "My partner from the Benevolent Union has been wonderful. She's only in the country till New Year's. But it's been good for me to have her as a friend."

"That's sweet," Eri offered. "Not a prospect?"

He felt himself blushing. "No – no. It's not like that. She has other prospects. And – no, she's from a good family, and she's going home to Nessiny. And it's just not like that." The thought of Agna as a – prospect – made him feel as though he were standing at a cliff's edge, queasy and exhilarated. It would never work. She didn't seem interested in having children, she wanted to travel, and she meant too much to him to risk; it would never work. "Anyway, I'm happy to have her in my life, and that's all."

Eri made a soft sound in her throat, not a word, or more than a word. Her hand rested on his knee. He looked up; she had leaned forward to bridge the space between them. "I'm glad you have someone like that," she said.

He freed a hand to cover hers, and she let him stay that way until he could speak. "Thank you."

Eri sat back. Keifon cleared his throat. "If I find a job in Wildern, I'd be about a week away. Do you think I could..."

Eri took a deep breath and nodded. "Of course. Under our agreement. But yes, of course."

"Thank you. I won't break the agreement. Thank you. This... I would be so happy." He was warmed and fed now, but exhausted, and perilously close to saying something he would regret – or crying in front of her, thinking about the possibility of visiting Nachi every year. Or even more than once a year, if he could carve out the time from his work. He would try.

"I really... appreciate that you'd do that for her," Eri said, and Keifon focused. "You know I've never agreed with this leaving the country idea. But I appreciate what you're planning. I know you're trying to do right by her. Even with all that's happened. ...I want you to know that I respect what you're doing now."

He bit his lip and pressed the corners of his eyes, but the tears slid free. It buried so many years that he'd spent miserably recounting the things she'd said about him. The bad times had happened. They would always be real. But if even Eri could come to forgive him, then –

"Thank you," he whispered. He couldn't come up with any other words.

Eri let him compose himself. She poked at the fire and took his empty plate to the kitchen. She poured him more tea and a cup for herself. They sipped together, not quite companionable, but at peace.

"So," she said. "Tell me more about the Benevolent woman."

"Um. She's Nessinian. She's a healer, like a Tufarian healer, except pantheist. Sort of. She..." He couldn't speak of Agna to Eri, of all people in this complicated world. He couldn't even name her out loud.

"She's good to you?"

The lump gathered in his throat. "Yeah. We're... we get along well. I love being with her. We talk a lot. And read." It sounded pathetic out loud. He couldn't tell Eri about the way Agna laughed, or how good it felt when she broke through her cautiousness for him, or how he felt like he had found a place that he belonged. "It's been good to have someone I can talk to."

She sipped her tea, cradling the cup in her hands. "Have you thought about marrying again, when you settle down?"

"Yeah. Of course. I mean... I don't know what it's like in Wildern. Kaverans mostly make love matches. But I think there are a few matchmakers, too."

"Hm. I've been thinking about looking. Now that Nachi is in school."

Keifon's warm thoughts plunged into chill. Eri deserved whatever happiness she could find, of course, the same as anyone. But Nachi... Nachi would have a new father, if Eri remarried. A replacement. ...An improvement, Keifon thought miserably.

He licked his lips and put the words together, one by one. "I wish you luck. I know... I know you'll pick better this time. And Nachi deserves – she deserves a father who can be there for her."

"It wouldn't replace you. Don't be like that."

He clenched and released his hands. "I'm sorry. It's... hard to face."

"I know it is. But do I have your support?"

"Of course!"

"All right, then." She smiled at him, though her eyes were tired. "She won't forget you. She loves you." She said it without resentment, and Keifon thanked her for that. "And I wouldn't let her forget. Even with... everything, I want her to know her Apa. As long as... well, you know."

"Yes. I know."

"She can have a father and a stepfather. Wouldn't be the first time."

"Thank you for that." Keifon wiped his eyes one more time and yawned. "Sorry. Do you think you could show me to your cousin's now? I need some sleep."

"Sure." Eri uncurled from the chair like a cat and collected their teacups.

She emerged from the kitchen with a handful of the money that he'd brought. She unlaced his money pouch and poured the coins in. Feeling her hands on his waist shot alarm and arousal through his nerves, and his fatigue flashed away. Wildly inappropriate, his brain argued, fighting against his body's reflexes. He began to stammer out a protest.

"Ssh. For your house in – Wildern?"

"Nngh. All right... all right."

For a moment, Eri's smile carried a trace of the wickedness and wildness that had drawn him to her so long ago. She had been the girl who got what she wanted, no matter who stood in her way. He had wanted to be her quest. He had wanted her to obliterate him with her personality, her indelible sense of self. He turned away and buckled on his backpack and slung his nanbur over his shoulder. He wasn't the boy she had loved. That boy had died over and over. And she had calmed, rooted, mellowed. The storm had become the rock.

She walked with him through the wet streets. "Tomorrow. Apa will pick up Nachi at school at three. If you want to come over after that, I'll tell him not to kill you. I'll be home at seven."

"Yes. I'd love that. Thank you."

Her cousin's room for rent had a separate door for lodgers, and that was where she left him. "I'll see you tomorrow, then. Rest well."

"You, too."

He worried about sending her off alone, and watched until she turned the corner. In her cousin's rented room he unpacked, needing this time to let everything that Eri had said unfold in his head. He came across the package that Baran had given him and untied the strings. The toymaker had given him a present for Nachi: a carved wooden puzzle with bright geometrical pieces. Keifon laughed to himself. In the morning he could write a note of thanks back to the caravan. It would reach Baran before he did. He would write to Agna, too.

He pulled out the vial that Nelle had given him and gave it another cautious sniff. Lavender, which was achingly familiar. Rosemary? There were other components that he couldn't place. He hardly needed help to get to sleep, for once, but it couldn't hurt. Keifon tipped a few drops onto a handkerchief and left it on the bedside table to scent the room.

Keifon crawled into the wide feather bed and slept until his body had recovered from all of its insults. He might have woken a few times out of nightmares, but in the end it wasn't important.

■ ■ ■

He walked Ceien's streets much of the day, after greeting Eri's cousin and paying for the room for two weeks. He remembered the rough layout of the streets, though several of the businesses had turned over in the intervening years. He tried not to notice the store where Eri worked – at least a bookkeeper would be in the back room, where she wouldn't see her ex-husband haunting the street outside. He passed the school where she sent Nachi, where Eri's mother taught.

Their lives were complete here. He had seen it during his previous visits, and had felt crushed. Their lives were complete, he'd thought, and they did not need him. He was superfluous. An interloper. But what Eri had said last night... maybe he could fit into their lives, somehow. She believed that he could, and would leave the door open for him. Keifon had to believe that she was right, that he deserved such an honor.

The thought straightened out his spine as he walked and retreaded last night's conversation. Eri respected him, despite her not-unfounded reservations. Agna respected him. Their patients and the Army and the Benevolent Union approved of him as a medic. He could act as though they weren't wrong, and over time he could come to believe them.

When the hour came and he knocked on the Sans' door, he greeted Eri's father with a respectful bow and a smile. The older man's mouth relaxed just a little. He turned to speak over his shoulder, but Nachi was already mid-flight. Keifon had just enough time to hand off the package from Baran to Nachi's grandfather before she struck.

"Apa-Kei, Apa-Kei, Apa-Kei!" She latched onto his stomach, and he stooped to hoist her up. She was too old for this. It didn't matter. His heart hammered and his soul sang. Finally, finally. Where he wanted to be, finally. He couldn't have failed her if she still greeted him like this. Nachi nearly strangled him with her hug.

Eventually he heaved a step over the threshold so that Eri's father could close the door. Nachi leaped to the floor. Keifon reached out for the gift, and Eri's father handed it back. "Thanks. – Hey, sweet girl. One of Apa's friends in Kavera made this for you."

She carted it to a table by the fireplace to open it. "Thank you!"

Keifon knelt beside her as she rearranged the pieces into birds and ships and trees. Eri's father moved on after a while, heading for the kitchen.

"How's school?"

"Good," she shrugged. "We're reading *Toki and the Six Foxes* right now. It's pretty good."

"Ah yes."

"You read it?"

"Lots of times. I've read all sorts of things."

"I know that," she said, exasperated. Of course it was self-evident; he was a grownup.

They talked about school, and the games they played in breaks, and math, and history. Nachi carried the box of puzzle pieces up to her room and bounced back out to pester her grandfather about dinner. Eri's mother came home to find them both helping out; Nachi stood on a stool to chop vegetables on the counter. Keifon looked up guiltily from the pan he was scrubbing, remembered his determination not to grovel, and gave Eri's mother a soapy salute. Nachi informed her that Keifon had arrived.

"Is h– are you staying for dinner, Keifon?"

"Oh – hm – I wouldn't want to impose." He calculated the pitfalls: he couldn't make them look like the villains in front of Nachi, but he couldn't invite himself if it would further alienate them. "I'd like to ask Eri, when she gets home."

"Fair enough," Eri's mother concluded. She passed by Keifon and Nachi to give her husband a kiss, then left them to their preparations.

Eri came home as Nachi was reading one of her schoolbooks by the fire, leaning against Keifon's chest as he sat with his back against one of the chairs. Eri paused, watched them, and said nothing. Keifon rested his chin against the top of Nachi's head and hoped.

Eri let him stay for dinner. He came back for dinner every day for two weeks.

Agna: Return

"Thanks for coming by, ma'am. And please check with Solei and Merkal when they come through in the spring. We'll keep checking every six months like that. – Have a good day."

Agna looked up, and her smile crystallized. She was barely aware that some of the remaining patients turned to track her gaze toward the door. She was barely aware that the clinic was there at all.

"Hi." Keifon shrugged to shift one of his backpack straps. "Um..."

"H-hi. Hey. Welcome back."

Half of the patients were silent; the other half all started talking at once. "Welcome back! I heard you went up to Yanwei. Whereabouts? I can come back later, Healer. Hey, Medic, the pain in my foot has started again, you were so good with that last year..."

They all went quiet when Agna hugged him. He lifted one gloved hand to her back and bent his face to her shoulder.

She kept it together in front of the patients. She was glad for their presence, after all. "I'm so glad to see you."

"I'm glad to see you, too." He stepped back, casting an embarrassed glance at the small crowd. "Hi, everyone."

The villagers chorused their greetings. Keifon's clinical manner began to slip into his voice as he waved and greeted them and thanked them for their well-wishes. "I've got to put this pack down, and then I'll be right back to help out."

"You don't have to—" Agna began to say, but he had already gone. She caught her breath, straightened her belt, and faced the next patient in line. "What seems to be the trouble?"

■ ■ ■

The patients kept their queue around the tent and out the door, and their conversations continued. When Keifon returned, Agna handed over his case of tools. He bowed, and a couple of the patients applauded.

Keifon took his place by the unoccupied stool and smiled at the next person in line. "Well, who's next?"

Agna heard the basics in passing fragments, as he explained his trip to half a dozen patients. He had gone to Ceien to see his six-and-a-half-year-old daughter. She was in good health and doing well in school. Everyone was charmed, as they always were. But Agna realized that he wasn't telling them this as part of his charm. It was a part of his real self. He didn't have to put on a cheerful act when he talked about Nachi.

Agna found herself buoyed on his new high spirits, rallying the energy that had begun to flag over the last few stops. Even working entirely by her healing arts, she was able to keep her focus together for the rest of the day. She reflected, warming her hands over the brazier in a rare idle moment between patients, that she might buy herself some medical equipment after all. It was a good fallback. It wasn't how the Academy instructed, but it was more important to do the best she could for the patients.

Keifon waved to a departing patient. Agna turned. They smiled, edged with the beginnings of fatigue. Neither would stop, not yet, even if Keifon had traveled all night to get here. Their team was back together. Nothing could stop them.

Another villager poked her head into the door. "Excuse me?"

The team worked together, as it once had, as it was meant to do.

■ ■ ■

The stream of patients slowed in the late afternoon, as the sun began to slide behind the mountains. Agna crunched into the apple that Masa had packed in her lunch. Nelle had learned of Keifon's arrival when she'd delivered Agna's lunch. They had shooed her off at the time, too busy to talk. Agna thought about inviting her back to their tent later for a little welcoming party. Later.

"So... it seems like you've been doing well."

She looked up. He was repacking his valise, lining up the bottles and tools across the examination table. Agna looked around the tent. "I think I have."

Keifon pulled a neat roll of bandages out of the valise. "The crowd management is working beautifully."

"Yeah, you know, it calms people down if they chat beforehand. Takes their minds off of whatever the problem is, I think. Though some of the time, they're giving one another bad advice."

"Heh."

"I hope it's all right that I used your stuff. It was a big help."

"Oh, it's fine. I'm glad you got some use out of it." He swirled the contents of one of the bottles and made a note. "How have you been? Otherwise."

"...All right." She rushed on, embarrassed. "But tell me about your trip! I heard that Nachi is doing well, that's great." She silenced the rest, because it would come out more petty and selfish than she meant it to sound. *How's her mother? Did you see Kazi? I'm glad you came back at all.*

"Yeah. It was so good to see her. Just... I needed to." He crossed his arms, leaving the tools aside. "I can't thank you enough for taking care of things here."

Agna shrugged and leaned against the edge of the side table. "It's what we had to do. Work together. Right?"

"Right."

Interrupted now and then by a few straggling patients, he told her about the trip. He told her about taking his daughter to the park, listening to her thoughts about school and her friends and her life. Agna wasn't sure she had seen him this happy before – this much at peace.

"She's happy there," Keifon concluded. Night came early now, and the two of them sat by the examination table in the lamp's circle of light with the brazier on the floor between them. Agna doodled in ink in the margins of her logbook as she listened. They could have gone home by now, but she didn't want to move. Not yet. Keifon seemed happy to stay late tonight, too. "I did a lot of thinking about... what to do, how to do right by her and by – by everyone. And... by me, too. Thinking that I should remember to do right by myself, somewhere in there, too."

"You should. I'm glad you've been thinking about it."

"I think... I think after you go, I am going to ask for a transfer to the base at Wildern, after all." He took a long breath. "Eri said she would be all right with me visiting."

"That's... terrific," Agna made herself say. *After you go.* She cleared her throat and tried to be sensible and strong. They were having a reasonable discussion about their plans. The spring was real; it was coming. It would happen whether she wanted it to happen or not.

Agna folded her hands into her sleeves, because it was less obvious than hugging herself against the chill. *After you go. After you go, I'm leaving.* The winter was just beginning. They had a long time yet. She had time to tell him about her foolish plans about staying in Kavera and opening her own gallery. She had time to become brave enough to tell him. But first she had to figure out whether she was making the same mistake all over again.

Keifon went on. "And... I think I could... I think I could start to make a life there." His voice strengthened. "I could have a place that's mine, and a position in the base. And... and live." He fell quiet, watching the flickering light on the table between them. "I want to try for those things we talked about at Midsummer. All of them, a little at a time."

She remembered his goals, all domestic and heartbreakingly simple. Agna covered his hand with her own. He turned his wrist to squeeze her hand. "I think you could," she said. "I believe."

His smile made her want to cry. "Thank you." He left his hand in hers. "It could be hard. For a lot of reasons. I'm old, for an apprentice. But the Benevolents should help. And... with other things, well. There are matchmakers. Or I could try to go it alone."

Agna's voice stuck in her throat. She had nothing to add on the topic, nothing but academic curiosity about matchmaking and arranged marriages.

Keifon saved her the embarrassment. "Do you have matchmakers in Nessiny? Or is it all your parents? Or love matches?"

She jumped on the tangent away from the personal. "Well, both. Mostly – mostly not arranged. Sometimes parents do it, or more often they just pester you about it. They've thrown my sister at as many of their colleagues' kids as they can find, because she doesn't want to be in the art trade." She remembered what Keifon had conjectured about Marco, which, of course, wasn't true.

"That sounds like a lot of pressure. It would be easier just to arrange it directly."

Agna shrugged. "Yeah, probably. Though I can't imagine an arranged marriage. I mean, I can't – not for me, I mean I can't imagine what it's like for somebody else."

"Hm. I wasn't... I wasn't in one, but I was supposed to be. My parents were still looking when they died." He slipped his hand out of hers, drumming a soft rhythm on the tabletop. "The thing is, the decision is made. There isn't as much pressure. You have the situation, and you make the best of it. It doesn't always work, but it usually does. My parents' marriage was arranged. They respected one another so much. I knew that, even as a kid."

"Hmm. *Alaste*, maybe, more than *amane*."

He considered this. "Family before romance? I suppose so. But romance is there. The expectation is that you build it – grow it – after you're married. And..." He shrugged. "For me – I mean – it's not the same for everyone. But I've always – for me, the willingness to – to build a family and a future with me is very attractive." His voice faltered, and he cleared his throat.

"It's sweet," Agna offered, covering his embarrassment. "I'm sure you'll find someone you love both ways. All ways. *Inire* and *ente*, too." *I like you more than peach pie,* she recalled, and had to smile.

The thought of another person entering his orbit cast ripples through her that she couldn't quite untangle yet. It wouldn't be the same as with Edann, though the apothecary's attitude toward her had shifted during their relationship – more pointed and guarded. If Keifon found someone who would marry him and treat him well, she would be happy for him. But she would miss him, all the same. If they both lived in Wildern, she was sure that they would find time for one another, but it would never be the same as this. It wasn't his fault, nor the fault of his potential spouse. It was the sadness that came along with the joy, that was all.

"I'm sure you'll find someone wonderful. Just make sure they get along with me, too, huh? I don't want to feud."

Keifon gave her a strange look. "Of course. ...Should I have you screen them for me? I'll give you a checklist."

Agna realized that she had taken their future proximity for granted, and that he had taken it as a joke. She scrambled to join in. "Oh, I can write a checklist. It will be extremely thorough."

"I'm sure it will. No one in the world would measure up."

"You deserve nothing less."

They broke down the tent eventually and went home together. Keifon said no less than four times that he was glad to be back. She agreed every time.

Keifon: Fairy Tales

Nelle settled her basket on her arm. "Fall in!" Keifon shot her an unamused glare, and she grinned and stuck her tongue out. "All right then, line up!" Agna shifted and shrugged against the clanking bag over her shoulder. Nelle spun to face them. "Stay safe. Watch out for one another. Meet me here at three; this'll be our base camp. Compass?" Keifon tapped the compass in his pocket, and Nelle nodded. "Know what you're looking for?"

"I have the list," Agna said. "And I remember last time."

"Good. I'll be over that way. Difficult terrain for newcomers." With one more flash of her teeth, she bounded through the snow and between the trees.

Agna sighed and surveyed the snowy landscape. "How about that way? The trees are thicker, but there's less snow."

"Mmn. Works for me."

They tramped through the snow toward the thicker cover. Agna tugged her scarf up to her lower eyelids. "I'm sorry we dragged you into this."

"You didn't drag me. It sounded fun."

"Yeah, but it's *cold*."

If I wait till it's warm, I won't have the chance again. "I think it'll still be fun."

"I guess." She swatted at some snow-covered branches.

"Walking will warm us up. How do you say 'hiking' in Nessinian?"

She told him, and stopped complaining about the cold. His conversational skill in Nessinian was not much more advanced than a child Nachi's age, though he had a burgeoning vocabulary in medicinal terms and words related to camping. He couldn't sustain much of a conversation with a native speaker. But Keifon was thankful for every word.

Agna paused in her etymological monologue to hop over a fallen log. Keifon climbed after her. She shifted sideways out of his path, pulling at her coat as if it didn't fit. Keifon paused beside her. "Is everything all right?"

"Ehhh. I just... I don't know. I look stupid."

"What? No, you don't."

She snugged her face into her scarf and grumbled. Maybe it was the trousers. She had never seemed to wear them before, but she had bought a pair while he was gone. They were heavy leather lined in wool, intended for plant-gathering outings much like this one. Nelle wore a similar getup, and the two of them looked like they could conquer the wilderness. Keifon found himself charmed in a way that he couldn't quite justify. Even though Agna moved and stood as though she weren't quite comfortable, she looked ready for adventure, and Keifon had found himself eager to go adventuring with her.

"I... kind of like it." He realized that he'd spoken out loud. "I-I mean. You look warm. And functional." Keifon sucked in a deep breath of the frigid air and walked ahead of her, sending her scrambling to catch up.

The woods thickened as they pushed through brittle canes and detoured around brambles. The snow was indeed thinner here, screened out by the boughs overhead. Agna pulled out Nelle's list and studied the trees. "Hmm. I think that bush over there might be darkberry. What do you think?" She held out the sketch she had made from Nelle's samples.

Keifon considered the drawing and the shrub. "It isn't far. We may as well try."

Agna nodded. "Fair enough." They headed toward the shrub, cutting an angling path between two patches of bramble. "Ever had darkberry jam? It was a mountain thing in Nessiny. Only place cold enough for these things to grow, I guess."

"Yeah. Too sweet for my taste, but I've tried it."

She chuckled. "Everything is too sweet for your taste. More for me."

"Heh. Well, Nelle's making things out of it."

"I mean metaphorically." She compared the plant's leaves to the drawing. They plucked off the frosted berries with their gloved hands, dropping them into one of the empty jars from Agna's bag. Agna cut a sprig of leaves with her penknife, for drawing later.

"So how do you say 'hiking' in Yanweian?"

Keifon told her, and she practiced the phrase until she got it right. Her tones were still flat. It was endearing, in a way. She was trying, even if it was difficult for her. And as strange as the sounds were, they belonged to her. The words were dear to him no matter how wrong they sounded.

They filled two jars with the berries and packed them at the bottom of Keifon's backpack. He had insisted on carrying it this morning, emptying out his belongings onto his cot, despite Agna's protests. He strapped the pack back on and looked for a likely path. Agna decided for them, ambling along a level swath overlooking a dry streambed.

"What happened next with Lun and the ghosts?"

Keifon smiled behind the collar of his coat and recalled where he'd left off in the story the previous night. He was probably embellishing it wrong as he went along, remembering a fairy tale he hadn't heard for years, but that seemed fitting somehow. Agna had already admitted to stylizing her Nessinian stories.

"Hmm. He had gone to the wisewoman to have his sword repaired, after swinging it at a ghost and chipping it on a stone. And she'd said that he had to journey to the edge of the afterlife to get the whetstone to sharpen it."

"Of course."

Keifon chuckled. "Of course. So he went around asking everyone he knew whether they knew the way to the edge of the afterlife..."

The two of them rambled through the snow as the watery sun climbed the sky. As he told the story, Keifon kept half an eye on the sun's direction and progress, noting where they were headed and how they could get back. Agna paused to compare another plant to her notes, and they stooped to scrape some lichen from a tree with their knives. In a clearing they stopped for an icy drink of water from their canteens, took their bearings, and began a wide, looping path that would take them toward a lake in the distance. Agna spotted some seedpods from Nelle's list, and took off her mittens when the seedpods began to stick to the fibers.

Keifon waited as she pulled on her mittens and flexed her hands to get the blood flowing. "Nelle had better appreciate your dedication as an apprentice."

She grinned. "Think I can get some darkberry jam out of it?"

"You can get some darkberry jam out of your natural charm. Aim for some of those walnuts she was looking for. We can cook something good out of those."

Agna shrugged the bag onto her shoulder. "You're just saying that because of your unrefined palate, Yanweian. Charm your own walnuts out of her."

Translated into Yanweian, that would sound obscene, but Keifon bit his lip over his snickering. "Yeah. I'll consider that."

At the water's edge, they found three more of Nelle's plants. Keifon and Agna tackled them one by one, trimming a few stalks from one with Keifon's knife, pulling some weeds from the soft ground, and finally wielding Nelle's trowels to dig up some roots. They swished these in the lake to wash the mud off, reaching out from a slab of stone that leaned over the water. Agna elbowed Keifon as they stretched out in a thin layer of snow, dangling roots into frigid lake water. He looked over at her and saw the smile in her eyes. They were absurd and deadly serious in the middle of nowhere, and being with her lent it a perfect logic. He laughed, and she laughed with him.

■ ■ ■

The sun hung low and orange in the sky at three. Nelle was flushed and bright-eyed under her layers of wool and leather, and the basket at her feet overflowed with stalks and leaves. She let out a triumphant whoop as Agna and Keifon stomped out of the trees, and leaped up from her makeshift log seat by the fire. "Yes, yes! Give 'em."

Keifon unstrapped his backpack, and Agna unshouldered her bag, now full of bark, soft pine buds, lichen, and a few mushrooms that they had found sheltered among the tree roots. They warmed their hands over Nelle's fire as she rifled through their finds.

Keifon flexed his hands. "Uh, I'm gonna need the pack back."

Nelle waved it off. "'Course. Counting, cataloguing tonight, and have it back to you tomorrow morning."

"Thanks."

"This is for everyone, right?" Agna reached for one of the fish skewered over the fire.

"Yeah, of course. We're celebrating."

As Nelle continued her gleeful survey of their haul, Keifon and Agna tucked into the grilled fish, hot tea, and toasted walnuts – she'd found them after all, and shared them without any extra application of charm. Agna gave up on pulling her handkerchief out of her pocket every half a minute, and finally tucked it into her sleeve. Keifon palmed his continually, dabbing his nose as the sudden heat made it run. They didn't joke about this business; they didn't need to.

Keifon's throat closed over a swallow of tea. This was his last winter with her. This was probably his first and last plant-collecting jaunt with her. They'd already had their last Lundrala and their last summer. Spring was far from this snowy corner of the western woods, but it wouldn't stay away forever.

Nelle finished her inventory and reached for the last skewers of fish. "S'wrong?"

Keifon snapped his eyes up to her firelit face. "I – um, sorry." He felt Agna's hand on his elbow and shoved down a swell of regret. *I should have enjoyed my time with you more. I should have done more. I should have...* "I just... I've had a good day. That's all."

Agna sighed. "Happiness makes him sad," she clarified for Nelle. "That's my boy."

Nelle regarded him kindly as she chewed. "Because it passes," she said. "Right?" Keifon had pulled his collar away from his face as they basked at the fire, and so Nelle could see him flushing. She took a pull at her canteen. "Misses you," she spelled out for Agna.

"I'm *still here*," Agna protested.

The herbalist shrugged. "Yeah, but..."

"I don't – I don't want to talk about this right now. Later, Agna, please, when we get back. Not now."

Nelle held up her hands in surrender. "Sorry. Didn't mean to upset you."

"It's...it's all right."

Agna squeezed his arm, and he offered her a thin smile. She was right; she was still here, for now. He would enjoy it for as long as he could.

■ ■ ■

"I'm sorry about today."

"What?" She turned, half-in, half-out of her long wool coat. "I had a lovely day."

"No, I mean – later. With Nelle."

"Oh. Don't worry about it on my account." She finished shrugging out of the coat and dashed outside to hang it next to Keifon's, then danced back inside, shuddering with cold. She fastened the tent flaps and sat on her cot to strip off her snowmelt-dampened socks. "Are you all right, though?"

He sat on his own cot, mirroring her in his stocking feet. The brazier had begun to warm the tent, and he hunched forward to spread his hands toward it. "I just – I like how things are now. I miss it, somehow. I know that isn't fair."

Her face was readable now, wind-pinked but bare in the indoor warmth. She watched him, puzzled. "I'm still here. And..." She sighed, motioning for him to wait. She removed her layers of socks and replaced them with dry socks. Then she hesitated, her hands idle on the rail of her cot. "Listen. I have to talk to you about something."

They'd talked all day, it seemed, when they weren't breathing in the fresh air and appreciating one another's silent company. But there was always more to say. Keifon warmed his hands and waited, listening.

"I've been thinking," Agna began. "And writing to Marco. About what I should do next, where I should go."

Keifon imagined her in a Nessinian art salon, draped in silks and velvets, surrounded by paintings framed in gold. She would be magnificent in her element. "Yes," he said. "They have a position for you, I assume."

"Well – yes, but..." She swung her legs onto the cot, folding up with her ankles crossed. "Mostly we've been writing about Kaveran art. And the state of the community here, and where the galleries are, and things like that."

"I see."

"I've learned so much since I've been here. If I went home I'd be one of hundreds of agents, even if I specialized in Kaveran art."

He heard the qualification, the *if* that replaced the *when*. Still, he could not bring himself to grasp for any misplaced hope. She would not risk her future. She would be a specialist in Kaveran art in the halls of her people, and she would shine all the brighter for her unique training.

"You aren't one of hundreds," he insisted, translating his own stampeding thoughts. "You're – you're you."

"Listen. I should have told you." She took a deep breath. "In Wildern, when you were gone, I met with some people. Historians, and local collectors. About whether there's enough of a following to open a gallery there. I think I can do it."

"Do...what?"

"Open a gallery in Wildern." She sat forward, and as she spoke her stockinged feet scuffed restlessly against the floor. "There are some private collections, but no public galleries. The local historical society is trying to open a history museum, too. We think we can open a combination of historical and art space. It would be small, but it's a start, and it's something the city doesn't have yet."

The lump in Keifon's throat stopped him from saying what he wanted to say. It rerouted into a weak "Could you do all of that from Nessiny?"

Agna lunged forward to nudge his forehead. "Don't be dense. But the problem is..." She withdrew, clinging to the cot rail. "I don't know whether it's the right thing to do. I made a mistake last time, even if I tried to make the best of it. I don't want to be that stupid again." She clenched her fists and released them. "I really want this. I know I can do it. But – am I just doing the same thing? I mean, I was thinking about Wildern's potential before you said you might move there. But maybe I'm fooling myself. It's your city. I shouldn't just follow along."

"I want you in my city," Keifon blurted. He saw Agna stand as he hunched over, resting his head in his hands. The dam-burst of relief dizzied him. "I want you to be your best, I want you to get all the good things you deserve, but – if I could see you, I'd be so happy."

Her hand lighted on his shoulder, and he felt her body settle next to him. "You're sure."

He straightened. "Yes! Of course."

Agna sighed. "Following a boy again," she muttered, but Keifon heard the irony in her voice.

"You should – you should go back for yourself, though. For your career."

"This is for my career. I'd rather do something new than follow my father. That's what I've come to realize, I think."

"Don't jeopardize your future just to spite him."

"I'm not doing it to spite him," she retorted. "He doesn't know yet, and he's going to be angry, but I don't care. It'll expand our name in the end. Let Marco take over Murio. I'd just end up competing with him anyway."

Keifon was left breathless by her cavalier rootlessness and her obliviousness to tradition and propriety. It wasn't right. Yet he also pictured her throwing open the doors of a museum she'd founded, and pride swelled in his chest. She would be magnificent wherever she went.

He found a path through his worry. "I know you know what's best for your career. I just – you know how I was raised. It's hard for me to accept breaking with the establishment."

"Yeah." She rubbed his shoulder, smiling. "I won't take it personally. And I'm not breaking with the establishment; I'm just taking it in a different direction."

He had to trust her appraisal of the situation. It wasn't his decision to make. He could only watch her fly, and worry for her, and be there if the wind picked up.

"I'm proud of you," he said at last. That was the truest part. "You're so brave, and I know you'll do what you set out to do."

Agna snuggled in against his side. Her arm around him was all the reply he needed.

"And I think it's all right," Keifon went on, not sure where his voice would lead. "To want to go where you know someone. You can make new friends, but... it helps. I know I'm..." He took a breath, trying to sort through his thoughts. "I'm so happy you'll be there." He already saw a timbered house on the edge of Wildern. Part of him wanted her there with him, just like this; he wanted to come home and make dinner with her and read by the fire. Part of him shied away, not wanting to hope for too much, not ready to consider where that might lead. Instead he imagined Agna coming to visit him, opening the front gate to be tackled by his adoring children, her own bursting out from behind her to run and play. She laughed, and his children called her *Aunt Agna*. He wiped his sleeve over his eyes. Agna would stay in his life. That would always be enough.

Agna ruffled her fingers through his hair, which only weakened his resolve. "You can cry if you need to," she murmured. "It's from happiness, though, right?"

"Yeah." He sniffled, but her voice had broken the spell. "I'm just thinking about the future. How it could be."

Agna's shoulders hitched in a near-silent laugh. "You – *you*, Reji Keifon the Medic – thought about the future, and it made you so happy you almost cried." Her voice cracked, and she let go of him to wipe her eyes. They laughed unsteadily together. Agna leaned back as her giggling subsided. "Did Nelle feed us something hallucinogenic out there?"

"If she did, we need to get more of it." Keifon gave her a hug, getting used to being unafraid. If he got attached – if he admitted that he was already attached – it was all right now. She wasn't leaving. Someday he would have to be less afraid of having his heart broken. But for now, she would stay, and that was all that mattered.

When they were ready, they drew apart. Keifon reflected, now that he felt calmer, that in his beautifully outlandish daydream, he'd given her a couple of children that she'd never said she wanted. That was presumptuous of him. Besides, they had been pale-skinned and dark-eyed like her. If she did ever get married and have children, they would probably be half-Kaveran. As, Keifon reminded himself, his own would probably be. It was strange to think about, though not at all unpleasant.

"So," he said, distracting himself, "what do you call your aunts in Nessinian? I can't remember the family terms right now."

"What?"

Keifon realized that his question had no context. "Um. I, uh – it was part of my thoughts about the future. My – well, my future kids called you *Bita* Agna. – Outside aunt," he translated.

"Outside?"

Another thing that foreigners apparently didn't do. Keifon repressed the urge to pace. "From the side of the family that has a different name than you."

"Yanwei is too complicated." She ruffled a hand through her hair. "Aunts and uncles on both sides are *Ceisi*. Kei-*ceisi*," she added, her voice dropping to a whisper. "Not that I'll...well, you get the idea."

He squeezed her hand. "Agna-*ceisi*?"

It made her smile, as he hoped it would. "Yep."

It was the most important word he learned that day.

Agna: Homecoming

Agna dropped off her letter with the master of records. Mail runners were thick on the ground this close to the major cities. She trusted the letter to get to Prisa before the caravan arrived.

She and Keifon took a seat near the front of the passenger wagon. Agna propped her stationery box on her lap, opened her sketchbook to a fresh page, and nestled her tin of pastel crayons on the seat between herself and her companion.

"I know what somebody's getting for her birthday." Keifon let go of his backpack strap and steadied the tin against the wagon's vibration.

Agna selected a warm brown, underlaid with orange. It was one of the longest remaining pastels in her collection; over half of it remained. Most of the greens were worn down to nubs.

"If they last that long. I think I'll look for more greens in Prisa." She drew the lightest lines she could finesse in such a bold medium. The paper's tooth grabbed and released the pigment, bringing texture to the lines.

"Then somebody's getting an easel, or paper, or whatever it is you can use when you are an artist who lives in a house."

"Beds, I hear. Bathroom facilities. Houseplants."

"For making art," Keifon elaborated, stomping resolutely off the nervous sidetrack she'd attempted. "Because somebody always looks relaxed when she draws."

Agna suggested some details on her sketch with twining shadows. "Paint," she said, and kept her voice steady. "In a house you can paint."

She swapped out the first pastel for a cool yellow-brown. Keifon watched her lines form a boxy, familiar shape.

"Are you scared?"

"Of painting? My mother is Alfia Despana; I'd say I'm intimidated."

"Of Wildern. Of... changing."

Pastels did not allow many mistakes. She could not rub them out with a chunk of rubber, as she could do with graphite. She could only incorporate the mistake into the drawing and keep going, or start over. That was always possible, too.

"Yes. And no. Yes and no."

Keifon squeezed the arm that supported her makeshift desk. "Me, too."

She chose a darker brown, like freshly turned earth. "Worth it. Is the thing."

"...yeah."

The wagon's wheels turned on the stone road that connected Wildern to Prisa, that wound into the forest, that linked town and homestead and city like the delicate map of arteries in the human body. Only a few stops remained. Fort Unity was where she had fought with a partner she'd barely known, and where she had played darts with a dear and patient friend. Vertal was where the Benevolent Union waited for her reports, and where the ships back to Nessiny would depart without her.

The next stop was Prisa, just over the horizon. It was where her people had made a foothold and built lives and homes and places of worship far from the rolling hills and olive groves. It was where one old friend from Nessiny had forgiven her for all she had said and not said. She would incorporate her sins and keep going.

Agna replaced the last pastel into its slot and closed the tin. Keifon leaned in to see the sketch, so she slid the book toward him.

Nelle's wagon, wreathed with painted leaves.

The camping tent, with the suggestion of a lighted lamp inside.

Keifon's lute, leaning on a bonfire log bench.

"It's beautiful," Keifon said.

"...Yeah. It was."

■ ■ ■

Marco's most recent letter, filed in her backpack, said *Good luck. Write me when you get to Wildern.* Violetta had drawn a flower under his signature in purple ink. Lina's most recent letter said *Send me your new address! I'm so happy for you.* She had enclosed a sprig of sweetmint, its scent lost to the paper and the weeks of travel.

Agna carried Rone's most recent letter in her pocket. It said *I miss you*, and *I'm sorry I hid things from you.* She did not have a copy of her most recent letter to him. It said much the same.

She stood before a modest storefront. Garlands of New Year's paper flowers looped behind the glass, over a series of signs lettered in Kaveran in a hand she didn't recognize. *Rone Sidduji. Nessinian Combat Arts. Classes Daily.* She recognized the writing on a larger sign: *Closed on New Year's / Spring Festival.* Beyond the glass she caught glimpses of movement. Laughter and battle cries and the dull crack of wooden swords mixed with the street noise behind her.

Agna knocked on the door and waited.

It opened on the full clamor of a practice room full of swordmastery students, framing the body of her old friend. Agna dropped a little formal bow to hide the molten flush rising up her neck. "Swordmaster Sidduji," she said, her treacherous voice wavering.

"Agna," Rone said quietly, chiding, affectionate, made real after too many years. He bent to throw his arms around her, and Agna gritted her teeth against the urge to cry. Not out of disappointment, not out of grief, not even out of rage. Nothing so simple or so sad. Love, she supposed. The lifeblood of all creation. Nothing more or less than that. It was not the same as with Laris, or Esirel, or Keifon. Each was its own particular, beautiful, heartbreaking thing.

"I missed you," he said.

She nodded against his chest. "I missed you, too."

He stepped back after a little while, and she saw him swallow hard. "Please come in. The students can practice without me."

She thanked her old friend and followed him inside.

Acknowledgements

This process took longer than it should have, though it was always a joy. The completion of this book owes so much to:

My husband, Jay, who admitted that he doesn't generally read fantasy or mushy-emotional books, but who gamely read multiple drafts and always believed in me.

The readers of the first draft: Jay, as noted; Dan, who pointed out the preponderance of tea and bathing; and Scintilla, my internet neighbor of umpteen years.

The readers of the second draft: Jay, who said I should put the beginning back in; Dan, who said that some of the "boring" stuff was fine after all; Stacie, who took the time to read despite being in the throes of grad school; and Martha, whom I've never met, but who sent me notes that kept me up till 2 a.m.

And thank you for sharing this story.

ABOUT THE AUTHOR

S.E. Robertson lives in Pennsylvania with two cats, one husband and a garden. *The Healers' Road* is their first book.

Visit **www.serobertsonfiction.com** for announcements.

Made in the USA
Coppell, TX
26 October 2021